GRANT'S
★WAR★

BLOOMINGTON
ST. JOSEPH
INDIANAPOLIS
SPRINGFIELD
TERRE HAUTE
KANSAS CITY
ILLINOIS
INDIANA
ST. LOUIS
JEFFERSON CITY
EVANSVILLE
LOUISVIL
MISSOURI
PADUCAH
CAIRO
HENRY AND DONELSON
(1862)
NEW MADRID
FT. HENRY
NASHVILLE
TENNES
JACKSON
SHILOH (1862)
MURFREESBORO
FT. SMITH
CHATTANOO
MEMPHIS
SHILOH
ARKANSAS
CORINTH
CHICKAMAUGA
(1863)
HELENA
FT. HINDMAN
VICKSBURG (1862-63)
GRENADA
ALABAMA
MISSISSIPPI
MONROE
SHREVEPORT
VICKSBURG
MONTGOMERY
JACKSON
LOUISIANA
TEXAS
MOBILE
PENSACOLA
BATON ROUGE
NEW ORLEANS

A Novel of the Civil War

GRANT'S ★WAR★

TED JONES

★

PRESIDIO

Grant's War is a novel. Although the sequence and general framework of this book are based on historical fact, specific events portrayed by characters other than historical personages are fictitious. Except for historical figures, any resemblance of characters to persons living or dead is purely coincidental.

Copyright © 1992 by Theador E. Jones

Published by Presidio Press
505 B San Marin Dr., Suite 300
Novato, CA 94945-1340

Library of Congress Cataloging—in—Publication Data

Jones, Ted, 1937 Oct. 22-
    Grant's war : a novel of the Civil War / Ted Jones.
      p. cm.
    Includes bibliographical references.
    ISBN 0-89141-434-7
    1. Grant, Ulysses S. (Ulysses Simpson), 1822-1885—Fiction.
  2. United States—History—Civil War, 1861-1865—Fiction.
  I. Title.
PS3560.05418G7 1992
813'.54—dc20   91-37635
                                                   CIP

Typography by ProImage

Printed in the United States of America

For Vonnie, for all her patience and understanding.

Acknowledgements

Any author who hears for the first time those sought after words "we want to publish your book" knows the gratitude sincerely expressed here. To Joan Griffin, Senior Editor of Presidio Press, who had the courage to say those words and to take a chance on a novice author and his first manuscript, thank you for your confidence. To Dale Wilson, who worked with me through the editing process and who shared with me his expertise on the Civil War period, thank you for your patience and encouragement. But most of all, to my wife—who read every word, from my first feeble attempt at writing fiction to the finished manuscript that comprises *Grant's War* and who sat at home alone while the endeavor moved slowly along—thank you, Vonnie, for your love, encouragement, and patience.

1 Them Was Glory Days

The midmorning heat, its intensity magnified by a blanket of misty haze, pressed oppressively on the clay clearing that passed for a farm. If one looked hard, there occasionally sparkled a vapory light through the dense, green growth that bordered the West Field. I never understood the reason for calling it the West Field, and I never asked. I never saw an East Field, or a North or South Field for that matter.

A low-lying swamp surrounded the patch of land, creating a perfect isolation. During the wet season, which seemed about always, the only way in led to two twelve-foot two-by-twelves, their ends overlapping where they met in the middle. These joining ends rested on a large, flat-topped rock that rose to a height three feet lower than the two banks anchoring the outer ends of the weathered planks. The makeshift bridge spanned a stagnant, brackish swamp where a colorful assortment of varmints made their home. Getting to this place required a commitment.

It mattered little if it never rained on this small corner of the world, although it often did. A man needed to bore less than two feet to create a permanent well.

Just beyond to the east, a half mile at most, the Mississippi River flowed southward. It required a careful study to detect its turbulence, but the vast, murky surface churned and surged with an infinite array of miniature whirlpools, undertows, and lesser forms of agitation. As with storms on the earth, this microscopic violence coexisted in stark contrast to the generally placid grandeur of the Father who sired them. The river reminded me of the war: quiet for the most part, even serene at times—when assessed in its whole—but boiling all the same, as irresistible forces met with explosive compulsion to move what refused to move except through a radical metamorphosis of the balance.

Square in the middle of the eighty-odd-acre plot stood a shack that appeared long since abandoned. I remember it being a comfortable place, a place with that familiar well-worn, lived-in look, but I doubt I would have lived there given a choice. Not a trace of paint remained on even the most shielded patch of wood. The original support held up one corner of the porch. A rake handle with the business end still in place supported the other corner, although the handle missed fulfilling its task by over two feet. The entrepreneur who devised this technology had contrived a bridge for the gap. The rake head itself rested precariously on two weather-worn bricks; a rusty wash tub bridged the first fifteen-inch expanse above the tip of the rake handle. The tub rested precariously on what used to be the business end of a serrated weed cutter. It stuck out far enough to promise a hazardous exit for anyone attempting careless departure from the porch in its direction. An odd assortment of boards segmented by a piece of corrugated tin siding bridged the top dozen inches. Except for one, all the boards had been weathered black. Either the porch had been settling, or the support had been compressing. A nearly new board made the closure with the rotting plank extending from the shack. Except for the cans of beans stored in an interior cabinet, that top board most likely was the only item less than thirty years old on the whole place. Except, of course, for me. I was only twenty-two at the time and barely two months past graduating from Harvard College.

For a variety of reasons, I had established for myself the task of writing about the Civil War. The visit to this lost corner of the world marked the first day of a journey that was to consume more than three years of my life.

Pulling cautiously on the door, which hung by one hinge, I entered the house, followed by the arthritic old gentleman who spoke fondly of this place he called home. During an earlier brief inspection of the premises, he informed me that he had lived here for more than fifty years. Considering that he had been well past thirty when he first arrived, that seemed about right. During my brief time in his company, when he insisted that I accompany him on a tour, I had reached out several times to support him when it seemed certain that the light breeze was about to topple him to the sod. He had, however, grown accustomed to fending for himself, so he always pulled away. Despite his insistence on self-reliance, it was futile for him to ignore the scars of advancing

time that had disfigured the dwelling and had obviously been as unkind to its inhabitant.

"That river was the key to the whole shebang," said the gaunt old
man without turning to look at me. "Grant saw this before almost anyone
else. Cuttin' the country in half became his obsession; the river was
the belt with which he planned to throttle the South."

I remember him smiling faintly as he sucked on a corncob pipe
stained black both inside and out. The pungent aroma of the smoke
fouled the air in the confinement of the dark parlor-kitchen that stretched
across the full width of the clapboard shack. He exhaled, as if carrying out a carefully planned act, then he let his eyelids drop. His thoughts
seemed absorbed in the swirling smoke flowing through the oblique
beams of sunlight. Its movement modeled the turbulence of the great
river just beyond sight, through the trees.

His eyes opened to two narrow slits as he fought off his weari-
ness. "I came to know him when he was just a common man," he
continued, "in a state of financial disgrace—his commandin' officer'd
forced him out of the army for drunkenness—cuttin' wood an' sellin'
it for four dollars a cord on the street corners of St. Louis."

His mind wandered, then his features twisted, as if he had experienced a sudden gas attack. What pained him, I suspected, was speaking
ill of Grant, but hard times were as much a part of the man as his general's
stars, so the old soldier continued.

"My family had a little money in them days," he said smiling, "and
nary a one of the men was partial to cuttin' wood. Usually, they sent
me to try to haggle down Grant's price, but he always held firm. That
trait served him well when he was fightin' Lee. As hard as times was
for the cap'n—we all called him the cap'n in those days—things only
got worse for him. By the winter of '59 he'd sunk so low that poverty would'a been a step up the social ladder."

The old man snickered devilishly as he flicked his head and clicked
his tongue against his teeth. I sensed in his mood no ill judgment of
Grant's financial status, but rather a kinship for a condition he had
learned to understand, if not appreciate.

"Them times were hard temperin' for a man about to be called upon
to supervise the killin' a two hundred thousand men."

The old gent's concentration frequently seemed to weaken. He spoke
a few sentences, then his thoughts drifted away. He had, after all, a
ton of memories to sift through, and his mind was nearly as enfeebled
as his body. That frailty, however, seemed to affect only his ability

to recall events in the present. The times of the war and before were as graphic as if being played out before him on a stage larger than life.

To me, writing feverishly in an attempt to capture every critical phrase on my writing pad, the old man's mind seemed anchored in a different time, a time of violence unequaled to the present. It was a time when to live meant making history, unless one worked hard at avoiding it. The old man had avoided none of it. His sad, sunken eyes offered fleeting, pantomime reviews of the tumult churning behind a face that seemed to have the dusty trails of marching armies etched in its furrows.

I welcomed the pauses, the respites granting relief for the cramping muscles in my hand. Yet pausing seemed a risk. The old soldier, every bit of eighty and looking ten years older, appeared as if he might die at any moment from no malaise greater than the weight of his years and experience. He had been there, seen the blood and suffering, walked into the eye of the storm and returned. I remember thinking: their experience will pass from memory, as though it never really happened, when his generation passes from our presence. The thought of it made me sad and redirected my urgency to tap his experience. Even a fleeting memory of what the old man knew was important. His memories were too precious to chance losing for the sake of pondering a whiff of smoke or a cramped muscle in a weary hand.

"That was his greatest virtue," the old man continued finally, "and his greatest failing. He always remained that common man we all knew, even when he became president. He was always direct, carvin' the simplest path to survival. Grant worked equally as well in adversity to keep his family alive as he did to keep his nation alive and well. How can that mark the passin' of a failure, as some will have you believe?" He thought for a moment, obviously reluctant to press the point. "But it's true," he added, speaking more to himself than to me. "What served him well as a general failed him utterly as the president. But I'll tell you this, if there lived a man still able to speak to you now, and you asked him if Grant was any kind'a failure, he'd tell you straight. That man was Lee. In all these here United States there has existed only one man with a more tenacious fightin' spirit than Robert E. Lee. That man was U. S. Grant."

The old man smiled to himself, obviously savoring a secret thought, measuring its meaning, and wondering at the wisdom of sharing it with an uncaring world. He must have decided, why not? "There's only one thing Lee ever done better than Grant," he nodded, as if affirming his conviction in the belief, "an' that was ride a horse. What's remarkable 'bout that is, I heard tell that Grant was the best horseman in his class when he was at the Point. He was all right, I suppose, but Lee had him beat, at least as I remember it.

"When we was fightin' in the Wilderness I got close enough to Lee to shoot him, and I just didn't have the heart. I felt in awe of him settin' astride that white horse of his. I think his name was Traveller—the horse, I mean. If the only way to win this damn war, I remember thinkin', is to shoot that man from off'n that animal—well, I just decided I could make it eatin' black-eyed peas and corn bread, if it came to that. A volley from my regiment would'a killed him twenty times over, but he never got so much as a scratch. Let me tell you. A merciful Providence was watchin' over him that day. Thinkin' back on it, if I'd'a killed Lee that day, fifty thousand men that felt the coldness of dirt in their faces probly would'a lived to know again the comfort of a warm woman's flesh. But I didn't know none of 'em that died because I let Lee live, so I figure, what the hell. Besides, what were fifty thousand souls more or less? I witnessed more'n'a tenth as many die in a bloody half hour at Cold Harbor. I damn near was one of 'em. It was that kind'a war."

The old man rocked back. Lifting quickly his one good leg, he rested his heel on a window sill crumbling with dry rot. Another stream of smoke sparkled and swirled in the stiff rods of light drilling their way through the cracks in the wall. During the pause I looked around. The old shanty spoke of nothing so eloquently as abject poverty. In the whole place, by actual count, there were thirteen dilapidated remnants of what few would give credit to being pieces of furniture. Besides the old man's stiff-backed rocking chair, there was a leather-covered—almost covered—love seat making a triangle of the west corner of the room. In the kitchen stood an oval dinner table with the normal four legs. That would have seemed unremarkable except that it had once had a fifth leg supporting the broad middle leaf. The wooden appendage reflected the most obvious infirmity of its owner: the old man had lost his right leg just below the knee. According to him he was the last casualty of the last great adventure of the war—the Battle of Appomattox. I never questioned that. The middle leg of the table was also just a stub; the lower ten inches had long since broken free. Time, or perhaps the rough wool of a grimy sock covering a foot with a persistent itch, had worn the jagged edges smooth.

Pushed under the table were three chairs designed with nothing so much in mind as to break a man's back. Against the wall stood a strange-looking cabinet without any doors. Cans of pork and beans lined its dingy top shelf. Counted among the thirteen items was the potbellied stove. There was also the once-elegant armchair in which I rested precariously, its most prominent feature a steel spring extending ominously upward between my legs. In the only other room of the shack stood a handsome but tarnished brass poster bed. Beside it stood a small bedside table straddling a slop jar and topped by a washbowl. Across the room were another wooden chair and a three-drawer chest of drawers with only two drawers. The old man did his cooking in the massive stone-faced fireplace in the southeast corner, or in the single saucepan that rested precariously on the top edge of the potbellied stove.

"I was a colonel, y'know," the old man said, as if there was nothing incomprehensible in the pronouncement, "a lieutenant colonel of infantry."

I flinched at the declaration. How was it possible for a man of such former prominence to sink to this level? I asked myself. But I realized that if I questioned him on this, then I must question everything he said.

The old man looked at me knowingly. "Hard to believe? That's what you're thinkin'. But it's true, every word. When we departed Washington, on May 4 of '64, I was a first lieutenant, second in command of a comp'ny of men. At nightfall, as we crossed the Rapidan, the cap'n in command drowned, so I became a cap'n. The next mornin', barely an hour into that dungeon of growth called the Wilderness, the regimental commander, Colonel Harder, had his head shot off'n by a ball. By sundown of that day all the regimental field-grade officers were dead or wounded. At five the next morning a cap'n on Grant's staff shook me outta my perch in the Y of a tree and told me I'd been assigned to take command of the regiment with the brevet rank of lieutenant colonel." His nostalgic expression told me there was more. "That wasn't so strange, when you think about it. When we started, my comp'ny had eighty men, and the regiment had nearly six hundred. By the time I took command, the whole regiment could muster only ninety-six, and a third a them was damaged in one way or another, but not enough to pull 'em from the line. I guess you might say I had command of a large comp'ny-sized regiment workin' on becomin' a platoon." He smiled, and I reflected the expression. "It was that kind'a war," the old soldier said again.

"An hour after sunup I was standin' as close as I am to that cookin' pot to Grant himself. He called a meeting of all the field commanders he could round up. There I was, improvised silver leaf on my shoulder and all, plannin' for the great killin' yet to come. God! When I think on it, it seems impossible. Here I was, six days past my thirtieth birthday, never gone to school a day in my life—my pa had no use for formal education, so I taught myself to read from the *Gazette*—an' in command of a regiment of men." He shook his head slowly as a peaceful smile spread across his weathered, wrinkled face. "Them was glory days, all right, an' Grant was hittin' his stride." His voice trailed as his thoughts wandered backward across the intervening fifty-two years. "Them was glory days."

2 Grant Made Things Happen

A quaint little place, Galena, Illinois, I thought as I stumbled at twilight down the riverboat ramp. My footing felt more secure as I stepped onto the worn planks of the wharf, so I stopped for a moment to survey the surroundings. A long, winding path, occasionally broken by a line of stairs where the path grew too steep, led up the hill to the town proper. The people living there were not the ones I sought. I turned and looked to the southwest.

Strung along the face of the hill were all manner of supply shops and assorted other establishments. The more respectable of these addressed the affairs of the river. The others fulfilled the pleasures and needs of the night. The men I sought were beyond the wants or needs of either. Their bodies now were too frail to sustain the necessary day's labor; their services to and by the river were past. They could savor only fond memories of long-lost cravings of the flesh. No matter. I had in mind tapping their memories of a time when a thirty-mile march was the order of the day between a bacon breakfast and a hardtack supper. Morning would come soon enough and the seemingly endless row of bleached, battered chairs that lined the wharf would fill again with the old men presently departing to escape the sharp sting of a hundred varieties of river bugs.

At the near end of the single row of crumbling, weather-worn buildings stood the tallest of the lot. The lone word on the sign hanging in front gave the necessary direction: HOTEL. Placing my carpetbag under my left arm and lifting the two larger bags in each hand, I moved quickly to reach my destination before darkness engulfed the unfamiliar wharf.

"A room, if you please," I said to the bearded attendant as I rang the small bell next to his hand.

"One night or a week?" the clerk asked, the words difficult to understand around the cold cigar extending from the corner of his mouth.

"Let me try a week to see how that does," I replied. "What's the rate?"

"Fifty cents a night, three dollars a week," replied the clerk. "Sign here. Room 209, second floor, end of the hall to the right."

I signed the register, witnessed by the attendant looking over the top of his half-circle glasses.

"What's that?" asked the attendant, unable to read my name.

"Arthur Kelly. Just call me Art." I smiled, trying to ease the gruffness in his eyes. "You're one up on me now. What's your name?"

"Just call me Reb," replied the attendant, "or whatever strikes your fancy."

"Have you lived here long?" I asked.

"Could be," he replied. "Why you askin'?"

"No reason," I shrugged. "Just trying to be friendly."

The attendant stiffened his arms and, shifting his weight forward, pressed his hands against the counter's edge. "That room you're stayin' in, 209, I was born there January 1 of '49. That must be what, sixty-six years now—nigh on sixty-seven?" Only a year short, I thought.

"If a man wanted to look into the history of this town," I asked, "especially around the time of the Civil War, who would you suggest contacting?"

"Depends."

"On what?"

"What you want to know."

"What are the options?" Priming Reb is difficult, I thought.

"Wellll," he replied as he stroked his beard, "let's see. If you want to talk about money makin', you want to talk to someone named Ferguson. Them's the bankers. Any one will do. If you want to know about the fightin' and the dyin' and the excitement, well, I 'spect I'm 'bout as good as the next fella."

"You served in the army during the Civil War?" I asked.

"Not exactly."

The answer caught me by surprise, and he detected the confusion in my expression.

"Navy. I served as gunner on one a them ironclads that patrolled the river. But I did some soldierin' for a time, after they blew my boat from under me down by Vicksburg. Grant captured me, or I should say, some a his men did. The first time I saw Grant himself, in the spring of '63, I had just turned fourteen. Rowed him 'cross the Mississippi twice, I did, he and his man Rawlins." He shook his head. "Had a hard time tellin' the general from the colonel. That Rawlins fellow never stopped talkin'. Cuss? That man could outcuss a sailor last in line for a whore. Grant never said a word. He grunted and nodded a couple a times, but mostly he just slept as I rowed across. It was a long pull 'cross that damn river. It tumbled so hard I had to start a mile upriver from where I wanted to dock."

"Would you describe Grant?" I asked, now thoroughly involved in what the attendant had to say.

"Quiet," he said, nodding. "I'd say he was very quiet."

Ask a stupid question, I thought. "Other than that?" I asked, prodding for more detail.

"Can't say. I only saw him twice, an' both times I was too busy to dwell on it. Y'interested in Grant?"

"Yes, very much."

The attendant shifted his weight and pointed toward the corner. "In about an hour a man will come down those stairs and plant himself in that corner chair. If you want to know about Grant, ask him. He'll be hard to talk to though. Can't hardly hear a word. But you mention Grant, and he'll fill your ears all right. He served on Grant's staff, almost from the start." He leaned forward and whispered out of the side of his mouth. "He was a bastard relative of Rawlins," then he elevated the volume, "but Grant liked him, so he appointed him to his staff during the time he made his way down to Cairo."

I nodded. "Thanks. You've been a big help. Where is a good place to eat?"

"Depends."

I sighed. "On what?"

"What you like. There is catfish places, and there is ham places."

"I'll try the fish."

"Galena River fish is better'n Mississippi fish," he said, sprinkling his directions with a little advertisement. "Not as muddy tastin'. Next door's as good a place as any. They water down the whiskey a bit, and the ladies have seen better days, but the cook knows what to do with them fish."

"May I leave my luggage here until later?"

He nodded. "I'll carry it up for you, if I get time." He immediately returned to reading the paper spread out next to the bell.

I reached into my pocket and found a dime. "Thanks," I said, slapping the coin on the counter. "Fish sounds good." I looked at the clock on the wall. Eight-thirty.

The attendant knew his fish places. I felt stuffed as I downed the last of my third cup of coffee. At 9:30 I returned to the hotel. I glanced toward the corner. As foretold, I saw an old man sitting in the corner chair reading the paper. This is no river man, I thought as I studied him carefully. A white, neatly trimmed and combed beard extended from his large, almost regal head. He wore a brown, neatly pressed wool suit with vest, and his brown oxford shoes glistened in the dim gaslight. He's probably a vain man, I thought as I watched him read the paper at arm's length. He won't wear his glasses, although he owns a pair. The steel rim was barely visible sticking out of his vest pocket.

"Pardon me," I said loudly, remembering the advice about his hearing. "May I talk with you for a moment?"

The old man flinched, obviously startled by a stranger's approach. "Don't have time," he replied diffidently.

"Oh. That's too bad. The hotel clerk told me you knew something about Grant, General U.S. Grant."

The old man's eyes lit up. "Grant, you say? I might have a minute to spare." He folded the paper neatly and placed it on the table by the chair. "Seat yourself." He said it more as a command than a request. "Grant, you say, huh? I served on his staff, you know, as Grant's personal doctor and surgeon to the officer staff." With his right index finger he pointed to a vacant spot on his left hand. "Had this middle finger blown away by a Minié ball at Shiloh. Wasn't much of a bother, though. I cut with my right hand." Leaning forward with considerable effort he lifted his left pant leg. "A ball exploded under my horse at Chattanooga. Killed the horse on the spot. Good thing, I thought at the time. We all were starving, and horse doesn't taste half bad if properly boiled." He rubbed a foot-long scar an inch across at the widest point. "Shrapnel blew through my calf here. Thought I'd lose this leg for sure." He struggled to remove his coat, then rolled up his shirt sleeve. "Took another Minié through the flesh here. Just missed the bone. That hurt some, even more than the leg. But the finger hurt more. Thought I'd die from the pain. Almost decided to quit that war, it hurt so bad. But Grant needed me. He had no taste for keeping track of the little things, like orders, but he sure knew how to keep track of an army, especially Lee's. When I wasn't cutting and dispensing I helped out around staff headquarters. I got to know Grant well."

The attendant judged him correctly, I thought. Just the mention of Grant set the words to flowing. The next thing I knew, the clock chimed 2:30 in the morning. The old man had hardly stopped talking in nearly five hours. What I most remember about the last thirty minutes of that conversation was never needing to piss so badly in all my life. But I just clamped my legs together and kept writing. I filled twenty pages with what that old man had to say, and at that he never got past the fall of '63—when Grant saved the army at Chattanooga by ordering the capture of Missionary Ridge. That strikes me as the most mystifying day of the war. Even now nobody believes what happened, including those who were there. In all the years I spent trying to look into the mind of this man Grant, I've heard a thousand different descriptions of him. One depiction stands out most. Wherever he went, things happened. That may not make him a great man, but it sure makes him an interesting man.

Finally, the old doctor just stopped talking in mid-sentence as he nodded off to sleep. I rushed to the outhouse to relieve the pressure before struggling wearily up the stairs to bed.

I rose at first light the next morning. The old doctor still slept in the corner chair. The outside chairs had already started to fill as I walked out the door into the blinding light reflected from the river. I felt a softness to the walk along that wharf. Strange, I thought, that I had not noticed this before. The weathering whittlings of a hundred knives cushioned each step. In places, the chips were an inch thick, and that only from the gathering since the last stiff wind. I learned later that a good whittler reduced a six-foot-long two-by-four to chips between sunup and noon, if the discussion proved exciting enough. That almost always proved so, especially when the first half of the 1860s was the featured topic.

It is my belief that not one coward occupied any of those chairs. They all had served, in one way or another, from private to colonel. The generals all must have lived up those steps. At first, one fact struck me as strange: I found the service of these men about equally divided between the North and the South. That seemed odd for the state of Illinois, as this was a state usually counted among the strongest for Lincoln and Union. It's just as well, however. A man had to learn about Lee to learn about Grant. The perspective varied only by degree. To a man who fought for the South, Bobby Lee always remained "The General," and Grant just got lucky. To the Union soldier, Grant whipped Lee, and that ended the comparison. These old soldiers were willing to give Lee his due, but that never changed the ending. "Unconditional Surrender" Grant accepted Lee's sword in the farmhouse parlor at Appomattox, and that about summed it up. On one point, however, they did agree—the tussle on the road to that farmhouse made their lives dangerous and interesting for a while.

The hotel attendant called himself Reb for a reason. He had spent all but three of his years living in Galena. He spent those three years serving in the Confederate Navy, but he never did talk about it. I learned from one of the men who had participated in his capture that he had been a prisoner for nearly a month when he rowed Grant and Rawlins across the Mississippi. The attendant neglected that small point when he recounted the story. Rawlins just took a shine to him, I guess. The attendant went south later in a prisoner exchange, and he immediately shipped out on another ship heading north, only to end up a prisoner again at New Orleans. As the old farmer said, it was that kind of war. There were no prisoner exchanges by then. That might explain his reluctance to dwell on the subject. From what I have learned, living in a prison operated by either side took the starch out of the strongest of men. For a boy it must have been hell.

I used up my three dollars' worth of room listening to whomever would speak about those glory days, then I bought three dollars more. In more than fifty recorded conversations I never heard the same point of view twice, yet they all wound up at the same ending. In the end, it came down to two critical points: Lee always emerged as a brilliant general and a patriot, but he fought for the wrong cause. Hardly a man I talked to in Galena acknowledged any virtue in slavery—then or now. Even those who cast their lot with the South rested their convictions in other quarters. But what of Grant? Grant saved the Union for Lincoln, and for you and me. They never said it just that way, but it's what they meant.

"Grant and Lee turned war into an art form," said a philosophizing former infantry major. "They painted broad strokes, then left the paint to run to fill in the details. They brought their spirit and their genius to the task, and they left it to the men on the line to pull the trigger. Both fervently believed that one man's death was too many, and fifty thousand deaths were too few if victory escaped or occurred in half measure. As in all wars, the battles they joined were far from perfect. They were more the art of turning disaster into victory. Lesser men—both the armies, North and South, had such men in abundance— made a habit of running when disaster seemed imminent. They must have thought there was a tolerable quota for the killing, and when they satisfied that quota, it was time to leave. Neither Grant nor Lee saw any of that. Men die in war, and the only way to stop the killing is to push on undaunted toward the final victory that ends the killing. There is no way to make war glamorous or to transform the killing into a virtue. Killing just dominates the portrait of war."

I asked of those men only one common question: "What made the Civil War different from other wars?" Allowing as how they knew little of other wars, they confined their answers to what they knew, what they believed to be real. I have no doubt that their most common answer was different from that of any philosopher. Philosophers, such as the major, invariably look for the deeper meaning in conflict carried out on a grand scale. Although they express themselves in picturesque words, they never quite touch the pulse of the process; they feel more of its death than its life. These old men knew, nearly every one of them, and they remembered it fifty years later. "The rifled bullet," they identified as the one critical difference, "the Minié ball." That is a personal answer. Every one of them, at one time or another, found himself having to dodge a chunk of that deadly lead. As one man expressed it: "When you hit a man in the little finger from a hundred yards with one of those damnable bullets, the impact lifted him a foot from the ground. It spun him around twice before laying him out flat, leaving him to think he had lost his arm." That has nothing to do with generals or strategy.

The Minié was a terrible innovation. No bone ever grew with the strength to resist its force when set free from a hundred yards. By way of proving the point, several of the men seated along the wharf had a stub where an arm or leg used to be.

A few soldiers added a more personal touch. "It never changed with me," Sgt. Jeremiah Clemmens told me long after I left Galena. "Each time, before a battle began, I had two wishes. First, I always tried to be where a Reb wasn't aimin'. Failin' that, I prayed, 'Let me die quickly.' I failed on both accounts." He had suffered four wounds—on the same day and at the same moment—at the Battle of Spotsylvania Courthouse; he lost both arms and both legs.

As many soldiers confirmed, competence in battle infrequently set the standard for promotion. That may have been one reason the war dragged on so long. The most aggressive soldiers, the ones willing to put everything on the line, usually died quickly. The trick was to survive, to draw back from the point of ultimate risk. A man had to know something, however, to survive a conflict where an eighteen-inch oak was whittled to the ground, cut down by a hail of Miniés, during a short afternoon of battle. The evidence is on display at the Smithsonian.

"To my view," said a former lieutenant and general's aide during the last days of the war, "the ultimate test for assessing the purpose of war comes down to the last man on one side killing the last man on the other side. At that instant, beyond dispute, command of the field is established. Then both victory and right are determined. The understanding on that point separated Grant from Lee by a country mile. Lee sought always to prevail at home—south of the Mason-Dixon line—but was content to let the other army go home to lick its wounds. He fought out of duty to his state; an army camped around Washington presented no immediate threat. Grant, at Lincoln's constant urging, found contentment only in the thought of saving the whole nation. Letting Lee's army out of his grip meant that the fighting must continue, and with it the killing."

As usual, the common soldier assessed the meaning of war in the purest sense. "Grant was a hellion," said one Confederate lieutenant. "By my count, Lee knocked him down six times. The difficulty was, Grant came at Lee seven times."

Grant did not so much defeat Lee's army as just kill it, one man at a time. No matter how high I climbed trying to get a sharp view of Grant, I always come back down to that.

One of my favorite stories, once I get past the horror of it, first came to me from a former second lieutenant. "It happened just before the slaughter at Cold Harbor," the lieutenant said. "General Meade sent a line of skirmishers out across a field. I can only guess at the purpose. I suspect he had in mind getting a feel for the other side. With Grant at his side, Meade watched from the south edge of a flat plane that dropped off sharply about a hundred yards to the north before it rose about five feet some thirty yards beyond. I got to know the area well the next morning when we all went across.

"Just beyond, the rebels had entrenched out of the line of sight of our position. Forty Federals, at intervals of ten feet and led by a young lieutenant—his name was Joe; he was my close friend—started walking north across that field. A volley shattered the stillness as they walked into view at the top of the far rise. First I saw the smoke, then heard the sound. Surprise was complete. Thirty-nine of those men fell dead or wounded. Only the young lieutenant, sword still held high in a stern posture of command, remained standing and whole. When he realized what had happened, he stopped in mid-stride, his rigid form silhouetted against the cloudless sky—more like a statue than a man. He looked slowly to the right, then to the left, before calmly inserting his saber back into its scabbard. Then he walked to the nearest of his fallen comrades and picked up the man's rifle."

Whenever I think of this story, I wonder at the reason for that act. The only explanation I have found is that, somehow, that lieutenant considered a saber too flimsy a weapon for the trial he faced. Then again, there is no explaining what men think during war.

"Joe cradled the rifle at the elbow of his left arm," the story continued, "as he began walking slowly back toward our lines. For a short time he disappeared from sight as he moved down into the shallow depression. Then, almost as if the ground was pushing him slowly upward, he rose to full view at the south rim. 'Get down, you fool,' I thought, 'they will kill you sure if you keep moving.' Some twenty yards south of the depression stood a lone ash tree, and Joe angled toward it. Just before reaching the tree, he looked over his shoulder. He must have had a premonition of what happened next. There was not a breeze stirring or a sound to be heard as everyone watched. Then I heard the distant echo: 'Reeeeeady, FIRE.' He stepped behind the tree just as the volley exploded." Three men I talked to remembered this part, and they all gave the same estimate of a hundred or more muskets firing directly at that tree. Following the volley the tree resembled a tall, freshly pruned fence post. When the bullets had passed, the lieutenant peered cautiously from behind the stricken tree, then pulled his head back. My primary witness concluded the story this way: "Joe leaned back against what remained of the tree, took a deep breath, then let out a long sigh. Without looking back, he stepped out and continued walking toward our line. As he passed beyond range of the rebel muskets, the Confederate soldiers climbed on top of the earth piled in front of their trench and gave a loud cheer."

It was that kind of war.

Those Confederate soldiers must have shared in the small, temporary victory of life over all but certain death. My guess is that the event represented to them a sign of their own hoped-for destiny during the war stretching endlessly before them. As the cheering subsided and the soldiers returned to their trenches, a single rebel soldier remained in view. "Don't you come again, Yanks," he yelled, "or death'll take you all." My guess is that many a man wished he had heeded that warning.

Shortly thereafter, the story goes, Grant motioned for his chief of staff, General Rawlins, to come to his side. They spoke for a moment—the words were private—then Rawlins sent a captain to get Joe. Still carrying his borrowed musket, the lieutenant ran to Grant's side and saluted. Grant stood calmly as he talked for a while. Then Grant turned away and went about his business. Joe followed Grant everywhere he went for the remainder of that day—it was June 2, 1864—coming always to a stop only a few feet away from the general, but never saying a word.

Perhaps Grant just wanted a quiet, personal association with a lucky man. Perhaps he viewed the lieutenant as the bravest of all men simply because he had walked rather than run from that field. Somehow, running says one thing about a man, and walking says another—even in retreat. In the end, however, it did not matter. Death may be betrayed for a moment, but it always takes its revenge. Joe fell the next morning, along with seven thousand others, during the bloodiest twenty minutes of this or any other war.

Now, as I read the paper about what is happening five thousand miles away in Europe, it appears war is being transformed again, this time into a science, a perfect science of killing. I now realize I must become a part of it, because my country now is part of it. But I learned something that I never set out to learn from talking to those old soldiers. To know war, we must experience its horror, its honor, and such glory as there may be in it. I suspect it will be more horror than glory. If there is any honor at all, I suspect it will have infrequent association with brave deeds. It will be, simply, in deciding not to run away.

3 Please Call Me Abby

I stood at the rail, mesmerized by the whish, whish, whishing sound of the rolling paddle wheel of the river steamer. The water sparkled from the light of a full moon skipping along its surface. The stars made a perfect backdrop. Even above the sound of the churning wheel I heard the croak of the frogs singing their mating songs in the shadows along the shore. Occasionally the flickering light of a lantern illuminated a small boat, its occupant poised with an arm held high, waiting to gig one of those frogs. Frog legs are big business in these parts and all along the river. I never developed a taste for them myself. Somehow, eating an amphibian only slightly removed from a tadpole never quite sat right with me.

The boat cruised uncomfortably close to the bank. Strange, I thought, that the captain is chancing coming so close to shore. There was a mile of river width at his disposal. Then I saw the darkened trunks of several trees protruding ominously from the rippling surface off toward the center of the river. Sand bar. The captain knows the way along this river. I felt more at ease.

"Aren't you chilled without a wrap?" said a soft, melodic voice from the darkness.

I turned to the sound of the female voice. Three feet away stood the most beautiful young lady I had ever seen. The shadows cast by the flickering moonlight on her porcelainlike face gave her an air of mystery. Stunned, I was unable to reply.

She cocked her head and waited for my acknowledgment. "I'm sorry to intrude," she continued. "You just looked so lonely standing out here by yourself."

"I didn't know how lonely I was—until now," I said, recovering quickly. Poor, I thought, very poor.

"You seemed startled by my approach," she said, ignoring the double meaning in my statement. "Were you pondering the mysteries of the universe?"

I was too shy to speak the truth, so I changed the subject. "No, not exactly. My thoughts were on Grant."

"Grant?"

"Yes, Ulysses S. Grant."

Her features hardened as she planted her hands firmly on her hips. "I hate that man," she said emphatically.

"Why?" I asked with unmistakable surprise. Something new emerged from this short, already perplexing encounter. No one had ever expressed hatred for Grant to me before.

"He captured my grandfather and nine thousand more fine Southern men at Fort Donelson, down on the Cumberland River. That has been an enduring disgrace in my family. Grandpa commanded a regiment at Fort Donelson where General Buckner surrendered, almost without firing a shot in defense of his men. It was a family disgrace for that drunkard to capture and humiliate a Southern gentleman." Venom permeated her words; she spoke of it as if the experience somehow had been hers.

"The man had to do his job," I replied. "There was nothing personal in it."

"How can you be so frivolous?" Even in the dark I saw her eyes squint and her lips tighten. "Disgrace is the most personal of things." She hesitated before moving back to the real issue. "How can you even speak of that wretched man? He drove the South to its knees, and in doing so killed all the grace and beauty in this country."

I thought of only one response. "He also freed the slaves, or at least Lincoln said it would be so, and Grant made it happen."

"You think that's something wonderful? Look at them now, lumbering around aimlessly, no idea what to do with themselves. My grandfather took care of his darkies." I sensed, even in the dark, her pride in that assertion. "They never wanted for anything. If he had food, they had food. Wherever he went, Grant took the food from their mouths."

My Yankee breeding flashed to the surface. "But no one ever asked them if they wanted to be slaves. Men like your grandfather made a self-fulfilling prophesy of the condition of the Negro. They chained him, then rationalized that it served a necessary purpose. They made a virtue of promoting the Negro's ignorance, then venerated themselves as his benevolent protector, while at the same time beating him into submission." My anger rose with each word. "Your Southern gentlemen did that, never acknowledging the result. They called it that 'peculiar institution.' Peculiar institution, indeed! What kind of term is that for treating a man worse than a dog? Slavery is slavery, and no fancy words ever devised make it a virtue."

She crossed her arms tightly across her breasts. "I see I was mistaken to try to ease your loneliness. I take my leave of you, sir," she snapped as she turned her back to me and strode sharply toward the stairs to the next deck.

Regardless of their gender, Southerners have a way about them. They say "sir" in a way that lets a man know he is a notch below being civilized. Still, the woman intrigued me. She had surfaced a different point of view. I struggled to retain my objectivity. I had already talked to at least two score rebel soldiers. They had expressed a wide variety of opinions about Grant—they were, after all, the ones who had dodged the bullets from Grant's men—but not one of them had expressed hatred for the man.

My anger eased toward passion as I watched her walk up the stairs; definitely a dichotomy, I thought as my hormones assumed control of my emotions. With my anger rising again, her beauty faded in my mind. So young to be so hard, I thought. Now I felt cold, so I climbed the stairs leading to my second-deck cabin.

The experience with this Southern lady had shaken me. Am I missing something? I asked myself. For nearly a year now I had been researching my book on Grant. Yet to this very moment I had been unable to write the first word of my manuscript. Grasping the true essence of the man seemed always just beyond reach. The words of my professor at Harvard rang in my ears from half a continent away: "Never write about something if you lack thorough understanding of what you want to say." I was not sure just what I wanted to say about Grant. How do you explain an enigma? The experience on the deck only increased my uncertainty. The minutes became an hour as I contemplated my self-appointed task. I began to wonder if my goal exceeded my grasp.

I rose from my chair to answer a knock at the door. I recognized the caller as the captain.

"You're Arthur Kelly, am I right?"

"Yes, Captain. What may I do for you?"

He seemed unsure of himself. "I don't know exactly how to put this. Did you have a confrontation with a young lady on the afterdeck a while back?"

I sensed trouble. "Yes," I answered reluctantly.

"The young lady in question, a Miss Abigail Conklin, wishes to extend to you her apology."

I sighed in relief. "Yes? Is that all?"

He waited. "I think not, sir, but that is all she said to say." Then he smiled. "Shall I introduce you to her?"

"That will be unnecessary. Our introduction has been quite complete, thank you."

"Then shall I give her a message?"

I thought for a moment. "Yes. Tell her I reside in Upper Deck Cabin C. The door will be open—all proper, as befits the station and reception of a Southern belle. If she wishes to convey her regrets personally, tell her I am eager to receive her. Tell her exactly that."

I watched his eyes as he struggled to retrieve my words. Then he smiled broadly. "Will she want a chaperone?" he asked hopefully.

"That will be quite unnecessary," I replied, trying to sound self-assured but knowing down deep that I had exposed the full range of my foolishness. "I expect I will be spending the remainder of the evening alone."

The captain squinted as he cocked his head to the side. "Somehow, sir, I doubt that." He turned and walked toward the stairs.

I returned to my chair and slid it up to the small desk. I turned the gas lamp as high as possible. At my side lay my carpetbag. Inside were all the notes I had written about Grant. From my seated position I had difficulty lifting them to the desk. In all there were fourteen large, thick, writing tablets completely filled with facts and impressions. Also included was an assortment of other papers, including several napkins on which, in desperate moments, I had scribbled bits of data. Several books added to the bulk.

It all must have meant something when I wrote it down, I thought. Now, as I examined material more than a year old, the need for reconstructive translation became obvious. For the first time the urge pressed upon me. Whole paragraphs, then whole chapters, flashed through my mind. I had learned something new, something more real. Grant was loved, hated, respected, detested, scorned, esteemed—all of those things—and for a time he wallowed in a quagmire of failure, too. I had come to think of him, somehow, as a god, or at least larger than life. Neither now rang true. He had been a man, like any other. Had it not been for a great and terrible war, he most likely would have died a pauper. Then I remembered: poverty precisely described his condition at his death. From pauper to president to pauper. Confronting that only made him seem more real.

There is a saying in the halls of knowledge back at Harvard that men rise but once. When men fall, they never rise again. They just struggle along until death relieves their burden. Delay the rise, if you must, but at all cost avoid the fall. Grant beat the odds, a fact that only added to his mystique.

Grant spent fifteen years in the army and rose only to the rank of captain. Then, yielding to drink, his most obvious frailty, he fell as far as it is possible to fall. After being driven from the army for drunkenness, he proceeded to do nothing so completely as to make a profession of failure. There was nothing unremarkable about this man. Whatever he did he did completely. With the war, the times and the man merged. "Hard tempering for a man about to be called upon to supervise the killing of two hundred thousand men," the old farmer had said. I realized that while I fancied myself being a writer, I lacked any capacity beyond being the messenger for ideas long ago etched in the minds of the participants in that greatest of all effusions of blood on this continent. That made it easier for me to begin.

The soft rap on the open door interrupted my reverie. I shifted my chair and turned. There she stood, as beautiful as the first time, with just a bit of the mystery washed away by the light. I made a conscious decision to appear stern, then I lost my will. "Come in, Miss Conklin. My name is Art." Despite my best efforts, a smile crept along my lips. "May I call you Abigail?"

"I think not, Mr. Kelly." The haughtiness remained, but then, one doesn't discard breeding so easily. "Please call me Abby."

I realized two things at that moment: I was ready to begin writing my book and I had a passionate determination to make Abby my wife. There remained many miles between this point on the river and New Orleans, or wherever she planned to disembark. The boat's shrill whistle sounded twice, then after a moment, the sound echoed back from the high bluff on the far shore. Moving with such pitiful grace as I possessed, I walked across the room and closed the door. I waited a decent period for the protest that mercifully never came.

4 Shiloh

Deep in depression after reading a report on the war, Lincoln slouched in his chair. The limp bags under his eyes sagged more than usual. The red lines in the president's eyes revealed that he had not slept in days. To the only other person in the room, Secretary of War Edwin M. Stanton, Lincoln appeared old and worn beyond his years. Lincoln shifted his weight, then sighed. "Who is this man Grant?" Lincoln asked Stanton.

Stanton smiled. "I wondered when you would get around to asking that question, Mr. President." Stanton rose and walked toward the door. "Will you excuse me for a moment, sir, while I get my notes?"

Lincoln nodded, but Stanton had already departed. Lincoln rose, then walked with slumped shoulders toward the window. Hints of growth were just beginning to show on the trees on the White House lawn. The trees were not much to speak about, most having been planted within the past three years. Still, the faint signs of new life brought a queer smile to Lincoln's lips.

"Mr. President?"

"Uh-huh," Lincoln replied as he continued to study spring's handiwork.

Stanton shook his head as he studied his notes. "I'm not sure if what I have learned will impress you, Mr. President. The man appears to be more of a ne'er-do-well than anything else. The one fact in his favor is he is a professional soldier. West Point, class of '43. Graduated twenty-first in a class of thirty-nine."

"What was his prior military experience?" Lincoln asked.

"He went to Mexico in '46; served under Taylor and Scott. He was a second lieutenant at the time," Stanton replied.

"So, he has had battle experience," Lincoln replied. Something in the way he said this had the ring of increased confidence, even hope.

Stanton nodded. "It appears so, but nothing much to speak of."

Lincoln ignored the modulating disclaimer. "Anything else?"

"His fitness reports were modest, until the last one, when he was forced to leave the service."

Lincoln turned. "Forced to leave, you say?"

"Yes, sir. He got drunk after being warned to leave the bottle alone, and his commanding officer, Lieutenant Colonel Buchanan, gave him the choice of resignation or court-martial. He left the army in '54 after serving eleven years on active duty. He was a captain at the time."

Lincoln shook his head. "This is the only man who gives me victories?" He turned again toward the window. "Our army is in trouble, Mr. Stanton."

"That's not the worst of it, Mr. President. The man did nothing—worse than nothing—with his life after leaving the army. He moved from job to job, never lasting at anything more than a few months. He failed at teaching, farming, and raising chickens, had some small success cutting and selling wood, worked for a pittance as a tanner—nothing worked for him. He even had a difficult time getting back into the service after the war started. Finally, Governor Yates appointed him colonel of the 21st Illinois." Stanton hesitated. "Sir, you gave him his star, at the recommendation of Congressman Washburn, on July 31 last year. Congress approved the recommendation a month later."

Lincoln shook his head. "I have appointed so many general officers. Am I expected to remember them all?" Lincoln often pondered, fussed and fumed, lamented, took counsel of others to make them feel important—all of these things he did in the company of his advisors—but he almost always acted in isolation. Confronted with deficiencies in high-placed men that were far greater than suffering in poverty or occasionally nipping at the jug, he walked to his desk and withdrew a sheet of paper from the open top drawer. "Please grant me the privilege," he wrote, "of congratulating you on your success in the capture of Forts Donelson and Henry. I pray for your continued success. As of this date I am sending forth to Congress my recommendation that you be promoted to the rank of major general."

He handed the brief note to Stanton. "Send this at once. Prepare the papers for Congress. I want everyone to know that success brings the reward of promotion."

"Are you certain this is best, Mr. President?"

Lincoln looked hard at Stanton.

Stanton knew that look. Lincoln had an infinite patience for listening to others. That look signaled the time for action. "I will attend to it today, Mr. President." Stanton moved toward the door. "There is something more you should know," he said as an afterthought. "General Halleck is not pleased with Grant's performance during this campaign. He thinks Grant moved too fast and without proper authority." Maj. Gen. Henry W. Halleck was the commander of Union forces in the West.

Lincoln appeared lost in thought. Then, he smiled. "Imagine. This Grant told the Confederate commander he would accept nothing but immediate and unconditional surrender." He clasped his hands together behind his back. "And he got it!" The smile grew broader, then Stanton's comment took root. The sad look returned. "You say Halleck is not pleased? My dear Stanton, if the subject ever comes up, as I am sure it will, and if you have the opportunity to speak on it, you just say that the president is pleased." Stanton began to move again toward the door. "Keep me advised of this man's progress, Stanton."

Stanton nodded and left the room.

So Grant emerged from the Forts Henry and Donelson campaign promoted to major general. By March of 1862, only a month after his capture of Fort Donelson, the lofty sounding title of "Unconditional Surrender" Grant echoed all across the North. The capture of the fort had a sound destined to catch the attention of Lincoln, desperate for victory, and whatever caught Lincoln's attention became important. Fort Donelson, the source of Abby's disgrace, had fallen without serious battle. In the space of a week Forts Henry and Donelson, along with fifteen thousand Southern prisoners, fell into Union hands, or more precisely, Grant's hands. "No terms except an unconditional and immediate surrender can be accepted," Grant wrote to Simon Bolivar Buckner, the Confederate commander at Fort Donelson and Grant's old friend and benefactor. "I propose to move immediately upon your works." The message, directly to the point, offered no possibility for misunderstanding.

My grandfather, then a captain in the signal service, arrived on the scene the day following the capitulation. Why I neglected to make his presence in the general vicinity known to Abby, I cannot say. At the time, I certainly had no regard for her self-esteem; my anger was such that I would have welcomed the opportunity to upset her in any way possible. Grandfather was there, however, in time to be among the first to see the rebuke that arrived by telegraph. Chance established that he was in the message tent when the key began to chatter, but it is his place to tell what happened then and in the weeks that followed.

*   *   *

"I carried the message to the general," Grandfather Kelly told me with a nod as he refreshed his mind from his diary. "I flinched at the pain in his eyes as he read it. I learned to hate General Halleck at that moment when I saw the moisture gather in Grant's eyes." Grandfather spoke of this often in my presence as I grew to manhood.

Captain Kelly wrote in his diary:

Strange thing, victory. You'd think that men sharing a common purpose would also share the adulation brought on by its successful achievement. Not so. General Halleck—nicknamed "Old Brains," and General Grant's immediate superior—has proved to be a jealous man. To Halleck's way of thinking, there are ways of doing things and ways of not doing things. Setting aside for the moment the facts of Grant's success in capturing two important forts, Halleck is anything but satisfied with the *way* Grant captured those forts.

Halleck's message to Grant said:

YOUR NEGLECT OF REPEATED ORDERS TO REPORT THE STRENGTH OF YOUR COMMAND HAS CREATED GREAT DISSATISFACTION AND SERIOUSLY INTERFERED WITH MILITARY PLANS. YOUR GOING TO NASHVILLE WITHOUT AUTHORITY WAS A MATTER OF VERY SERIOUS COMPLAINT AT WASHINGTON, SO MUCH SO THAT I WAS ADVISED TO ARREST YOU ON YOUR RETURN.

Grandfather's diary continued:

In the days that followed that terse message, word of the "seriously interfered with military plans" drifted down from Halleck's command center. Halleck intended to take those forts sometime during the summer—after a proper degree of planning and strategizing. Now, apparently, he has no idea what to do with himself or his strategy. Fortunately, following a stressful week of conflict within the high command, Grant's offer of resignation came to nothing—again as a result of advice from Washington, but fingered on a different telegraph key and sent by a different author than the first. The first message, to which Halleck referred in his personal rebuke of Grant, came from General McClellan. The second, I understand, came from the secretary of war at Lincoln's insistence.

Now, with Grant in command, we are on the move again. Some say the war will be over by summer's end, but from what I know on the matter, wars have a way of hanging on. The dot on the map marks Pittsburg Landing. I'm on my way there to anchor communications for the command post. My destination is a backwoods church building known as Shiloh Chapel. I look forward to having a roof over my head again.

Two weeks passed before the next entry.

Grant has the habit of gathering about him men like himself, men, shall we say, taking a circuitous path to public advancement. One such man is William Tecumseh Sherman, a man publicly pronounced as crazy late last fall. It is of benefit having a U.S. senator for a brother. Crazy or not, Sherman is back in command of his division. I was in the communications tent, five feet away, when Grant and Sherman casually began discussing the upcoming campaign. Sherman leaned against the front tent pole; Grant sat on a wooden-slatted, folding chair, facing toward the back, arms crossed on the top of the back support.

"This is a good place for a base of operations, Sam," Sherman said to Grant. "I suggest you bring the army here, where we have a hundred-foot bluff to guard our back and a clear field ahead for defensive operations. In no time at all we can establish a strong defensive perimeter that General [Albert Sidney] Johnston will think twice about attacking."

"I don't know, Sherman," Grant answered. "Bringing the men here seems a sound idea, but I have in mind doing battle with

Johnston. I fear a strong defensive perimeter will put him off a bit."

The words did little to ease my mind. Did Grant have a trap in mind? Was I part of the bait? I remember sarcastically thinking that retreat will be no problem; the only escape is off that hundred-foot bluff into a rampaging, rain-swollen river that could drown a weak-swimming fish. With the approach of April, the temperature continues to rise, and so do emotions in anticipation of what everyone knows must come.

"What makes you think Johnston will come to you?" Sherman asked.

"Sidney's a proud man," said Grant. "I remember him from the Mexican campaign, back in '46. After the loss of Henry and Donelson, he'll be itching to reverse his fortunes. He'll come like rolling thunder when conditions are right. I just have to make it worth his while to move his men from Corinth. It strikes me as counterproductive to make our defenses appear too strong."

That's one peculiarity about this war. Everyone knows everyone. Unless he knows someone high up to provide a lift, a man has to be about forty or more to be the right age to be a general. The only ones that age with battle experience served in the Mexican War. The lieutenants, captains, and majors young enough to do the fighting then have reached the age to be generals. Grant is one of them. Johnston is older, but he's one of them. Half the Union generals know half the Confederate generals well enough to call them by their first name. It has been a small army these past fifteen years. Their paths all crossed at one time or another.

Hell, I hear many of them courted the same girls. It's enough to make you wonder at the real reason they will be going at each other. If I took away a man's woman, I wouldn't want him coming at me ten years later with a fifty-thousand-man army. From what I hear, Grant was woolied around a lot before he first left the army in '54. Some of those Reb generals may have some accounting to do for that. Grant is a quiet one. It's the quiet ones who tend to note most what goes on around them. Grant sure didn't have any trouble going at Buckner at Donelson, and Buckner is his friend. What might he have in mind for his enemies?

Grandfather made it clear that Grant wanted Johnston to come at him, but I suspect he just as soon would have had it happen a smidgen later, after Buell's army came down from Nashville. Johnston had his own ideas.

Johnston's men formed in double regiment lines. At the sound of the drums, they boiled out of the woods on General Prentiss's front at about seven o'clock this morning, Sunday, April 6. A day of living hell has just concluded. You might say Grant got his wish. The only problem is, he wasn't here when it broke loose! As I understand it, he was just finishing a leisurely breakfast back at the Cherry Mansion, nine miles up the river.

So this was Sherman's day, and by my estimation, he saved Grant's bacon and his reputation—barely.

I learned something about battle today. Although trained as a signal officer, I have suffered through some classes on tactics and strategy. Generals spend endless hours around the campfire talking about this great general doing this and this one doing that. So far as I can determine, it's all a futile attempt to put order into the least orderly of human endeavors—war. I suspect that even if a man knew what was happening it still would overwhelm him, general or not—but he doesn't know. Strategy, for sure, goes out the door when the first general yells "Go after 'em, boys." From that moment on it's a mad rush for personal survival, and more than a few don't make it.

Tactics are a bit more useful. When they don't work out, which is usual, you have immediate information to explain what went wrong. A quick learner may get a second chance to do it right, if he ever finds himself in the same fix again.

Strategy and tactics had nothing to do with saving the Union Army during this day's battle. Sherman did that, at least in the early fighting. Shouting and waving his hat, he seemed to appear everywhere at once. He refused to run. It's hard for a private to run when he sees his general sitting proud on a high horse facing the battle. A thousand mistakes occurred this day, about equally divided between both sides. I saw a battery of guns captured here, a regiment cut down there, but everyone was so busy it meant little at the time, although to some it seemed like the end of the world, which of course it was. Battle lines almost never joined the fight as their commanders envisioned. They won't tell you that, but it's so obvious that even the private soldier sees it clearly. No one would plan these disasters!

Words from the past, but they seemed as fresh as yesterday's paper. The same messages are coming from France. There is a temptation to think of war as titanic struggles flowing in an orderly manner from elaborate designs. Yet, the real impression, compressed from the expressed experiences of real people, is of contests settled by the side that makes the fewest mistakes. Grandfather, at least, thought so.

Little, individual decisions, made by unimportant men such as privates, sergeants, and lieutenants, saved particular situations, or led to temporary disaster in another. Often, the choice was as simple as to run or die. Generals don't count much when chaos takes command. If they do make a difference, it's whether they run or stay. The private soldier knows little of war. His task is to load and fire and load and fire again. Generals should know what is going on! The private soldier figures that if the general stays, things must be going all right. If the general runs, there is no chance the private will protect the general's ass by staying around to load and fire once more. Sherman stayed on this fateful Sunday, and enough of the privates stayed with him that it made a difference.

The irony of war is always present. Men march a hundred miles over many days only to find that inches of distance and moments of time make all the difference. Grant arrived at the battle site about midmorning. Looking up from tying a tourniquet on the two remaining inches of a major's leg, I first saw Grant riding up in full dress to talk to Sherman. Grant turned to one of his aides who sat on his horse looking at the battle through a telescope. Grant handed him a message, obviously intending that an order be delivered to some hazardous place. For some reason, after accepting the message and saluting smartly, the staff officer brought the glass to his eye for one last, brief look. A Minié passed through the front glass, moved perfectly along the tube to the back glass, then passed squarely through his eye and out the back of his head. As he fell, he still clutched the blood-spattered message, which another officer retrieved and carried to its destination. I'll never forget the surprise in the sightless stare of that officer's remaining eye.

Later, as Grant rode to his headquarters, a battery of heavy guns found his range. One of the balls smashed his saber, which hung just about even with his hip. When asked about it here at headquarters I heard him say that he failed to discover this until later, and at the sight, "I broke into a cold sweat." Then he smiled faintly. "Rawlins," he asked, "do I have another saber?"

"No, General," he replied, "and I have no idea where to look for one."

As with everyone, generals are flesh and blood, too. So, when they stay on, leading by example, it means something. Yet sometimes they die, and in their dying the tide of battle changes. According to the report from some Reb prisoners, Gen. Albert Sidney Johnston died this afternoon from nothing more than what a line soldier would call a nick on the knee. In his frenzy to address more important events, he left the wound unattended. His life drained out through a severed artery and flowed into his boot. Did it make a difference? I don't know. He came to his death by an inch, and Grant missed a critical wound by the same measure. At that point, in the early afternoon, Johnston's men nearly had the battle won. With Johnston dead and Grant alive we are back at even odds.

Reflecting on Grandfather's words, I realized that many men died as an indirect result of Johnston's death. The Confederate general died at a place considered, at the time, to be on the fringe of the battle. If he had remained alive he might have continued to push in that direction, as had been his intention when he led his troops forward, the act resulting in his fatal wound. Unknown to his men, perhaps unknown even to Johnston, had they pressed forward they might have won the battle there and then.

"Except for a few provosts and skirmishers," Grandfather recorded, "and of course, me, nothing stood between them and Pittsburg Landing, then the far rear of our whole army."

They would have rolled right over Grandfather. Leaderless as a result of Johnston's death, the Confederate regiments stopped, shortly to be turned by Maj. Gen. Braxton Bragg in another direction, toward the sound of the heaviest fighting. I shudder at the possible result of that fateful hour. If Johnston's men had moved on without him, might the battle have ended in a brilliant Confederate victory? More to the point: would I be here to wonder at the outcome?

The place has become known as the HORNET'S NEST, and for good reason. I write it in capital letters because I think men will talk about it for a long time. Because it marked the place of the heaviest dying, the Hornet's Nest was the place in greatest need of communication. Rawlins sent me to give such assistance as possible. Accompanying a party of medical aides, I came up from the southwest to join a reinforcing brigade led by one-armed Colonel Sweeny. Along the way a fragment ripped into his remaining arm.

Men fight differently for different reasons. Sometimes they fight because there is nothing else to do. That was so at the Hornet's Nest. Within the hour our situation became untenable, or so it seemed. With the option of running removed, the men set about the task of killing Rebs. They performed with the vengeance of a farmer dedicated to removing the last stump from the middle of his prized field. The Rebs kept coming in waves, urged on, I heard, by Bragg's order to go where the fighting was. I only learned of this later, while attending a wounded Confederate colonel who asked me to get a message to his wife telling her that he died with honor. How do you suppose he thought I could do that? In the process, Bragg's order became a prophecy. Men came forward in lines packed so closely that their shoulders touched. The rifled shells of the Union Enfields, supported by the cannon canister raining down from a western hill, cut them down in groups of a dozen or more. Sometimes, after a volley when the men were reloading and waiting to fire again, the smoke cleared to reveal a whole line of the enemy cut off at the knees. The order to shoot low had, in a grim sort of way, paid off. Sometimes, it seemed the wounded filled the air with one sustained scream. Dying, by contrast, is a relatively quiet process.

As it worked out, Bragg's men inflicted considerable suffering, both on our soldiers and on themselves. In the end, the Rebs prevailed. More than two thousand of those around me marched off to prison. Nearly as many died or suffered wounds. Reasoning that about the most useless person around was a signal officer, I went out with the last remnant given orders to try to escape the trap. Pulling with me a wounded corporal with a foot missing, I crawled for perhaps two hundred yards along a small ravine behind the Hornet's Nest. The corporal lived, and by nightfall I was back at Grant's headquarters.

There are water smudges on the the diary's pages at this point. I thought once to ask about their source, but let the opportunity pass. There was room enough for tears in the meaning of the words, but it also rained that night. Grandfather spoke from the past:

> Grant knows the price paid by the men in the Hornet's Nest. He must have known. By drawing Bragg's men to them, those men saved our army from capture, cut off as we are by the river at our back. For a short time, again, tactics held sway. The dying in the Hornet's Nest gave us time to reform a defensive line.

If ever there existed a contrast to Grant, it was Sherman. In a roundabout way, Grandfather noticed this difference. Grant seemed always composed, quiet, and in control. Sherman ran with his emotions, exuded impatience, and spoke in loud, bellowing tones—to everyone but Grant. Grant liked Sherman, and Sherman returned the feeling. More important, Grant trusted Sherman. Each probably saw something in the other that he wished was a part of himself. Whatever it was, each man complemented the other, bringing to the conflict what the other lacked.

Grandfather gave Sherman much credit for the army's performance during this long, grueling Sunday, but that unfairly diminishes Grant's contribution. While Sherman rode up and down the lines trying to rally the men, Grant detected a more subtle meaning to what evolved as the afternoon progressed. Refusing to panic, or perhaps conditioned by his life never to see the worst in events, he performed in the only way possible to save his army. The conflict at the Hornet's Nest was a part of what he saw, and in it he detected a meaning that escaped Sherman. Grant reasoned that the day must eventually end. If only he could prevent a rout, Maj. Gen. Don Carlos Buell's army would arrive before the next day to replenish the ranks. So, while Sherman concentrated on the men, Grant moved quietly but firmly among his officers telling them, "It will be all right." Somehow, in the midst of all the noise and turmoil, they accepted his assessment of conditions, and they responded.

To be sure, the Hornet's Nest was a cruel and costly tragedy, at least for the men directly involved, but all the dying and killing served a useful purpose in tipping the balance of the overall battle. The

dying men were using up the daylight as the rebels concentrated all
their energy to subdue that pocket of resistance. Grant used the time
to steady his line. Slowly, he pulled the bulk of his army back to the
high ground and massed his cannon for maximum impact when the
final rebel push came. It was war at its worst and leadership at its best,
and Grant had the insight to think it through and respond. He did a
general's job.

"Had you not best be preparing for a retreat across the river?"
an agitated officer asked Grant, not far from where I stood.

"No," Grant replied calmly. "Before that happens I will have
used up so great a portion of the army that not enough will remain to worry about."

One last time the Rebs came forward toward our men, and a
half-mile-long row of our guns, eighty or more, anchored by six
giant siege guns, expelled their fire and steel. Making the sound
of a fading echo, the explosions rolled down the line from gun
to gun, only to begin all over again when the last in the line had
fired. The shot and canister blew large, gaping holes in the advancing rebel ranks and the advance began to wither like vines
do when brushed by a flaming torch. Faced with this unpleasant
circumstance, the Rebs decided they had suffered enough for one
day, and the lengthening shadows of late evening chased them
in their retreat.

During the worst of this, I saw Grant, his left foot propped on
a busted wagon wheel, standing on a ridge as night approached.
He puffed on a cigar. He must have been anxious. The smoke
pouring out of his mouth reminded me of a locomotive laboring
up a steep grade. The only movement in his body was the clenching
and relaxing of his fist as the unending chain of explosions rolled
down that line of cannon. As I looked up and down that line of
men, I thought of a hundred orders I would have screamed. Grant
just watched, never saying a word, as the last of the Confederate infantry blended into the night. When the last Reb faded from
sight, Grant reached down and took hold of his broken saber. He
looked at it briefly, with the look of a man who had lost a close
friend, then he let it drop to his side as he turned and walked toward
his horse. He spoke briefly to Rawlins, but they were too far away

for me to hear his words. It must have been unimportant, for they rode off slowly together.

Looking for a deeper, more profound meaning in what Grandfather observed, I have often wondered what Grant thought at that moment. For the second time that day, a resolute charge by the enemy could have scattered his army over a hundred miles. Yet, the hour was late. Tired from their labor, the Rebs held back. Except for what he had already done, Grant was powerless to stop them. His calmness at the point of final confrontation suggests he knew as much. I swear I would have had to do something, throw a rock, fire a pistol, or just scream, "Go get 'em, boys."

That which preceded and followed that failed charge has inspired much criticism and hardly any praise. No matter. Grant just stood puffing on that cigar, saying nothing. History records that it began to rain, gently at first, then in torrents. I prefer to rationalize that the rain would have made movement too difficult for the rebels to have succeeded even without Grant's planning. Grandfather may have had similar thoughts.

At the time, the meaning of the rain escaped me. Lying before me, shoulder-to-shoulder, foot-to-head on a plot covering three acres, were the men who chose not to run. All were bleeding. One in four would be dead by first light. More than a few were assisted in their departure by the occasional burst of a cannon shell landing in their midst. A constant moaning filled the air. The multiple amputees and those with their guts hanging out were the most pitiful. They prayed to die, to put an end to their suffering. The rain only added to their misery. The appalling suffering drew me into their midst, where I moved among the battered bodies hoping to grasp the terrible meaning of death. I learned nothing. The most common word spoken, even more frequently than God, was Mama. I found that perplexing. It was as if, at the moment of confronting the fragile nature of life, they wanted to return to the womb in the futile hope of trying to begin all over again.

Those men were there when Grant watched the hesitant attack, but never did he turn to dwell on their suffering. He just stood, puffing and thinking. How great his burden must have been!

What he did, how he stood so calmly while the world seemed to be ripping asunder, must have meant something to the men. There isn't a man in sight of this dismal place that dares to think that the dying is over. Most generals would have been overwhelmed by panic and frantically organizing a retreat. Not Grant. I doubt he even considered it. Before, because Sherman stood firm, the men stood with him. Now that those men have stood firm, thousands at the price of life and limb, Grant can do no less. I wonder what tomorrow will bring?

"What do you think?" Grant asked Sherman as he munched a strip of jerky back at headquarters.

"I think, sir," Sherman replied, "they will come at us at first light with the force of Hell."

Grant nodded. "Do you think we will hold?"

"Now that Buell's men are coming in, I think so."

"Then make your plans," Grant said as he swung his leg over the saddle.

Grant wasn't much on strategy or tactics at the time, Grandfather emphasized in his writing. Much had to be done before morning came, but mostly it involved getting men in place to hold the line. So far as I know, no particular plan was in place, except to be ready to respond to whatever happened. Buell's men jumped into the ranks as fast as they marched up. The rain kept coming down, making any movement difficult. "It seems like the Lord is rubbing it in," Grandfather heard a nearby soldier say.

It had been Grandfather's reminiscing about the war that first got me interested in that time. He never let his diary out of his sight, but he always let me read it when I asked. There must have been a hundred pages. In all of it, one short yet profound passage stands out above all the others as the most important:

War is a strange thing. When you endure the worst the other side can fling at you, when the pit of despair is at its darkest, morale starts to rise. When you pour all you have into it, however, and then victory stays just out of reach, confidence begins to sag. It's nothing solid that you see, nothing with form to feel, but you know it's there. A general can't give a speech to make it happen or to keep it from happening. It's a private assessment, in more ways than one. On this, the most miserable of nights, it happened fifty thousand times all along both lines. Something told our men that conditions must improve. Across the way, something about the day's events convinced the Rebs they had squandered their best chance. At some moment during the night these points of view crossed and resolved the eventual outcome without a shot being fired. As difficult as the night had been for our troops, it also rained on the rebel camps.

*   *   *

I have read everything about this battle that I could get my hands on. Many called it a defeat for the Union; hardly anyone called it a victory. Grandfather was there, however, and he felt something in the misery of that cold, wet night. To me it seems almost mystical, at the very least a mystery. He felt the shift in the men's thinking, a shift from defeat to something else. If not to victory, I cannot say to what, but the rebels faced a vibrant, revitalized army when the next dawn appeared. Grandfather concluded:

Things happened today just about the way Sherman predicted, but never with the intensity of hell, or at least the hell of the first day. There were attacks all along the line, but the Rebs lacked the energy to press hard. It was more like they were going to work but were unwilling to give their boss more than he paid for. By midafternoon, the Battle of Pittsburg Landing, as our side calls it, or Shiloh, as the Reb prisoners call it, concluded. If there are any Hebrew-speaking soldiers present, they must be surprised by the pure irony in the meaning of the name—Place of Peace. The greatest battle of the war has concluded, the last shot fired at defiant Confederate general Nathan Bedford Forrest as he galloped from the field. I pray I never experience the battle that makes this second.

In two days, nearly twenty-three thousand men fell dead and wounded. The majority wore blue, but given the disparity of population between North and South, the Union had more to spare.

At the time something was taking form, a statistic that acquired meaning only at the end of the war. As long as Grant lived, as long as he did battle, he never retreated in fear.

In the years since 1862, historians have fought the Battle of Shiloh many times. A clear victor has hardly ever emerged. At the time, the Northern papers and politicians were highly critical of Grant. No one was more critical than his commander, Halleck. So incensed was Halleck that he removed Grant from direct command and threatened again to send him away in disgrace. As was often the case, however, Lincoln spoke the last words, or at least the only words that mattered. "I can't spare this man," he said. "He fights."

The paramount axiom of battle is simple: when the fighting stops, whoever holds the field wins. One fact is beyond dispute. When the echo of that last shot faded, Grant's army held Shiloh field.

"Show me an army of lions led by sheep, and I will show you defeat," an ancient warrior observed. "Show me an army of sheep led by a lion, and I will show you victory."

5 Hardly Anyone Wanted War

Drift down the Galena River to the Mississippi and you enter one type of waterway. Walk down the bluff at Vicksburg to the crumbling boat ramps and you discover a different river. The river has the same name, Mississippi, but there the similarity ends. For one thing, by the time the river reaches Vicksburg it has picked up the waters from dozens of lesser streams and rivers. At Vicksburg it is difficult to determine where the river ends and dry lands begin. Actually, it is a gradual transition, often involving miles of swamps and snake-infested backwaters. Over the centuries, the river has changed course many times. History and the river have passed by places once on the river's banks that now are high and dry. Vicksburg has withstood the river's pressures.

Below the cliffs of Vicksburg, at the time of the war, the river stretched out like a long, narrow sea, and, looking at the city from the west, the city resembled nothing so much as a bustling seaport. It is also that way now, but only because Grant failed to make it otherwise.

Vicksburg grew at the turning place of a long river bend. A cliff of a hundred feet or more plunges from the west edge of the city down to the water. The river tumbles toward the city from the northwest. Some distance downriver it moves back to the southwest. The result of this changing direction created in Grant's mind a possibility. If his men dug a channel, he surmised, from a point north to a point south of Vicksburg, the city would be left high and dry. This would straighten the river's course and would, in effect, create an island of the land left isolated to the east of the new channel. Perhaps from the outset it was an impossible scheme. One fact is certain: Grant had the men to attempt the task. He had an army. But that came later.

*   *   *

As so often happened in his life, both in war and peace, Grant descended on hard times following Shiloh.

"As boisterous and joyous as the reporters and politicians had been in their praise of Grant after Fort Donelson," an old war correspondent who wrote for a Chicago newspaper at the time told me, "they were belligerent in their utterances after Shiloh. The killing and the maiming caused part of his problem. His tardiness at the start of the battle added substance to their sounds of outrage. You have to understand that the nation moved slowly toward grasping the fact that men die and are maimed in war, at least in the numbers killed and wounded in the two days at Pittsburg Landing. The numbers, thirteen thousand for the North and ten thousand for the South, were appalling enough. Expressed another way, however, twenty-three thousand Americans had died or been wounded. That made it sound much worse. In effect, at least in the early stages of the war, Grant was being held accountable for all who died on both sides. In contrast, fewer than four hundred Confederate and five hundred Union soldiers died at the first Battle of Bull Run, and the press screamed when those figures became known. At the time, Shiloh stood out as the greatest single conflict ever experienced on the continent. The sight and thought of men, as one reporter recorded, 'cut down and stacked like cordwood' left no room for redeeming analysis. General Halleck, Grant's commander, had an especially negative view of this development."

A few days after the battle Halleck came down from St. Louis.

"Were you there when General Halleck arrived?" I asked.

"Not at the time when he met with Grant. A number of guards were posted about the area, and they had no trouble hearing the conversation. I pieced together the essential points from their recollections." His eyes brightened. "Wait a minute. I still have my notes from that time stacked around here someplace." The old reporter walked across the large pressroom and opened a creaking door to a dusty storage room. "I kept all this material," he said in a muffled voice, "thinking I might write the great American war novel. Of course, I never did. Let me see. Here it is, 1862." He blew the dust from the journal as he kicked the door shut. He thumbed through the crisp, yellowing pages. "Here it is." Reading from his notes, the old man reconstructed the meeting between the two generals.

" 'General Grant,' Halleck reportedly said, 'in all my years as a military man, I never have heard of such wanton disregard for the lives of men by a commanding general.'

" 'Sir,' Grant replied, 'you were not there and therefore are unfit to judge the events of the battle.' " The reporter looked at me and smiled. "That proved to be an unfortunate beginning to the conversation, I suspect. Halleck was not the type of man to yield gracefully to rebuke.

" 'I've read your accounts, sir,' Halleck retorted, 'and the accounts in the papers. What have you accomplished, sir? I'll tell you: nothing!'

" 'Nothing, sir?' Grant replied. 'We drove the rebel army from the field. Even now our army is in pursuit.'

" 'But at such a fearful cost in lives!' Halleck cried out."

The old reporter looked over the rim of his glasses. "It kept coming back to that," he said, "and Grant possessed no means of moderating the arithmetic.

" 'Johnston set the tone, General,' Grant said. 'Would you have had me retreat? If so, then when will we fight? War is not all moving and countermoving. The purpose of such movement as is necessary is to bring the armies together. Then men die. If you expect to resolve this conflict without men dying then let us send the men home and bid the rebels well. I feel certain they will be content with that arrangement.'

"Halleck reportedly hit the tent with a fist. 'You are impudent, sir,' Halleck replied. One witness said the two shadows in the tent came together as Halleck yelled in Grant's face.

"Grant moved back a pace. 'Perhaps, General Halleck, but I think you fail to see war for what it is. It is bleeding, maiming, and, yes, killing. I never have found the right number to die, but I know this: for the South to live, its men must have land to stand on, to grow crops on, to move their armies about. There now is less of that land, and final victory is closer, but only if we persevere.'

"Halleck shook his head and threw up his arms. 'Are you mad, sir?' Halleck went to the opening of the tent, then turned toward Grant. He said something to the effect that Grant and he lacked the same perspective of war. To that he added: 'I will take field command of the army now that I am here. You will serve as my deputy. You will take no action without my personal approval, and report to me only through my adjutant. I will demonstrate the way to move the army about the field.' His final statement defined his problem. To Halleck, moving armies about the field defined the art of war. Halleck's directive effectively removed Grant from any part in the army's operation, especially since Halleck refused to receive Grant's counsel, even through his adjutant."

*   *   *

Halleck, for all his knowledge of strategy and tactics, had missed Grant's essential point. He failed to accept the horror of war or, for that matter, to understand what war might become when the opposing sides became serious in their disagreement. "War is not chess," Sherman responded to a journalist's criticism of Grant, "with pieces moved quickly and quietly from the board through the skillful move of an opposing piece. War is all Hell."

Grant, however, had endorsement for his sentiment, support that mattered.

About this time another drama, this one of more lasting importance, evolved in the city of Washington. It was after midnight, and Lincoln sat silently in his study observing the flickering tongues of flame in the fireplace. Although the days were now warm, a damp, cool breeze usually blew in the early morning hours. Lincoln knew this well; he seldom slept during this spring of '62. Secretary of War Stanton sat a few feet away, deep in thought, while across the room Treasury Secretary Salmon P. Chase sat studying a stack of papers as if they were the most significant documents of the time. Actually, there were two documents, one quite long and the other short, and both, in their own ways, *were* the most significant documents of the time. Assessment of the positive or negative meaning of these two documents, however, depends on one's particular values. The official list of the Shiloh casualties comprised the longer document. The other was an early draft of the Emancipation Proclamation. It still remained unnamed, and the text remained jagged and disjointed, but the meaning was there, and that meaning promised to be as explosive an issue as the war itself.

Lincoln appeared tired. He propped his right elbow on the arm of the chair, and with his midsection shifted to the other side, he leaned sideways to rest his head on the upstretched right hand. "They just won't fight," he said softly.

"What?" Stanton said as if shaken from a trance.

"My generals. They just won't fight. They maneuver well enough, but they avoid the enemy. They spar a bit when contact is forced, then they back away." A long pause followed. "All except Grant," he added finally.

Satisfied that Lincoln had nothing new to say, Stanton settled back in his chair and let his eyes close again. "Halleck wants to fire Grant, you know," Stanton said.

"Yes, that's what I hear," Lincoln answered. "McClellan supports Halleck, and the Democrats support McClellan." Lincoln's thoughts merged with the flames as he contemplated the generalship of Maj. Gen. George B. McClellan, who was both commanding general of the army and commander of the Army of the Potomac. "For all his virtues, the man simply will not fight."

"Grant?" Stanton asked in surprise.

"No, McClellan. If it will help, I will gladly hold his horse." Lincoln shifted his weight and straightened up, then placing his elbows on his knees, he leaned forward and placed his chin in the cup of his hands. He sighed. "I think he wants to be king."

The comment caught Chase's attention. "Who?" he asked, his words carried by a small laugh.

"McClellan," Lincoln answered sharply. "He fancies himself the savior of the country." Lincoln shook his head. "God! If only it were true. The man consumes a million dollars worth of supplies a day marching his army up and down the Peninsula. He refuses to understand that I have no desire to capture Richmond if it means Lee's army breaks loose. What will I do with the city if he gives it to me? We don't have the men to garrison it, at least not with a force that will keep Lee out if he chooses to take it back, which he will." Lincoln rose and walked to the window, then turned and looked at the clock. "It's after one, and look at this! If I close my eyes and throw a rock, I'll hit at least one general. What do they all do?" He shook his head. More than a minute passed before he continued. "Stanton, how serious is Halleck in his intent to fire Grant?"

"I think he is very serious, Mr. President. Grant is a threat to 'Old Brains,' as well as to McClellan. McClellan's message to Halleck stopped just short of ordering Grant's dismissal. So long as Halleck is out there he will blame every setback on Grant and save all that goes well for himself. There will always be Grant's love for the bottle to blame."

Lincoln sighed again, then walked toward his desk. "There may be little enough I can do," he mumbled to himself, "but I am still the president." He opened a drawer and withdrew a sheet of writing paper, then began penning an order. After he finished, he knelt by the fire and read it carefully to himself. Satisfied with the content, he smiled.

"Here," he said as he handed the paper to Stanton. "Send this to Halleck. With it, send him a personal note from me telling him he is too important to our efforts to risk his being killed by a wayward rebel bullet. Mention something about General Johnston's death to emphasize the point."

Stanton adjusted his glasses and casually read the order. As he neared the end, his alertness improved. "This relieves him of his field command!" Stanton exclaimed.

Lincoln said nothing. He knew what it meant. No commander liked to give up leadership of troops in the field. But Lincoln saw more in this conflict than was apparent on the surface: he saw an opportunity to address a variety of concerns within the army's command structure. An obvious by-product of his action was to free Grant to do what he had demonstrated both a willingness and an aptitude to do: engage the enemy and produce victories.

But as part of Lincoln's broader plan, he intended to make Halleck commanding general of the army, relieving McClellan of the dual responsibilities of commanding the Army of the Potomac and managing the overall war effort. Although Halleck had hardly distinguished himself as a field commander in the months following Shiloh, his overall management of the army in the western theater—especially its strategic direction and coordination of administrative and supply operation—was laudatory. Known as "Old Brains" throughout the army, Halleck would prove to be an able administrator as he coordinated the efforts of the various bureaus charged with supporting the armies in the field. Despite their earlier differences, Grant and Halleck would, later in the war when their respective talents were applied to maximum benefit, develop a complementary if not warm personal relationship.

Last, but far from least, relieving McClellan of his broader command responsibilities removed any further excuse McClellan might raise for his failure to move his army decisively toward General Lee.

"What plan have you for Grant?" Stanton asked.

"With Halleck back in Washington," Lincoln replied, "the western army will need a commander." He paused as he leaned forward and rested his outstretched hand on the fireplace mantle. "I cannot spare this man," Lincoln said. "He fights. If saving Grant means removing Halleck . . ." He let the sentence drop. Lincoln had to do something, so he made a simple choice. In making it, he altered the course of the war more than if he had ordered a hundred thousand men into battle. He did not, of course, know this at the time.

McClellan, who was then lumbering around in seemingly endless preparations to attack Richmond, also had no taste for killing. He had, however, considerable personal power resulting from having many friends in high places, most of them in the Democratic Party. In time, when it best served Lincoln's purpose, he also removed McClellan, but only when the general's flame had lost most of its flicker. For the present, Lincoln contented himself with keeping Grant in the field and moving Halleck to Washington. Lincoln had never met Grant, but he knew all he needed to know about the man. He fought, and at the time Lincoln needed nothing so much as a general who knew why he wore a uniform.

There was, however, more to it than that. This always had been a political war, and the political issues were beginning to manifest themselves in the way people in authority acted. Lurking submerged under the roar of battle and the chanting in the streets was the real but as yet unspoken reason the nation had gone to war. That reason was the Negro.

*   *   *

"Good morning, Senator," I said as I entered the large office decorated with ornate paneling and an array of neatly framed and matted photographs. Massive golden drapes hung from the broad window. Stitched in the middle of each of the four pleated drape panels was an eighteen-inch-diameter embroidered seal of the president of the United States, the gift from a grateful president for some long-forgotten service. On the mahogany wall behind the desk were two flags, their gleaming brass poles crossing at the point where the base of the banners fastened to the staffs. One was the United States flag, the other for the state of Kansas. In front of the massive oak desk stood three leatherbound chairs with silver-headed brads holding the covers in place. I felt the chairs needed to be behind glass rather than on the floor. I held back when the senator directed me to take a seat, but there was no other place to sit.

"Senator Potter," I said as I studied the room, "I'm doing research for a book about General Grant and his part in the Civil War. I know you were in Washington at the time, but I've received conflicting reports on your purpose for being in the city. You were too young at the time to be a senator."

"I was elected to the Senate more than twenty years after the war ended. In 1861, I worked as an aide to Secretary Chase in the Treasury Department. I had recently graduated from Harvard with a degree in economics—the first to receive such a degree, I might add. I'm quite proud of that."

I reviewed my questions. "I understand that paying for the war presented a considerable burden."

"Worse than that," he said. "For all intent and purpose, the nation was broke by the fall of '61, and the war had hardly begun."

"I was informed," I said, "that you developed the plan for tapping business profits to finance the war."

He smiled. "That's an exaggeration," he said. "Actually, we were just sitting around talking one evening—we were wondering if there was enough money in the Treasury to pay our salary—and I mentioned that the big businesses were booming and getting rich off the war, and they ought to pay part of the bill. One suggestion led to another, and the nucleus of a plan emerged. But Secretary Chase pulled it together and transformed raw ideas into a workable plan. He was a genius in economic theory, and I don't know that he ever had an hour of formal training in the subject."

"What did you consider to be your most important contribution to the war effort?" I asked.

"I drafted the first plan for the economic strangulation of the South. When I realized how severe financial problems were for us, I knew how much worse it must be for the South. I had traveled a little down in Kentucky and Georgia, and even made it down to Florida. Southern industry was worse than primitive; in many respects, it didn't exist at all. I mentioned to Gen. Winfield Scott one day that the South would fight forever unless we cut off their supplies. I didn't think he even heard me. Then, a few days later, he asked me to draft a plan addressing this issue. A young supply clerk and I sat down that evening and studied a big map of the South. It soon became clear that the Mississippi was the key to everything. To me, this meant that the early war effort had to be in the West, and we just had to hold on in the East. That idea wasn't very glamorous to politicians who thought of Washington as the center of the universe."

"Why were there so many problems during '61 and '62?" I asked.

"Simple," he replied. "The plan for conducting the war emerged very slowly. The process for building the army typified the confusion. First, men went in for thirty-day enlistments, then for ninety more days, then for a year. In time, when it became obvious that the war might drag on past the summer, many extended their enlistments for three years. The point is, without knowing the magnitude of the job, no one had an accurate measure to determine how long its accomplishment might take. The critical problem, though, was leadership. The common soldier tended to accept the war in terms of survival and drudgery, the drudgery in the marching, with survival becoming the problem when the marching stopped. The generals, however, tended to conceive the war in terms of personal glory and what that glory might mean for them later within the political arena. At the outset, more than half of the generals were political appointees with no significant military training. It took the first two years or so to sort things out."

"Why did Lincoln let those people get in control of the military?" I asked.

"Politics," the senator replied. "Every decision revolved around political considerations. Lincoln had to build a consensus before he could even fight the war. If Congress had been in session at the time the war began, it's doubtful it would have approved the war. Lincoln spent millions of dollars without a single congressional appropriations act. He even suspended the writ of habeas corpus. Many in the government had Southern sympathies. Even Lincoln had trouble grasping the crux of the need. He often told his cabinet: 'We must eliminate their capacity to conduct the war.' What this meant, exactly, no one knew. This was forgivable during the early stages of the war. There were more pressing problems, such as organizing the army, establishing a production and supply system, and neutralizing the border states. The time was approaching, however, when addressing the central problem could no longer be ignored."

"When did priorities begin to change?" I asked.

"Following Bull Run. Before that battle, everyone thought the South would surrender as soon as we killed some of their men. That myth exploded along with the cannon and muskets of that first public battle. Slowly, the emphasis shifted from purely political considerations to a cohesive economic and military strategy.

"One has to understand that, before the war, a large portion of the South's needs came from the North. Economic ties were strong. Cotton was king, and cotton prices determined the rate of exchange. The South had economic power far in excess of its ability to produce the goods necessary for the growth of a powerful nation. Actually, even before the war, slavery was slowly killing the economic structure of the South. If the price of cotton doubled, so did the price of a slave. Plantation owners paid three or four thousand dollars for a good field hand, more than he could ever return on the investment. Slaves meant status for a Southern gentleman, and the process of acquiring slaves squelched all incentive for capital investment. It almost was an aristocrat-and-serf economy with slavery the cornerstone of all economic activity. They saw no gradual way out of their dilemma, so they clung to slavery against all rational consideration."

Senator Potter walked to a large framed map fastened to the west wall of the room. He made a sweeping circle with his hand. "Overall, the South was totally unprepared to engage in a war. Their vulnerability escaped no one who understood the requirements of a wartime economy. Many of the Southerners who populated Washington—most of the population was Southern or of Southern persuasion—knew this. All except the radicals privately believed that the South was committing suicide, but in public they spoke of swift and certain victory. In truth, hardly anyone wanted war, and no one knew how to prevent it.

"With supplies and finished goods cut off from the North, everything had to roll in from the West or be shipped from Europe. As the eastern sea blockade stiffened, much of the necessary war materials first had to go through Mexico before being moved through Texas and across the Mississippi. Cattle, grain, guns, ammunition, even many of the men necessary to carry on the struggle moved along this trail. But to accomplish anything, they had to cross that river. The Mississippi was both the salvation of and the greatest problem for the South. Although only a mile wide at critical crossing points, control of that mile was paramount."

To comprehend this it is necessary to understand the river, a river unlike any other anyplace on earth. Grant knew the river; he knew its importance and the difficulties it presented. He understood that controlling this lifeline required his turning the river into a barrier more restricting than simply a troublesome wet road. Once he accomplished this, if doing so was even possible, the river might as well be a hundred miles wide, at least for the South's purposes.

"There is something few people think about," said the senator. "Once the southern end of the Mississippi came under Union control there remained only two critical battles. We had to take Vicksburg, and we had to whip Lee. Grant did both. All of the other battles were interesting historical events, but none was critical to winning the war." He thought for a moment. "There might be one exception, in a roundabout sort of way. Antietam gave Lincoln the excuse he needed to issue the Emancipation Proclamation, but that could have been done after any victory. Yes, Grant made the critical difference."

6 Unvexed to the Sea

I thought of my conversation with that former Kansas senator as I sat on the hotel balcony one evening, looking west into the sun only a quarter visible above the horizon. For reasons difficult to explain, the shadows wavering about the Vicksburg square formed shapes new and different from any I had seen before. It was like a name that rumbles around in your thoughts. First you have it, then it slips away. In time, it becomes an obsession, and the effort to grab hold drives you nearly mad if it eludes you long enough. That's what I had experienced since my arrival in Vicksburg. Here, especially, I learned that shadows are a major portion of substance.

When my mind occasionally shook off this tantalizing obscurity that troubled me so, I wondered what Grant thought about the task given him by President Lincoln. I know what he did about it. That perhaps was the most remarkable accomplishment of the war, yet the doing seems a contradiction as paradoxical as the man himself. Grant never gave textbook strategy or tactics much thought. His detractors made much of this commonly known fact, yet it did them no good. What he did during '62 and '63 evolved into a campaign, a campaign unrivaled in its complexity and tenacity, that already commands a chapter in military textbooks around the world.

Despite my best effort to concentrate on Grant, I failed. As I sat on that balcony observing the movements and happenings around the square, my thoughts drifted to those shadows that troubled me so much. One critical question kept haunting me. The answer constantly eluded me. I asked everyone who would listen to me: "What made the men of the South fight so hard?" My concern was less in the generic sense of men than in the man himself. What compelled a man to pick up a gun and march off to fight a war in which he had no perceptible stake? The answer seemed important in a roundabout way. For four years these men fought as if their women were just beyond sight, awaiting mayhem and rape by the onrushing bluebellies. This was untrue, of course. Until Sherman made his march through Georgia, most of the South had avoided the horrors of war. Virginia and the border states had taken the point of the spear. These men fought just the same. Subduing them eventually required men such as Grant and Sherman to grind them into the ground.

Again I reached for what was missing, only to feel it slip away. It was, however, emerging more often, staying longer, and leaving an image behind each time it faded. The war, and what it meant, is living history in the South. Everywhere I look I see defiance. The Confederate flagpole is a full foot taller than the one on which the lesser banner of the United States flutters in the breeze. Even slavery, thought by those in the North to be dead, has not so much been eliminated as craftily disguised and transformed by insidious design. Any conversation that moves past the price of a dozen eggs evolves to include the war or its aftermath. In all of this, square in the middle, around the edges, hidden in the background, there is the Negro. I often wonder what Southern people would do without the Negro to blame for their problems.

To the old men I talked with in Galena, the Civil War was a memory of an event that absorbed their youth and their passions. They moved on from there, however, to live out their lives in pursuit of more relaxing ambitions. To the old men who gather around the courthouse in Vicksburg the war is more, much more. Here, people think of the war as the beginning of a subjugated present cutting them off from a glorious past crushed by an invading, foreign army. Saying it is as awkward as the reality. Never mind that the glorious part of the past exists mainly as an illusion, the idea persists—most of all for the common man.

Is that it? Is the answer buried in the past where it is invisible to searching minds? Here, however, past and present are no different. What existed then exists now. The shape may be fluid to adjust to varying constraints, but the mass and composition remains unchanged. I let my thoughts run unrestrained.

Never more than a small percentage of the people in the South ever owned a slave; those few "masters" usually owned large numbers. Then as now, the overwhelming majority of the white population subsisted in a state of poverty only slightly elevated from the Negro. The poor whites often existed without the barest signs of security commonly attributed even to the Negro. The men of property, the Southern aristocrats, the men who owned slaves, had a vested interest in satisfying at least a wretched standard of living for their property. For men and women to work they at least have to eat.

During the war, few of these men of property carried a gun into battle. They declared the production of cotton a virtue. Then, with that virtue self-asserted as a national priority, they professed themselves free of military obligation. When they did carry a gun, it most certainly was the pistol commonly carried by an officer. A man committed to slavery is by natural exclusion a man unlikely to defend with his life the virtue of that act. His most usual contribution to the war was to send off his son, or his neighbor's son, to do the fighting for him.

What happened to the common man? As their numbers were far greater, it fell to them to defend the plantation owners' property, whether living or inert. It is amazing to me that they performed this task with such a vigilance that they held off twice their number with half the resources for four entire years less two days. I asked myself until the thought of it numbed my mind: why?

The days of a Vicksburg summer are hot and damp. The heat and moisture drain a person of energy and wilt the passion necessary to pursue labored tasks or thought. As the sun set on the last of a series of such days, I sank into my wicker chair and disconnected my energy from my thoughts. Only my eyes and ears were at work watching and listening to the comings and goings out on the courthouse lawn.

"Come here, nigger," Jeff Monroe—I had met him before—said to a passing Negro carrying a large sack of grain. "Take this cup and fetch me some water."

The tall, overweight old man of color placed the sack on the lawn before he shuffled over and took the tin cup. At the time, I sensed no sign of defiance. He simply submitted as a rat conditioned to run a maze complies with the obvious task defined by his surroundings. He returned shortly and handed Monroe the cup. Monroe took a sip before pouring the remainder on the ground. Thinking back on the event, it is evident that he had planned his action from the start. "When I tell you to get water I mean cool water, boy. Now you scurry on over to the well in the shade of the livery and get me some cool water."

"Yassuh," the old gent replied. This time he moved more slowly, but he returned in good time.

"Boy, how old are you?" Monroe asked.

"I is eighty-one," the Negro answered.

"So am I," Monroe replied, "and I sure can move faster than that." He emptied the cup on the grass and extended it again. "This time, boy, move faster so the water doesn't get hot before you get back."

"Mistuh Jeff," the Negro said, "I has gots to get this grain ovuh tuh Mistuh Jackson afore he gets angry."

"What!" Monroe exclaimed. "Are you refusing to get an old man some cool water?"

"No suh. I has done it twicet already. Now I has gots to get this grain ovuh tuh Mistuh Jackson so we can get on home by suppuh time."

Defiance? I don't know for sure, but a hint of it showed.

Monroe threw the cup at the Negro but missed. "Do it, boy, and do it now!" he hissed. His voice was soft, the meaning hard.

The Negro looked to his right toward a horse-drawn wagon tied to a hitch near the street's end. A well-dressed, portly man of about fifty stood by the wagon. With one extended arm he braced himself on a pole supporting the tin roof over the board walkway. He watched intently, but he remained calm and silent. I only guessed at the man's name, but I suspected Jackson. Then the Negro looked back at Monroe.

Although hardly perceptible, Monroe's anxiety rose. I had difficulty reading his eyes from some forty paces away, but something had changed. All I knew was, the passiveness faded, and with that there occurred a change in the rules of the game. The new emotions were a combination of fear, hatred, and shame. I wondered which would prevail. The fear prevailed in action; the hatred prevailed in the form of the action. The old black gent snapped up the cup, but the glare that remained fixed on Monroe must have warned him that there were limits to the Negro's willingness to comply.

Quite by accident, Monroe looked over his shoulder and saw the man leaning passively against the post. The man smiled, nodded slightly, then tipped his hat. Not a word passed between them. "Get along with you, boy," Monroe said loudly as he accented the command with a flippant flick of his wrist, "and the next time I send you to fetch water, do it with more respect."

By now six young men, each as shabbily dressed as the Negro, had gathered around. All were above the age of consent. They knew better, but they laughed and punched each other at the spectacle of one old white man shattering the spirit of one old black man. "Do it, boy," one of them taunted at the last command to get some water. "Show us you know your place." I had the feeling that this spectacle had been a vital part of their education.

My guess is that Mr. Jackson seldom found cause to berate his Negro employee. Unlike in the glorious days, the old black gent might just move on down the road during a long summer night, and his labor was necessary. Mr. Jackson saw nothing wrong, however, in someone else sending a message from which there might emerge some vicarious benefit. Just by doing nothing other than passively watching the drama, he sent his employee a vital message. To the old Negro the message resonated as clearly as the long drum roll of an advancing rebel army. So he picked up the cup. With the point clearly understood by that time, the sport wore thin. Besides, darkness approached, and baiting Negroes was in part a spectator sport, unless the baiting was serious. Then hoods were necessary to prevent the tormentors being recognized.

There, in the fading light and shadows, the mystery emerged clearly for the first time. I knew then why the South had fought so hard and so long. The aristocrat saw nothing wrong in speaking gently to his darkies, so long as they did as he commanded. Yet he felt perfectly free to whip or kill one to ease the stress of even the slightest hint of defiance. Now sharp, hostile, demeaning words pass for the whip, but the effect is the same, and he lets the common man speak for him, where before he depended on his overseer.

There must exist in this illusion of kindness a distorted form of virtue. The Southern "gentleman" is nothing if not educated in the virtue of control, but still, a man must salve his emotions and indignation in some way. It prevents, after all, an unseemly hatred from boiling violently to the surface. Society expects less of the poor white. Back then, at the time of the war, there existed between him and the Negro hardly any difference at all, except for their color. It all comes down to status, I realized. If the poor whites were to find any self-respect at all, they must have felt it necessary to keep the Negro "in his place." If he ever escaped his shackles, well, who knew what might happen?

Both were victims. One looks up, but he sees no hope. The other looks only down. There he finds a man beneath him, placed there by virtue of nothing but skin color, and never thinks to look up to see how high he might rise. It seems so simple and so ludicrous. The white man bled and died for no purpose other than to shackle himself to an anchor of hatred. He hated because he feared, with good cause, what might happen if the black man became free. Nothing else explains it. The process demands constant vigilance, and during my two weeks in Vicksburg I witnessed it in a hundred forms.

If slavery is mainly the ability of one man to force another to do something against his will, as I suspect it to be, slavery is alive and well in the South. I think it will be for a long time.

So what of Grant is there in all of this? He had no interest in slavery one way or the other. But keeping the South poor and unfettered with the troubles of conducting serious commerce, other than the sale of cotton, did consume the time of Northern men with vision. This assured the opportunity for a Northern man to make, without fear of competition, a profit selling an abundance of goods. "Let slavery live in the South," reasoned men such as General McClellan. "What is its harm?" More than a few supported his position. Confine it, by all means, so it presents no troublesome interference with expansion and growth in the West, but that is enough. Actually free the slave? No. That went too far. So McClellan sparred with Lee, and Halleck pretended that war was a board game. Unencumbered by political confusion and enterprise—he never experienced success at business anyway—Grant did what war required.

*   *   *

Jeff "Davis" Monroe often looks at that flag, the one rising a foot above the other. As he looks, one truth is obvious by the faraway gaze in his eighty-year-old eyes. Although his body has progressed through time, his conception of the world remains impaled on the past. As I watch him it is impossible to mistake the impression. Although there is a quiet resignation about the half-century-old outcome of that conflict, no part of that acquiescence includes acceptance. That acceptance is most absent when a Negro comes too close.

Coming here and talking to these old men has expanded my viewpoint. I find that talking to the Southern soldiers now living in Galena and along the river from St. Louis north is a world apart from talking to these men. There, I talked to many Northern men who made a rational decision to fight for the South. When the war ended they put it behind them. I find none of that ambivalence here. These are—first, last, and always—Southern men, and the conflict gathers together in their collective minds as a cause rather than just a war. Each gives the impression of an absence of hesitation to die on the spot to reverse the outcome. Even so, I must confess I have found little expression of hate for Grant, at least not at the volatile level voiced by Abby. There is, to be sure, no love for Grant in these parts, but they hate the man less than what he did. Allowing for the possibility of reversed circumstance, as in fact was true at Chattanooga, they confess the possibility of having done the same as Grant did to Vicksburg. These are men of the river, and they give Grant his due. They witnessed what he accomplished, were amazed at his persistence, and they all agree that it seemed, at the time, an impossibility. Fully half the men I have talked to here in Vicksburg saw Grant when he rode into town or during the days following. Two confess to touching his coat.

"What do you most remember about that time?" I asked Jeff Monroe.

"Hunger," he replied without giving it thought. "We were outta food by the middle of June, or at least food as I'd come to know it. We were on quarter rations of boiled mule before the first of July. Children just went to sleep at night and failed to wake up in the morning. Mothers lacked the energy to cry for their loss.

"Hunger does strange things to the mind. I remember one night about three days before the surrender. I was assigned to guard duty. Hot! Hell would have been a breather. At the time I was all of eighteen. Out of this house pranced this young woman—her name is Sara, she still lives somewhere about—naked as the minute she took her first breath, headin' for the outhouse. I'd a been on her like a new saddle three months earlier, and never said thank you. The thought never crossed my mind that night. I just kept walkin' and never looked back." Almost expressing sorrow with the gesture, he shook his head slowly. "Hunger does strange things to a man's sense of purpose. Now, of course, I'd leave her alone, too—but for a different reason." A wry smile lit up his one good eye.

"Were you here from the beginning?" I asked.

"Born and raised about a mile from where we are a-jawin'. Joined up the day I turned sixteen. There wasn't much goin' on then, but Grant sure changed that. For a while, as I now understand it, the eyes of the world were on this town. If we'd a won, and if Lee'd whupped Meade at Gettysburg, that would'a been a whole different war. Half of Europe appeared ready to recognize and support us, provided our success seemed assured. The victories by Grant and Meade ended that."

"Did you go to prison after the surrender?" I asked.

"Nope. They still exchanged prisoners at that time. After a while they just sent us on our way. I had enough food to last three days. I ate mine the first day, however. I had seen many good men never make it three days, and I had hard memories of my recent hunger. To tell the truth, I never quite got over bein' hungry since."

"Where did you go after that?"

"They told us to stay out of the fightin', havin' been captured and all, but the South had a shortage of men. The provost picked me up about a week later and sent me out to Virginia, so if I got captured again no one would know. Grant looked me square in the eye one day, right over there by the livery. When I fought with Lee at Spotsylvania I became more scared of bein' captured than bein' kilt. I just knew Grant would remember me, and I had no idea what he might do. I said 'Thank you, Lord,' when I got wounded and the doctor sent me back to Richmond. It seems I just went from the pan into the fire. I starved here for a month. In Richmond I went ten months without a full belly."

"So, you were in the fighting?" I asked.

"Here, you mean?"

"Yes."

"Some of it, what there was of it. Grant came at us six ways from Sunday durin' the winter and spring. Our defenses were strong, so he backed off and lay in the siege. The Union controlled the river and all the ground around in a big half-circle. Grant had the patience of Job. He couldn't get in, and we couldn't get out, so he just sealed us off and waited for us to wither away in the summer heat."

I filled many pages with what Monroe had to say, both about Vicksburg and his fighting with the Army of Northern Virginia. He lived the war as a private and, as privates often do, he had a lofty yet self-centered view of generals. It seemed only natural to him that he would be remembered eighteen months later if captured by Grant, and Monroe expected Grant to inflict all manner of misery on him.

Some men had a closer view of Grant's war. One of these, Edward Stone—Col. Edward Ambrose Stone late of the Confederate States of America Cavalry—had a unique idea of the reason men go to war.

No prouder man ever rode a horse or killed a Union soldier. According to him, however, he confined his killing to men of equal or near equal rank. As an officer he knew the value of officers.

"No man is worth a damn without a head," he said. "So it is with a body of men." His chest puffed out as he spoke. "Many a fine Harvard man never went home," he told me so often that I dreamed about Harvard men feeling the saber. It somehow seemed inappropriate to tell him that I, too, was a Harvard man.

In truth, there were far too few trained soldiers to lead the armies on either side. Most officers, even many of general rank, had never served in a military unit. Many, however, had been to college, part or all of four years. Colonel Stone was such a man.

"Cavalry was the glory unit," he told me, "still is and always will be."

He must hear little of what is happening across the Atlantic, I thought. Riding a horse across a field swept with machine-gun fire impresses me as a careless way to go into battle. In his war conditions were different, but not much.

"Grant tried everything to get at Vicksburg. He tried frontal attacks, and we drove him back with a fearful loss of men. He sent Sherman to try to sneak around our flank, with the same result. He even tried to divert the river—a stupid thing to try, I thought at the time. Still do. That river goes where it wants to go.

"My job, or at least the job of the division in which I served, was to tie Grant in knots, to give him no peace. We ferried across the river at night, rider and horse, and hit him where we could. All winter and into the spring it continued. Then he did an unbelievable thing."

As the old man talked, my thoughts drifted back to another conversation. Maj. Thomas Quip, himself a cavalryman, served with Grant during the Vicksburg campaign. With the discovery that horses had little use in the swamp, headquarters temporarily reassigned him to Maj. Gen. James B. McPherson's engineers. He joined the ranks of men digging that channel trying to redirect the river. One evening, Grant rode up to inspect the works, and a gathering of generals followed.

"How is it going?" Grant asked.

"We will have a nice lake for fishing in before long," McPherson told him. "As for telling this river where to go, I would just as soon try to tell the ocean what to do."

"How are the men's spirits?" Grant asked, changing the subject.

"The men are in good spirits, but they sometimes wonder at the wisdom of generals."

A thin grin ruffled Grant's whiskers. "Keep them busy, General. There will be time enough for fighting soon enough."

"What are your plans?" Sherman asked.

Grant looked around to see who might be listening. "I'm gathering a fleet of gunboats up the river. Come the next new moon, when the weather is right and the current is strong, I mean to load the men on those boats and run them down the river so we can come at Vicksburg from the dry land to the south."

"The whole army?" Maj. Gen. John Logan asked.

"As much of it as will fit," Grant replied.

"No ship afloat can pass under those guns on the bluff without being blown from the water," Sherman countered. "We'll lose the army and the war. It's against all military logic."

"Maybe so," Grant replied, "maybe not, but that's what I mean to do. If it works we can come up on their blind side and take them by storm."

"Pardon me, General, but it's impossible," Logan said, bolstering the collective complaint. "Even if we get the men through the fire, where will we get supplies? There aren't enough boats on the whole river to carry an army and the necessary supplies."

"We will carry our weapons and ammunition and enough food for a week. After that, we live off the land."

"What about our horses?" asked Maj. Gen. James H. Wilson, the cavalry commander.

"Your men better start limbering up, General," Grant replied solemnly. "My horse is a Northern horse. He's reluctant to go that far south. I suspect they all feel the same." That ended all talk of horses.

Defying all military logic, Grant pointed his armada south on the night of April 16, 1863. Bringing a large part of his army with him, he ran the gauntlet under the Vicksburg guns. In addition to the army guarding Vicksburg, another smaller army roamed to the east—an army headed by Gen. Joseph E. Johnston. Grant split his army in two and, living off the land as they moved, half headed for Johnston and the other half for Vicksburg. Horseless at the start, Grant confiscated a horse from Confederate president Jeff Davis's plantation—he even named the animal Jeff Davis—and managed to ride much of the way. Most of the cavalry soldiers were less fortunate.

Grant's men fought five battles in the span of three weeks. All ended in Union victories. Then the prize appeared on the horizon: Vicksburg. He attempted to take the city by storm, but the attack failed. The siege followed the attack.

There is a story, a small sidelight to that attack, that came to my attention while at Galena.

I saw Colonel Stone, the Confederate cavalry colonel, almost every day during the nearly three weeks I spent in Vicksburg. He always wore the same clothes, including an officer's jacket that still hugged his slim hips and hung down to mid-thigh. No doubt it had once been gray, but long hours in the sun had faded it nearly white. Although I paid no attention to him at the time, I had the impression there was something different about this man. Later, while talking to an old rebel captain, I saw the colonel rise from his bench and walk toward a bar, his right hand stuck deep into his coat pocket. I had noticed this before.

"Why does Colonel Stone always keep his hand in his pocket?" I asked the captain.

"He doesn't," the captain replied wryly. After letting the remark hang for a moment, he added: "There's no hand there."

"What happened?" I asked.

"A bluebelly cut it off near the end of Grant's last assault on Vicksburg."

"How did it happen?"

"A Yankee sergeant cut it off. I saw him do it. That same Yankee son of a bitch ran me through right after." He refused to elaborate, so I let it drop there. Later, I remembered that the tale had a familiar ring. It kept buzzing through my brain like an irritating bee. Then, back in my room, it came to me. Frantically, I dug through my notes. After ten minutes of searching, I found it: "Reminiscences by Sergeant/Colonel Smith," the heading read.

On May 17, 1863, Grant launched a frontal attack against the men holed up in Vicksburg. After discussing the situation with Sherman and other unit commanders, he had decided to try to take the city by storm. Smith played a small part in that attack.

"It happened near the end of the battle," Smith told me. "All of the company officers had been knocked out of action. The regimental commander gave me temporary command of a platoon of men. We went forward with grenades to try to break loose a group of Rebs blocking our way down a ravine. In that sector the approach to Vicksburg led down a hill into a ravine filled with cane. Just beyond were a series of rises separated by more small ravines. It formed as natural a defensive line as I saw during the war, and all of those ravines were filled with Johnnie Rebs.

" 'Corporal, come with me,' I yelled to the nearest man—I can't remember his name now. 'We have to work around their flank and throw in these grenades.' He turned up a little draw and I went ahead, keeping low in the cane. Then, off to the left, I saw it. A small unit of Reb cavalry came charging down that ravine directly at a group of our infantry that was trying to bust through their line. At the head of the charge, swinging a long, gleaming sword, I saw a colonel. He hacked and slashed at our men with a fury. First, I saw him swing that blade into a major's head, splitting it like a melon. How I heard it over all the noise, I don't know, but I'll never forget that sound. It sounded like when you step on a fat frog. Then the colonel went after a lieutenant. He went out of his way, I thought, to get at that pup of an officer. With a mighty swing, he cut away the lieutenant's head. I clearly saw the smile on the colonel's face; then something snapped inside of me.

"Unable to stand up against charging cavalry, our men started to run. Down the ravine ran a riderless horse, and I grabbed him and climbed aboard. A scabbard, still holding its saber, hung from the saddle. I pulled out the blade and rode right into those screaming Rebs. Christ, what a dumb fool thing to do! But watching that colonel slice our men made me angry as hell. I ran three of them through before they realized I wore blue. Then the colonel, his sword held high, that evil grin on his face, came at me out of the sun. I gritted my teeth and went at him. We both swung our blades at the same time. Mine caught him at the wrist just before his reached my neck. His hand, still holding that saber, popped off so easily that my swing kept going right on around. I nearly threw myself off that horse. I'll never forget the look on his face: it wasn't pain, but more a look of disbelief. I heard him whimper, then he stuck the bleeding stub in his pocket and rode off. When the other Rebs saw their colonel leave the field they lost heart—right after I rode into their midst and stuck three more of them.

"Then, on the verge of exhaustion, I turned the horse to head back to our lines, and there, holding up their caps and yelling, were the men that the Reb cavalry had routed." He paused for a moment before adding: "I got a Congressional Medal of Honor for my work that day."

He smiled broadly—I recorded the smile in my notes—and reached into his pocket. He pulled out the medal and held it up for me to examine.

"Later, when Grant pinned this on me, he said the day was mine and I could have anything within his power to deliver. I remember looking at those two stars on his shoulder, and it came to me. 'General,' I said, 'I've always had it in my mind to go to West Point.'

" 'Can you read and cipher?' the general asked.

" 'My mother was a teacher,' I told him, 'and she made me learn about everything she knew.'

" 'Then you shall go to West Point,' Grant said, and I did. I graduated eighth in my class and was a colonel myself when I left the service thirty years later, after fighting the Indians in the West." He rubbed the medal with his hand. "Are you writing a book?" he asked, looking up.

"Yes," I replied. "It's about Grant."

The old colonel just smiled.

A good description of war is the coming apart of things. War is a destructive process on all accounts. Yet sometimes, over a wide expanse of time and from faraway places, events come together again. A sergeant who had no use for a colonel on a horse cutting down infantry officers took matters into his own hands. As a result, his career took off like a shooting star. At the same moment, a colonel took off down a ravine minus the hand that directed the killing. The event forever reduced him to living his life for that brief moment when, with great advantage on his side, he had cut down some Harvard men. I met and learned to like many veterans on my travels up and down the Mississippi, soldiers who fought on both sides. I feel comfortable in saying I liked that Reb colonel least of all.

*   *   *

After the failed assault on Vicksburg, Grant dug in and decided to wait. Facing east and west at the same time, he kept Johnston out and held the army at Vicksburg in. History records that Sherman told Grant: "I want to congratulate you, General Grant, on the success of your plan. And it's your plan, by heaven, and nobody else's. For nobody else believed in it."

The remainder is history. Grant kept Vicksburg locked up until early July. Finally, Lt. Gen. John Pemberton, a native Philadelphian and one of many Northern men who fought for the South, sent up the white flag. So the siege ended with a whimper. No major victory during the war caused so few deaths. Shocked by Shiloh, the press and politicians finally had their way. I doubt it mattered, however, because the war had worked its way around the innocence of the spring of 1862. The day before Vicksburg fell, Robert E. Lee sent a substantial portion of his army across a Gettysburg field—twelve thousand men under the command of Maj. Gen. George E. Pickett. Only about a hundred of his men reached the Union lines on Cemetery Ridge; the rest were strung out along the way, many filled with shot or worse. In an hour, as a result of Pickett's charge, there were more casualties than in all the Vicksburg campaign.

Disaster had an opportunity to crush Grant at a dozen points along the way. Everything about the campaign ran counter to military logic. Nevertheless, it worked. Many commanders have devised good plans, only to lay them aside when doubt entered their minds. Not so with Grant. Once he settled on a plan and an objective, nothing distracted him from it.

Many events have taken place on July 4. A nation emerged on that day, later divided, and then came together again. Two presidents, John Adams and Thomas Jefferson, died on that day, fifty years to the day after they signed the Declaration of Independence. Lee retreated from Gettysburg on that day, his army beaten and broken for the first time, never to be the same again. On that day, too, Grant took Vicksburg. Nearly three generations have passed, and still the people of Vicksburg refuse to celebrate the nation's independence.

Perhaps Lincoln best summed up the result: "The father of waters again goes unvexed to the sea."

7 Why Men Run

The ride to the front has been a hostile introduction to this war. Two of the men in the truck died without ever seeing what war is about. Jerry—I don't even know his last name—died when we were less than an hour on the road. A Fokker triplane came out of the sun and strafed the convoy. Jerry took one square in the back of the head. I doubt he had time to feel it, to know death had arrived. He just stiffened, and his eyes opened wide. They never closed.

Frank Sawyer had less luck. He talked all the way up; he was talking when the shell hit. A seventy-five, one of our own, fell short and exploded about twenty yards off the road. Two fragments hit the truck, and both of them found Frank. It is obvious luck plays a part in this war. One fragment cut off his arm at the elbow, then it passed through the shirt sleeve of the man sleeping beside me. That man never even woke up to know of his close brush with death. The other fragment severed Private Sawyer's spine at about the fifth lumbar. He had time to dwell on his death. We just never got the bleeding stopped, and he drifted into shock about twenty minutes from here. Now he's dead.

"Lift them down gently, boys," I said to the first sergeant.

"What's the problem, Lieutenant?" he replied. "They are past the point of feeling anything."

"Think of them as your sister," I replied.

"All right, men, these are your comrades-in-arms," the first sergeant yelled. "Treat these boys gentle."

"Lieutenant?"

I turned toward the sound.

"Are you Lt. Arthur Kelly?"

67

Off to the right about ten yards stood an officer. The insignia on his shoulders looked like a major's leaves, but the grime on his jacket made it difficult to tell. I saluted anyway. "Lieutenant Kelly, reporting as ordered, sir, up from the rear with replacements."

"How many replacements do you have?" he asked.

"Started with nine and made it here with seven," I replied sharply. "Eight counting me."

"Rough ride, huh?"

"Yes, sir."

"You're assigned to the 125th, Lieutenant. Is there a First Sergeant Stone with you?"

"Yes, sir. He's attending to the two we lost on the way up."

"Well, when he's finished, he's to go with you. Do you have a list of the replacements?"

"Right here, sir."

"Write DOA on the two that were killed and give it to my sergeant. He's in the tent marked HQ."

I saluted and moved toward the tent. "A major told me to give this list to you, Sergeant."

He looked at the list. "Lost two before you got here, huh? Yesterday a truck rolled in, and all nine in the back were dead, plus one of the ones up front. Blood sloshed out the back end. God, I want to go home. The Hun is getting ready for an offensive. They've been softening us up for three days now."

"Where will I find the 125th?" I asked, eager to get on with the war.

He looked at me and shook his head. "You been assigned there, huh?"

"Is something wrong with that?" I asked.

"Not if you got your will made out. That 125th colonel must be bucking for a star. His regiment is always the first in and the last out. Glory hound if you ask me."

"I didn't ask, Sergeant."

"Yes, sir. Just trying to be friendly."

"How do I get there?"

"Out that flap is the road. Cross the road and three miles west is the front line. You will find the 125th there, probably digging a new trench to get closer to the Hun."

I gave him a hard look.

"Sorry, sir. Just trying to be friendly. The more you know up here the better your chances of staying alive, although with your going to the 125th nothing will probably help—sorry, sir. Is that all, Lieutenant? I got all the casualty reports to fill out. See this big pile? All are from the 125th. See this other, smaller pile? That's from all the other units in the division. Yes, sir, that 125th sure keeps me busy." He didn't look up as I departed.

"First Sergeant," I yelled, "you're to come with me. We're headed for the 125th."

"Yeah, Lieutenant, I heard. I heard something else, too."

I read his mind through the look on his face. "I don't want to hear it, First Sergeant. Let's get going."

"We got to walk, Lieutenant?"

I slung my rifle over my shoulder and headed west.

The first sergeant and I were heavily laden, and it wasn't long before I noticed he had a slight limp. I pointed to his leg. "Do you have a problem?" I asked.

"Shrapnel, sir. Took one in the thigh about two months ago. Walking still gives me trouble."

"What are you doing here, First Sergeant? You shouldn't be sent back to the line until you're fully healed. That's regulation."

"This is where the war is, sir. I was getting fat sitting around."

"You're young to be a first sergeant," I observed.

"Got off the boat as a buck sergeant. Got three promotions in four months, one of them a double jump. Experience is worth a lot up here, sir. If you survive until summer, you'll be a captain."

"If I survive?"

"Those Huns love to shoot lieutenants, sir. Those bars sparkle like a spotlight. In the first regiment I fought with, the Huns shot every officer below major in the first month. The Hun has been at this war three years now. He knows how to shoot. If I was you, I'd take those bars off, and hide your whistle, too. They love to shoot at whistles. When a whistle blows you can just see their guns moving in that direction, like a forked birch stick going to water."

My apprehension rose by the moment. Why had I spent three months learning to be an officer if now I had to hide it? I removed the bars and studied the landscape as we continued to walk. With spring here, the ground should be green by now, I thought, but there is nothing but a wet, muddy brown cast all around. That wasn't the worst of it.

Shell holes pocked nearly every square yard of ground. It looked like pictures of the moon I saw in college.

Litter covered the ground: boots, tattered bits of uniforms, pieces of rifles, helmets with holes in them—the look and smell of war fouled my senses.

As we moved closer to the front we began to encounter stragglers moving back, most of them wounded in one place or another. None of the stragglers saluted. I began to feel more comfortable.

"Where is Colonel Ross?" I asked a private in the headquarters area.

"That's him, over by that truck looking at a map," the private replied.

"Sir, Lieutenant Kelly reporting. I have a First Sergeant Stone with me."

"A first sergeant, huh. Can we use him!"

The comment severely bruised my ego. I started to say something, but kept quiet. "You are assigned to F Company, second platoon. Try to keep your head down, will you, Lieutenant? You're the third new lieutenant in F Company in three weeks." Studying our orders, he turned. "First Sergeant Stone?"

"Yes, sir."

"You will be assigned to F Company, also. Report to Captain Logan, men. F Company is about a thousand yards off to the right, in that front line of trenches."

"Yes, sir," I said, saluting.

The colonel got his arm about half up before becoming distracted by his map.

"Captain Logan?" I asked of the first captain I saw.

"Not now, Lieutenant. There's a Hun patrol out there sniping at us."

I ducked into the nearest trench. It grew strangely quiet, so I closed my eyes and let my thoughts drift. It had been a long boat ride over. I hadn't slept well since embarking; the first three nights I hadn't slept at all. The constant rolling of the boat made me sick. I found peace only when I thought about Abby. After a stormy courtship, we married on Christmas day. She is a warm, passionate girl. Never is this more true than when I mention Grant. Early on, I came to one conclusion. Never mention Grant. Every time I mention that name to Abby a crimson glow spreads over her face.

I have finished the first half of my book, but I am having a difficult time with the last half. As I wrote, I began to feel I lacked an understanding of battle, what the men felt, why they reacted as they did. Why, for example, does one man run from danger and another climb on a runaway horse and charge into a cavalry unit swinging an unfamiliar weapon? There had to be more to this than fear of death. Anyhow, President Wilson has solved my problem. An old captain swore me in on August 15, 1917. Following eight weeks of basic training, I moved on to officer training school. I married Abby while on leave. I received my shipping orders on March 1, and here I am, hiding in a trench.

A grip on my shoulder jarred me from my slumber. "You Lieutenant Kelly?" a corporal asked.

I adjusted my helmet. "That's right, Corporal."

"Captain Logan wants to see you." He pointed. "He's over in the HQ bunker."

I felt my ass as I approached the bunker's entrance and realized my trousers were wet clear through. "Captain Logan, I'm Lieutenant Kelly."

"Where are your bars, Lieutenant?" he asked sharply.

"First Sergeant Stone advised me to remove them, sir."

"Hum," he replied.

I continued to stand at attention.

"At ease, Lieutenant. Christ! We aren't much on formality up here. I see you're fresh from the States. I also see you've had infiltration training." He continued to study my file. "A Harvard man, huh? I'm from Michigan State, myself." I read in his eyes that he wanted to say more, but he held back. People from Ivy League schools have a habit of making light of graduates from other universities. They know it too, those from other schools. I suspected he had no use for a Harvard man.

"Yes, sir," I said proudly. "I never got captured once on exercises."

"You don't say. You'll find the Hun has a bit more dedication along those lines." He leaned to the side and studied me closely. "Only thing is, they will shoot off your wet ass."

I moved my hand to my rear. The captain just smiled. I fidgeted. I felt like a fifteen-year-old kid. It's not supposed to be like this, I thought.

"Come with me, Lieutenant." The captain led the way to a narrow slit trench that projected at a right angle from the main trench. At the end of the trench someone had embedded a steel plate about four feet high and wide. Someone had cut an opening about two inches high and four inches wide in the middle of the plate. The captain pressed his binoculars to the small opening. "About a thousand yards west is a man looking at me through his binoculars. He's the enemy, Lieutenant, and I'm tired of looking at him. After dark, I want you to take three men and go capture him. We will see if you're worth your salt at infiltrating. Take experienced men."

"How will I know if they're experienced, sir?"

The captain just looked at me. I felt humiliated. I felt like crying. Actually, I felt stupid.

"Take off at 1:00 A.M."

"Yes, sir."

Sleep was impossible. Even worse than the dampness were the bugs that populated the wall of the sleeping bunker. Every time a shell went off in the vicinity, a frequent occurrence, the concussion showered a dozen or more bugs onto the bed. I went to the jump-off point at 12:30 and waited. Soon, the men I had asked First Sergeant Stone to select joined me.

"We go at one o'clock, men. My name is Lieutenant Kelly."

The men introduced themselves unenthusiastically. They preferred not to be too well known by their officers. The corollary to "Never volunteer for anything" is "If they don't know my name, they can't volunteer me." Both are practical rules.

My anxiety increased. It bothered me that the men seemed so calm. They probably thought the same of me. "We go in five minutes," I said in a whisper. "Keep noise to a minimum. We cross no-man's-land and head for the German command post. It's only about two-thirds of a mile. Our mission is to capture an officer. Look for the one with field glasses." I had no other way to explain it. It seemed inappropriate to tell them the truth: the captain has grown tired of that man watching him, men, so our mission is to stop him. It depressed me just to think it.

I studied my watch. "Let's get it over with," I said as I waved them forward.

The trip across the field went smoothly and quickly. As we approached our objective, my anxiety rose again. Men were moving all about.

"What now, Lieutenant?" asked the ranking soldier, a corporal.

I thought for a moment. "Do you have any ideas?"

"Yeah," he said gruffly. "Let's go home."

"Besides that, Corporal."

Without answering, he crawled the few yards to the top of the German trench. Removing his helmet, he looked over. Then he slid back down the slope. "The command post is about thirty yards to the south," he whispered. "There's not much activity there, and there appears to be a slit trench at that point extending out from the main trench. I think one of us—you—could crawl in and get him, if you think best, sir."

My first test as an officer had arrived. Should I send one of them in, or go in myself? What would I find? What if there were twenty men in there? How was I to find the officer I wanted? How could I keep from waking one or more in the strangeness of a dark bunker? I had such a simple task, and there were so many unknowns. Every unknown demanded an answer. The more attention I gave the options now, the better the chance for survival when action began. What must Grant have felt? I thought. He had fifty thousand men under his command, fifty thousand decisions to make. I climbed up the rise and looked over just to confirm the corporal's report, then slid back down.

I thought back to Galena and a captain I'd talked to. "A man can die only once," he told me. "The thing I learned early was to reduce the chances. I always went first, the first time. Then I felt comfortable asking the men to do the same thing. It was always a long time until my turn came again." Good advice, I realized now. The trick is to survive the first time.

"Corporal, you take one man and move about ten yards past the slit trench. You other two come with me and stop about ten yards this side of the slit trench. I know what I'm looking for. I'll go in."

Moving at a crawl, it took nearly twenty minutes to get into place. I bellied into the shallow trench and slid along the wall to the main trench. There was enough of a bend on either side that none of the men stirring around had a clear view of the command post. I dashed to the entrance and peeked inside. It was quiet. There were five cots in the room and a small desk at which an enlisted man sat working on some reports. Another man was asleep on one of the cots. A pair of field glasses hung from a peg sticking from the dirt wall. I withdrew my .45, took a deep breath, and moved toward the desk. I pressed my body against the man's back as I grabbed him around the neck, at the same time bringing the pistol butt down with all my strength. I heard a sharp crack, and his body went limp. I looked at the other man. He moved, but remained asleep.

Dropping to my knees, I moved toward the officer. I placed my hand over his mouth and pressed the pistol against his head. At the feel of cold steel, his eyes popped open. "Shhhh," I said. "Don't say a word." His eyes rolled in my direction. I slid my free arm around his neck and prodded him to a sitting position with the pistol. "Do you speak English?" I asked.

"Nein," he said.

"Parlez-vous français?"

He looked surprised. He didn't know I was a Harvard man. He nodded.

"Good," I said in French. "Now get up slowly and go where I push. Don't make a sound."

He tensed, but remained seated.

I brought the .45 to his ear and cocked it. "I'm going out that opening in five seconds. You can go with me alive or stay here dead. Either way, I will fulfill my mission."

He rose, and I pushed him toward the opening. Pushing his face against the side of the bunker, I looked both ways, up and down the trench. Satisfied it was clear, I pushed the Hun major toward the slit trench and out into the open. "Let's go," I said, just loudly enough for the others to hear. "Stay low. Major, trust me when I tell you, if you do anything to reveal our presence, I will kill you sure."

He nodded acknowledgment.

We had moved out about four hundred yards when it seemed like the world began to explode. A walking barrage moved toward us. The first five shells went off about two hundred yards away, halfway between the front of the German lines and our position. Ten seconds later, five more shells exploded twenty-five yards closer. We were right in the path, right on the target line. "Run for it," I yelled. They were moving on my command. "Move it, Major, at a trot."

I soon realized it was impossible to outrun the advancing shells and still watch the major. I pushed the German into a shell hole half filled with water. I turned and looked toward the advancing shells. In my mind, I calculated the rate of advance. "In thirty seconds that barrage will blow us to Hell," I screamed in French. "We have to move between the projectiles."

It was too late. The next rounds moved twice the distance, and I ran as fast as possible. I moved a hundred yards and dove into another hole. The barrage stopped fifty yards away, then started moving back in the direction from which it started. God! I thought. The major didn't follow me. In the flashes of the explosions I saw him stagger to the rim of a nearby hole and collapse on the open ground. Without a thought I ran back. I reached the point of the third burst of the retreating barrage, and then felt myself flying through the air. I landed on my knees in the hole, just below the major. He looked up as I dragged him into the relative security of the depression. The barrage passed over as I covered him with my body. My hand felt sticky; then I realized why: the explosion had shattered the major's leg. I lifted him to my shoulders and stumbled back toward our lines.

"I never saw anything like that in all my life," the corporal said as I lowered the major into a hole a hundred yards in front of our lines.

"I told you men to get back to the trenches," I said.

"You looked like you might need help, Lieutenant, so I came back."

I smiled, and patted him on the shoulder. "Thanks, Butch. I'm glad you did come back."

"Here," he said, "let me carry this Hun. He looks a bit beat up."

"Watch his leg. The barrage got him."

When we were back in the trenches, I directed the corporal to carry the major to the aid station. Leaving the major in the hands of the medics, I found a dry spot and collapsed. I must have been asleep in two seconds.

Sensing someone watching me, I sprang to a sitting position. "How do you feel, Lieutenant?" the captain said. Arms crossed on his knees, he squatted beside me.

I rubbed my eyes. The first ray of light was just illuminating the dark fields around me. "Frankly, sir, that's the best night's sleep I've had in weeks."

"I don't know what to do with you, Lieutenant. Sleeping out in the open like this will get your ass peppered." He paused. "We operate kind of strangely around here, Lieutenant. One of the things we do, when we come back from an assignment, is report to our commanding officer."

My hand snapped to my mouth. "I'm sorry, sir. I just forgot. God, I'm sorry. Actually, I wasn't feeling too good."

"I know. The corporal told me you did a flip when the barrage hit too close. You made some friends out there last night."

I maneuvered to my knees. "How is that, sir?"

"Well, the way they figure it, if you're willing to run back through an artillery barrage to get a Hun, you'll crawl through Hell to get one of your own men." He smiled. "Why did you do it?"

"Orders, sir."

The captain looked surprised. "Orders?"

"Yes, sir. You told me to bring that man with the binoculars back, and he was the one."

"I'll remember that, Lieutenant, the next time I have something important I want done. I must confess something, however, and there's no one else I'd tell this to. For some reason, I trust you. I was just tired of that son of a bitch spying on me. But I never wanted you killed, or even hurt, just to bring him back." He hesitated. "But now I'm damn glad I sent you. It turns out he's some sort of general staff flunky—but an important flunky. Judging from the papers he had on him, he was sent here to map the ground in front of their trenches. He appears to be a trained artillery spotter, also. Our general staff wants to talk to him badly."

I looked surprised.

"Lieutenant, he won't talk to a damn person except you. Seems you made a friend in him, too. He keeps asking for the officer who carried him from the field. He says he'll talk to you—in French?" There was a questioning tone in his voice.

"Yes, sir. I speak French. So does he."

"Then let's get with it, Lieutenant."

I spent the next hour in seclusion with the German major. He seemed pleased to be out of the war. He wanted to survive to get back to his work as a historian. We had a long talk about Grant. It seems Grant's reputation is as solid here as at home. Anyway, he did have important information. The Germans were planning a major offensive, and he'd sent a message off at sundown expressing the opinion that this sector offers the best advantage. I told the captain. He took me to the major, and the major took me to the colonel.

"Come with me, son," said the colonel after I told him what was coming. "You have to give this directly to the general." So, I told the general. The general told me, in private, that he was recommending me for the Distinguished Service Cross. I never got it, but I got what I had come for.

Nor did the captain ever again bring up the subject of my failure to report after I completed the mission. He must finally have realized that Harvard men aren't perfect, either. I could have told him that. In football, Michigan State beat us by forty points my senior year. I wonder if the captain knew that?

*   *   *

There is a sidelight to this adventure. Remember First Sergeant Stone? The name Stone caught my attention when I had time, later, to think about it. After the battle—he had been wounded again and awaited shipment to the rear, then all the way home—I went to him in the aid station. He had been wounded during an action in which he led a squad of men to protect a field mess that was in danger of being overrun. As is common in our army, most kitchen personnel are Negroes without any significant combat training. Stone had scrounged up some weapons and trained them on the spot. More than fifty dead Germans were scattered around the area, so the cooks obviously learned fast. Stone got the Distinguished Service Cross for his efforts.

I gave him a cigarette, and he took a long drag.

"Where you from?" I asked him.

"Mississippi," he replied.

That was the first time I noticed his accent. "Where in Mississippi?"

"Vicksburg," he answered.

"Much of your family live there?" I asked.

"Everyone still alive, back to my grandpap. My mother was born in '69, the last of eight children. I mean to go back there, Lieutenant, soon as I heal up a bit."

I took a chance. "Is your grandfather a white-haired man with one hand who likes to wear a Confederate colonel's cavalry jacket?"

His mouth dropped open. "How did you know?"

"I met him once. It seems a lifetime ago." Colonel Stone had redeemed himself a bit in my eyes, having in his line a man like First Sergeant Stone. There had been a moment or two in my life when the thought crossed my mind that one too many Confederate colonels had survived the war. Had events turned out otherwise, however, there never would have been a First Sergeant Stone. That would have been the country's loss.

Passing judgment on fate is a futile task.

*   *   *

It is apparent that I survived the attack that started at dawn four days later. We massed our artillery and were ready for them. We lost just short of two hundred killed and captured. As happened at Shiloh, we piled up their men like cordwood. At least a thousand Germans died that day, with three times as many captured—a small number by the standards of my war, I now realize. The massed artillery barrage caused a barrier of fire through which they were afraid to retreat. The Germans threw up their hands en masse when our men piled out of the trenches. It is becoming clear that everyone is growing tired of war. Everywhere I go there is talk by the men that nobody wants to be last to die. The same apparently is true for the Hun.

In this war, I have yet to see my first silver-bearded general ride a white horse along the line trying to rally his men. Now the generals rely on reports from a new breed of cavalry, the airplane pilots, to tell them what is happening. The Germans, however, also have airplanes, so there exists a precarious balance. Balance regulates the fortunes of war, I have learned. If the stability becomes skewed, large numbers of men die on the disadvantaged side. When equilibrium exists, large numbers of men die on both sides. Our general had the balance skewed in his favor as a result of the information provided by one grateful German soldier. Charity pays, even when extended to the enemy. The charitable act of saving one German's life led to their side losing five times our number. Next time, I suppose it will be our turn to fall in windrows.

This time, however, my general looked very smart indeed, as did the colonel and the major. The captain looked especially smart for having sent me out to capture the German major. I never told anyone the real reason I went on that mission. Something tells me the captain also kept it to himself. Two days after the attack the captain became a major, and the general elevated me to first lieutenant, breveted to the rank of captain. By then I had seniority, since all the other officers in my company were dead or wounded. Our regiment took the most casualties repelling the attack. As usual, the colonel sent us out at the front of the line. Even with two bars on my shoulder I still felt as silly and as lost as ever, but I kept it a secret. The major insisted I take temporary command of the company. That condition persisted for three months until the general elevated me to the permanent rank of captain and assigned me to the general staff as a brevet major.

I learned something about soldiering that night in the field, and I learned even more about command during the weeks that followed. Not even during my first night with Abby following our marriage had I felt so alive. The worry and the fear comes when you have time to think, before or after the event, or when there is a lull. I never felt as scared in my life as when I looked back at that German major trying, on one good leg, to get away from that barrage. Then the fear passed, and he became just a man needing help. I lied to the captain. I didn't go back because of orders. I just went back.

My own experiences helped me to understand Grant better. He knew what men think during battle. There is no doubt that the majority of the Civil War soldiers were brave—hundreds of thousands of them. When the officers said go, they went—into the fires of Hell if asked. Recorded in all of history are but few instances where men flatly refused to go into battle. Running is common practice, however. What happens? I think I know. It's somehow wrapped up in leadership. If the general runs, the men are sure to run. I think, however, that hesitation, or a conveyed sense of uncertainty, is just as bad. A great many generals hesitated during the Civil War—during any war.

I have always mildly criticized Grant for his drinking, but no more. He must have saved his hesitation, his fear, for a time when he was away from his men, away from the demands of command. In battle he was always certain, or somehow kept his uncertainty buried deep inside, out of sight from his men. Even Rawlins, who watched over Grant with the principle purpose of keeping him away from the bottle, failed at times. A man can take only so much, general or private. So Grant drank a bit when it did the least harm. When he required a clear head, however, he chose to puff hard on a cigar or run his horse wildly along the line. All good officers have their own way of fighting fear. That will have to do until there is no fear. I wouldn't want a man who has no fear leading me into battle. Such a man must be a fool.

8 Waitin' for Someone to Lead Us

Few generals have ever found their armies in a more precarious condition than did Maj. Gen. William S. Rosecrans at Chattanooga. There is something different about this battlefield, something distinctive in its character and design. Sitting here studying the terrain, the eventual outcome seems almost mystical. I cock my head, close my eyes, and I almost hear the heavy sound of a cannon rolling across the land, dust boiling up with every blow of the bouncing wheels. In the distance, I hear the cannon's shot explode. Then, after a brief moment of silence, the cry of a gut-shot horse. It is more of a whimper at first, as the signal from the torn flesh moves to the brain, then a bellowing wail of pain. I imagine it struggling to remain standing, instinctively knowing that falling to the ground means never rising again. The sound blends with a thousand noises all around, then it disappears altogether as the animal slumps to the ground. The sun flashes from behind a cloud, and in an instant there is the long, glistening light reflecting from a thousand advancing bayonets held high by a battle line of terrified infantry.

"It is good that war is so terrible," Lee had said a year earlier at Fredericksburg, "or we would grow too fond of it." Looking out across this special place helps me understand what he meant. The "terrible" in his comment is the link to sanity. The "fond" speaks of how close we always are to returning to our origin in the trees.

There was death in this valley, yet also life, the life of the nation.

Each battle leaves its own special meaning inked on the pages of history. Gettysburg, ended only four months earlier, marked the high tide of the Confederacy. Shiloh brought the hard reality of war to both

North and South, teaching everyone that when men meet to do battle large numbers of them usually die. Antietam opened the way for Lincoln to begin the process of ending the blight of slavery. Vicksburg spoke eloquently of the virtue of hard work to fulfill a distant goal. Chattanooga was somehow different. Here, the salient fact seems to be the act of battle itself. I have thought about the battle for years, but the mystery lingers.

At Gettysburg, General Pickett led a mile-wide line of twelve thousand men across a rolling field. Few consider it anything less than the most spectacular charge by massed infantry during the war. Barely a handful of gray-clad men reached the other side to breach the Union defenses. There they surrendered quickly or faded back across the field. As I looked at that peaceful stretch of land, it amazed me. It is difficult to believe that Lee thought his men could survive the mile-long walk into the massed infantry and cannon coiled like a deadly serpent to strike at their ranks. Each man on the eastern ridge, where the Union soldiers stood, had time during the Confederates' long walk to load and fire a dozen times or more. Solid shot from the cannon skimmed the ground like ricocheting hail, cutting men down in long, bloody rows. Then, as the distance narrowed, canister and grape blew gaping holes in the ranks. Yet they proceeded on, earning a hallowed place in history.

Lee should have seen it coming. He should have remembered seven months earlier at Fredericksburg, where on the hill behind the town he witnessed the effect of massed fire and reflected on its terrible result. There the Union Army tried to storm the rebel position in a sunken road. In four desperate assaults, five thousand men paid with their lives and limbs. Fredericksburg ominously foretold the human destruction in my own war. Eight thousand men gathered in a natural defile gouged into the side of the hill. The depression was the result of an endless procession of wagons rolling down the one-lane road. A four-foot stone wall kept the dirt from crumbling into it. At the time, with the weapons of the day, a man required between fifteen and twenty seconds to load and fire. The Confederate infantry moved to the firing line in four rotating groups. In a single minute they could send twenty-four thousand chunks of lead tumbling down into the ranks of the Union infantry advancing on a half-mile front. Nothing I faced in France, even with the use of massed rapid-fire machine guns, equaled the carnage faced by the Union men at Fredericksburg as they advanced across that open field.

As deadly as the fire at Fredericksburg and Gettysburg became, conditions there seem as a difficulty contrasted against an impossibility when one assesses the Union's chances of successfully charging up Missionary Ridge here at Chattanooga.

I am studying the field from Pulpit Rock, or what they once called Pulpit Rock. Jeff Davis, the Confederate president, delivered a speech from this precise spot. He had as his objective inspiring his army to subdue the Union forces trapped within his sight. The speech failed. Later, when the Union owned this site again, the rock on which I sit had its name changed to Devil's Pulpit. Given the times in which that transformation took place, the name change is easy enough to understand.

"Strategic location" is a term with significant meaning to a military man. Now that I have experienced war, I feel more at ease exploring the idea. Lookout Mountain, a twelve-hundred-foot protrusion—hardly a mountain by the standards of the Rockies—is a strategic location, or so any reasonable military mind would conclude. One sees the mountain first, then the surrounding terrain. Sitting here, looking north and west, it is almost possible to feel what the men who fought here felt. The men of the Southern army entrenched here must have felt nothing so certain as their invincibility. The Federal soldiers, on the other hand, must have felt their confinement in Chattanooga was simply preliminary training for the hardships of prison life. It is difficult to conceive of a more confining prison, yet they had placed themselves there.

The Tennessee River flows a stone's throw to the north of my perch. From my vantage point, on the lower, west face of Lookout Mountain, it is plainly visible, just as it must have been then. The river, rolling down from the north, aims straight for Lookout Mountain. With no place to go, the river veers a few hundred yards east and south. Then it turns abruptly north, carving with its suddenly reversed course a mile-wide isthmus called Moccasin Point. From there, the river flows north for another mile or so before turning sharply west, forming in its arc a convex quarter-circle of land on which the city of Chattanooga sits. Just beyond, permanently distracted from its mission but recovered from its confusion, the Tennessee River turns to the northeast and blends with the mist and forest as it vanishes from sight. The Union Army found itself confined in that quarter-circle, with the rampaging river to its back and the Confederate Army to its front. It was the morning of September 24, 1863.

The Chattanooga Valley spreads eastward from Lookout Mountain. Two miles in the distance a sharply rising string of attached mountains confines the valley. The locals refer to this string of mountains as Missionary Ridge. The rebel army had its right flank anchored on this ridge and its left flank anchored on Lookout. This army must have represented an imposing barrier to the men in blue only a mile away.

Nothing appears so insane as the idea of a commander placing his army in Chattanooga. General Rosecrans, however, did precisely that, although circumstance played a part in his decision. That circumstance was the army's defeat at the Battle of Chickamauga, its site just beyond view, on the far east side of Missionary Ridge. It is amazing that the Confederate general, Braxton Bragg, was content to leave the Union soldiers alone. You may remember General Bragg; it was he who directed his men toward the "sound of the fighting" at the Hornet's Nest, thereby snatching defeat from the jaws of victory. I suppose one had to be at Chattanooga in '63 to understand the decisions people made.

*   *   *

"I swear we had the Rebs beat at Chickamauga," a Northern major confided in me. "We had taken everything they threw at us, and still we held. Then it happened. Just a damned accident, that's all, and they had us on the run."

The major had been a Pennsylvania man, but he liked the Chattanooga area so much he returned there after the war. "It was a hard decision," he told me, "but an enterprising man could make some money here." He must have been correct. Three businesses bear his name. "If it had been in the heart of the South I probably wouldn't have come back," he told me, "but Tennessee is a border state, not quite Southern and not quite Northern, so I stayed on."

"What happened during the battle?" I asked.

"Which one?" he asked.

"Chickamauga," I replied.

"Some call it the fortunes of war," he said, looking disgusted, "but I call it plain, stupid generalship. Our army formed lines east of this little creek facing east with the Rebs facing us. The battle lines were classic Civil War, with whole divisions fighting shoulder-to-shoulder, except the trees made it impossible to see much to the right or left. For most of two days General Thomas's corps took the main force of the Reb attack and held its own. I was in General Wood's division, off to Thomas's right. Then the damnable order arrived directing us to move our line to the left to close on General Reynolds's division. The problem with that was Reynolds was nowhere in sight. So we pulled out of the line and marched behind the division on our left. At precisely that moment, General Longstreet attacked the area we had moved from. The result was catastrophic. Longstreet's men split our army in half, leaving the two interior flanks exposed. The Rebs began to roll up the flank leading to Thomas's position while the other half of the army retreated through the gaps in the mountains. Have you ever seen what happens in a flank attack?"

"No. Tell me about it."

"There isn't much to tell. The reality about a line of men is someone has to be on the end. A good general always anchors his flanks so no one is in a position to come at those ends. A river will do, or a hill— any terrain that's difficult to cross. When a line breaks in the middle there's nothing to hold against, so the man on the end of the line looks to his side, and what does he see? He sees the whole of the enemy army coming straight at his position. Stonewall Jackson did it to Hooker at Chancellorsville, and everyone knows the result. Longstreet did it to us at Chickamauga with the same result.

"Did anything in particular strike you about what followed?" I asked.

The major thought for a moment. "Well," he finally said, "I learned something about disaster that day. Disasters are made by generals and they are avoided by generals. During two years I fought in three major battles and half a dozen minor ones. All along I kept hearing how this army was going to destroy that army if this or that went according to plan, and no armies ever got destroyed. If ever anyone had a chance to destroy an army, it was Bragg. 'Old Rosey,' our commanding general, panicked and ran, and his men had a hard time catching up with him and his staff. Abandoned, George Thomas was left to hold off the whole rebel army or surrender. He pulled together the remaining units on a nearby hill and settled in for a fight. No general ever mounted a better defensive stand than the 'Rock of Chickamauga'—that's what we called Thomas after that—and he saved Old Rosey's ass, by

God. He and those Sharps repeating rifles one regiment had saved all
our asses."

"What happened then?"

"What do you think? We were nearly out of ammunition with night
rolling in. With all of Bragg's army about to surround us, we retreated
to Chattanooga." His mind seemed to drift. "It's strange, you know.
Bragg let us go." Then the major caught hold of himself and looked
at me hard, as if the glare bore a special message about the war. "I
guess both sides had a fair share of incompetent generals, but sometimes I think we took a larger sifting of the lot." He walked across
the room and picked up a faded, yellowing picture sitting on top of
the rolltop desk. "This is a picture of my company when we mustered
in. I was among the youngest in the company. They're mostly dead
by now, even those not killed in the war. Two of them settled here.
One died last summer; the other's in a home." He shook his head. "Do
you know what Chickamauga means in the Cherokee Indian language?
River of Death. No truer words were ever spoken. Thirty thousand men
fell in those woods, Union and Confederate, and the dying had just
begun."

"What happened to you?" I asked.

Pride sparked in his eyes. "You remember I told you how Thomas directed our defense? The only thing he did better was direct that
retreat. I consider it a thing of beauty. One regiment would retreat for
a quarter mile or so before establishing a defensive line. Then the next
retreated beyond the first. Over and over again, all the way back to
Chattanooga, the army leapfrogged itself. I made it back to our lines
at dawn the next morning."

He laughed. "In all that happened during that day and night, the
last moment of that retreat stands out in my mind. I remember this
captain—never knew his name—calm as you please. He commanded
the last company of men to reach our lines. His men were backing toward
our lines all crouched over, and he was in front of them—the last man
in. Not one of those men ran. They were probably too tired. They just
sidestepped in with their captain out front holding up his saber. About
a hundred yards out, the men picked up speed and left their captain
out there all alone. He turned toward our lines and realized his precarious position, with a regiment of Rebs not a hundred yards away.
They could have popped him with no trouble. He hesitated for a moment,
then he ran about ten yards. He must have realized that a fair portion

of the men in two armies were watching him, so he stopped and faced the Rebs again. Calm as you please, he drew his revolver and kneeled on one knee. He raised the pistol to get good elevation and slowly squeezed off all seven rounds. You arrogant son of a bitch, I thought, they'll kill you for sure. The last bullets were still on their way when he yelled: 'That's as far as you come, Johnnie Rebs.' He was right. They never came a step closer, ever. Two of those Rebs dropped wounded from those bullets, and our men cheered. Two months passed before the next cheer.

"After that, we dug in to wait for the final attack that never came. I wish it had. I still think we could have whipped them then and there."

"To your way of thinking, Major, what saved your army?" I asked.

A broad smile wrinkled his face. "Not what, who. General Grant pulled us out, or I should say, gave back the army's self-respect, and the army did what needed to be done. But I wasn't there when that happened. My regiment had been assigned to guard the wagon-train route along which we attempted to bring in supplies. I was north when the end came. Wish I'd been there, though. I heard tell it turned out to be the damnedest hoopla ever witnessed by mortal eyes."

I've heard the same from a dozen or more men with those mortal eyes that saw or were a part of what happened.

Grant always seemed to end up with the tough assignments. Chattanooga must have been the toughest of all, or it probably seemed so at the time.

That old farmer I talked to on the Mississippi farm appears to have been right about Grant's horsemanship. After Vicksburg, while parading in New Orleans, Grant tumbled from his horse and suffered a painful injury. The war moved on without him for a couple of months. When Grant had partially recovered, Lincoln gave him command of the western army. It was in that capacity that he came to Chattanooga, arriving on October 23, 1863. Previously, Grant had relieved Rosecrans and made Thomas commander of the army in the Chattanooga area.

In recounting what happened after the first day at Shiloh, I stated that something happened there in the minds of the men that altered the logical outcome. No less happened at Chattanooga. Somehow, Grant learned—there is no evidence that he learned it at West Point, at least not formally—that men have to see something happening that stands in their favor. With that in their minds, they marshal their efforts to endure the worst, or make something better of it given the chance. At Chattanooga, Grant gave them the chance.

For weeks the army had been trying to subsist on supplies brought down from the North. A private assigned to this detail put the futility of that effort into perspective.

"At Bridgeport Base," he said, "we loaded a wagon full of forage for the stock at Chattanooga. If the journey went right and we made good time, the horses pulling the wagon ate the last of the forage just outside Chattanooga, and then were too tired to make the long pull back."

An exaggeration? Perhaps, but the story described the problem. In time, if the army stayed in Chattanooga, starvation appeared to be the only outcome for soldier and animal alike. The only other alternative was to abandon this strategic location and thereby admit defeat, an option both Lincoln and Grant rejected. Grant, therefore, had to lift the siege and do it quickly.

One fact speaks poorly for the Union: unlike at Vicksburg, the siege at Chattanooga never was complete. Only the facts of an army in front and a river behind were similar. The men were in an uncomfortable situation, to be sure, but the Tennessee River is not the Mississippi. The Confederate Army, even at its greatest strength, never had enough men to completely surround Chattanooga, and it never tried. Old Rosey seemed to accept the fact of siege without that fact being established. He made no attempt to maneuver into a more satisfactory position. Except for the feeble effort to supply the army from Bridgeport, nothing of consequence had been attempted. Common sense dictates that if wagon trains could come and go, so could the army.

Grant spent a few hours studying the terrain before approaching General Thomas.

"Do you have a plan?" Grant asked him.

"Yes, General, if I am given the authority to act."

There had certainly been plenty of time to think about a plan.

"Let me see what you have," Grant replied. Grant listened as Thomas described his situation and outlined the plan. The task required less than thirty minutes. After suggesting a few minor revisions, Grant asked: "How soon will you be able to move?"

"Night after next, with your approval."

"Then do it."

That simple command started the army moving.

"The men saw what happened," a lieutenant named Carter told me. "Even without food in our bellies, our energy surged. Finally, something was being done. We never asked for more."

In five days, after a sharp encounter across the river, the siege collapsed. Supplies began flowing in over a shorter route as "an abundance of ammunition was brought up," Grant recorded, "and a cheerfulness prevailed not before enjoyed in many weeks. Neither officers nor men looked upon themselves any longer as doomed. The weak and languid appearance of the troops, so visible before, disappeared at once."

Grant had arrived, and with his arrival all thoughts of disaster faded. Everyone prepared for the finale. The army had suffered extended privation and was in bad physical shape. Bragg had a force capable of crushing any attempt to break out in a way not considered as a retreat in defeat. Leaving, however, meant abandoning the western Tennessee Valley, and Grant's plans included nothing like that. Thinking it prudent to bring in fresh troops, men not infected by the earlier defeat, Grant sent for Sherman's division as the final phase of the campaign began.

"After the initial shock of Chickamauga wore off," Sgt. Bradley Smith of the 118th Ohio told me, "I don't think anythin' but our own generals could've held us in Chattanooga. We were Westerners—not runners like in the Army of the Potomac. We never did accept defeat. We were just waitin' for someone to lead us. We knew Grant had come to do something. We knew that when he was ready to leave Chattanooga we all would leave, and we expected that to happen soon."

By this point in the war, the reality of Grant's presence meant something. In eighteen months his reputation had grown from nothing into an irresistible force. First, at the beginning of the war, there had been the capture of Forts Henry and Donelson to whet the Northern taste for victory. Then Shiloh, where he recovered from initial near-defeat to drive the rebels from the field, added to the growing myth. After Vicksburg the man began to assume the aura of legend. It is strange how, after Vicksburg, the shrill cry of defeat following Shiloh was transformed into an acknowledgment that perhaps the event had been less dire than first thought. Something more, but not much really, was required to give the legend a sense of permanence.

At the bottom of everything that might be said about Grant was a simple truth: men acted because Grant acted, and each time the anticipated result became fact. The army had acquired a sense of seasoning, and with that seasoning the soldiers gained confidence to do anything asked of them. Their confidence, however, was linked to Grant—or the idea of Grant—not to a vague, glorious ideal. There was no rush to rashness in them, but neither would they hold back if someone said a job needed doing.

Later, after the war concluded and the western army was parading through Washington, Sherman—he had made the army his by then—reportedly observed, "It is my belief that if this army were transported across the sea to Europe, it could fight through any force placed before it and rule the continent in a year."

Sherman came to know the army best. He was a part of it as it marched through Georgia and the Carolinas during the last months of the war. Yet whatever it is that makes an army invincible, the necessary tempering ended here in the south of Tennessee, and Grant's hand stoked the billows and guided the hammer.

So as the winter of 1863 approached, the tide of war took a sharp turn—at least in the men's minds. Nothing much had happened yet, but they felt the time for action was approaching. Grant had arrived.

9 He Was My Commander

The terrain around Chattanooga presented an interesting challenge for any army commander: it was a striking contrast to what I encountered in France. The conflict in Europe involved millions of men maneuvering over a vast expanse of territory. What the men of the Civil War started with their "works," as they often referred to them, the men of my war perfected. Most of the time we lived like moles in tunnels without roofs. Trenches snaked for miles, seemingly in every direction. Long stalemates set the tone until both sides saved up enough men to begin the killing all over again. Around Chattanooga, everyone must have been able to see everyone else. It is amazing that either side permitted this condition to persist. The Union Army, seemingly locked in its self-imposed prison, was no more locked in that position than the rebel army that everyone presumed had the key to the lock. Grant, with a minimum cost in casualties, effectively lifted any resemblance to a siege five days after his arrival. Although getting supplies to the troops remained a problem, the difficulty proved no greater than other armies faced throughout the war.

Both the Union and Confederate presidents viewed the Chattanooga area as a strategic necessity. Lincoln saw it as necessary to restrict the overall supply capabilities of the rebellious states. Davis's point of view, obviously, was just the opposite. The irony was that as long as the Union Army stayed put, the stalemate served the Northern cause as surely as if there were no Confederate Army at all. Stalemates, however, cry out for resolution, if for no other reason than that such conditions eat away at the morale and resolve of those encumbered by the condition. Grant found it thus when he arrived on the scene. Grant had heard that

Old Rosey had it in his mind to evacuate the city, so his first act as western commander was to replace Rosecrans with Thomas. His second act was to lift the siege. This left the main problem of Bragg's army unresolved. Grant had a variety of options for dealing with this obstruction. In the end, the solution came from unanticipated quarters. In fact, the solution violated his basic plan.

I realized that uncloaking the mystery of the battle that followed required talking to men who had fought there. With that in mind I traveled to Knoxville, Tennessee. Tennessee, like Kentucky and Missouri, was a border state, a state where slavery existed at best as a limited institution. I suspected that among the men this allowed a more tempered point of view.

At Knoxville I generally found that if one shook a dozen veterans from a larger batch, about half fought for the South and half for the North. For me to understand what finally happened on the field at Chattanooga, I needed a balanced assessment.

Having nothing better to do, the old veterans in Knoxville hang out at the train depot. They whittle through the day and watch the trains go by. I found the same at Galena, except there they watched the boats. Along about evening, the Knoxville veterans drift into one of several taverns that have sprung up in the depot's vicinity. There they play dominoes or pitch until the small morning hours. It never varied six days of the week. It varied on Sunday only by cutting the daylight hours in half in order to attend to matters of the spirit. Even in this, their conditions were different. At Galena there flourished one impression of God, a perception that He had, after all, been on the side of right. In Vicksburg, the idea of God was quite different, the general conclusion being that God had made a mistake in abandoning the South. They added to this the conviction that the nation was still paying for this lapse.

In Knoxville there existed a collective view of a Great Spirit who simply permitted things to become confused until men sorted it out, a task completed with the ending of the war.

One thing I noticed quickly: partners in these contests of cards and "rocks" carried out after sundown were as likely to be men who had fought on opposing sides as the reverse. Such a relationship would have been impossible in Vicksburg, where an enemy always remained an enemy.

Lincoln saw this difference as early as the first days of the war.

This uncertainty, this mixed allegiance of the men in the border states, guided Lincoln's actions up to the Battle of Chattanooga and beyond. While it was then impossible to make these states go with the North, it was enough, for the time being, to keep them from going with the South. In such a condition, each man was free to make his own choice about what to do. Yet no matter the decision, these men had to come back together after the issue was settled. I feel this explains what I found in Knoxville.

I selected as my target a run-down old building with a faded sign nailed to the front: Chattanooga Bar. I learned the moment I walked in that the old men of Knoxville are wary of strangers—especially strangers from Boston. I thought they talked strangely, but I soon learned that the majority decides what is strange. Word circulated quickly that a Harvard man was snooping around. That gave them another common reason for banding together to exclude me. At first, they simply refused to talk to me about anything. Only after I wiggled my way into a cutthroat domino game played for a dime a game, winner take all, did I gain a measure of respect. Two Sundays passed before that day.

"What are you doing here?" an old Union corporal asked bluntly after I had won my third straight game.

"Playing dominoes," I said with a straight face.

He sat for a moment trying to decide, I'm sure, if his original judgment of me had been correct. "I mean besides that?" he added, unwilling to be put off.

"I'm a writer," I replied. "I write about the Great Rebellion."

"Whoa there, young fellow," a Confederate lieutenant at the table said sharply. "We don't know about any rebellion. There was a misunderstanding, a condition common even among reasonable men, but we worked it out."

"All right," I replied, trying to get a fresh start. "I write about the War Between North and South. Do you agree there was such a war?"

A broad smile spread across the lieutenant's face. "There was a war, that's for sure, and we gave them a run for their money."

The corporal's nod confirmed his agreement.

"What do you write about the war?" the private across the table asked, an ominous squint in his eye suggesting that he had already made up his mind about my answer.

I was unsure of the color of his uniform, but this was a "veteran's only" establishment, although there seemed to be no preference or prejudice about which wars. I had learned this earlier and left a few pictures of myself in a major's uniform lying conspicuously here and there. The word got around.

"I'm almost afraid to say," I replied.

"Try me," he commanded, choosing age above rank to determine who asked and who answered the questions.

"I'm writing about Grant," I said. I mentally recoiled, waiting for the hostile response that never materialized.

"U.S. Grant?" the lieutenant inquired.

"The same," I replied.

A hush developed as all eyes turned toward my table. They all are listening, I thought. It must have been driving them mad this last week wondering what I was doing here. Immediately one of the games broke up, and the four men drifted toward me, bringing their chairs with them.

The first man to approach slapped me on the back. "No trouble telling which side you were on," he said loudly.

"I wasn't on either side, oldtimer. My mother wasn't born until after the war."

"Well, I bet your mother lived in Boston when she was born."

I had to smile. "I guess you could say that," I replied. "Which side were you on?"

He placed his large hand on the knee of the man sitting beside him. "My brother here, Sam, he fought on the losin' side. I was older, and older is smarter. I went with the winner."

"Why did you fight on different sides?" I asked. "Did one of you own slaves?"

"I was seventeen when I went in, and Sam was fifteen. We didn't own nothin'. It just seemed the thing to do at the time."

Soon I had a crowd of twenty men gathered around. We talked for a while, about the war in general, then I moved the conversation to the subject of Chattanooga. "I've written a lot about Grant," I told them, "but I'm having trouble writing about Chattanooga. It seems things got turned around there. The early loser ended up winning, and Bragg, who had the Union whipped, ended up defeated."

There was near-unanimous nodding at my conclusion.

"That about sums it up," a tall, self-assured man said, "and you're about on target. It was Grant who made the difference."

"Were you there?" I asked.

"I shot six men that I know of at Chickamauga, before one of them shot me. They carried me back to Chattanooga when Thomas retreated. I barely had recovered from losing my little toe when the last battle began. I still stumbled a bit, but nothing was going to keep me from going up that hill." His jaw muscles tensed. "They'd been shooting their cannon at me for weeks, and it was getting personal."

"What unit were you in?" I asked.

"I came with Sheridan, and I rode with him till the end of the war." He shook his head and made a clicking sound with the side of his mouth. "Now there was a general! Didn't weigh a hundred twenty pounds soaking wet, but that just made him a smaller target."

"Are you saying you went up Missionary Ridge?"

"All the way, stumbling and all. Even so, I suspect not more than fifty men beat me to the top."

"You lyin' old coot," said a man on the perimeter. "My regiment must've kilt the first fifty to reach the top, and I didn't see you no-where around. If I had, you wouldn't be boastin' your oats now." He sounded serious, but the sparkle in his eye signaled forgiveness.

I looked at the man, who obviously had no plan for yielding any-thing in this discussion. "You were with the Confederate forces on the top?"

"Proud of it, young fella," he said with a defiant air.

"Did you run?" The old man stiffened and his fists clinched, and I realized immediately that I had phrased my question badly.

"I went where I was ordered," he said sternly. "I never ran, not once. Runnin' ain't in my nature."

I believed him. "But you did leave the hill?"

He replaced the anger with a look of nostalgia. "I don't know for sure what happened. All I know is, from where I was standin', it 'peared as if the whole damned Union Army was coming straight at me. I saw nothin' 'cept what was in front and below me, and they was all wearin' blue. So when the colonel said get, I got." A strange, bewildered look glazed his eyes, as if he had just discovered something previously unanticipated. "But there's more to it than that. For better'n two months I'd looked across that valley straight at Lookout Mountain, higher'n the mountain I was on. It seemed impossible for anyone to scale that hill and fight a battle at the same time. But them Yankees did, and their flag had just went up on the highest point of that hill. If they could'a got up there, I said to myself, what was there to keep 'em from gettin' at me?"

I had learned, both vicariously from talking to the veterans and from my own experience, that wars are decided by more than terrain or the willingness of men to shoot at others. A seemingly impossible objective is as likely to be simple as a simple one is to be impossible. What matters is what men think about it. Is that what happened? Did the men on Missionary Ridge change their minds about the impossibility of its being scaled? I hadn't considered that.

"That's excuse makin'," another man retorted. There was firm agreement among several of those present. "I was with Wood's division, and I remember it like yesterday. We'd been whupped at Chickamauga, no doubt about it, but not by no Rebs. Our own generals didn't know what they was doin'. But whupped is whupped, and I spent the next months eatin' grain I plucked out'n the mud. I was tired of it, like all the men. When Grant came, he said we didn't have to do that no more, and I believed him. He made us believe that whupped wasn't whupped after all."

"Yeah," said the man standing next to him, "but that wasn't the reason I went up that hill."

"Why did you go?" I asked. "Didn't it seem impossible at the time?"

"Sure it did," he asserted. "Even Grant thought it was impossible. We weren't even supposed to be a part of the fighting. Our job was to hold the middle and move to whichever flank got into trouble. Sherman was attackin' from the north with the main force while Hooker came up from the south. They planned to move along the ridge and meet in the middle. But things went badly for both of them.

"I was a runner sitting on my horse there on Orchard Knob, with all of those staff officers, assigned to carry messages from Thomas to Wood. I guess Grant became frustrated with how things were going. Late in the afternoon, Grant turned to Thomas and said, 'Don't you think it's about time you went after those trenches at the bottom of Missionary Ridge?' General Thomas motioned me over and told me to tell Wood to take those trenches. Wood told me to tell Sheridan, and that's what I did. I was there, so I stayed.

"So we just went across, straight at those trenches. We must have been a terrible sight to those Rebs with their backs to the mountain and no place to run but up. So, that's what they did, and we moved into their trenches." Then he looked surprised. "No one ever thought to ask what would happen when we took those trenches. Every Reb gun on that hill started firing down at us. Bullets were coming at such an angle that they traveled two feet through a man before coming out his back. I remember thinking three things: if we stayed there, death was certain; if we ran, we would be humiliated again; or, we could go up that hill. No one said anything. It was as if everyone, general and private, saw the problem the same way, so we started up the mountain. Anything was better than dying like gophers in our holes."

"So you never really came to the conclusion that scaling the mountain was possible, only that there was no other choice?" I prodded.

"What would you have done?" he asked.

I pondered his question for a moment before answering.

"I suppose, with the conditions you describe, I would've gone up."

"There you have it. It wasn't as bad as you might think, though. We were right behind the Rebs, and the men on the top had a difficult time shooting at us without hitting their own men. Shooting his own makes a man cautious, makes him stop and think. There were rocks all around, however, so we had plenty of cover. After a while, I just got too tired to worry about it. That damn hill is nearly straight up, about eight hundred feet of it."

"How long did it take to reach the top?" I asked.

He turned to the man standing next to him who was leaning on his cane. "How long did it take, Jake, an hour?"

"Not that long, Tom. Three-quarters, maybe. I was kinda hobblin', though. I sprained my ankle when I jumped into a trench about halfway up. Remember? We spent about five minutes in hand-to-hand there, then started up." He nodded. "I'd say less than an hour."

"What happened when you got to the top?" I asked.

Tom looked at Jake and shrugged. "I sat down," he replied. "I was tired."

"I crawled under a cannon," Jake added. "My ankle was swole up bad by then. Anyway, all the Rebs were runnin' down the other side of the hill, and conditions were about as wild as I ever saw 'em. They were fresh, so they had no trouble outrunnin' us. Besides, I didn't want to catch 'em. I just wanted 'em to stop shootin' at us anymore. But I remember bein' mad earlier. What kind'a man would shoot at another man as if he was a rat in a hole? Damned inhospitable, I thought."

"What happened then?" I asked.

"I curled up and went to sleep. It was about dark, and the day's work was over. With no more Rebs to shoot at, I just went to sleep."

"Did you feel a sense of victory?" I asked, expecting general agreement from the Union veterans.

"I guess there was something of that in what I thought," said Tom. "But mostly I thought, 'Them Rebs will sure be mad when we catch up to them, making them run like that.' I knew sure as sin we would be going after them in a day or two. That was what Grant was there to do, chase the rebels. So I took the rest I had coming and left the hooting and hollering to the generals."

"Anything else?" I asked, speaking to the crowd.

They looked at their neighbors and acknowledged general agreement with a series of nods.

"I got shot twice," said a short, simple-appearing man. Everyone turned.

"Where at?" I asked.

"On the hill," he replied. Everyone except the simple man laughed, and I felt bad.

"No, I meant where did the bullets hit you?"

"One in the arm, and the other in the head." I felt worse.

"Did that end the war for you?"

"I don't remember much until '73," he said, a vacant stare revealing the confusion in his mind. "I went down when Grant was a general and woke up with him as the president."

I rose and walked toward him. A path opened up as I moved. I placed my hands on his shoulders and looked him in the eye. "What rank were you, soldier?" I asked. I expected him to say private, or corporal at best.

"I was a lieutenant colonel," he said smiling, "second in command of a regiment, they tell me." The smile faded to a look of uncertainty.

A tear came to my eye. War is cruelty, I thought.

"Come with me, oldtimer. I want to buy you a beer."

A toothless smile revealed his pleasure.

I heard a commotion behind me and an old soldier supporting himself on two canes pushed his way through the gathering. He walked to the old colonel and faced him. Almost losing his balance in the process, he shifted the cane in his right hand to his left and gave what passed for a snappy salute.

"Sir," he said with a weak, wavering voice to the colonel. "May I escort you to the bar?"

New strength entered the colonel's frail frame as he came to attention and returned the salute.

"He was my commander," said the man with two canes as he turned and looked at me. "Sometimes that's difficult to remember. Thank you, sir, for reminding me."

A tear rolled down his cheek and his lips quivered. His eyes reflected a perplexing mixture of sadness and remorse. He grasped the colonel's arm, and with each holding the other up, they moved slowly toward the bar.

For a long moment no sound entered my ears except the shuffle of four tired feet and the thump of the canes. Then, adding a sense of drama to the moment, a distant train whistle broke the spell. The man standing next to me, a man younger than most of the others, placed his arm around my shoulder.

"Major," he said, "I've never been to Harvard College, but it must be a nice place."

I turned and looked at the men gathered around.

"Come to think about it, men," I said, "I want to buy all of you a beer."

Life and laughter returned to the gathering as they moved toward the bar. After that, I never had any trouble getting those men to talk.

10 Lieutenant General Grant

The door to Willard's Hotel squeaked open. No one noticed at first. A rumpled, wholly unpretentious man with graying whiskers held the door open as a young boy of thirteen shuffled past carrying a carpetbag and moved on to the counter. The man pushed the door shut and followed the boy. The man wore the uniform of the Union Army. This attracted no particular attention, as uniformed men were a common sight in Washington these days. The battered condition of the uniform, however, seemed a bit odd. This, and the rough, weathered look of the man, attracted the attention of several people in the lobby. One who looked at the weather-beaten face later remarked that the general had "rather the look of a man who did, or once did, take a little too much to drink." At another time the major general's insignia might have commanded more respectful attention, but not now, not with the end of the war's third year only weeks away.

Get the price of the room in advance, the clerk thought.

"May I be of service?" he asked.

The general pounded his hands against his jacket. A small cloud of dust drifted into the air, part of it settling on the counter. "We need a room," he said in a soft voice.

"Will you want a separate room for the boy?" asked the clerk.

"No. Since the government will be paying the bill, one room will be enough."

I'll need authorization for this, thought the clerk. "Please sign the register."

As the general signed, the clerk motioned to the manager. The two conferred for a moment, each stealing a glance or two at the shabby officer during the conversation. The manager finally nodded as the clerk returned to the counter.

During the course of their brief conversation three soldiers, each immaculately dressed in the uniform of a brigadier general, walked past the major general at the desk. None gave him any notice, although one did smile at the boy. This was Washington in the late winter of 1864, and the city had no shortage of generals. Perhaps five hundred generals were in the army, and most of them, at one time or another, found their way to Willard's. The plethora of generals had prompted Lincoln to remark how easy it would be to hit one with a rock thrown from his office window, even if it were thrown during the small hours of the morning.

The man signed the register as the clerk watched.

The clerk squinted as he tried to read the upside-down signature. "I'm—unable—to make that out," he said haltingly as he slid the general a key.

The military man seemed distracted as he searched through his pockets. Without answering, he placed a small envelope on the desk. "Just present this to the Treasury," he said, "and the bill will be paid."

The clerk had accepted many such envelopes in recent years. It'll take three months to get the money for this room, he thought. He continued to study what the general had written.

"Grant," the man in the uniform finally said. "I hope you don't mind my just using my initials. U.S. Grant."

"U.S. Grant and Son—Galena, Illinois," the clerk read casually. Then, as if the power of what he had read finally hit him, he stepped back and placed his hand over his mouth. "Gen. U.S. Grant?" the clerk asked. "The man called by the president to be general-in-chief of all the army?" Everyone had heard of Grant, although hardly anyone outside the army had seen him.

"The same," Grant replied as he bent down to break a chunk of dried mud from his boot.

The perception of those in the lobby changed immediately. One man who earlier had observed that he had "blue eyes," now detected that the general had "a clear, blue eye." On second look, a formerly observed "seedy look" yielded to a more accurate assessment of "a man with a quiet dignity that obviously set the man apart, a quality not apparent on first sight."

The clerk now moved with excited urgency. "Sir. We received orders to hold Parlor 6, the Presidential Suite, for you and your son. It's *much* more comfortable. There's room to stretch out. You'll have your own tub and facilities."

The attendant had seen many generals before, but never *this* general. His excitement showed. He slapped the bell, and a bellboy ran to the counter. "Take Mr.—I mean General—Grant's luggage to Parlor 6," he commanded.

By now the general had been completely transformed, at least in the minds of those who had been attentive enough to draw a conclusion from the time he entered the building. Another observer noticed a "rough dignity of surface," the look of a man who "habitually wears an expression as if he had determined to drive his head through a brick wall, and was about to do it." All that was favorable about Grant was observed only after his identity became known, however.

Grant stooped to pick up his grip to hand it to the bellboy. The young man looked surprised, then he rushed to relieve the general of his burden. "Just throw it on the bed," Grant said, the words slightly distorted by the cold cigar extending from the corner of his mouth. "The boy is hungry," Grant said to the clerk. "Will you have something sent up?"

The clerk looked disappointed.

"Is that a problem?" Grant asked. He had accustomed himself to hearing what men thought, even when they remained silent.

"Oh no, sir." He hesitated as he looked around the lobby at the gathering observers. He leaned closer. "It's just that business has been slow this winter," he said softly, "and the sight of General Grant and his son eating supper in our establishment, well, you know, sir."

Grant pursed his lips; the clerk remembered it as a soft smile. "Order a small steak for me and a large one for the boy. Well done. I personally will pay for his. We'll be down as soon as we clean up a bit. You say the room has its own facilities?"

"Yes, General," the clerk said smugly. "Put in especially for the president."

"Well, I'll be." He placed a quarter on the counter.

"Thank you, General. Your steaks will be ready when you come down."

As Grant washed his face, he heard a timid tap on the door. "See who's at the door," he said to his son in a muffled voice through the towel.

The boy opened the door. A tall young man, splendidly dressed in the uniform of a brigadier general decorated in gold sash and braid, stood at attention. The young brigadier presented a snappy salute as he saw Grant standing on the other side of the spacious room. "Sir. My name is Thomas Laird. May I have a moment of your time, General?"

Grant studied the young man, who appeared to be fifteen years his junior.

"General, that is all the time I can give you. The boy is hungry, and his meat is in the skillet by now." The young brigadier stood as if fastened to the floor. "Well, General," Grant motioned, "come in."

The officer walked briskly into the room and stood at attention. "Sir, forgive my tenacity, but I have a request."

Grant waited.

The young officer relaxed, but only slightly. "General, I wish to request a field assignment. I feel the war will end soon, and I have been stuck here in Washington since its beginning."

Grant dried his hands. "I wish I shared your confidence that the war will soon be over, General, but that is not what is important here. What type of position do you seek?"

"A position in the line, sir, in command of troops going into battle."

"You are a brigadier, sir," Grant replied. "Do you envision yourself in command of a brigade?"

"Whatever the General thinks is correct," he replied, extending his chin even more.

"I see. You have no experience in battle, but you want to lead a brigade of fifteen hundred men into battle. What might the men you lead think of that?"

The young officer appeared puzzled. "It's not for them to say," he said.

"Perhaps, General, but they do think. What they think about the man who leads them into battle is important. We're dealing with veterans here, and every one of them wishes to be alive at the end of the war."

"Sir, some are going to die."

"That is correct, General, but it's my responsibility to see that their dying serves some useful purpose. What is your rank, sir?"

The young man stiffened; then he looked at his shoulder boards as if in confusion: "Sir, I am a brigadier general."

"No, General, your permanent rank."

He hesitated, as if embarrassed to answer the question. "My permanent rank, sir? I—I'm a captain."

Grant nodded. "And your age?"

"Twenty-seven, sir."

Grant nodded again. "That sounds about right for a captain. I was twenty-six when I made captain. I remained a captain until I left the army eight years later." Grant walked to the bed, lifted his new longcoat, and put it on. As he buttoned the coat, he looked sternly at the young officer. "Tell you what, General. I have an abundance of generals. What I'm short of is captains. They keep getting killed, and replacing them is a constant strain. If you are willing to take command of a company, I will grant your request for a transfer."

The officer appeared indignant. "As a captain, sir?"

"As a captain, General Laird. I'm unwilling to entrust more men than that to anyone without experience at dodging bullets."

"But I graduated from West Point, sir!"

"A professional soldier, eh? All the more reason to take a field command. After this war is over there'll be no place for officers without combat experience, West Point or not."

"I don't know, sir. Being a captain after being a general is a difficult decision."

"Well, I need captains, sir." He walked toward the door. "But now, my son is hungry. You think it over and let me know. Now if you'll excuse us."

Polite applause greeted him as he entered the dining room. Word had circulated by this time that Grant was having supper at Willard's. A large number of people who had never before given the place a thought suddenly found it necessary to pay a visit. Grant was history in the making, and shortly there would be nobody who was anybody who had not seen, and preferably talked to, the general. Grant and his son spent a stressful hour in the dining room. "It proved annoying," he recalled later, "having reporters record how I held my fork or how many chews it required to grind up a piece of meat."

Just as Grant pushed back his chair in anticipation of returning to his room, his attention shifted to a young military man holding his cap under his arm moving briskly toward the corner where Grant sat. He looked familiar to Grant, but he could not place him.

The young officer approached to within several feet of Grant, then he snapped to attention. "Captain Laird reporting, sir."

Grant studied the young officer carefully. "Were you the young brigadier with a beard who talked with me earlier?"

"Yes, sir. I figured if I'm going to die I want my men to know what I look like. I shaved it off." The enterprising young man had already removed the stars from his shoulders and replaced them with captain's insignia.

Grant smiled. "How does it feel, sir, being a captain instead of a general?"

The young officer smiled broadly. "I've earned the rank of captain, General Grant," he said proudly. "What I do with it is up to me. I was made a general because of who my father is, but he insisted that I remain in Washington where it's safe."

"That no longer appeals to you, Captain?"

"There's a war out there, General, like none this world has ever seen. I want to be a part of it. If I die I'll never know the difference. If I survive—well, I have a one-year-old son, sir. I'm a professional soldier in the middle of the grandest war ever fought. How could I ever explain to him that I avoided the fighting?"

Grant placed his hand on the young captain's shoulder. "Captain," he said, "go over to that desk and get a piece of paper. Write out your full name and unit, along with the name of your commanding officer. I'll write out the order directing that you be assigned to command a company of men in a combat regiment."

"Thank you, sir."

"Just remember one thing, Captain. If you serve your men, they will serve you. They don't know much about generals, but they know captains. One other thing. I'd keep quiet about having been a general. They might get the idea you were demoted for reasons other than your own decision."

The captain smiled. "I see what you mean, General Grant."

"Now write out that information for me," Grant said, "and bring it to my room."

My grandfather told me the little-known story of this young captain. He met him just before the army moved south into the Wilderness during the spring of '64. "I never met a man more eager to smite the enemy," Grandfather said, "or less in the proper state of mind for the encounter. At the time, I had the feeling that this would be a mighty lucky man if he lived past the first week."

This story has a double meaning. The first is the manner in which Grant was introduced to Washington after the president had summoned him. There may have been men who by that time had never heard of Lincoln. I doubt there were any who had not heard of Grant. Such was his fame. Sen. James Doolittle, the grandfather of a friend, totaled up Grant's accomplishments to that time. Besides having been presented a special gold medal created in his honor, Grant had won seventeen battles, captured one hundred thousand prisoners including all of two armies, and captured five hundred artillery pieces. That record, in part, was the reason for his summons to the capital.

The second, the anecdote about Captain Laird, will in time become apparent.

*   *   *

Lincoln always had a personal and sometimes unique view of the Great Rebellion. At the outset it never occurred to him to try to impose his will on the South, at least to a burdening extent. Long after the war began in earnest he repeatedly counseled tolerance, even for that "peculiar institution" called slavery. He did object, however, to having the South dictate that the people in the several states would have slavery imposed upon them, against their will, even from a distance.

For the Southern politician, the only alternative for protecting slavery demanded, at the least, an inability to vote it out. This meant keeping an equal number of free and slave states. Each time the subject came up, eyes turned West to where new states lay in the making. The bickering continued all though the 1850s. By 1860, the noise was becoming unbearable. In the South, of course, the discussion seemed to be leading in only one direction: slavery had to go. Rarely do there exist issues for which compromise is impossible. Here they found such an issue. Here they had found an issue that could be settled only by force of arms. The addition of even one free state without a compensating slave state would shift the balance of power to those states demanding that all slaves be freed. The Southern politicians concluded, perhaps correctly or perhaps incorrectly, that slavery's doom was at hand if this occurred. So, the war began on the pretext of preserving states' rights. The underlying objective, however, from the South's point of view, was to preserve slavery—at any cost. The problem defined the solution, and the solution became the problem.

Now, fifty-seven years later, the only solution for this clash of values appears obvious. In 1861, however, conditions appeared more clouded. So the country drifted into war.

Politics, however, knows no borders. Slavery or no slavery, few could imagine a strong Northern economy without the South to purchase Northern goods. For the South to buy Northern goods, it needed hard currency. This meant cotton, and cotton needed picking. Whatever the Northern farmer and storekeeper might have thought, the manufacturers and the wholesalers thought something else. Each time the subject rolled around to this point, convictions on the virtue of slavery grew fuzzy. In time, even in the North, discussions grew hostile.

Always present, just under the surface, were those westward-turning eyes. Every man with nothing saw something for himself and his family in all of that land just waiting for the plow.

The issues ran deep and were infinitely complex. Lincoln undoubtedly faced the most complex dilemma encountered by any American president.

Lincoln recognized, perhaps more clearly than anyone, the struggle to balance the issues. Lincoln found no balance. There either is slavery or there is no slavery. Half-measures, however well designed, are ineffective for holding a man in bondage. The Supreme Court's Dred Scott decision made that clear. On the other side, a Union either is a Union or it is not a Union. Stated another way, as Lincoln often did, if the children had the right to tell the parents what to do, the family must perish. In effect, if such attitudes persisted unresolved, the Union must, in time, break apart—with war or without war.

The long-range threat reached farther than just the North and South. The nation had to grow. The land mass west of the Mississippi was larger than the North and South combined. Just as a Southern mentality had developed, what might happen if there evolved a Midwestern mentality? Or, perhaps, a Northwestern and Southwestern mentality? What about a Plains States mentality or a California mentality? Where would it end? Nothing about Lincoln suggests that he had any idea of presiding over the dissolution of the nation. To him, the meaning of the name "United States" existed in the word "United" rather than in "States."

As the war progressed toward the conclusion of its second full year, Lincoln took hold of the political realities of the war with both hands. With the Emancipation Proclamation he had limited his grip to one hand. That proclamation left open the door to slavery, especially in the border states that had stayed with the Union. The problem was the Constitution. He lacked the authority to abolish slavery outright, even if he wanted to do so, which he did not, at least at first. But attitudes had evolved, and along with them Lincoln's own.

The more Lincoln thought about it, the more he realized there could be only one solution.

"The problem always moves in a full circle," he told Stanton. "I think it is impossible for the nation to survive if slavery remains a viable institution. That vile institution must be destroyed, utterly." The Constitution might end up a bit tattered in the process, but total war called for extraordinary action. "Besides," he told his cabinet, "the Southern senators and judges are gone. Who is left to protest?" McClellan? He had passed from the scene, sacked once and for all after the battle at Antietam.

Lincoln knew history. He knew that the Founding Fathers had been reluctant, even unable, to confront the issue of slavery directly. They, however, had an escape route; they had the task of creating a nation. So, they had put off looking for a solution, a luxury unavailable to Lincoln. He had to settle the matter once and for all. The problem was in finding a general with the conviction to drive the issue home. As Sherman later wrote, the time had come for hard war.

*   *   *

"Lincoln's problem," said Sam Fortney, a veteran of forty years in the House of Representatives, "was letting go of the war. For my father—a United States senator at the time—the war dominated every conversation he had with me from the first time I remember. From the beginning, Lincoln always fancied himself an armchair general. I suppose that is understandable." He reached into his vest pocket with a shaking hand, withdrew a sack of Bull Durham, and began to roll a cigarette. Five minutes passed before he continued to talk. "Lincoln had difficulty," he said with a snicker, "finding a general capable of reading his mind. Even if that had been possible, I doubt much good would have come from it; he himself didn't know what he wanted. By '64, everyone understood one thing: if Lincoln ever was to let go of the harness, there had to be a general in charge who knew what it took to end the war."

"He sure used up a bunch of generals looking for the right one," I said.

"Do you know what's ironic about that? Right from the beginning, I think McClellan read Lincoln's mind."

My mouth dropped open. "What makes you believe that?" I asked. "Lincoln never found a way to make McClellan fight except when Lee had him backed into a corner."

As I saw the congressman's wry smile, I braced my mind for a new point of view.

"Think about it," he said with a nod. "Lincoln was the president. McClellan was an intelligent man, nearly top in his class at the Point. It seems impossible for a man to so completely defy the president when that president did everything within his power to get the man to fight. I think my father spotted the problem. McClellan knew what the president wanted. The thing was, McClellan wanted something different. Lincoln was president, all right, but McClellan had the army. McClellan also had the support of his soldiers and a fair number of politicians. What soldier wouldn't support a general who did everything possible to keep him from getting killed?

"History is important here, young man," he said with a stern look. "After leaving the army a decade earlier, McClellan had gone into railroading. There were powerful railroad people who wanted to preserve the status quo. They realized only later how a war generates money. My father told me how, when these men realized fully the money they were making, they began to have a change of heart. Only then were they willing to sacrifice McClellan, or more precisely, to let Lincoln send him packing."

I nodded. That explains several things, I thought. Halleck shied away from the fighting because he came of age thinking of war as an expanded form of chess. McClellan's motives might have been more practical, politically speaking. Yes, it offered an answer if not the answer. There were other possible answers. McClellan was full of himself, arrogant to the core. This led Lincoln to think that McClellan wanted to be a king. McClellan also thought Lincoln was a baboon, or worse. It may have been simply that he resented taking orders from the man. I have found, not surprisingly, that given a variety of reasons for how a man acts, the practical reason usually proves true.

"How did Grant figure into all of this?" I asked.

"Simple. The political winds shifted. These men had to get on with the business of business. They had locked up about all of the war concessions—even cotton flowed freely into the North during the war—and they had railroads to build. They knew about the land, millions of acres of lands, waiting for settlers to give it value. Before anyone could move West, however, the war had to end. It would not do to kill off all the settlers. About that time they began to add up the numbers—these were men who understood numbers. Grant had won every battle he fought. By this time, others had converted even Shiloh into a victory, seeing as how it had not been a defeat.

"So, the idea developed—I never knew with certainty where it first came from—to create a more powerful military leader. By this time there were a hundred or more major generals. A man needed a log book to keep track of date of rank to know if he ranked or was ranked by another general. The idea to create the rank of lieutenant general took root and grew like fire in a drought. Only George Washington had held that rank. Winfield Scott had been a brevet lieutenant general, but that was mostly an honorary status. An honest-to-goodness permanent rank of lieutenant general was something new for this generation. It meant power. It meant no more doubt about who was in command. So Congress created the rank and left it to Lincoln to appoint the right man. Grant was the only man ever considered."

"So far as you know," I asked, "did Grant ever express reservations about accepting the responsibility?"

"Grant was a good soldier; in some respects, a perfect soldier. He had this creative way about him of taking an order, however obscure, and making it work. When Lincoln said he wanted Grant to be the new commander of the armies, Grant simply said 'yes, sir'—but there were some conditions. He wanted his own men around him, and he wanted to have his headquarters in the field away from Washington. His intent was to stay close to the Army of the Potomac. This meant putting Sherman in charge in the West. Those concessions being acceptable, he came to Washington to get his third star."

"Did you ever meet Grant during the war years?"

"Yes. Twice."

"What was your impression?"

"The first time I met him we were out for a buggy ride at twilight. The weather had turned pleasantly warm after months of hard winter, so my father took my sisters and me for a ride. On the way, he saw some senators talking on the fringe of the White House lawn. He parked the buggy and walked the few paces to meet with them. I suppose ten minutes had passed when Lincoln and Grant strolled within sight. They noticed my father and the others and walked over. I felt terrified. All I could think about was all those men I heard he had killed. I thought he, personally, had killed them all. For the longest time I studied him out of the corner of my eye. Considering his small stature, the fear gradually lifted, and over the hysterical objections of my older sister, I crawled out of the buggy and walked over. I stood in the shadows of a tree and listened for, oh, perhaps ten minutes. In all that time Grant said only three words. These were no, yes, and sir: 'yes, sir'; 'no, sir.' He shook and nodded his head a number of times, but his only comments were in response to direct questions. I remember asking myself: what do they see in this man? Later, I recalled that Lincoln hardly said anything, either.

"You never forget a moment such as that. The moment grew in significance as I grew older. I often found myself being noncommittal about an issue I wanted to keep close to my vest. I concluded, many years later, that expressing their intentions to a bunch of senators was about the worst thing they could do. There were no secrets in Washington, then or now."

I marveled at this old man. He hardly had the strength of body to lift a pouch of tobacco, but his mind had the crispness of youth. It made me glad that fate had placed me at this point in history. Ten years from now, all these men would be dead or too old to remember anything. How many people could claim they'd seen Grant and Lincoln together—a thousand at most? Perhaps no more than fifty of those remained alive. Lincoln and Grant met only twice, once here in Washington, and once just before the war ended, shortly before Lincoln's assassination. Their destinies, however, were as firmly linked as if they had spent their lives together. Their roots were similar, one coming from Galena and the other from Springfield, both from Illinois, but nothing else bound them together except a desire to end the war. At the time, there existed nothing more important in the nation.

"Did you know Grant as president?" I asked, breaking new ground.

"Yes, unfortunately. I ran for the House during Grant's last term. I must confess, I did not think much of him as a president. As a commander, the men he selected to work with him were the best this country had to offer. How is it possible, I asked myself many times, that he possesses such poor judgment in selecting the men who serve him as president? The man simply lacked a head for business, and no larger business ever existed than the government of this nation." He sighed. "Those were difficult years, for the nation and for Grant."

"More so for Grant than when he commanded the army?" I asked.

The old man appeared surprised by my question. "I think Grant found no greater pleasure in his life than during the Civil War years. Sure, he had some problems, but on balance, conditions suited him well. In my judgment, he was the most powerful man in America. Lincoln, the philosopher-statesman, held the nation together so that a man like Grant could flourish. But those were war years, and Grant was commander of the military. Grant had the power of life or death for a great many young men."

"Why, do you think, did Lincoln like Grant so much?"

"That's an easy one. Grant was unthreatening. At the time, Grant had no political ambition, except possibly to be the mayor of Galena." He laughed. "He said that once, do you know that?"

I smiled. "Yes. I heard that he said that. He did become president, however."

"Given the choice between being president of the United States or mayor of Galena, which would you choose?"

"I see your point."

I regretted having pushed the congressman to discuss Grant's presidential years. I have read volumes about that time, most of it uncharitable beyond reason. Few men ever rise to anything approaching greatness. Hardly any achieve the greatness that Grant achieved over a sustained four-year period. The man never existed who had no limitations. Not more than a dozen men ever lived who achieved worldwide prominence in two fields, and most of those had the luxury of controlling the reports, so the accounting is suspect. Of this there is no doubt: Grant was a great general. Whether directing small units or an army, he did it with skill, confidence, and success. So, what is there in us that makes us think we have a right to be so self-righteous in our criticism of the man as president?

As I sit here in the refurbished Willard's Hotel looking out on Pennsylvania Avenue, I am in awe of this small city's history. George Washington walked here when it was nothing but a swamp. Every president since Washington has added something to the fiber of this city. This includes Grant. But being made a lieutenant general was of little importance. That was merely a reward from a grateful Congress and president for past accomplishments. More to the point, it offered a way for that Congress and president to tell him that they expected even more. March of 1864 had arrived, and the end of the war seemed hardly closer than on the day it began in the spring of 1861 back at Fort Sumter. Now, however, the army was professional, and it needed a professional at its head. The time had come for constant, unrelenting killing and dying. Within two months of his promotion and assignment as general-in-chief, Grant led the army south. From that day forward, the men of that army never again broke contact with Lee's army. Never, that is, until Appomattox.

11 A Master Plan

After Grant's appointment as lieutenant general in the late winter of 1864, he spent two months devising a comprehensive strategy for ending the war once and for all. He wrote in his memoirs: "My general plan now was to concentrate all the force possible against the Confederate armies in the field. Before this time these various armies had acted separately and independently of each other, giving the enemy an opportunity, often, of depleting one command, not pressed, to reinforce another more actively engaged. I decided to stop this." Decisive words, and he meant them.

Grant initiated his grand strategy by appointing Maj. Gen. William T. Sherman to command the western army. Grant traveled west to meet with his friend. The six hundred miles from Washington to Cincinnati, Ohio, required the better part of three days by train. The loan of Lincoln's personal coach and a second coach generally reserved for the president of the railroad made the journey as comfortable as possible. Accompanying him were General Rawlins, three staff planners, and his personal aide.

"General," Rawlins said, shaking Grant's shoulder. "It's time to wake up, sir. We will arrive in Cincinnati in about fifteen minutes."

"What time is it?" Grant asked as he rubbed his eyes.

"Nearly six, sir. The sun is just coming up."

Grant swung his feet to the floor. "It's good that I've had the time for some sleep," he said as he pulled on his boots. "There'll be precious little time for sleep after I return to Washington. Has there been a message from my wife?"

"Yes, General," Rawlins answered. "There was a telegram waiting at the last wood stop. She expects to meet you at the station."

"And Ulysses Jr.?"

"The boy is with her."

Grant smiled, but said nothing.

The loud, shrill sound of a whistle fractured the cold, morning air. Then another. "That's the signal, General. We're within sight of the station."

"Where's my aide?" Grant asked.

"I sent him forward to gather our luggage together. Shall I call him?"

"No." Grant moved to the small clothes rack and took down his full-length jacket. He hesitated as he studied the shoulder patches, each with three gold stars.

"May I help you, General?" Rawlins asked.

Startled from his daydream, Grant looked at Rawlins. "I wish that was possible, Rawlins. I think Mr. Lincoln sees more in me than is there. He placed a terrible burden on my shoulders when he gave me this third star."

Rawlins placed his large hand on Grant's arm. "Sam, President Lincoln is the smartest man I know. He proved that by selecting you to lead this army."

Grant sighed. "The country needs me, Rawlins, is that what you're saying?"

"Something like that, sir. Here, let me help you with your jacket. We're pulling into the station."

Grant turned his back and Rawlins held out the coat. Grant slipped his arms into the sleeves and began to button. "Are you sure this damn coat is necessary, Rawlins?"

"It's below freezing out there, sir. The country needs a general, not a hospital patient."

"Very well."

The train lurched, then screeched to a stop. Grant moved to the window. The sun had hardly pierced the horizon, but people covered the station platform. Standing at the front of the crowd were Mrs. Grant, Ulysses Jr., and General Sherman. Grant shook his head. "Is all of this necessary, Rawlins?"

"You're the commanding general, sir. How would it look if no one came to welcome you?"

"Hummmm," Grant said. "Well, let's get on with it."

As Grant stepped into sight the band began to play, and all of the military personnel came to attention and saluted. Grant returned the salute as he stepped onto the platform.

Ulysses Jr. moved first. "Hello, Father," the boy said over the noise.

"How are you, son?" Grant replied with a special smile reserved for the boy.

"Fine, Father. Will you have time to take me fishing?"

Grant placed his hands on the boy's shoulders. "I think the war will wait an hour or two while we test the water in these parts. Perhaps this afternoon."

Ulysses Jr. smiled broadly.

"Now, son, I must speak to your mother." Grant extended his arms, and the handsome woman moved across the platform. As she approached, Grant pulled her to his chest. "I've missed you, Mother."

The band stopped playing. "And I you, Mr. Grant," she replied in a whisper. She always called him Mr. Grant, even in private. "How was your trip?"

Grant turned his head toward the Pullman. "Look at that thing, Mother. One would think they made me king. It even has a water closet!" He looked fondly at her. "How was your trip?"

She pointed to a Pullman sitting on a side track. "The president of the railroad insisted I use his private car," she said.

Grant studied the car. "Hell, it's more luxurious than that of the president of this nation."

"The president of the railroad has more money than the president of the nation," she replied with a wry smile.

"Probably more than the government," Grant added seriously. "I have only two days, Mother. That will have to do us for a long time."

"I understand," she replied, letting her head drop. "This has been such a long, dreadful war."

Grant stepped back and held her at arm's length. "God willing, Mother, it will end soon. Where are you staying?"

"The mayor has provided us with several rooms at the hotel. There's even a cook. Do you want breakfast?"

"I'm starved. Where are your bags?"

"Already at the hotel."

"I need to talk to Bill for a minute," Grant said. "Wait for me and I'll walk you to the hotel."

She nodded.

Grant walked toward Sherman. "Good to see you, old friend," Grant said as he extended his hand.

"I see the politicians did you no harm, Sam," Sherman said smiling. "How was your trip?"

"Comfortable," Grant nodded. "Have you had breakfast?"

"Not yet, General."

"Come, then, and join us. We have much to discuss. May as well get at it."

"General, your bags are on their way to your quarters," Rawlins said. "Nice to see you, General Sherman."

"You too, General Rawlins. I'm glad to see you were able to stay with General Grant. Everyone knows you're the general behind the general."

"Thanks, Bill. It makes an old country lawyer feel a bit uncomfortable, however."

Grant smiled. He knew the meaning of Sherman's words. Grant had been accused of drunkenness following the Shiloh battle. Later, with Grant still stinging from the considerable public criticism, Sherman had made a well-publicized statement. "Grant stood by me when I was crazy," he said, "and I mean to stand by him when he's drunk." The statement spoke of more than loyalty; it spoke of unquestioning friendship. Grant never forgot.

There had been but one hesitation in placing Grant in charge of the Union Army. Everyone, especially those in Congress, was aware of the persistent rumors of Grant's "problem." They were equally aware that Rawlins had sworn to keep Grant dry, so long as he had the power to make it so. In effect, Rawlins had appointed himself to guard Grant's honor. His position as Grant's principal staff officer and advisor gave him official sanction to do so. His resolve, however, was more than a simple commitment given credibility by some official appointment, it was a personal passion. Unstated, but taken for granted, was the belief by Congress that "Rawlins was the man who would save the man that would save the country." But Rawlins also had merit as an organizer, so his assignment to Grant's staff served a double purpose. Seldom did anyone see one man out of the company of the other.

"Let us have some breakfast, gentlemen," Grant said.

A young lieutenant stepped forward and saluted. "Permit me to show you to your quarters, General. Follow me."

After breakfast, Grant pushed away from the table and withdrew a cigar from his breast pocket. "Feel free to smoke," he said. "Now let's get to work."

Grant, Sherman, and the three aides followed Rawlins to an adjacent room. There, Rawlins had placed several maps on a large table moved in for the meeting. The top map displayed the area stretching from northern Tennessee in the north to the Gulf of Mexico in the south, and from eastern Mississippi in the west to the Atlantic in the east.

Sherman studied the map in silence as Grant walked to the window.

"Looks like rain," Grant said. "How goes the war in the West, Bill?" He knew the answer, but it was an opening.

"Joe Johnston will resist all the way to the sea, General, and that's where I plan to drive him. It would have been easier if they had left Bragg in charge. He was more daring and would have been easier to destroy. I think it will be difficult to draw Joe into an all-out battle."

"Have you formulated an overall plan?" Grant asked.

"As we discussed earlier, I mean to drive the rebels toward Atlanta. Johnston will have to defend the town. It's like the second Confederate capital."

"It's also a major source of production," Rawlins added. "When it falls, a major source of war supplies will be lost."

"Sam," Sherman said, "may I speak frankly?"

Grant turned from the window and nodded.

Sherman pointed at the map. "I should be able to take Atlanta by July—August at the latest. This will move us out of the hill country and into the open. My plan is to leave our supply lines behind and strike south across the middle of Georgia."

"Leave your supply line behind?" Grant asked. "Isn't that risky?"

"No more so than when you did it at Vicksburg, Sam, and we'll be able to move much faster." He hesitated. "But that's not my main reason. As I understand it, your objective is to end this damn war as soon as possible. I'm convinced that doing that will require bringing the war into the heart of the South. We must make the people understand the meaning of hard war. If I set my troops loose to live off the land, the people down there will begin to understand what hard war means. I never have seen a place for chivalry and niceties for the civilians while men are dying by the thousands in the trenches. The war will end only when the resistance to carry on is destroyed. The people must suffer. They wanted war. I propose to give it to them in all of its forms."

"Hummm," Grant said. "Go on."

Sherman pointed at the map. "Once Atlanta is secure, I propose to head southeast toward the sea. Once there, we'll be resupplied. You can arrange for the ships to meet us. Then I'll come up through the Carolinas and bring the war to those who have avoided it, but who deserve it the most."

Grant smiled. "Do you propose to salt the earth as you go?"

Everyone laughed.

"No, Sam. I can't carry that much salt with me, and the South is in short supply. But my men are hungry for ham and chicken. I plan to cut a swath through the middle of Georgia, leaving nothing for those devils to ship to their armies."

"Don't you think Joe Johnston will have something to say about this?"

"He has but two choices. One is to stand and fight. The other is to run and preserve his army. Either way, the same purpose will be accomplished. I think he'll run. The South has a dilemma. It can't afford to have its western army destroyed. Fighting all-out opens it up to total destruction. Nor does that army have the strength to stand and fight. Besides, by the time Johnston figures out where we're headed, he'll be out of position to do anything." Sherman leaned forward and placed both hands on the table. "Sam. If my army is raising hell down there, it'll drive the leaders in the Deep South into a panic. They'll have to stop all northern shipments of men and materials. That'll make it easier for you when you go at Lee."

"Hummm," Grant said as he nodded. "I like it. You know the Northern Copperheads will scream if the war hurts the Southern people, though."

"Let them scream. How does anyone think this will end if the South is left untouched? It had to come to this, sooner or later." He appeared thoughtful. "Will Lincoln support it?"

"Mr. Lincoln has only one objective," Grant said nodding, "to end the hostilities. Do you have this planned in detail?"

"I do. May I suggest we go to my quarters down the hall? My staff has everything laid out."

So there it was. Sherman planned to strike at the heart of the Confederacy, and Grant would "go at Lee." Simple, direct, and absolutely necessary if the struggle was ever to end. What is simple in words, however, is often difficult in application.

All along, the Southern leaders had offered a simple alternative for ending the struggle. "Leave us alone," Jefferson Davis said, "and we will leave you alone." What the South wanted most was to leave everything alone, to preserve the past and keep slavery alive. Fully eighty percent of the slaves remained secure in their plantation shacks. The Emancipation Proclamation had no meaning at all down there. Any solution to the war that left that condition unchanged offered little more than a dream of a restored Union. The governors of Georgia, Alabama, North and South Carolina, and Mississippi would continue to languish in leisure, content to have Lee battle it out in Virginia or points north or west, if only they remained beyond the hardship of war. Sherman proposed to end all of that. For the South to die, Southern gentlemen had to lose their comfort and treasure. So what if a few of them lost their lives in the process? Getting at them was the problem. Stretching a supply line all the way from Knoxville to the sea was impossible. Nathan Bedford Forrest, Johnston's cavalry commander, would see to that. Even if Johnston could not fight a pitched battle, his cavalry could play havoc with a train of wagons stretching across three hundred miles. Living off the country meant Sherman would have no supply line to protect, and it would force his army to consume everything in its path, bringing the reality of war home to those Southerners along the route of march.

There was a third advantage, a political one. The South's political structure was different from the North's. Part of its reason for leaving the Union had been the Southern obsession with states' rights. The South's central government was weak, always having to act with agreement from the states. With the security of those states threatened, men and supplies were required to remain close to home to defend those who started the war in the first place.

Whether Sherman and Grant actually saw the heart of the issue is difficult to say. Evidence on that subject remains uncertain. But Sherman had discovered the ultimate weakness of the South. In the design of this would-be nation, the Confederacy had sown the seeds of its own destruction. If its leaders would not yield the perceived rights of the states in order to stay in the Union, there was no reason to believe that they would sacrifice their principles now. Even Lee, the epitome of the Southern aristocrat, but still a rational man, had stated that his state was everything—more important than nation or life.

So Sherman would rape the South, starting in Georgia and extending the terror to the northern border of North Carolina. He did not say it now, but he had special plans for South Carolina, where the rebellion had begun in a small bay guarded by a fort called Sumter.

There was another part of the plan, also unspoken. Both Grant and Sherman knew that Grant had selected the most difficult task for himself. No one doubted Lee's resolve to fight until utterly vanquished; it was not in the man to quit while he possessed the means to resist. If Lee had not been whipped by the time Sherman made his giant swing through the South and back to the northeast, there would be two armies to hammer on Lee's trenches. Lee's men could load and fire only so fast. With the massive power of the North hurled relentlessly toward them, only one outcome could result.

12 Never Sound Retreat

Between Washington and Richmond there is a swath of land and inland waterways that, by actual measurement, spans a hundred miles north to south. From an imaginary line that links the two cities, the land extends eastward toward the sea across a stretch, although more irregular, about as wide as it is deep. These ten thousand square miles of solid land and inland waterways are, without a doubt, the most fought-over area on the North American continent. Even in the spring of 1864, before U.S. Grant had trod a single footstep on this bloody landscape, the land had achieved this distinction. It is more so now thanks to Grant and the Army of the Potomac. Here lie Yorktown of Revolutionary War fame, the two Bull Runs, Fredericksburg, Chancellorsville, and a dozen or more other battle sites of greater and lesser importance. The blood of scores of thousands has nourished this ground in the effort to harvest and preserve a nation. But these early battles were nothing, as measured by the effusion of blood, compared to what was about to follow. In prospect, as Grant honed his army for the last, longest, and most costly campaign of the war, were battles of unparalleled horror and perseverance.

Sensing political danger if he established his headquarters in Washington, Grant placed himself in position to control a significant portion of the history of this region. After his appointment as commanding general of the army, he assigned himself to personally oversee the conduct of the Army of the Potomac. Gen. George G. Meade would command the army in the field, but Grant would command Meade.

For three long years this luckless army, marching to and from a string of defeats, had ground to fine powder the soil of this area. Grant established as his objective the ending of that sad, laborious process.

At sunset on May Day, 1864, Grant brought together all of his corps and division commanders. It was less a council of war—Grant never called a meeting for such a purpose—than a final briefing before the spring offensive now scheduled to begin at midnight three days hence. Gouverneur K. Warren, the V Corps commander, arrived first, followed by Philip H. Sheridan, the newly appointed commander of the Cavalry Corps. George G. Meade, commander of the Army of the Potomac, arrived next. Warren's division commanders followed close behind.

John Sedgwick, the VI Corps commander, rode up just before Winfield Scott Hancock, the II Corps commander, rode into view. Last to arrive were Henry J. Hunt, the artillery commander, and Ambrose E. Burnside, the IX Corps commander. Within a brief period, forty-seven general officers crowded noisily into the thirty-by-forty-foot rough lumber building that served as the winter officers' mess for VI Corps. An assortment of lesser generals, colonels, and majors waited outside.

Although the air was warm for the first day of May, Rawlins had issued orders to nail all the windows shut and to cover the glass with black paper. The right information in the wrong hands could cost a thousand lives and perhaps the war. A large table, specially constructed for the meeting, sat squarely in the middle of the room. Other than the twenty-one chairs that surrounded the table and the racks from which hung roughly drawn maps, the room was bare. Most of those present had to stand. All the better to keep them awake, Rawlins reasoned.

Grant had previously expressed to Rawlins his reluctance to call these men together in one room. The arrest three days earlier of a sergeant major as he conversed with an infantry lieutenant colonel had caused this anxiety. The sergeant major's uniform had given him away—it was new. None of the enlisted men had even seen new field uniforms since early in the fall of '63. The colonel had objected to "this rude intrusion on our conversation," a protest resulting in his prompt relief from command. Too much was at risk to take chances. If the colonel turned out to be an innocent victim, selected by chance to supply vital information to the Confederacy, his court-martial would sort it out. In the meantime, everyone was expendable, especially staff lieutenant colonels, and more especially if they were political appointees, as was this particular lieutenant colonel. His brigade commander had been eager to point out that "I never really trusted Lieutenant Colonel Todd, but I never knew why until now." Hindsight is a blessed gift. This comment did not enhance Colonel Todd's chances. No doubt the comment had been self-serving for the brigadier who made it, but in times of war someone has to be wrong. Better a colonel than a general.

By any standard, the colonel fared better than the spy. It had taken less than an hour to establish that the sergeant major possessed no means of confirming his place in the Union Army. Within another hour, the provosts had tied him to a fence post and shot him three times through the heart.

At any rate, as a result of this unsettling affair Grant had expressed concern for the safety of his general staff. Rawlins had assumed the implied responsibility and nailed shut the windows and papered over the glass. No one approached within a hundred yards of the building without written and then confirming oral approval by Rawlins or appropriate staff officers.

Even before the meeting began, the air had the consistency of an iron smelter's exhaust. Half the men smoked cigars. The thick haze made it difficult for Grant to identify the men at the far end of the room. Several of the nonsmokers, suffering one discomfort to avoid another, stood next to a wall hoping to find a crack through which an occasional whiff of fresh air might pass by.

"Gentlemen," Rawlins said, slapping his hand on the table to gain attention, "some of you have a long ride following this meeting. Shall we begin?"

Grant cleared his throat as he stepped forward. "Gentlemen, I've talked personally with all of the corps commanders. Each knows his assignment. I will clarify any uncertainty in that regard, but that is not the main purpose of this meeting. It is my intent that each man here fully understands the strategy I have devised for this campaign." He turned and briefly looked at the map, then turned again toward his generals.

"For over three years," he continued, "we have struggled to crush this rebellion. It is fair to say that this task is hardly closer to success than on the day the war began. There are rebel pickets less than ten miles south, just across the Rapidan. It was thus three years ago on this date. That must change. Mr. Lincoln wants it so and I want it so. Slightly more than two days from now we will move the army across the Rapidan at Ely and Germanna Fords. We will field a force of nearly 120,000 men. It is my intent to move at General Lee's army by the most direct means possible. We will recross the Rapidan only when Lee is defeated or our army has been destroyed." The comment brought shifts in position and a number of sideways glances. There rose even a murmur here and there. "If so much as one division can stand its ground," he continued as he leaned forward, placing both palms on the table, "we will fight." Grant looked slowly from right to left, taking time along the way to study the faces of those present, insofar as they were visible through the smoke. His impression displeased him. "Some of you will be missing at the end, either dead or injured. That's war, and the price of this campaign will be high in lives and material. But this war must end."

He stopped for a moment to let the message sink in. "Let me repeat: this war must end! During each of the past three years, this army has moved south numerous times only to be driven from the field back toward Washington." This was not a revelation to any in the room; more than half had made the round trip at least once. Along the way, more than a hundred thousand Union soldiers died without securing a fraction of one percent of the land claimed by those in rebellion. Although many in this room had participated in those defeats, still much in doubt was if the experience had taught them anything. Grant looked directly at Burnside, the hapless commander at the Battle of Fredericksburg a year and a half earlier. In his discomfort, Burnside looked away.

Something was needed to shock them into belief. "I tell you this as fact, gentlemen. If I knew of some way to secure the final victory on the first day of this campaign with the loss of fifty thousand men, I would select them personally and count the Union fortunate."

A collective gasp filled the room, followed by the predictable physical agitation indirectly expressing regret for the uncontrolled emotional response. Sensing these men still were missing his point, Grant slammed his fist against the table. "I fear, gentlemen, that you do not grasp the full significance of my message. Lee will meet us with sixty thousand men or more, and so long as there is an army to absorb them, more will come up every day. Every one of those men will be a crack shot and nearly every one a veteran. They'll have the advantage of knowing the terrain and fighting from the defensive. For every one of them we kill or wound we likely will lose one and a half, or more. But understand me: I consider it cheap at twice the price compared to continuing as in the past. My objective is to kill them all if such is required to secure the peace. I will never sound retreat."

They had heard similar words before, from McClellan, Burnside, McDowell, and Hooker—and each time a retreat had followed. Who was this Grant, who thought himself a better general than Bobby Lee?

Not a man present, with the exception of Rawlins, lacked a healthy skepticism. McClellan had seen a vision of Lee's army expanding like buds popping into leaves on a giant tree. What McClellan believed to be a force of a hundred thousand men, twice its actual size, had grown in his imagination to a force of two hundred thousand as justification for his retreats. Burnside had gone the other way. Realizing his force outnumbered Lee's by at least three to two, he had proceeded to sacrifice his men in a headlong frenzy to eliminate his advantage. Hooker, if possible more arrogant than McClellan, eventually grew to see a Reb behind every tree in the Wilderness, and the Wilderness had an unlimited supply of trees. Consumed and overwhelmed by fear, he had retreated with greater haste than the others.

And now Grant's turn had arrived. Somehow, he failed to grasp Lee's greatness. At the start of the war, everyone, including Gen. Winfield Scott, considered Colonel Lee to be the best soldier in the Union Army. Lincoln had offered him command of the Union forces. Lee declined. Instead, he selected the South, or more precisely, Virginia. Nothing had happened since, with the possible exception of Gettysburg, to diminish the mystical reputation that they all honored and feared.

"The only way this army will break contact with Lee's men," Grant continued, "is if I am dead, relieved of command, or their army no longer has the capacity to fight. Any man who lacks the stomach for this form of war needs to tell me now, before I find it out for myself. I offer each of you a medical leave, no questions asked. The offer is good until dawn." The offer placed a bit more starch in the words, but still, what about Lee?

The air began to clear up a trifle. Mostly out of sense of self-preservation, the men had stopped smoking. Even Grant, seldom seen without a cigar in his mouth, found the willpower to slack his habit. "Does anyone have anything to say?" Grant asked.

Several seconds passed before Sedgwick leaned forward. "General Grant, I understand what you expect. I have no doubt the men will do what you ask, as difficult as it will be, but when those casualty reports start flowing into the War Department, what then? Many think too many have died already. Horace Greeley and his like scream at the death of a thousand. What will happen when the daily toll is five times that many?"

Grant sighed. Sedgwick had rubbed the raw nerve, and it needed soothing. "The situation is this, General. This is an election year. Whatever is to be done needs to be completed, or well on the road to completion, by the November election. President Lincoln understands what will follow the news of high casualties, but he has promised me he'll support our efforts without complaint. Our responsibility is to fight the war and end it as soon as possible. We'll fail if we watch the rebels with one eye and the politicians with the other. It's as simple as that. I want all eyes on Lee."

Sedgwick nodded. "General Grant, I've waited a long time to hear that." Sounds of agreement filled the room, but were they sounds of belief?

"Is it your intention to capture Richmond?" Burnside asked.

"No," Grant snapped. "My intention is to capture Lee's army. If he goes to Florida, then we will also go to Florida. If he goes to Richmond, we'll follow him there, but that means a siege. I hope to avoid a siege. This is a critical point, gentlemen. I have no interest in territory. Every inch of ground we fight on is Union territory temporarily lost to our control. There is no North or South, only the Union. No one spot is more important than any other. The only land I want is the land on which Lee's men stand unarmed and unable to fight. Then we'll have Richmond, and all of the South. Nothing more is required; nothing less will do."

Grant waited. "Anything else?" he asked. "Good. General Rawlins will finish with a general review of the campaign. It's my hope that we can pass through the Wilderness before Lee makes contact, but I expect it will be otherwise. His smaller army will be at a disadvantage in the open, and I've never heard of Lee accepting a disadvantage without protest."

Aha, thought Burnside. Now he's beginning to lose his certitude. Lee will protest, all right, with the declaration written in fire and steel. Grant will see, as have all the rest of us. Grant will see when he meets General Lee.

There would have been no surprise if Burnside had screamed the words rather than taken counsel with a passing thought. Grant recognized his central problem. In simple truth, every man in the room feared Lee. The difference in Grant was his approach to the problem. To him, the answer resided in the numbers: kill or maim two Confederates and accept the death or maiming of three on the Union side. Do that over and over again and, at some distant crossroads, Lee would find himself standing alone. What happened in the interim was war—hard and cruel to be certain, but a necessary part of the process. Both Lincoln and he anticipated the price, but at stake was the nation. In all of the

Union, with the possible exception of Sherman, Grant was the only man alive with the combination of skill and resolve to see it through. In the numbers, or more precisely, in Grant's willingness to accept the hard meaning of the numbers, lay the answer.

"General Rawlins," Grant concluded, nodding in the direction of his chief of staff.

Grant's mind wandered as Rawlins finished the briefing. As short as the meeting had been, the words spoken were different than these generals had heard before. Perhaps they had understood. Perhaps not. There always had been confusion as to the true objective of the war. Many believed it would be easier to capture Richmond. Destroying Lee's army represented a far more difficult task—some would have said impossible. From the beginning, Lincoln sought to protect Washington while trying to destroy Lee's army in the field. Grant had found this to be the most difficult idea to shake from the president's mind. A small army remained constantly quartered within the city's defenses, an army that could serve a better purpose shooting rebel soldiers. With the cream of the Northern manpower pool now skimmed, Grant had need of these men for more dangerous work. He had transferred most of them to the Army of the Potomac and intended to send them south. If Lincoln could part with the security offered by these troops, the generals could put Washington out of their minds. But Grant recognized the problem: the pretext of protecting the capital was a crutch in the minds of these men. It offered a ready-made excuse to break and run north at the first sign of difficulty—or when the casualty count climbed too high. The city had always given promise of a safe haven for defeated generals, a place to lick their wounds and dwell on Mr. Lee's luck. No more. Each day forward would be rough—with any licking of wounds, if time permitted, done in the field. If they believed nothing else of Grant's words, that was essential.

"That's about it, gentlemen," Rawlins said in conclusion. "General Meade will be in overall command of this campaign. General Grant, however, will accompany the army and maintain his headquarters in the field. He chooses to operate away from the prying eyes of all those politicians everyone is so concerned with."

Everyone laughed, but it was hardly a laughing matter. Grant had learned from his earlier brief stay in Washington that any given ten politicians had ten different ideas for winning the war. Grant wanted no part of listening to that, and he meant to have it his way. To Grant's way of thinking, the front promised safer haven.

*   *   *

I caught up with Jacob Gattlin in the upper reaches of the Ozarks in southern Missouri. After asking his wife where I might find him, I spent two hours walking and climbing along a woodland trail south-west of Branson. I finally found him sitting on a folding canvas chair next to a small, gurgling stream. He had nodded off when I first saw him. Six inert cane poles lined the bank of the stream, the lines extending into water as clear as a new mirror. I saw that fish had nibbled all the bait from the hooks, but Gattlin apparently had no concern for this temporary disadvantage. This isolated bit of Heaven on earth was about as far from Washington as one could get and still remain on the planet, and as the day progressed, I learned that Gattlin had more interest in catching up on his share of life's authorized tranquility than in catching fish. I failed to extract from him all that I desired, but I heard enough.

Gattlin had been among the first of a new breed of military men, men who fought with their brains rather than guns. Such men acquired real importance during my war, but in the early 1860s, true military men considered officers such as Gattlin just a notch above shirkers. A man had to possess a better than average military mind to have any hope of surviving in an army where tradition and advancement virtually demanded glorious achievement on the field. I sought out Gattlin because others had told me he was such a man. My mission was to get a firmer grip on the political intrigues that hindered the war effort, especially as those intrigues applied to Grant after he assumed overall command.

What Grant and Rawlins failed to clarify at the meeting with the generals, or at any other level so far as I have been able to establish, was the grand strategy Grant had devised for winning the war.

There were, of course, abundant clues offering glimpses of Grant's ideas. The clues took more solid form as the last year of the war progressed, but to acquire a hindsight view of what he was thinking in the spring of 1864 I had to rely largely on Grant's recollections as reported in his memoirs. Few men, Sherman being among the exceptions, saw the grand design. Gattlin was another who had figured it out for himself. I wanted a more detached view, so Gattlin was my man.

"There may have been several reasons for Grant's reluctance to lay it all out," Gattlin told me. At the time, in '64, Gattlin worked in the War Department. He held the rank of captain and spent all of the war years immersed in planning operations. He described himself as being thirty-sixth in command of the War Department—that is, there were thirty-four officers in direct line above him before reaching General Halleck. In reality, he was several hundred down the line in the decision-making process. He was there, however, and saw and heard much that happened.

"For one thing," he continued, "the armchair generals had difficulty finding fault with or improving upon what they did not know. There would have been an abundance of both activities had Grant spoken openly on the subject. Then there was General Lee. Anything that reached a politician's ear was bound to appear in some newspaper within a week. Lee would have heard about it the next day. But mainly, I think, Grant had doubt about the competence of his generals. Although his grand strategy was quite simple in its overall design, it was complicated in the linkage of its several parts. Had any one part come unraveled, all the other generals would have had a built-in excuse for their failures, seeing as how they could reason that their failure resulted more from the prior negligence of others than any failure on their parts.

"The hard part in attempting to understand this war," Gattlin said, "is realizing how political everything became, right from the start. This applied on the battlefield as well as in Washington. The attitudes of support for the war efforts rose and fell in direct relationship to the most immediately concluded battle. Spirits were high when we won; everyone seemed ready to run up the white flag when we lost. Little things, subjective things, made all the difference. For example, it became very important for a general to hold his position when the killing stopped. The battle was generally considered a defeat if the commanding general withdrew his troops while the rebels clung to their positions.

"Politically, our overall strategy early on became one of avoiding defeat rather than winning. In a sense, the army's survival became more important than winning the war, the theory being that so long as the army survived there could always be another battle. That might have gone on forever. It remained so right up to the day Grant took command. What few realized was there was a limit to our ability to sustain this conflict. By 1864, when our industrial capacity had reached a point where the war hardly taxed our ability, the critical limit became political."

Suddenly his attention shifted to the water. "The fish took all my bait," he said. "Sort of reminds me of Grant and Lee. Grant kept dangling opportunities in front of Lee, sort of like bait, but Lee never grabbed the hook. Some mysterious sixth sense apparently told Lee that if he met Grant head-on it would all be over, and not in Lee's favor." Gattlin took his time as he baited the hooks. When he had finished, he turned to me. "Let's go for a walk and give the fish some time to think about their next move."

The day had turned warm and bright, about the same as in early May when Grant was smoothing out the rough edges of his plans. If ever I hoped to understand what followed, I had to understand the circumstances that controlled those plans. I had to move beyond Grant before I could return to him. We walked a short distance before coming to the top of the hill. The view took my breath away. It was a perfect analogy for my objective: I had to emerge from the forest before I could understand the grand view spreading before me. We sat on a large rock hanging over the broad, green valley.

"Do you agree," I asked, "that Lincoln shared a portion of the responsibility for the problems until this time?"

Gattlin smiled. He had continued his work for the government well into the present century. He shared with most government workers, inside and outside the military, a reluctance to speak ill of those he considered his superiors. For Gattlin, that list had shrunk over the years; he received a brevet promotion to major general the day before his retirement. He had seen them all come and go: Lincoln, Grant, Sherman, Sheridan, and a dozen more with lesser merit. "Of course Lincoln was part of the problem," he said finally, "but I find no fault in him for this. The generals had the luxury of fighting on only one front at a time. Lincoln always had to keep one eye on the war and the other on the politicians. It's difficult to say where the greater danger existed."

He sighed. "Take Gen. Ben Butler, for example. There was a politician for you—you notice I didn't say general. He outranked, by virtue of his major general's rank and date of appointment, just about all the generals. In that sense, Grant ignored him at his peril. Grant at first formed a modestly warm personal relationship with Butler, but the more Grant observed Butler in action the more the relationship cooled."

"Did this relationship affect Grant's grand strategy for the war?" I asked.

"Did it ever. As you probably know from all your research, Grant had a hard-hitting, straight-ahead attitude about fighting. He had a natural instinct to attack, and attack with everything at his disposal. He could

not have encountered a man with a more contrary motivation than Butler—
McClellan might have been worse, but at least McClellan had the virtue
of an organized mind—and Butler was the worst kind of soldier to have
in command of a major portion of his army, especially considering what
Grant had in mind during the spring of '64."

"What did he have in mind?" I asked.

"You want it all?"

"No. Just a rough outline."

"Well, I guess I'd have to say he had an eastern strategy and a
western strategy. Grant had recognized this as far back as the fall of
'62, when he went about trying to capture Vicksburg. Cutting off the
West was essential if we hoped to deny to the Confederacy the men
and materials available to it from across the Mississippi. The real winning
strategy became possible once Vicksburg fell under our control. Grant
recognized that Lee's army had to be captured or destroyed. That became
General Meade's task. Meade had orders to make contact with Lee's
army and never let go. As Meade moved south, General Butler was
expected to move with about thirty thousand men up the James River
to City Point and, if possible, to Richmond. If Lee was still on the
loose by the time Meade arrived in this area, Meade and Butler were
to join forces and go after Lee together.

"Meanwhile, out in the West, Sherman had orders to go after the
rebel army in that area. He had Atlanta as his immediate target. That
industrial base in the South's heartland had to be destroyed for two
reasons. First, its industrial capacity was enormously important in
sustaining the rebel army. Perhaps of equal importance was the anticipated morale impact if Atlanta fell. Although many a good Southern patriot conceded that Richmond might fall, the Confederate high
command considered Atlanta beyond reach. That city, more than any
other, had become the South's symbol of defiance."

"All of this happened," I observed. "I fail to see the problem."

"Butler was the problem. A short distance upstream, before the James
and Appomattox Rivers join, there is a rather substantial double bend
in the James. The protrusion in the landscape created by this double
loop of the river is called the Bermuda Hundred. Butler unloaded his
army here, almost within sight of Richmond. For the next three months
he contented himself to remain there, rendering his army about as
ineffective to the war effort as a large frog on a lily pad. Lee had to
place only a small blocking force across the neck of land at the bot-

tom of the Hundred—the river kept Butler hemmed in on the other sides—and go on about his business. Nothing Grant tried succeeded in getting Butler to move. In desperation, he tried to have him removed from command, but Lincoln would have no part of that."

"Why not?" I asked. "It's my understanding that Lincoln gave Grant a free hand in conducting the war."

He smiled. "History makes of relationships what it pleases. There're always exceptions, and it's naive to think otherwise. You see, Butler was a member of one of the most powerful families in the country. More important, he was a Democrat. Since Lincoln was a Republican, and there was to be an election in the fall, he wanted Ben Butler kept as far as possible from an active part in the election process. Lincoln must have snickered to himself that the Bermuda Hundred was the perfect place for a man such as Butler. One of Grant's unique qualities was his ability to see this for himself.

"Had Butler performed as Grant wanted, Lee would've been required to reduce the size of his army and send help to keep Butler from capturing Richmond and Petersburg. Virtually all of Lee's supplies moved along the railroads that converged on the Richmond–Petersburg complex. Union success in capturing these two cities would have forced Lee to abandon Virginia. If Sherman had captured Atlanta by that time, Lee's army would have wilted on the vine, so to speak. Grant would have had Lee caught in a vise between his army and Sherman's forces. Between them, they could have rolled up the South. The war most likely would have ended that fall."

"If that's correct," I observed, "the war dragged on until the next spring and another hundred thousand men died for nothing."

"You haven't dabbled much in politics, have you?" Gattlin replied.

"I confess, you've found me out," I said.

"In everything I've said, I qualified it with 'could have' or 'might have.' I outlined Grant's strategy, but Lee was a different matter. And then there was Lincoln. If Lincoln was to survive politically, to see the struggle through, he had to win the November election. Everything on the political front might have changed with Butler on the loose up North. And I failed to mention the Shenandoah Valley. Lee could have turned north with his still substantial army and moved against Washington through the Valley. It's unlikely he would have made the Gettysburg mistake a second time. Grant would have had to abandon his grand strategy. He had counted on General Sigel to establish control in the Valley, and that part of his strategy came unstuck by summer. It wasn't until fall that Grant sent Sheridan into the Valley to sweep it clean."

"So what is the crux of what you've told me?"

"The crux is that Grant had a strategy, but to bring the strategy to a successful conclusion he had to acquire a sensitivity to both the military and political components of the war. He also had to rely on many people to make it work. If he'd discovered by this time another half dozen Shermans or Sheridans it might have moved along with greater speed. I doubt there were another half dozen military men of their caliber in the whole country, North and South combined. Grant's good fortune was in finding two such men while, during the critical middle phase of the war, Lee was losing his best two field commanders, Stonewall Jackson and James Longstreet."

War involves more than fighting and glory. My conversation with General Gattlin made that clear in my mind for the first time. This Civil War had evolved to become an incredibly complex undertaking. Grant somehow found it within himself to see this complexity and to develop within the limitations imposed a plan that offered a chance of keeping the nation together. I have grave doubt that the phrase we all take for granted—one nation, indivisible—would have any meaning today if Grant had failed in his military endeavors. On the political side, the threads that bound the people's will to Lincoln's valiant struggle quite likely would have unraveled if the November 1864 election had moved McClellan into the White House. Three desperate years had passed with Lincoln having no real objective other than to find the right man to join with him to see the struggle through. Now that his efforts had been rewarded, these two men were historically linked, and, for better or worse, they would ride the same horse to the end.

Grant at least offered a chance, and that offered more than Lincoln had seen with his other generals. What to this day remains incredible to me was Lincoln's faith—faith in a man he hardly knew. Lincoln had tried everything, and nothing had worked. He had tried deep involvement in the planning; he had begged for success; he had even offered to hold a general's horse if that would help bring the struggle to a close.

Now, with Grant, Lincoln accepted the most desperate gamble of all: he elected to do nothing. At the end of April 1864, he wrote a note to Grant. In it he said: "Not expecting to see you again before the spring campaign opens, I wish to express in this my entire satisfaction with what you have done up to this time, so far as I understand it. The particulars of your plans I neither know nor seek to know. You are vigilant and self-reliant; and, pleased with this, I wish not to obtrude any constraints or restraints upon you . . . and now with a brave army, and a just cause, may God sustain you."

Words of faith if ever I saw them. Now there could be no retreat.

13 The Beginning of the End

On May 4, 1919, I rented a buckboard at the Culpeper Livery. From there, Abby and I set off toward the Wilderness. We considered driving our new Ford, but I wanted to get a feel for the country, to absorb the history that permeated this place of epic struggle. We had traveled to Washington for a belated honeymoon denied us earlier by the demands of a great world war.

It was fifty-five years to the day after Grant pointed the army toward the Rapidan River and moved it south. Grant had reached an accommodation with Lincoln, and the time had come to earn his pay. "The particulars of your plans I neither know nor seek to know," Lincoln had written to Grant, and in so saying had lifted a large portion of the burden from his own shoulders and placed it on Grant's. Doing so offered the last, best hope for winning the war.

It's a pleasant ride from Culpeper down to the Rapidan. Small farms line the way, and the people are friendly. We reached Ely's Ford about noon, and there we stopped to feast on a picnic of chicken, slaw, potato salad, and sweet rolls that Abby had prepared before we left Washington. Abby spread a blanket under a budding tree overlooking a riverbank. A cool breeze blew across the placid river.

Just as we were about to have lunch, an old man in his late sixties crossed the bridge built over the ford and pulled his wagon to a stop. "Whoa," he said as he strained on the reins. "Whoa, ya damned mule." He wrapped the reins around the brake handle and slowly eased his way to the ground. He winced slightly as his knee popped, but he appeared resigned to the limitations imposed by advancing age. His clothes revealed his occupation. His baggy overalls had faded almost

137

white; a wide-brimmed straw hat battered by wind, rain, and sun hung wilted about his head. A long straw of dead grass extended from the corner of his mouth. "You people just out for a lark," he asked, "or ya head'n some place in particular?"

I walked toward him and extended a hand that he clasped and pumped with the persistence of a man priming a pump. The firmness of his grip surprised me. I involuntarily gasped at the pressure. "We rode down to see the Wilderness," I said. "This is my wife, Abby. My name is Kelly."

"I'm Jubal," he said proudly. He stuck his hands in his pockets. His shoulders followed in a sagging slouch as he scanned the far shore of the river. "The Wilderness!" he exclaimed in mild surprise. "Why'd anyone wanna see the Wilderness?"

"Two armies fought a great battle here," I answered. "In fact, two great battles were fought here."

"Ya don't say," he replied. I sensed he was poking fun of me.

"Have you lived here long?" I asked.

"All my life. My grandpa settled that farmstead ya just passed, a hundred acres all together. I've doubled it durin' my lifetime, an acre here, five acres there." He looked up. "In fact, young man, this's my tree you're sittin' under."

"Oh. I'm sorry. We didn't mean to trespass."

"Never mind. I'm 'customed to Yankees eatin' under my trees. They say Grant stopped at this grove to watch his cavalry pass by back in '64."

"How do you know I'm a Yankee?"

He cocked his head and the twinkle in his eyes seemed to say "that's a rhetorical question," but courtesy compelled him to remain silent.

"Will you join us for some chicken?" I asked.

I sensed immediately that the offer restored the balance for the loan of the tree. "Don't mind if I do," he replied as he pulled his hands from his pockets and wiped them on his dusty pants legs.

"If you've lived here all your life, you must've been here when Grant passed through."

"Yup," he said nodding, "but not exactly right here. I'd just turned fifteen. A month earlier, on April 8—that's my birthday—I walked south to join Lee's army near Clarke's Mountain. Paw wouldn't let me go before then. He'd been wounded the year before at Chancellorsville and was still recoverin'."

"So you supported the rebellion," I said.

His lips tightened, and his eyes narrowed down to slits. My assertion had touched a sensitive spot. "I was a Virginian," he replied sternly, "and damned proud of it. We never owned a slave or ever thought of ownin' one. But the bluebellies had invaded my state. We don't take lightly to things like that down here."

"I didn't mean anything personal," I said apologetically. "It's just that the term is in such common use."

"Have you got a breast?" he asked as he looked at my wife.

She looked shocked. Her mouth dropped open and her arms instinctively crossed her chest.

"Chicken breast," he replied quickly in an effort to ease her mind.

Abby relaxed; then she smiled; then her face turned red. "Four pieces—breasts," she said. She raised the basket lid. "Take your pick."

Jubal ambled up the slight rise and bent stiff-legged at the waist to examine the contents of the basket. It pleased me to see the delight in his eyes. "Just as my wife used to cook it," he said with a sadness in his voice. "She died of consumption a year back. Don't get much chicken now."

We ate our meal in silence. The two chickens Abby had prepared were just bone and gristle when we finished. Something about a picnic elevates the appetite. As he tossed a leg bone over his shoulder, he wiped his hands on the grass. "Thank you, ma'am. That shore tasted good. I had my teeth set on buttermilk and bread, but this does fine." He hesitated. "I meant no offense before, by what I said."

Abby smiled; then she placed her soft hand on his knee. "None taken, Mr. Jubal."

"Wilson," he said. "My last name is Wilson. Actually, my first name is Raymond. They just call me Jubal 'cause I fought in Jubal Early's army. My regiment shipped up to the Shenandoah right after Spotsylvania. Sheridan's men captured me in October of '64." His eyes glazed. "God, there was a man."

"Jubal Early?" I asked.

"He was all right, too, I guess, but I mean Little Phil."

His comment surprised me. "But he was a Union general," I said.

"That didn't keep him from bein' a man," Jubal replied indignantly. "He whipped us up an' down that valley all fall long. I fought in one of General Gordon's divisions right up to the end. We had the Yankees whipped until Sheridan rallied his men and chased us clear back to Richmond. A band of Custer's cavalry captured me. That was the day I knew the war was lost. To that day, I'd never heard a good word 'bout Yankee cavalry. But those boys shore knew how to ride. I give Sheridan credit for that."

I looked across the river toward the Wilderness's edge. The leaves were just popping out here in an unusually warm early May. The branches were still bare fifty-five years ago, the purple cast of violets the only signs of spring. It is a God-forsaken stretch of land six miles or so wide and twelve miles deep. Nowhere do the heavens look down on a more useless scrap of earth. A hundred years ago a great forest of tall oaks covered the area. Enterprising and hopeful farmers cleared most of it to make farms, but the effort failed. Several iron smelters sprouted up and used the wood for fuel. They too failed. Then as now, nothing described the area so completely as "a dungeon of trees." No sooner had farmers cleared the land than second-growth sprouts sprang up. In time the growth formed a tangled jungle. Now it served mostly as an obstacle in the way of crossing from one place to another.

Now as then, small flickers of light reach the ground to give sporadic hints of day. Vines curl down from twisted trunks, forming a barrier through which only the most dedicated traveler can find passage off the narrow dirt roads. The limbs and vines intertwine to form a wind-blown canopy over rotting leaves and moldy tree trunks that harbor an infinite number of crawling things. Even in the winter, the branches are so thick that the sun's rays penetrate only here and there as the breeze moves the canopy around. It's impossible to see straight ahead for more than a few yards. Only here and there are there a few square yards of open ground. The largest patch of clear ground I saw was perhaps five acres. Other than that, it is nothing but twisted oaks, dark, water-washed gullies, and rocks. Here, during three days in early May 1864, North and South fought one of the most bone-breaking, blood-letting battles of the Civil War. Not a bit of it progressed according to plan, at least not Grant's plan.

"It's not a very impressive place, is it?" Jubal said. I turned and looked at him. "I saw ya lookin' across that river at those trees. It was hell on earth for a man carryin' a musket. Ya couldn't shoot ten yards ahead without hittin' a tree. That's what made it so bad. All the fightin' came down to close quarters. A Minié rips a terrible hole in a man at ten yards. To get a clear line of fire, we had to chop down the trees. The sound of the choppin' never failed to bring a flock of Yankees runnin' in our direction. Hearin' and smellin' was easier than seein' in there, so everyone moved to the sound of the muskets and the smell of powder. By the second day, the smell of rottin' human flesh marked the place of the previous day's battle. Even though it was spring, the heat pressed down like the blast from a cannon. The trees held in the smoke, and everyone had difficulty breathin'. To a lad of only fifteen, it was a rough introduction to war. I never stopped bein' scared."

"You'd been in the army less than a month," I observed. "You couldn't have had much training."

"Yeah," he said with a smile, "but I'd hunted squirrels in those woods since I turned nine. I knew how to shoot. I know of eight Yankees I killed personal like, and there probably were more. They were bigger'n squirrels, ya know." He nodded to accent the assertion. "I done my share."

"If your family never owned slaves," I observed, "why did you fight for the South?"

I saw the uncertainty in his eyes. Then he expressed the only reason that made sense: "There was a war on."

Is that why? Is it simply because there is a war that young men and boys fight? To a lad of fifteen, that reason made all the sense he required. In the fifty-odd years since, it had never occurred to him to question the simplicity of it all. This was a whole different perspective than I had heard in Vicksburg. Two different types of people were fighting on the same side and never questioning the rightness of their position. Grant had been correct. The only way to end it lay in destroying the Confederate Army. It was absurd to expect surrender while the means and will to resist remained. War generates its own warped form of logic.

We bid the old farmer well as Abby placed the basket back under the buggy seat. A one-lane bridge crossed the river where once the people relied on the ford. The Rapidan is a small river by Eastern standards, less than a hundred feet wide. At this time of the year it is a gentle enough stretch of water. When the spring rains settle in later, it will become a raging torrent for a month or two.

We had traveled no more than a few hundred yards into the thicket of trees when Abby turned to me. She had been strangely quiet for a woman who spoke her mind without a moment's hesitation on virtually every subject, and especially on the war. "What makes men fight in such a place as this?" she asked. "It seems insane."

"They fought because the armies met here," I replied. "It's as simple and complicated as that. Grant wanted to cross the Wilderness and attack Lee on the open ground to the south. Lee, on the other hand, had defeated General Hooker on this very site a year earlier, and that victory must have been foremost in his mind. The trouble was, he wasn't fighting Hooker. Grant had abandoned all the old restrictions. He had reduced the war to mathematics. The Union's men were double the South's. If Grant could kill one for every one and a half he lost, eventually the numbers had to produce the desired results. Failing that, he saw no reason to expect the war to ever end."

I pulled the wagon to a stop. "Come with me," I said. She climbed from the carriage, and we walked for a short distance along a trail. "See those," I said pointing to ridges of dirt extending deep into the woods. "Those are trenches."

"How could that be?" she replied. "It's been so long."

"The trees protect them. At one time, they were more deep and wide. Over the years, the dirt has washed back into the pits. There were, however, men in those trenches, and they fought for their lives. Many died. I expect that if we dug around we'd find bullets in the dirt. Lead doesn't deteriorate like steel and wood."

She looked around, as if the battlefield had suddenly acquired new meaning. "How is it possible for men to fight in a place such as this? It's impossible to see anything."

"Abby," I said, "that's exactly what they asked themselves." We returned to the carriage.

A dull, brown object lying under a rock just off the road caught my attention. I stepped down and walked through the rustling, brown leaves littering the side of the road. How did this survive in all this dampness? I asked myself. I bent over and pulled the object from a tangle of vines. In my hand I held the front end of a rifled musket with the rusted and pitted bayonet still attached.

"This is what did all the damage," I said as I handed the twisted metal and rotting wood to Abby. "By the standard Grant set, he had the best of it. He lost about sixteen thousand killed and wounded, but Lee lost more than eleven thousand."

"That's terrible," Abby said as she examined the trophy. "Did so many have to die to end it?"

"No," I replied, "but you forget one important fact."

I talked softly, but the words hung in the air, as if spoken in a cave. I felt as if this ground was somehow more sacred than any church I had ever been in. "The South started the war. Men such as your grandfather wanted to preserve a way of life that had become corrupt to the core. There was nothing gentlemanly about it. They spoke of it in such terms only to rationalize the result. Their objective was to keep other men in slavery. There was dissatisfaction, however, with just keeping what they had. They wanted to expand slavery to the West. At some point, it became necessary to say 'enough.' The violence in Kansas made it clear that the Southern aristocracy would stop at nothing to impose their will on the majority. They failed to understand, however, that the nation was coming of age, and in that new age, slavery had no future or virtue—if it ever had."

Abby remained silent, so I decided just to let the point sink in. Somehow, we had to find a formula to dissolve this barrier between us. To do that, she had to think about the cost of the war. There was more to it than her grandfather's humiliating surrender early in the hostilities. She spoke of a "Southern way of life" as though it was a safe harbor for a demented, inalienable right. It had become the cancerous exception to the Constitution. If they were willing to kill to preserve it, it seemed only right that they also had to die until they removed the yoke both from themselves and the colored.

If white men found glory and vindication in the clash of battle and charging forward on a swiftly moving horse with saber held high, the black man saw none of this. He had no say in it whatsoever. It wasn't enough for men such as Jeff Monroe to pass from this earth. He and his kind had created the blight, but they had also passed the heritage of the believed right in it on to their sons and daughters. Abby hated the killing, but never understood the reason. To her, Grant was the cause of the suffering rather than the result. I never had found the words to make her understand the difference.

I sensed the turbulence in her mind as we rode deeper into the tangled thicket and the light grew dimmer than dusk on a cloudy day. I had visited the battlefields at Gettysburg and Chattanooga and immediately recognized the difference. In those places, monuments rose from the ground like giant tombstones, proudly marking the places where regiments had fought or where a grand charge rolled across a ripening wheat field. I saw none of that here. Occasionally, along the road I saw buried in the poor ground a small stone with a bronze plate marking the place of a memorable event. That was about all. The explanation was simple. Nothing about this battle was conventional, and little that is ceremonial about memorial had a place here. This was nothing more than a killing place. There were no stouthearted cavalry charges or massive gatherings of infantry seeking to drive an enemy from the field. In fact, riding a horse in a straight line for more than a few yards was impossible. Even within a thousand-man line, no more than a few companions were visible from a given place.

To a man in danger loneliness means fear, and there were 150,000 lonely men packed into this forest of dwarfed trees and moss-covered rocks. As one participant wrote: "This was nothing more than bushwhacking on a grand scale. I viewed it as the beginning of the end of sanity." It surprised me to hear Jubal say he knew he had killed eight of his foe. Many of the men who fought here never had a clear view of the enemy. Only the noise and the smoke revealed the danger that waited to separate a man's head from his neck if he lifted it more than a few inches above the ground. Even so, men died by the thousands, as they do in every great battle. Transporting the Union wounded back to Fredericksburg required agonizing days in a seemingly endless row of springless wagons. There, only rudimentary medical care waited to ease their suffering. The experience of the Southern soldier was even worse.

I made the turn onto the narrow side road leading to Grant's Hill. Grant's perspective was no different from the average private's. No way existed to keep track of the battle, even for a general. Grant had pointed the way through the trees and waited to see what happened. If the opposing forces met, there would be killing—most likely a great deal of killing. It had to begin someplace, however, for Grant had established that as the immediate objective. Each death brought the war a moment closer to an end.

There is a small clearing at the top of a rise where Grant established his headquarters. Then he settled down to wait for news. As Meade was in charge of the unit involved in the fight, most of the news came to him. Only when a decision involved a major change in strategy did Meade even consult Grant. As usual when the Army of the Potomac marched into the field, bad news followed. Until late afternoon on both May 5 and 6, Grant sat under a tree, still wearing his gloves, whittling on a series of twigs. Little of the news that reached that knob of ground proved to his liking, yet none of it spoke of impending doom, so he continued to whittle.

Only in the early afternoon on May 6, when he learned that Longstreet's corps had joined the fight in force, did his agitation increase. By the narrowest of margins, the two men had avoided conflict at Chattanooga. The previous fall, Lee had detached Longstreet's corps and sent it to assist Bragg in southern Tennessee. As the siege dragged on, Longstreet's corps moved again, this time to Knoxville to be put to more useful purpose. Grant arrived after Longstreet's departure. Now he had returned to the Army of Northern Virginia.

Grant knew Longstreet. During their younger days the two men had bunked together. Knowing a man elevates his potential. Grant had liked "Old Pete" as a man and respected him as a soldier. He still did, despite their drifting apart toward different values. It must have seemed irrational to discount those feelings now. But if Grant knew Longstreet, Longstreet also knew Grant. Grant's coming foretold a new kind of war, and Longstreet forecast it from the start. He passed the message to all who cared to listen: "That man will fight us every day and every hour until the end of the war."

He probably said more than he intended, or perhaps he recognized the truth but hesitated, for obvious reasons, to say it outright. In his simple statement, Longstreet had spoken both of the means and the result, and the result was all that mattered. The message was clear that Grant *would* end the war. But he had no miracles in his pocket—all he had was the ability to hammer away and the willingness to use the hammer. If that proved sufficient, then the Union would prevail.

For a short while, however, here at day's end on May 6, 1864, there was room for doubt. For a while there was danger that Longstreet's force would, as a result of an aggressive flanking attack, roll up the Union ranks and drive them back to the Rapidan—with or without Grant's consent. For some self-destructive reason, however, the Army of Northern Virginia had a propensity for shooting itself in the foot—if not inflicting a mortal wound. It had happened at Chancellorsville a year earlier when Confederate soldiers shot Stonewall Jackson. He died a few days later. This time Longstreet was the one who paid the price for riding too close to the fighting. All through the war, for both North and South, it had been the same. The best, most aggressive field commanders met early deaths or suffered wounds. The impact in this instance was immediate. When Confederate pickets shot down their commander, the Confederate attack sputtered to a halt. In time, dusk settled in—it settles in here more quickly than at most places on earth—and with the advancing darkness, the crisis passed.

*   *   *

A man can resist only so long against so much. Personally, I think it is abnormal for a man to sit under a tree and whittle while the world is coming apart all around him. Muscles and nerves have a breaking point, and so it was with Grant. The rumor has persisted over the years that, as the sun set on May 6, Grant strolled to his tent after being informed of the repulse of Longstreet. The rumor also claims he broke down completely and cried. A reporter on the scene swore it was fact, although he reported it only later when the dying had stopped for good. I don't know. It seems out of character for the man, yet nothing seems more human. Given the circumstances, crying makes more sense than whittling on a twig.

I told the story to Abby, and a sadness fell upon her. This Grant was different from the one she had learned to hate. Forever after that, she spoke of Grant with a softer voice and more tolerant judgment. Fifty years after the war Grant still has a job to do, even in myth, if that is what it is. Only the organized killing has stopped. The hostility that brought on that killing still clutches at the hearts and minds of the people who populate the South.

"Grant was an irony," said a man who knew him well, "a man who ate only burnt meat because he hated the sight of blood. Yet he talked of killing thousands of men as if it was the most natural thing in the world." His irony, however, is a part of each of us. At a moment when compassion pushed aside common sense, I risked my life to save a German major. Then I pumped from him information that resulted in the death of thousands. A brief moment of glory, perhaps leading to a bloody irrationality, but it sustains me still. Whenever I do something I would rather not have done, I let the thought of that moment give me comfort. I always think of Grant at those times. Even so, I have only a fuzzy awareness of what Grant must have felt. How will I ever pass that awareness on to the woman I love more than life itself? The woman soon to give me a child.

*   *   *

It was at about this time, fifty-five years before, that Capt. Thomas Laird first found the glory he so desperately sought.

"Colonel!" Laird yelled over the sound of the cannon—neither side deployed many cannon during the Wilderness campaign. In the first place, there were only a few clearings big enough in which to deploy them. More important, it was generally impossible to be certain that firing them would kill only the enemy. Longstreet, however, had found a place, and the guns were pounding Laird's regiment into raw meat. Altering the situation became a necessity. "I think I can work my way south and flank those guns, sir."

Colonel Boyd studied the situation. "Those woods are filled with Rebs, Captain. You'll never make it."

"I'd rather try to stop them than stay here and be blown to bits, sir."

"What do you require?" the colonel asked.

"Just my company of men, sir."

"Very well, Captain, see what you can do."

Laird pulled his men into a knot around him. "Men, we have to stop those guns," he said.

"We have no chance at all of charging those guns," a sergeant objected. "They'll load canister and cut us to pieces."

"I agree," Laird said, "but we might flank them. That'll put the fear of God into those gunners. They won't know what to do."

That seemed reasonable, the sergeant thought.

"What I want is to circle south and come up through that ravine. If we move quietly, we'll be in the infantry's midst before they know it. We must hold our fire until we have them in clear sight; then we'll fire all at once and scream and yell like the demons of Hell are upon them. They may run from the surprise."

"May run?" a lieutenant asked.

"They will run, Lieutenant. Trust me." What choice had they? "After the infantry runs, we'll fire on the men manning the cannons. Then we'll charge them with bayonets and drive them from the field."

"What do we do with them guns when they is ours?" a private asked, as if the ownership was an established fact.

"Do any of you know how to load and fire a cannon?" Laird asked. None volunteered. "Well, they're too heavy to lug to our lines. I guess we dig in and wait to be relieved."

"That seems to be a whole lot of thinking for just a captain," a corporal said, "but it makes more sense than staying here and having my parts blown off." Just then, by way of accenting the corporal's point, a shell exploded in a cluster of trees less than ten yards away. Shrapnel cut through a man's arm and his screams punctuated the cost of waiting.

"Let's get them guns," yelled a private, and they rose as one man.

General Sedgwick, on his way to Grant's Hill, rode by at this moment. He noticed the advance, so he stopped to watch. Laird led his men through the woods to the ravine. It was less deep than he had hoped, but he had made the commitment. The men had to crouch to keep from being seen by the enemy. It required about fifteen minutes to reach the top of the hill, but still they remained undetected. Sedgwick watched their progress through his field glasses. Half the men placed their rifles on the rim of the ravine facing west, the other half east. Cool as you please, Laird rose to a standing position and yelled, "Fire!" Smoke boiled from the ravine. Unsure of who or what had crept into their midst, the rebels broke and ran during the brief span of time required for the unseen enemy to reload. Then Laird yelled again: "Fire!" Before the bullets reached their targets, he yelled a third time: "Let's get those guns, boys!" They advanced into the open field, the bayonets on their unloaded muskets aimed straight at the gunners. The commander of the battery of guns pulled his pistol and started to fire, then thought better of wasting the time, considering what must follow. He followed his men as they raced for the woods to the east. In less time than it takes to tell about it, the blue-clad soldiers swept across the small field to claim the guns, and fairly so.

Without even stopping to sort out what had happened, the men began to dig with cups and knives, working feverishly to prepare a defensive position around the guns. A few puffs of dust rose from the ground where occasional rebel bullets hit, and the men stopped their digging and reloaded their rifles. Then they returned to their digging. Off to the north, the men of the Union regiment watched these proceedings in admiration, but they stayed in the cover of the trees. General Sedgwick observed this and wondered why. Finally, he trotted his horse in the direction of the regimental commander. "Why don't you go to the aid of your men?" Sedgwick asked the lieutenant colonel.

"Sir, there are a great many Rebs still out there. They'll recover and want those guns back."

"So you think it unwise to try to keep them from getting their guns back?"

"Yes, sir." He thought for a moment. "I'm in command only by accident, General. The colonel had his head blown off and this is my first command. I can't risk the lives of these men to hold those guns."

"So why'd you let that officer lead his men out there?" the general asked.

"So he could stop those guns from firing on us, General," replied the colonel.

"I see. Who is that officer on the hill?"

"Captain Laird, sir. He's a new man, a replacement from Washington."

"Capt. Thomas Laird?" asked the general.

"Yes, sir. Do you know him?"

"Tell you what I want, Colonel," Sedgwick said without answering the question, "you take your regiment and march up that rise toward those guns. I assume the responsibility. When you get there, you call Captain Laird off for a private talk, and you tell him I've given him the brevet rank of colonel. That's full colonel—what is your name, sir?"

"Boyd, sir."

"That's full colonel, Boyd. With that he'll rank you. Tell him he's to take command of this regiment. Is that clear?"

Lieutenant Colonel Boyd saluted and replied briskly, "Yes, sir. I'll tell him, sir." He turned and started to move; then he stopped and turned again. "Thank you, General."

Relieved of the responsibility, Boyd moved his men into the open and up the rise. They held the guns against two counterattacks, and Sedgwick moved on toward Grant's Hill. As Sedgwick talked with Meade, he occasionally turned to look at Grant destroying twigs.

Meade read Sedgwick's mind. "He's been doing that all day," Meade said with a shrug. "I sometimes wonder if the man has a nerve in his body. Just seeing him takes the starch out of every general who rides up here to complain about his particular disaster."

Sedgwick smiled. "That comes from knowing your purpose and refusing to be distracted. We finally have a commander in charge." The remark just as easily might have offended Meade, for this was in truth his army. He evidently understood Sedgwick's meaning and simply nodded in concurrence.

Sedgwick strolled over to Grant. "Planning to build a fire with all that kindling, General?" he asked.

Grant smiled but kept his eye on the knife. "How's it going, General Sedgwick?"

Sedgwick pulled at his whiskers. "It could be worse, sir. Lee has all his forces up, so he's doing about as much damage as possible; but we're holding firm. You're getting your way, General Grant. A lot of Rebs are dying out there."

Grant nodded.

"By the way, General," Sedgwick added, "do you remember that captain you sent to me, Capt. Thomas Laird?"

Grant stopped whittling and looked up. "I remember."

"You've a keen eye for ability and courage, General. I just made him a colonel and gave him a regiment. He led his company and captured a battery of guns right out in the open. Damnedest thing I ever witnessed."

Grant smiled. "He still has a ways to go."

Sedgwick looked surprised. "What do you mean?"

"Well, when I first met him, he was a brigadier general in a staff assignment in Washington. He wanted to fight, but I told him I had all the generals I needed for the moment. If he'd take the rank of captain, I told him, I'd give him a company to command. He accepted the proposition."

Sedgwick laughed. "I'll be damned," he said, and shook his head. "Well, General, there've been only two days of battle. Give the young man a week and we'll see what he makes of himself."

"If he stays alive, General, if he stays alive."

So the captain who had been a general was now a colonel, and he had a battery of enemy guns to prove his valor to his young son—provided he survived.

For a man to lead, he must possess the ability to recognize leadership ability in others, and then he must entrust them with the power. Grant never supposed he had the ability to stop the war all by himself. Sedgwick, too, was a leader, but a leader already on a collision course with destiny. In less than a week he would be killed by a sniper's bullet—fired from more than eight hundred yards away. I feel certain he would not have hesitated a moment to praise the skill of the Reb who fired that bullet. He might have preferred to have avoided the discomfort it caused. He, too, had been quick to reward courage and competence—and just as swift to knock down the man who accidentally or mistakenly acquired too much responsibility.

Grant returned to his twigs as he shivered slightly from the chill of a cool breeze. Shortly, he looked up to check on the sun, then slowly slid his back up the tree and strolled toward his tent. He claimed later to have been nervous at this point, but not from the perilous progress of the battle. "Having nothing much to do all day," he said, "I smoked all of my cigars. The ones packed with my belongings had been lost, and I had not the slightest idea where to find more of my brand." For that reason, I concede that he might have had a reason to cry.

The dense growth distorted everything. Even morning arrived late in the Wilderness. The men snatched such sleep as was possible where they found themselves at sunset on the second day. Here and there throughout the night, musket volleys rang out, but mostly the men shot at shadows or the occasional movement of a rabbit venturing out of its hole. Fires started by muskets during the previous day crackled and slithered like snakes through the dense underbrush. Occasionally, as a fire drifted toward a man too injured to drag himself out of harm's way, there arose a loud scream. At such times, men return to the basics of life. "God, please help me!" rose the common cry, but most discovered that God had abandoned the Wilderness. So the man had to find his own solution. If the injured soldier had retained enough presence of mind to load his weapon, the sharp crack of his musket shattered the air, and with the report the screaming stopped. The men on both sides, neither certain if the man had been Reb or Yank, would close their eyes and utter a silent prayer. That which in a different time and place would have commanded solemn grief for days passed from their minds with a silent amen. War hardens a man's soul.

As May 6 wore on, it became obvious that a stalemate had resulted. The men had experienced enough of the bushwhacking. It became sufficient just to pop off a few rounds now and again at anything that moved, but no one looked for trouble. By this time, the men had learned the cost of moving above ground. Life-preserving trenches hacked from the root-entangled ground began to extend in every direction. On occasion, men from one trench or another yelled: "Volley coming, get your heads down." A few seconds later, the sound of muskets rolled along the trenches. If the men who yelled were lucky, the enemy across the way would return the favor when their officers gave the order to fire. Grant may have had killing in mind, but there would be time enough for that later. Besides, he had neglected to tell the privates what he had in mind. Even without a clear message to the effect, however, there exists a natural order in battle, so the killing continued at a steady if more relaxed pace.

"The moment arms were stacked," Grant wrote later, "the men entrenched themselves. For this purpose they would build up piles of logs or rails if they could be found in their front, and dug a ditch throwing the dirt forward on the timbers. Thus the digging they did counted in making a depression to stand in, and increased the elevation in front of them. It was wonderful how quickly they could in this way construct defenses of considerable strength."

With midnight of May 7 less than two hours away, Grant strolled over to Meade's tent. Meade was writing his daily report by the light of a lantern. He looked up. "Come in, General."

"It's time to move, General Meade." He handed Meade a number of orders. "Have these sent out to the corps commanders."

"When do we move?" Meade asked as he accepted the orders.

"Now," Grant said casually. "I want to be out of these woods by first light."

Meade started to protest. It required time to get a hundred thousand men moving.

Grant anticipated the protest. "We'll swing to the east, then move south while it's dark so General Lee is unaware of our movement. Order the men to leave their fires burning and to move out as quietly as possible. Send Sheridan ahead to screen our movement from Stuart."

At midnight, Warren's corps, farthest to the west, moved first. Movement was east and slightly south along the only road in the area. He moved behind the men still in line, leaving the next corps in line to cover his rear.

"We're heading back to the Rapidan," a sergeant yelled.

"It's Chancellorsville all over again," replied another.

Warren rode by. "General," a private yelled from the security of darkness, "why do we keep marching back and forth to the Wilderness?" After a pause, and after assessing the futility of it all, the soldier added: "I want to go home."

"Close it up, boys," Warren said, his voice carrying in the confined space like the vibration of rolling drums. "We're heading where it's warm all year 'round."

"We're finally goin' to Hell, huh?" said another, and everyone laughed.

"Hooker said the same," replied another skeptic, "and I froze my ass off all last winter."

"Keep moving, boys," Warren counseled. "Grant's here now."

They marched down Brock Road. Everyone knew about the crossroads just ahead. Experience had given it meaning greatly in excess of its importance. At this junction, one road turned north toward Washington; the other turned south toward Richmond. Last May, when Hooker had been in command, the army had turned north. No one expected differently now.

"Move aside," yelled a rider galloping down the line, "move aside." A small knot of men trotted along the fringe of the road. As the riders passed, the soldiers flinched, as if gently nudged into another, higher level of existence—then the tired, slumping shoulders of the men stretched upward a few inches.

"It's Grant," rang a voice from the night, "and he's turnin' south!"

"Grant's goin' south!" yelled another, and the message telegraphed along the line of marching men. Soon, the men still holding the trenches heard the calls, and a great cheer rolled through the night. So much for moving quietly.

"What did you feel at that moment?" I asked Frank Hawkins, a veteran of the march.

"For the first time, I realized this war would one day be over. I hated the Wilderness worse'n my banker. This was as far as we had gotten, in five trips south, since the war began. I didn't want to make a sixth trip. I knew enough to expect the hard fightin' ahead, but that didn't matter then. Everyone felt the same. Everyone said the same: 'Grant's headin' south, straight at Bobby Lee.' "

"Weren't you tired after three days of battle?"

"Certainly we were, but there was less stragglin' on that march than any I remember. Somehow, it just seemed unpatriotic not to get out of those woods. We helped anyone that was hurtin' stay on his feet. I remember seein' this one man up ahead with bandages wrapped all up and down his body—shrapnel had peppered him during the evening—waitin' for an ambulance. 'Where're you men goin'?' he yelled.

" 'We're takin' the war to Lee's front yard,' a marcher a few feet in front of me yelled.

"The wounded soldier slapped his leg. 'I'll be goddamned to Hell,' he said. 'Help me to my feet. I've been at this too long to miss out on the finish.' "

It's amazing what a symbol will accomplish, I thought. A different turn, a change in direction, and everything changes.

"In my memory," Hawkins told me, "nothin' like that ever happened before. Two men right behind me helped him up and off he marched with us, limpin' along into the darkness. The night separated us shortly after." He hesitated before adding: "I've often wondered if he made it."

The men marched all night, trying to "steal a march on General Lee." No one had ever accomplished that, and this time was no different. Lee somehow learned of the mass of Union soldiers headed south, and he pulled his men out of the trenches and raced toward a fateful reunion with his enemy. Lee's army had the more difficult task: his only available road angled too far to the west, so he put his army to cutting a way south through the trees. But Lee had the advantage of interior lines—a shorter distance to move. Still, the task was monumental, and only Jeb Stuart's cavalry was in a position to delay the Union march.

Chance had placed a small country courthouse at the junction of several important roads. The place, its name as large as the courthouse building, was a small hamlet called Spotsylvania Courthouse.

14 The Turning Point

All night long, the men in Grant's army marched around Lee's right flank—heading first east and then south. As they moved, they passed the endless line of converted wagons and ambulances marked by the distinctive black letters: U.S. Hearse. They were heading north filled with those who would miss the ending. "It was as if war, a great, clumsy device for maiming people, had at last been perfected," a noted author wrote much later. "Instead of turning out its grist spasmodically, with long waits between each delivery, it was at last able to produce every day, without any gaps at all." More than the generals, fate and geography were directing the destiny of the men moving closer to the next killing ground. Places that history otherwise never would have noticed were, as a result of this struggle, taking their place alongside Waterloo and the Alamo. The most unlikely of such places was Spotsylvania Courthouse.

One soldier who discovered the true meaning of pain during Grant's advance was Sgt. Jeremiah Clemmens—a man who both benefited and suffered at the hands of fate. Up to this time, his lot had been more pleasant than that of most soldiers. Early in the war, the army had assigned him to a heavy artillery unit stationed in the defenses around Washington. He had enjoyed this plush assignment with its soft clean sheets, three hot meals each day, and easy, relaxed duty. Grant's arrival signaled the end of such luxury. With the supply of trained men drying up, and with many in the army scheduled to be released within the next few weeks, Grant decided that the policy of defending Washington in strength must end. Lincoln protested only mildly, and Grant converted many of these soldiers to infantry and moved them south

into the Wilderness. Sergeant Clemmens was in one of those regiments.
Now they moved farther south, into the open ground leading toward
Richmond and the long ending of the war.

*   *   *

The first hint of winter was reflected in the large windowpane as
I looked out, watching a flood of leaves swirling toward the ground.
Although it was just past the middle of October, already a few snow-
flakes drifted lazily from the scattered clouds masking most of a steel-
gray sky. Winter comes early to South Dakota; it is no different even
in a town called Hot Springs.

"Do you want me to tuck in your blanket?" I asked Sergeant
Clemmens. "It's getting cold."

"There's hardly enough of me left to feel it," he replied with his
stiff, black humor. I tucked the blanket tighter around him anyway.
Sergeant Clemmens had suffered as much as any living survivor of
the Civil War. Even the colonel from Knoxville, the one shot in the
head, had been fortunate by comparison. He had too little recognition
of his malady to understand its meaning. This did not apply to Sergeant Clemmens. He understood everything that had happened, and
the memory haunted him every waking second.

Despite Sergeant Clemmens's conversion to infantry, the steady
attrition among those assigned to cannon batteries had altered his fortune
a second time when he had traveled only two days into the Wilderness. The army reassigned him again, this time to a cannon battery,
as the troops headed south following the battle.

On Monday, May 10, exactly eleven months less one day before
the war ended, an enemy shell exploded directly over the caissons of
the gun battery he manned. The explosion killed everyone in the gun
section except Sergeant Clemmens. He was less fortunate.

"I remember flyin' into the air with the memory of bein' a whole
man," he said, "an' landin' as nothin' but a lump of mangled, bloody
flesh."

The force of the exploding shells and powder in the caissons blew
off both his arms and legs. Ironically, the fire from the explosion kept
the spark of life burning. The blast seared his mangled muscles and
kept him from bleeding to death before help arrived to tend the wounds.
He emerged from the war as one of no more than a half dozen men to
survive the loss of all four limbs. He expressed no gratitude about
this fact.

There persisted in my mind the lurid irony of his existence. Only two conditions are necessary for a man to take his own life: one is the will, the other the means. I had learned that nowhere was there a man with a stronger will. The irony was that the very circumstance that compelled the will had removed the means. What is a man with no arms or legs to do except endure?

More than thirty years after the war ended the army built this veterans' hospital on top of the hill overlooking this small, sheltering valley. Even getting here demanded a desperate effort. The only path up moved along a shallow, rutted grade at an angle to the hillside. A fifth of the way up, it cut sharply back in the other direction. After four more similar turns, the road leveled out at the top on a plateau just beyond a barricade of large, densely packed blue spruce trees. The trees obviously shielded the place; whether from the outside or from within, I never knew. Scattered about the grounds were hundreds of evergreen trees, grown as part of the natural setting of the hill and the surrounding valley. None of these was blue spruce. Beyond, large red stucco-covered buildings rose from browning lawns, their color matching precisely the hue and tint of the surrounding hills and rocks. With the hill eighty feet straight up on three sides and the fourth side bordered by a facing hill that was even higher, the government must have had a secret objective in selecting this site. I probably looked for more in this coincidence than had been intended, but I sensed there had existed a devious intent to blend the place so perfectly with the landscape that no one would find it—unless by accident—or know what happened here if an error led him this way. This thought, however, entered my mind only after I ambled unknowing into the main hospital complex. I was not prepared mentally for what I found.

At first impression, the building was like any other constructed to house the sick and infirm. Three nurses in stiffly starched white uniforms scurried about behind a long admissions desk. A fourth sat working on patient charts. Record books littered the working surface hidden under a chest-high counter. More record books lined the shelves on the far side of the open space. The immediate impression was one of wild confusion. Short-tempered orderlies and ward nurses wandered in and out seeking this or that bit of information, but seldom getting it.

"Through that door and to your right," snapped the head nurse—clearly identified by her gruff, sharp voice. The gold major's leaf pinned to her collar added a measure of credibility to my assumption. The other three white-clad personnel wore insignia of lesser rank. I had directed my question at her in hopes of finding the location of Sgt. Jeremiah Clemmens formerly of the Union Army, assigned to the Army of the Potomac.

Clemmens was sent here in 1901 to live out his life in bitter remembrance. I am certain that was not the military's intent, but it has been the result. The existence of men such as Clemmens explains, at least in part, the seemingly secret if unofficial obsession with hiding this institution from prying eyes on what remains the last frontier of a rapidly growing nation.

Innocently, I pushed my way through a pair of massive brass-plated swinging doors into the main receiving ward. The sight—a strain on the senses—compelled me to stop, to somehow adjust to the horror that lay before me. Just to the right on the floor, barely ten feet into the room, a babbling man—his age somewhere between twenty-five and sixty; I had no way of establishing it more precisely—rolled around on a blanket smeared with his own excrement. His eyes, open unnaturally wide, seemed fixed on some distant horror that eluded his understanding. Or perhaps that was the problem: maybe he did comprehend its meaning. He wore only a dingy, soiled diaper. One pin had snapped loose and the point pricked his skin each time he rolled to that side. A dozen or more spots of blood within a square-inch area offered proof of his neglect.

A few feet away, in a battered wheelchair, another man of about forty sat naked. He leaned slightly forward, his drooling mouth persistently agape, his right arm—hanging between the wheel and the chair—shaking in a constant spasm. The massive scar on the side of his head identified imprecisely where a substantial part of his brain had once been.

With the one quick sweep that I forced my eyes to make, my mind absorbed at least fifty other such horrors—each different, each worse than the other. There were half as many workers moving aimlessly about; a few more shuffling quickly to squelch one crisis or another with nothing in particular being done for the patients, as if any of them would have known, one way or the other, if his needs were the concern of anyone present. Chaos is too mild a word to describe what occurred in this bedlam.

That was my first encounter with the place where the military had sent Sergeant Clemmens. I can think of one way to describe it: it was a compost heap for the human waste of war.

*   *   *

As we sat in silence, looking across the sparkling river flowing at the base of the red earth bluff barely half a mile west, I sank slowly into depression. For three days I had searched in vain for the words to bring a spark of joy into this old man's life. Only twice did he smile in my presence, both times when Lieutenant McFee joined us on the balcony. McFee's presence adds another touch of irony to the Clemmens story.

"Jeremiah went down during the early stages at Spotsylvania," McFee told me in a private conversation. "I was serving on the other side, in the 18th Virginia. Most of Lee's army was still moving south through the woods. We were trying to hold the crossroads with a single division. Each hour, men poured from the woods by the thousands and the sounds of battle grew in proportion to the increasing numbers. We were doing pretty good except for those guns blasting us from the hill to our north.

"For several hours we'd divided our attention between the guns and the gathering Union infantry. I commanded a company of men assigned to guard the cannon. 'Forget the infantry!' the battery commander shouted. 'Concentrate on those guns. We can't hold if they keep after us.' So we turned all the cannon on the hill. We had twenty-four guns—all that had made it out of the woods. We blasted them with star shells, trying to kill the gunners. Those shells had timers to make them explode above ground, spraying the area with shrapnel. They didn't hurt the guns much, but they rained white-hot steel down on the gunners. We had the range, so it must've been hell on that hill.

"Anyway, about ten minutes after we advanced on the guns, a shell exploded directly above a gun caisson. The hill seemed to evaporate in a cloud of fire, steel, and smoke. In the shock of the explosion, about half of their guns were silenced. 'Go get em!' my regimental commander yelled, and we charged across the field and up the hill. We fought hand to hand with the gunners until we drove them off. Then I saw Jeremiah. I'd been at war for three years, but I'd never seen anything like that. There was just this three-foot-long lump of flesh thrashing in agony in a pool of blood-drenched dirt. At first, I wasn't even certain it was human. I bent over double and threw up at the sight.

"After I recovered, still unable even to think, I dropped close by his side. 'Kill me,' he said in a weak, raspy voice. Blood spurted from his mouth with every word. 'If you believe in God, kill me,' he pleaded over and over. At one point, I picked up an abandoned musket and started to drive the bayonet into his chest, but it seemed like murder and I couldn't do it. I dropped the rifle and frantically began to tie off his stubs with strips of cloth I found lying about. All the time I was doing this he kept saying 'Kill me,' and I just kept wrapping those stubs of mangled flesh and splintered bone with dirty rags. I can still see it when I close my eyes."

As he told the story, I studied the lieutenant carefully. He had a whole body, but each breath he inhaled seemed a labor of agony. "That explains the sergeant," I said, "but what about you? How did you come to be at this same place more than fifty years later?"

He smiled. "Seems rather improbable, doesn't it? Jeremiah says it's my punishment for letting him live." He struggled to remain erect on the two wooden canes grasped by wrinkled fingers as he rose and walked to the balcony rail. He sighed as he let his head drop. "Federal forces captured me later that same day. The Union was growing short of men, although not as bad as the South, and about three dozen of us were offered the opportunity to go west to fight the Indians if we'd take the Oath of Allegiance to the Union. That seemed better than prison, so I formed a small company of willing Confederates and we converted to cavalry. They made me a lieutenant. I stayed in the Union cavalry until '79—when one of Sitting Bull's braves shot me in the chest with an arrow. Before I hit the ground, two more arrows hit me in the chest. Both lungs were pierced; then infection set in, and for over a year I barely hung on. I finally recovered enough to be sent east to a hospital. My wife had died by then and I had no one else. So years later, when I learned about this place, I asked to be sent here. I love the West. That's when I found Jeremiah. We've been together ever since."

"So you served under both Lee and Grant," I said.

"Yes," he said nodding, "and after Grant, I served under General Sherman, and in his turn, General Sheridan. I even met Grant, once."

It amazed me that the army had let Confederate soldiers that close to Grant. "How did that happen?"

"That sort of explains how I got into the Union Army," he replied. "I'd been wounded—that's how I fell into Union hands—and spent several days in a field hospital. While I convalesced they didn't watch me too closely. In all the confusion, while the army was getting ready to move down toward the North Anna River, I just walked away. During those days of captivity, however, I learned a thing or two. I learned that the Yankees were just like us, just Americans. You can't imagine how that surprised me. It embarrasses me now every time I think about it. Besides that, I knew the condition of our army. When I saw the men and materials the Union pushed down those roads I knew the war could end only one way.

"As I left the aid station I stole a Union corporal's jacket, so I could move without much trouble. I'd traveled about five miles southwest when I saw this troop of cavalry riding by. Then, off in the woods, I saw a bunch of Southern soldiers. They just let the cavalry pass without firing a shot. That's strange, I thought; then I learned why. Off to the northeast, I saw another group of riders trotting down the road. I knew from all the gold braid they were a bunch of officers. As they came closer, I recognized General Grant riding in the middle of the group. I'd seen his picture in a paper shortly after he'd been promoted. I just thought to myself that if those men in the woods killed Grant the war was certain to go on longer. I ran up the road, stopped them, and told the cavalry major leading the guard about the soldiers in the woods. Well, they whisked Grant off and waited for the rear guard cavalry unit to ride up. By that time, the men in the woods evidently figured out what had happened, and they scampered away. The cavalry captured one, and he told them about the ambush. Then they put me on a horse and escorted me back to the hospital.

"That night, the cavalry major came into my hospital tent. 'Captain McFee,' he said, 'are you up to a ride?'

" 'Yes,' I said. 'Where're we going?'

" 'Just follow me, Captain,' he replied.

"We rode for about an hour; then we came to the Union headquarters. There must have been fifty sentries roaming that area.

" 'Get down, Captain, and follow me,' the Union officer said.

"I followed him to a tent in the middle of a circle of tents.

" 'General Grant, this is Captain McFee,' the major said.

"General Grant turned and looked up at me—I'm about six inches taller than the general—and he extended his hand.

" 'Son,' he said, 'come into my tent.'

" 'Yes, sir,' I replied, and then I saluted.

" 'Have a chair, Captain. Would you like a cigar?'

"I didn't smoke, but I took the cigar.

" 'Captain,' he said, 'you probably saved my life today, do you realize that?'

"I was too scared to talk, so I just nodded.

" 'Why'd you warn us, Captain? They tell me you're a prisoner.'

" 'This war has gone on long enough, General,' I replied; then I began to cry. After I got control of myself, I told him about Sergeant Clemmens. 'I just can't be a part of any more maiming,' I said. 'I think you'll bring it to a stop before long. That's why I did it.'

"Grant's mouth actually dropped open. 'But I'm the one leading the Union Army and telling my men to kill your men,' he said.

" 'I know,' I replied, 'and I understand that more men have to die before this war ends. But General Lee is too good a soldier for the other Union generals. You seem to know what has to be done, as terrible as it may be.'

" 'I see,' he replied. 'You know something, Captain, I had a long talk with President Lincoln a few weeks back. He told me he wanted nothing more than for all of us to be brother Americans again. I think you're as good a place as any to begin that process. If you swear allegiance to the Union, I will commission you a lieutenant and send you out West to help settle that country—as soon as you're well, of course. What do you say?'

"For some reason, I stood up and snapped to attention. Three sentries moved toward the tent opening with rifles level, but Grant raised his hand and they stepped back. Without waiting for my reply, Grant went to his desk and wrote out an order. I'll never forget the words.

" 'To the Secretary of War,' it read. 'The bearer of this order is Lt. Joseph McFee, late of the Confederate Army. Lieutenant McFee exercised great courage by warning me of an ambush planned by Confederate soldiers in a field east of the North Anna River. For that reason, and because he has sworn to me his allegiance to the United States of America, I give him full pardon and assign him as a lieutenant to serve in the West in Indian Territory. Please extend to Lieutenant McFee the courtesy you would extend to me.' He signed it 'Ulysses S. Grant, General in Chief.' "

"Did you swear allegiance?" I asked.

"Right there in that tent," he replied with pride.

"Did you ever have any regrets?" I asked.

"Not until I came here and saw Sergeant Clemmens again. He's asked me to kill him every day since." He looked at me and smiled.

"I thought about it once or twice. He's a cantankerous old devil. By the way, young man, where's that woman I saw with you?"

"That woman, Lieutenant, is my wife. She's down the hill at the Evans Hotel. Why do you ask?"

"Oh, nothing much. Jeremiah just told me she's the only woman who ever smiled at him since the day he lost his limbs."

I walked down the hill to the hotel. The conversation with Lieutenant McFee had been instructive. I had always known that Lincoln and Grant realized that the faster the killing progressed the sooner it would end, and in the end the less killing there would be. But learning that even one Confederate soldier shared this view was a surprise. If he realized this strange truth, there must have been others. What occupied my mind, however, was his parting comment. Why had Abby taken a shine to that hostile old quadriplegic?

"Abby," I said as I entered the room, "what do you think of Sergeant Clemmens?"

She seemed surprised by the question. "I like him. Is something wrong with that?" she asked.

"No," I replied, "but I've never heard you say a good thing about a Union soldier."

She looked contrite. "He came from a small fishing village in Maine," she said. "He lost everything, his health, his lover, his family—and for what? He told me he'd never seen a black man until he joined the army, but when he learned about the meaning of the war, he saw fighting as the right thing to do. In that, he told me, he never had a single regret." She walked to the window; then she turned and looked me in the eyes. "Perhaps I've been wrong. If a man loses everything, even most of his body, and still sees the right of his cause—well, it made me think. It just drained the hate from me."

A blessing from strange quarters, I thought. All my attempts at reasoning had failed to subdue her hostility. Yet a single comment from this hostile old man had wiped from her mind the teachings of a lifetime. To reach this point we had traveled two thousand miles to a remote hospital nestled in the southern edge of the Black Hills of South Dakota. The result was worth the effort.

Now, as I reflect on the significance of that moment, I recall that throughout history there have been many attempts by one man to enslave another. On the scale of nations, slavery has never ended without the spilling of blood. Sometimes, however, within the solitude of a single soul, the idea gives way with only a reflection on the human suffering required to bring it to an end.

There were two turning points at this juncture of time. Circumstance had delayed one for more than fifty years. First, Grant had aimed his army like a deadly spear at the South's heart. A simple thing, perhaps, but something never before tried in three years of conflict. With this action he made a commitment to total war. Then, as a result of Grant's making this commitment, a soldier was horribly maimed, leaving him to travel a tortured path destined later to alter the fundamental beliefs of another person.

Two days later, just after we finished packing in preparation to board the Union Pacific train to take us home, I heard a knock at the door.

"Are you Mr. Kelly?" asked the man in a white hospital uniform.

"Yes," I answered.

"This message is for you," he said; then he turned and disappeared around the corner.

"What is it, dear?" Abby asked.

"A message from the hospital," I replied. I opened it and read aloud.

Dear Major Kelly: I thought it right to inform you that the orderly left Sergeant Clemmens unattended out on the balcony for several hours during the recent bad weather. I suspect Jeremiah made no attempt to remedy this oversight. You know that he had a voice that would ripple still water if he wanted something. Anyway, he took a bad case of pneumonia as a result, and he died at 8:30 this morning. He has, at last, found relief from fifty years of suffering. His last words were: tell that lady that came with Major Kelly how pretty I think she is. Your friend, Lt. Joseph McFee.

I looked up at Abby, who stood stiff as a board. At first, I detected no expression at all on her face, just the same porcelain beauty that had attracted me to her on that moonlit night in what seems another lifetime. Finally, her legs seemed to buckle and she caught herself on the bedpost. Gathering herself, looking the picture of composure, she then stood tall and straight before bending slightly to smooth an imagined wrinkle in her dress. Then, as she patted her hair, her lips quivered slightly and tears began to etch a path through the powder on her cheeks. This continued in silence for a few moments until, with a sniff, she bent gently at the knees and picked up her grip before walking past me out the door.

Not a word passed between us during that strange, almost ritual-like moment. Odd as it may seem, she has never spoken a word on the subject, and I have never pressed. What I remember most about the journey is that we spent a long, sad time on the train as it rambled along the tracks toward home.

15 Born to Be a Soldier

Grant pulled many men from the ranks and personally placed them on a short, steep path to advancement. Sherman was one, Sheridan another. In almost every way, except two, each man differed from the other. Neither general set any limit on his ability or ambition. Both had a strong sense of the core issues over which the nation was struggling. Although Grant had assigned Sherman to lead the army in the West, he brought the younger man, Sheridan, with him to the Army of the Potomac. He gave Sheridan, at the age of thirty-three, command of the ten-thousand-man Cavalry Corps.

Here, as the spring of 1864 turned into summer, a young man by the name of Emory Upton also came to Grant's attention. In time Grant promoted him, too, above others less able. On May 7, that action was a few days in the future, but the drum rolls sounding the advance of the steamroller called war were beating out a long, steady cadence. Nothing could stop it now, for Grant had turned south, driving the conflict toward the heart of the Old Dominion.

The battle at Spotsylvania Courthouse started with a dull, sporadic firing; then it moved rapidly to an overpowering crescendo. First, a few pickets popped off shots at each other, and a sprinkle of wounded drifted back to the aid stations. In time, regiments collided, then brigades and divisions, then whole armies. At this dusty crossroads hamlet, however, something new developed that is difficult to understand. Men who normally were cautious to a fault walked into a leaden hailstorm as though it was no more dangerous than a walk in the park with a favorite girl.

Actually, the battle began a few miles north of the courthouse, at another crossroads building called Todd's Tavern. The cavalry came first, the Union and Confederate forces arriving almost at the same time.

"Let me tell you," recalled Lt. Henry James of the New York Dragoons, "it was not my smartest day when I joined the cavalry. Besides the fact I wasn't from New York—I'd been pulled out of a Washington guard unit and attached to the Dragoons as a replacement three days before we crossed the Rapidan—I really wasn't even a cavalryman. Don't misunderstand me: I knew somethin' about horses. In fact, that was my job before the war. I started breakin' those critters at the age of seventeen. I'd been in charge of a part of the stables at Washington, so it must've seemed only natural to stick me in the cavalry."

I talked to Lieutenant James in a Philadelphia gentleman's club. At seventy-seven, he still practiced law and was the senior partner in his firm. What struck me as strange about James was his speech. He still talked like that horse breaker of seventeen. I found it difficult not to smile when he let himself go and lapsed into his stable jargon. Except for the history professor I met later, James was perhaps the most intelligent of all the men I talked to on my odyssey around the country.

"At this time," he said, "servin' in the cavalry was a disparagin' assignment. The common joke goin' around was that durin' all the war no infantryman'd ever seen a dead cavalryman. That was untrue of course, but the joke summed up the status of cavalry in the Army of the Potomac."

"Did you fight at Todd's Tavern?" I asked.

"Certainly did. Twice. Stuart drove us out shortly after we arrived the first time. For Grant's army to move south out of the Wilderness, however, that road had to be used. So Sheridan led us back in again." He inserted his thumbs behind his vest. "We advanced in grand style with our repeatin' rifles knockin' those Rebs outta their saddles by the dozens. All mornin' an' into the afternoon we pushed the Rebs back, sometimes advancin' on horseback, sometimes advancin' dismounted. But we did a job on those yelping Rebs an' gave 'em the first lickin' they'd ever suffered."

He hesitated; then his mood darkened. "If only I'd known what our efforts were leadin' toward, I doubt I'd'a been so pleased. The Devil himself brewed up what followed. No general would've been that cruel. By late afternoon, we'd pushed the Reb cavalry most of the way down the Brock Road toward Spotsylvania, but we paid a high price: in less'n six hours, my regiment lost nearly a dozen officers and more than eight score enlisted men. That turned out to be the heaviest loss of cavalry in a single engagement durin' the whole war." He smiled, as if enjoying a private joke. "After Todd's Tavern, the infantry stopped laughin' at us cavalry. Most of the army had to travel down that road, an' all about there lay ample evidence that cavalrymen had died tryin' to carve the way for the infantry." He held up his left hand. "I was swingin' my saber at a Reb when a bullet slammed into my hand an' severed these two fingers. It weakened my grip a bit, but if I'd quit to worry about it just then, they'd'a killed me, too."

"What happened after the fracas at Todd's Tavern?" I inquired.

"All hell broke loose," he replied. "That was the day Little Phil started comin' into his own. In my judgment, he was the best soldier produced by this nation in that century. A few I know will argue that point, but they've never convinced me."

"What brought this about?"

"Well, exactly what happened I can't say for certain, but there were plenty of rumors. All I know for certain is the cavalry broke free from guardin' wagons an' the infantry an' headed after Jeb Stuart. Less'n a week later, that wily Confederate was dead an' buried. With his demise— an' with Sheridan commandin' us—the Southern cavalry lost its aura of invincibility."

I let the matter pass and discussed other aspects of the battle with Lieutenant James. I remembered, however, that there was a man who had been a witness to much of what followed. I never traveled anywhere without my notes. By now, I had talked with two hundred or more veterans of greater and lesser rank. Keeping mental track of who said what over a period of several years was impossible. I felt, however, the importance of this historical incident. I went back to my room and began to dig through my files.

The more I thought about it, the more I concluded that the key to success and failure during the period of the rebellion seemed connected to the generals. This is not to take anything away from the men and other, lower-ranking officers. But looking back over fifty years at what happened, it is obvious that the men performed about as well as the general who led them. That was true at the brigade level, it was true at division and corps level, and it was true for the army as a whole— it just made more difference at army level. It is the man with the stars on his shoulders who possesses the power to give commands that the whole army must follow. The general has the power to say "Go north," as General Hooker commanded at Chancellorsville in May of 1863, or he has the power to say "Go south," as Grant directed at the same road junction a year later. What they said made all the difference in the world. Now I had no doubt that the temperament and tempering of the man who has such power controls the destiny of war as much as any condition—more so than most.

I dug through my notes for nearly an hour before I found what I was looking for: "Reflections of a Staff Officer/Capt. David C. Kennedy." Captain Kennedy was young for an important staff officer. Typically, such assignments accrued mostly to West Point men, young men on their way up. Staff assignments were the training ground for the most promising young officers. At some point, it became necessary to test their courage and judgment under fire, but that usually resulted after the mental training. Captain Kennedy was neither a West Point graduate nor in training for future glory. He was, in fact, a farmer and a Southerner, from Alabama.

While much has been said about the men from the North who crossed over into Dixie to fight for the South, the road ran both ways.

"Why did you go north to fight?" I asked Captain Kennedy.

"I wanted to fight. Isn't that stupid? I was seventeen with a war raging all about me. I wanted to be a part of it. But more than that, I was an idealist, a trait for which I give my father full credit, a trait that could be deadly in the South if the ideals were the wrong type. Mine were. I opposed slavery with every fiber of my being. My brothers and me—I had four brothers, two older and two younger—had been taught that no man has a right to tell another what he must do against his will. But I lived in Alabama, the state that gave meaning to the term 'Deep South.' There, if you were black, you weren't a man. In early '62 my older brothers, James and George, traveled north to fight in the Union Army. When my time came a few months later, I grabbed my rifle and headed out to join them. It required a month of sleeping by day and traveling by night before I reached some Union troops and joined their army."

"You were a seventeen-year-old private in the spring of '62," I observed, "and a captain on Meade's staff by the spring of '64. That's a big jump."

"Maybe so, but I earned the right to be there."

Young David had not arrived at this assignment along an easy road. In many respects, his story was the epitome of what the war was about. I hope I do him justice. It began on a warm spring night in 1862. Accounts of the battle at Shiloh were just filtering into the lower regions of the South, and tempers were at a boiling point. The Kennedy family suffered the full impact of that unshackled hostility.

* * *

"Come out here you nigger lover," a man shouted from the shadows just beyond the Kennedy house. "We won't tolerate the likes of you an' your kind in these parts no more."

Old David Kennedy opened the door a crack and looked into the darkness. "Is that you, Jake Redmer?" he asked.

"Yeah, you shit heel, it's Jake—an' the rest of your friends."

Rifle in hand, Kennedy moved cautiously onto the front porch. "What do you men want?" he demanded.

"We want you," another voice called out, "an' all your bastard children."

"This is my land," Kennedy called out. "You get out of here." He gestured menacingly with his rifle.

"Not tonight, Kennedy."

"Is that you, Mr. Fulton?"

"It's me, Dave," Fulton said with the soft drawl common to men of authority. "You know why we're here, so come on out now. The time of atonement is at hand."

Henry Fulton owned the largest plantation in Marion County. His word was law among the uneducated backwoods farmers and laborers in the area. All that was good and all that was bad in Marion County flowed from Henry Fulton. Even the sheriff was his sometime field boss when crime was slow.

By now, Kennedy was growing afraid. "I don't know why you're here. What do you want, Mr. Fulton?"

"You heard about Shiloh?" Fulton asked.

"Yeah, I heard some. What does that have to do with me?"

"Ten thousand good Southern boys were chewed up there, Dave, boys willing to die if need be to preserve our way of life. As I understand it, you don't cotton much to our way of life, and neither do your sons. I hear two of them went north to fight for the Yankees. Is that true?"

"That's none of your business," Kennedy replied. "I believe in live and let live. As I understand it, that's what this war is all about."

"There's more to it than that, Dave, and you know it. The South can't survive without slaves, and you're a damned abolitionist."

"I don't believe in slavery, if that's what you mean. That's my right as a free man. If you want to own slaves, that's your right, too, I guess."

"Well, Dave, that won't do. Look how you've corrupted your sons. They don't believe in owning slaves, either. Now, what would happen if that attitude started to spread? Where would we be then? No, Dave, that won't do at all. Now come on out here."

Kennedy stepped down from the porch and strolled a few steps toward the trees. As he moved, a dozen or more figures moved from the shadows into the dim light provided by the sliver of a crescent moon. All had rifles, all except Fulton. He let others carry out the violent acts. That way, he insulated himself from such official law as existed in those parts.

Fulton walked to the front of the gathering and moved toward Kennedy. He placed his hand on Kennedy's shoulder. "Dave, my sons are in the army, too, and they know what they're fightin' for. Do your sons know what they're fightin' for?"

"They know what they ain't fightin' for," Kennedy said, letting his caution slip. "They ain't fightin' to save your slaves, that's for certain. We never owned a slave and never will. We do all right on our own. Why should my sons fight to make you a rich man?"

"Now there we have it, Dave," Fulton said as he squeezed Kennedy's shoulder. "You're just against our way of life, and that's all there is to it. Something has to be done about that."

"And what's that?" Kennedy snapped. "You goin' to beat me like you do your niggers?"

"My nigras are dumb critters, Dave, and they need clear language to learn right from wrong. A whip helps them learn faster, that's all. But I don't think you have it in you to learn. That makes you worse than a nigra, and you know we can't tolerate anything worse than a nigra."

Fulton turned and slowly walked over to a large gum tree. "This looks about right," he said; then he faded into the shadows. As soon as he had passed from sight, the other men rushed Kennedy. For the first time Kennedy saw the rope with a large noose at one end. He kicked and yelled, but there were too many of them. Young David Kennedy ran from the house and dove into the yelling men. A rifle butt crashed into his back, and he fell limp on the dew-covered grass. He remembered hearing the yelling: "Kill the nigger lover, hang him from his own tree." Young David strained to rise, but the blow had numbed his nerves and his legs refused to move. Then, except for a gagging sound drifting into his ears from what seemed a long distance away, there was silence.

Watching a person die does something to the observer, even if the one killed is an enemy and hate motivates the act. Somehow, it's so final, so irreversible. "What if I was wrong?" one must ask. In killing David Kennedy, they had etched on the heavens for everyone to see the silent message that killing for a strongly held belief was all right. But they had also foretold their own vulnerability. What was right for them was just as right for others, and propelled forward by that reality, men went to war. A great many people, Northerner and Southerner alike, had seen enough of slavery, and they meant to end it. Within seven months of David Kennedy's death, Lincoln issued a proclamation giving official sanction to his conviction that the slaves should be freed.

Even without seeing, young David knew what had happened. "I just couldn't bring myself to look up," Captain Kennedy said, his voice cracking. He sniffed and, closing his eyes, squeezed a tear to the surface. It slid down the base of his nose and hung from his upper lip. He wiped it away with his sleeve. "I knew my father was hanging from that tree. If ever there'd been any doubt in my mind about hating what I had grown up with, those doubts were forever removed. I knew that I could get one, maybe even two of them, if I made it back into the house and got a gun. But they'd'a killed me, and my mother would have lost a son as well as a husband. Those men might've killed my whole family!"

That's what the report from Shiloh had done to everybody: it put violence in the mind and vengeance in the heart.

"But killing Pa wasn't enough for them. 'Get the bitch and her little curs,' one of them yelled. One of them lit a torch. I watched it crash through the window, and the house began to burn. Mom and the kids ran out screaming, right into the sight of Pa hanging limp and black from that tree. The men walked off laughing shortly after. After they departed, I got a ladder and cut Pa down. I'll never forget his black face, and the irony of it hit me like a rock between the eyes. In killing him, they'd made of Pa what they feared more than God—a black man.

"Pa'd stood firm against the vileness of slavery, and his neighbors had killed him for it. Pa'd always savored the hope that one day the people would see the evil of it all and slavery would simply fade away. I now knew better. A week later, after I'd guided my family to a safe home in another county, I took the gun that I'd saved from the burning house and a sack containing a ham and a loaf of bread, and headed north. I never returned, and that's been fifty-eight years."

As he spoke, I found it impossible to ignore the sound of self-imposed guilt in his voice resulting from his failure to act. Perhaps he felt his own death would have solved something, but we both knew better. Besides, he had found a better means of protest. War raged up north, and in war there is permission to kill as long as you have the stamina to stand and pull the trigger.

"I have to admit," he said, "that at that moment my only thoughts were on vengeance. It didn't matter who I killed as long at it was someone who supported slavery."

He rose and moved toward the door to his house. "You want to stay for supper?" he asked.

"Sounds good."

"I'll tell Mother. Wait until you taste Mother's cherry pie and ice cream," he said with a smile. "The thought of it keeps me alive."

We both laughed. He returned shortly.

"Tell me how you got to be on Meade's staff," I said.

"When I joined up," he replied, "they put me in a polyglot regiment with men from all over the North. That served me fine, for it made for less confusion about my loyalty. I just wanted to kill Southerners. But the thought never left me: what if one of those I kill is one of my brothers? I figured the one just younger than me had been drafted by them.

"My first battle was Second Bull Run. I charged a fence row of Rebs and killed three before the others wounded me and ran. For that they made me a corporal and wrote me up in dispatches. Next was Fredericksburg, in the winter of '62. I led a squad of men across a stream north of the town and captured a Reb command post. For that they made me a sergeant and gave me the Medal of Honor. Things were kind of slow until Gettysburg. Meade was in command by then. On the second day of the battle, when things were looking bad in the wheat field and around Little Round Top, I assumed command of a company—all the officers had been killed—and blunted the charge of a rebel regiment. They made me a lieutenant and then a captain the next day, after I led my men into Pickett's flank as the Rebs charged across the field toward Cemetery Ridge.

"I first met Meade later that evening. Conditions were rather chaotic, and Meade called in a bunch of officers to organize our defenses. During the discussion, I pointed out what I thought'd been some weaknesses in our dispositions. That got Meade's attention and he turned to me. 'Go through that again, Captain,' he said.

"I'm a lieutenant, sir," I said—I'd just had time to pin on my new insignia—and he said, 'Not anymore, Captain.' He listened to my suggestions and nodded. That night, a major summoned me to his tent to inform me of my appointment to the staff."

"Didn't that dampen your plans to kill more Rebs?" I asked.

"I managed to pop off a few now and again. Staff captains move about quite a bit, y'know, what with carrying messages and all."

I can still remember the smell of catfish frying in the kitchen of the small house where Kennedy and his wife lived. A man from the South never loses an appetite for Southern food—no matter where he goes. I enjoyed the meal of catfish, okra, and hominy grits. That night I even developed a taste for bread dipped in milk. Most of all, however, I remember the taste of Mrs. Kennedy's cherry pie and homemade ice cream. I had difficulty keeping my eyes open as I listened to the rest of Kennedy's story while we rocked on the porch overlooking Hudson Bay.

Kennedy stuffed tobacco into his pipe as he rocked. He lit three matches before the fire caught. He inhaled deeply, then blew smoke into the brisk east wind. "Don't misunderstand me," he began, sounding as if he had thought for a long time about the proper opening, "I had the utmost respect for the job Meade had to do. It's easy to look back in hindsight and say this or that should've been done. But Sheridan seemed to have an insight into the big problems that others lacked the vision to see. There in the Wilderness, Sheridan had just whipped what, until that moment, was considered the best cavalry in the world. He was feeling, as he later described it, 'in high feather.' He had only one objective: to drive the Rebs south across the Po River and secure the road for Meade's men as they moved south. By now, Sheridan's men were scattered over a dozen square miles. He wrote orders directing them to move to the Po and secure the bridges. He intended to send one division south of the Po to secure the ground around Spotsylvania Courthouse until the infantry arrived.

"Meade's advance units made it to Todd's Tavern earlier than expected, so Sheridan's orders hadn't reached his cavalry division commanders. Meade issued orders with a different effect. He sent most of the cavalry on a roundabout trip toward Spotsylvania, away from the vital Po crossing. He also ordered a portion of the cavalry to guard duty for his wagons. His overall purpose was logical enough: he wanted to clear the road of the nearly ten thousand riders to make the passage easier for his infantry. I heard him say that. In effect, however, he was a victim of the shortsighted attitude exhibited during the war by most infantry commanders. They saw cavalry as outriders, incapable of dedicated offensive action. But the war had changed. With their new Henry repeating rifles, what cavalry gave up in the way of punch with their shorter-range carbines they regained by the sheer volume of fire they could lay down.

"My bad fortune was in having to carry Meade's orders to Sheridan's troopers. Before long, they were riding out of sight, leaving only General Wilson's division of Sheridan's corps to head for Spotsylvania proper."

"If Sheridan was their commander," I asked, "why did the cavalry commander act on Meade's orders?"

"Simple. Although Sheridan was their commander, he was subordinate to Meade. But it didn't matter much by then. The Rebs had already moved into position across Brock Road. Lee's men, under General Anderson, had moved with greater speed than anyone believed possible. By morning, shortly after the Union cavalry division arrived and drove the Reb cavalry away, their infantry reached Spotsylvania and quickly drove off the Union cavalry. The cavalry division Meade sent to clear the way for the infantry ran into the stout rebel defense, and the whole Union Army came to a grinding halt. As many as thirty thousand troops—both cavalry and infantry—piled up before the stout rebel works.

"General Warren, commander of the lead corps, exploded and lit into one of Sheridan's division commanders. During the exchange, he made some unkind remarks about Sheridan, remarks that eventually reached Sheridan's ears.

"I was present when Sheridan caught up with Meade. The exchange that followed still rings in my ears. Sheridan as much as accused his superior of incompetence. Meade in turn blamed Sheridan for Warren's inability to reach Spotsylvania. He claimed that Sheridan's men, who were asleep at the time and blocking the road, had prevented Warren's movement to the bridges. Meade was probably right, if everything had gone as planned. But to escape the smoke and fires in the Wilderness, General Anderson had marched his men all night and had reached the vital crossing leading to Spotsylvania well ahead of schedule.

"But that wasn't the critical part of the exchange. Sheridan never had liked Warren. He believed Warren was too cautious and slow to move until everything was just right, which it hardly ever was. Sheridan stormed out after a while, but only after telling Meade that if he'd just stay out of the way of the cavalry he'd destroy Jeb Stuart and his infernal cavalry. His comments about Warren were even less flattering, with the result that a feud had been started that would end only fifteen years later—after Warren was three months in his grave."

"Is that actually what happened, or does it just make a good story?" I asked.

"It happened, just about as I said, but it left Meade with a problem. He was insecure about his status with Grant. He'd expected to be relieved after Grant announced his intention to make his headquarters in the field with the Army of the Potomac. He said so at least twice that I heard. He also knew how much Grant thought of Sheridan. 'That damned Sheridan thinks he's God Almighty,' Meade told Grant when they met the next day.

" 'Oh?' Grant said calmly. 'How's that?'

" 'He told me, if I'd just stay out of his way, he'd go after Stuart and whip him all the way back to Richmond.'

"Grant had several choices at that point, and the one he made turned out to be precisely right, although it strained military protocol to the limit. The decision he made set in motion a chain of events that brought death to one high-ranking officer and, eventually, disgrace to another. Before, Meade had more than sufficient grounds to relieve Sheridan for openly challenging his competence. Grant probably would've had no choice other than to sustain Meade if he'd removed Sheridan. But, at the bottom of it all, Meade was as cautious as Warren. He backed away from the decision, and Grant made it for him.

"It's as clear as yesterday. Grant dragged deeply on his cigar and let the smoke out slowly. 'Did Sheridan say that?' Grant asked. 'Well, he generally knows what he's talking about. Let him start right out and do it.' I remember thinking, as a result of that simple exchange, how different these two men were. Meade had made a questionable decision by giving orders to Sheridan's cavalry without first consulting with him. Then, at the point of confrontation with his subordinate, he'd defended Warren, but let the affront to his own authority pass unchallenged. He always thought of war in traditional terms. He failed to see even the possibility that the cavalry might be wasted if it had no purposes other than to protect the infantry's flanks and guard wagons. At the time, Grant may not have realized that the cavalry had real value as a fighting unit, but he believed that Sheridan thought so. That was enough to convince him to turn the cavalry loose. Two days later, a Union sergeant killed Jeb Stuart, and the South had lost one of its most capable generals."

"Yes, I agree with everything you've said," I countered, "but Sheridan's comment about getting Stuart was, at the time, nothing but the idle boast of a young and impetuous officer."

Kennedy looked sternly at me. "No, young man, you miss the essential point. Grant's army was full of general officers who always looked for the cautious alternative. They'd let things happen rather than make them happen. That's where Lee had it all over them. He was always willing to take the kinds of risks that lead to winning or losing all. If one of his gambles failed, he always had it in the back of his mind that his opponent would fail to follow up and he would somehow get away, even from the worst disaster. That's precisely what happened at Antietam and Gettysburg. McClellan lacked the stomach to go after Lee when he had him beat. Meade lacked the killer instinct when he had Lee penned up north of the Potomac. Nothing Lincoln said made McClellan or Meade act. McClellan was the same on the Peninsula. Hooker, Burnside, and the others were the same, too."

As Kennedy talked, my thoughts drifted back to young Captain Laird. His colonel had been afraid to assume the ultimate responsibility. He moved his troops forward well enough after Sedgwick relieved him of that burden, so it wasn't that he was a coward or afraid to die. A bullet moving toward a man when he is second in command is just as deadly as when he is the commander. It is as if such men see the unknown as an impenetrable barrier rather than a challenge or opportunity. As a result, they move only after careful planning and run smack into the inevitable uncertainty of war. Then they delay and let the opportunity pass.

Grant obviously saw something different in Sheridan—certainly more than just the belief he might actually get Stuart. Grant created the opportunity; that was all he could do. Lee said as much about his own leadership. What happened after that was up to Sheridan and fate.

Kennedy neglected to explain what he meant by a soldier's disgrace, but I knew. The seeds of another event were sown on that day of hostile recriminations, but they reached full growth only as the war was about to end. Warren, the hero of Little Round Top at Gettysburg, was another man of unquestioned personal courage. At Gettysburg, he had moved with the urgency necessary to save Meade's flank, but at the time he felt none of the heavy burden of responsibility if he had failed. As a commander, he always moved with an engineer's caution, a disconcerting trait unsuitable for men who hold in their hands the destiny of a nation. Grant saw this trait only later, and when it became visible he took the necessary action, if only indirectly, to solve the problem. What happened, however, is another story that must be explained in the proper context.

16 The Killing Field

I have never heard our generals utter a word of encouragement, whether before or after entering a battle. I have never seen them ride along the lines and tell each regiment that it held an important position and that it was expected to hold it to the last. I have never heard them appeal to the love every soldier has for his colors, or to his patriotism. Neither have I ever seen a general thank his troops after the action for the gallantry they have displayed.
Col. Emory Upton, 121st New York Volunteer Regiment

Lee had only his insight to guide him in determining where Grant might go after leaving the Wilderness. As so often happened, he guessed correctly. Luck, however, played a part. During May 7 the two armies backed away from each other, or at least they entrenched themselves following two days of savage fighting. Lee learned on the seventh that Grant's army was moving, but where? Needing somehow to react, he directed one of his division commanders, Maj. Gen. Richard Anderson, to move south on the morning of the eighth. Fires, however, were spreading throughout the woods, so Anderson moved on the night of May 7–8. The time gained was just enough. The movement was an accident, or at least Grant viewed it as such. Later, Grant wrote a simple analysis of this chance action: "accident often decides the fate of battle." This accident played a major role in placing infantry in front of Warren's men when they later moved south. It also contributed to the confrontation between Sheridan and Meade that shortly led to Stuart's death.

The armies were making things happen as much as a by-product of battle as by battle itself.

One other "accident" worthy of note followed these events. Warren did not believe that Lee had time to move any but cavalry troops to his front. Partly because of this, but mainly because Warren once again had failed to commit all of his forces to overpower the rebels, Grant ordered General Sedgwick to come to Warren's assistance. By the time he arrived, about all that was happening was a steady, long-range duel of sharpshooters. In an effort to get the men moving, he rode to a ridge to assess the size of the force holding up the advance. As he studied the terrain through his field glasses, he judged that the nearest enemy troops were eight hundred yards away.

"Those snipers are popping our men off like bottles on a fence," a private told him.

"Nonsense," Sedgwick said. "I'm ashamed of you, dodging that way. They couldn't hit an elephant at this distance."

Almost before the words passed from his lips, he stiffened and then slowly toppled from his horse. The bullet had entered just below his left eye. "He smiled strangely, as if to acknowledge the dark humor of what had turned out to be his last remark," reported an observer, "then he was dead." His death was a knee-buckling shock to the men of his corps. Besides, when corps commanders started toppling, alive one minute and dead the next, who was safe?

"Is he really dead?" Grant asked. He puttered for a few moments, then turned his ashen face to a member of his staff. "Is he really dead?" he asked again, a pained expression distorting his brow.

Sedgwick was dead, and the war shifted in another direction. Grant had failed to beat Lee to Spotsylvania. Now nothing remained but to go at him head-on.

"All through the day on the ninth and into the night and morning of the tenth, Grant and Lee fed their men into the line," Maj. Tom Terrill told me. "Slowly, the soldiers moved onto the killing field. I later came to look upon it as a magnet drawing bits of ferrous metal from all directions, pulling them together in an angry urgency to occupy the exact same space in time."

I met Major Terrill on a train going from Washington to Richmond. After visiting the Wilderness, my wife decided she had seen enough of battlefields for a while. I needed to do some research, so I left her in the hotel. I had about an hour to kill, so I had dug out some of my notes to consolidate some important points. Terrill watched in silence for a while before I dropped one of my original notes. He leaned forward and picked it up.

"These are Civil War notes," he observed. "Are you writing a book?"

"That's what I'm doing," I replied. "I've been at it for over three years now. It takes a long time to gather the data."

"Look out there," he said as he pointed across a field. "Do you know what that is?"

"No, I don't," I answered.

"That's the last leg of the Brock Road. I walked past that house in the spring of '64 on my way to the killing grounds."

"Do you mean Spotsylvania Courthouse?" I asked.

He turned with a surprised squint in his eyes. "You do know something about the war, don't you?"

"A little," I replied modestly. "It sounds like you know even more."

"I don't know. One of the hardest things is to see a war that you're fighting in. War is something you have to stand back from if you want to find out what's going on."

"I know," I said, "and even then it's difficult to know if what you see is the truth."

Although he was nearly eighty years old now, Terrill did not look a day over sixty. Even his hair had grayed only slightly. Except for crow's-feet around his eyes his face was nearly wrinkle-free. His speech had the ring of a college professor or an engineer—precise and sharp, yet descriptive and insightful.

When the war started, men of some importance formed regiments in their local communities. These men, mostly in their thirties with some sprinkled on either side, knew nothing of war. Only a few were like Grant, castoffs from a different time. Mostly they were politicians or men of substance with enough money to buy the uniforms and provisions necessary to get started. By 1864, most of those pretend soldiers were dead, except the ones who had decided that war was more than they had bargained for and had gone home to make money. Gradually replacing them were men of less financial substance, but who were better trained for the grisly work that war demanded. The war was coming under the control of professionals, men such as Major Terrill. Calling him a major, however, is an injustice. After serving thirty-five years as a professional soldier, he had left the service as a major general. When I met him he was on his way to Mobile to visit his grandson.

Terrill graduated from West Point in 1862, and at the time of

Spotsylvania he was twenty-three years old and had two years of war behind him. He had risen to assistant regimental commander. Only a year older was his friend and brigade commander, Col. Emory Upton. Upton had been his company commander at the Academy when Upton was in his last year.

"We didn't see much of Grant during the first few days of the campaign," Terrill said. "Now that we were out of the Wilderness, now that the trees were somewhat less dense and tangled, he seemed to be more interested in watching what happened. In our front the Rebs had dug a three-mile-long line of trenches. It seemed to me that God himself would have drawn back from charging those works. Colonel Upton had recently been given command of our brigade. Throughout most of the day we watched Warren's men try to break through Lee's line. All they got for their effort was a growing pile of bodies."

"What did the men think," I asked him, "when they looked across the field and stared at that line of trenches?"

"You had to be there to understand," he answered. "I remember when the war started, when men lined up as pretty as you please in nice, neat lines and advanced shoulder to shoulder across rolling fields. That's the way they trained us at the Academy. Tactics change slow and hard in the military. I've been as guilty as any. 'Dress right,' commanders yelled as men fell from the ranks. At that time, the Rebs had more smoothbore rifles than anything else. They weren't much good beyond a hundred yards. They were the same as those used in Napoleon's time. Loading them took what seemed forever. If we charged from within their range, it was possible to make it to their line with only one volley being fired. It required a half minute to reload. Gradually, as they acquired more and more rifled weapons, the journey across those fields became more hazardous. It's nothing to knock down a man at four hundred yards with a rifled Minié ball. Even by '62, a well-trained soldier could fire three or four times, starting when we were four hundred yards away, even if we scampered forward at a dead run. That's what made Fredericksburg so terrible. The war had reached its modern stage by then."

I listened intently as the train added its clackity-clack to the sound of his cadencelike voice. I had no trouble imagining him standing on a hill directing regiments to go here and there, watching dispassionately as men fell in bloody, twisted heaps. I had difficulty knowing if my thoughts were complimenting him or not. In my earlier assessment

I had been wrong, I realized. Talking to men of lesser rank had been important, but that provided only half a perspective. Such men told *what* happened, usually adding a liberal amount of subjective, emotional editorializing in the process. Generals, even future generals, knew *why*. They took the time to study all the details and make what previously seemed idiotic appear rational.

"Fear slows a man's reflexes," he said. "During the first years of the war, everyone was afraid all the time. But even fear gets dull with experience. The longer a man survives, the more he begins to feel immune to dying. Lee had only veterans by the time we reached Spotsylvania. I believe his fifty thousand could have whipped any half million new recruits, and you pick them from any place in the world. Like our veterans, however, they probably had decided that sudden death was just a matter of time. They were determined to make every shot count. Such deliberation relaxes a man. Even as short a time back as at Gettysburg I saw men stick their rifles out over barricades and fire without looking. More than a few fired with the ramrods still stuffed down the barrel. A flock of ducks flying over a battle was certain not to make it since so many bullets shot up instead of across. Men got excited and forgot to cap their rifles. We found the rifles of dead men with four or five loads stuffed down the barrel. With all the noise and confusion, they probably didn't realize their weapons had never fired.

"By Spotsylvania, the veterans moved like machines. They loaded without wasted motion; then they took their time and aimed at specific targets. Men who advanced into battle actually acted on an insightful reflex, drawing back just before a bullet hit them. I saw it so many times I finally figured out why this happened. Evidently, something across the way caught their attention, probably an enemy soldier taking a bead. You know how it is when someone is looking at you from the side or from behind your back. You sense it and you turn. They knew a particular bullet would reach them before they could move out of the way, so they just flinched, stiffened up to wait for the blow.

"By the time you reach their works, if you reach them, the actual close-quarter combat is a relief. At least then there's a chance to get even. Coming across toward those trenches, however, is just pure hell. That's the only way to describe it. Every man had his own way of dealing with it. Some actually closed their eyes. More than a few cried. Many yelled. The Rebs yelled like crazy. They sounded like devils straight from Hell. A man needed a stout heart to keep from running when they let out that rebel yell. Many of the men resented the officers for holding back. But if you ever sat a horse, your head seven feet in the air with nothing but blue sky as your armor, you'd understand why they held back. In the early days of the war, when chivalry was still in style, officers were expected to lead a charge on horseback. The smart ones, the ones who survived, moved in dismounted, mingling with their men so they wouldn't stick out so much." He leaned forward, smiling conspiratorially as he placed his hand on my leg; then he looked over his shoulder. "I admit to being one of the first to engage in this practice," he said softly, as if to keep anyone else from hearing. "Otherwise," he added solemnly, "I wouldn't be here to talk about it."

"Tell me about Upton's charge," I said.

*   *   *

It had become common practice by this time in the war to look for every advantage when digging in. This usually meant taking maximum advantage of the natural lay of the land. Lee's Spotsylvania trenches extended more than a mile along a generally straight line at the edge of a slight rise before reaching an outward projecting extension of the rise. "A large teat," one man described the lateral prominence. It probably seemed natural for the line to follow the rise. For whatever reason, the battle line jutted out in a U-shaped salient projecting more than a mile toward the Union lines. It was half as wide. Then it curved back to join the remainder of the trench line. From Lee's side of the field it appeared, because of the salient's elevation, to be an excellent artillery emplacement. From Grant's perspective, the jutting spit of land appeared isolated, susceptible to being taken by force. If that happened, the men could attack opposite flanking ends of the main Confederate line. The problem was getting a strong force of men into this Mule Shoe, as the Confederates called it, without being cut to pieces.

"Men," Upton said as he gathered his officers around him, "see that group of men back there on that hill." They all turned and looked. "That's Generals Grant, Meade, and Wright, General Sedgwick's replacement. Grant told Meade he wants us to assault those works. Meade told Wright, and Wright told me. Now I'm telling you."

"Emory," Terrill said, shaking his head, "Warren's divisions have been charging those works all up and down the line nearly all day long. What has it got them? Nothing. What can we do with just a brigade?"

"I know," Upton said with a nod, "but there may be a way. If we succeed, Mott's division will follow us across; then we can roll up the whole Confederate line—both right and left." The subdued groans of protest were an obvious signal that none of the others shared his optimism. "Here's what we'll do. Time is the critical factor. I've watched those men attacking across that field all day long. Most of those who didn't make it stopped along the way to fire and load. This gives the Rebs time to get a man in their sights. That's the most dangerous time, when you're standing still or kneeling to reload. I want you to order the men to load their rifles but to leave the percussion caps off. When we start, I don't want anyone to stop for anything. We'll be within a couple of hundred yards before the Rebs have a clear field of fire. At most, they can fire and reload only once or twice if we keep on the move. After we get there, we'll drive bayonets into them. I think they'll run. Then we can cap our rifles and fire a volley into their backs at close range."

If nothing else, it offered something new, and something new offered at least a ray of hope.

"By God, Colonel," a major said, "it just might work."

With those words of hope, the officers relaxed, but only slightly. One even offered a joke. The common soldier knew what was coming, and the sound of laughter caught his attention. The officers had gone into the huddle grim-faced and tense. Now they were laughing and relaxed.

"I thought they'd decided to cancel the charge," a Galena private told me, "and I immediately began building a fire to boil coffee. Only a pile of ashes remained, and someone else had gulped down the coffee by the time I returned, but for a moment there I breathed easy."

Wright knew nothing of these new tactics, nor did Meade or Grant. Looking back now, it seems doubtful to me they would have cared. This had become a war of attrition. Even a partially successful charge meant a few less Rebs to defend against the rush that followed—whenever that might be. Nevertheless, the general officers watched as Upton's men tightened their belts, pinned messages on their uniforms giving directions where to send the body, and gathered to make the effort.

*   *   *

"Our regiments moved out slowly at first," Terrill said, "bent over to make a smaller target, not worrying much about style or finesse. Then they began to trot. A few broke into a run, and the remainder followed. Out in front was Upton, advancing in line with the flags, waving his saber in the air. We aimed right at the outermost point of the curve. At about a hundred and fifty yards the first volley cracked the air and a wave of smoke rolled outward from the Confederate trenches. Here and there, as bullets struck flesh, our men slumped to the ground. The men ran faster. With luck, they knew, they had at least another fifteen seconds to live before the next curtain of lead came crashing down, this time at more deadly range and with more force."

He drew a puff on his pipe; then he began to regress. I wrote it down as best I could. "A fast man carrying a rifle and all that goes with it can run a hundred yards in about fifteen to seventeen seconds. The race against death was on. By the accounting of most of the men on the run, their counterparts in the trenches would get off one more volley before the race ended. Only a few of the faster Rebs were able to load their rifles and fire off another shot before the blue wave washed over them. Most of the Rebs lost their concentration as they sensed the enemy's legs moving faster than their hands. The men collided in a clash of steel and flesh as our soldiers jumped over the barricades into the breastworks."

Terrill clicked his tongue and flipped his head. "Emory had been correct." He turned toward me with a smile and a nod. "In war—I suppose in any endeavor—the most difficult condition to adjust to is surprise. Not one of those Rebs expected us to cross that field in so short a time. They fought hand to hand for a few minutes; then fear took over. For all they knew, a whole corps was following us in. Actually, no one followed us, not even Mott's division assigned to the task, but they didn't know that. If it'd happened as they'd expected there were too few of them to stand against that number, and they knew it. As we fanned out and moved on their flanks, many threw down their rifles and surrendered to anyone who agreed to take them prisoner. Even more ran. Those who resisted died or went down wounded.

"That was the most exhilarating half hour of my life. For a few minutes there, I actually felt invincible. It was an incredible feeling that I never experienced again, as if some invisible aura had formed a mystical, impenetrable shield around me. One Reb pointed at me with his rifle and fired. The gun was pointed directly at my chest, but nothing happened. I felt as if I had the power to look into that Reb's soul and see his fear. When one broke and ran, others followed as our men inserted the percussion caps into their rifles and fired. As with everything else, this caught the Rebs by surprise. More surrendered. Then it was over. We'd assaulted and captured their trenches and lived to tell about it.

"I'm convinced that if more men'd followed us in we could've rolled up Lee's line that day and ended the war. Of course, that didn't happen. The only good thing to come out of all of this was that Grant fired General Mott. Mott was an altogether unsatisfactory general if ever there was one. Grant had the power to tell his subordinates what to do, but that was as far as it went. The history of the Army of the Potomac was written in the sad performance of its generals in the field. Before long, when the Rebs counterattacked, we had to pull out and go back across that field to our lines. Emory had demonstrated, however, that it would work—or so we all thought."

*   *   *

Upton praised his men that day, and everyone knew they had accomplished something never before done on such a scale. Upton, of course, was not a general, so his assertion condemning the insensitivity of generals held true, but only for a short time.

"By God, that was a sight," Meade said to Grant, "but how did they do it?"

Grant just nodded. He had noticed. "I want to speak with that young man," Grant said to Meade. "Send someone to tell him I'll meet with him at headquarters as soon as he can get here." Grant mounted his horse and disappeared into the trees.

Escorted by troopers from Meade's personal guard, Upton arrived at Grant's field headquarters after dark. "General Grant, Colonel Upton," the troop commander announced as he swung out of the saddle.

"Come into my tent," Grant directed as he returned Upton's salute and extended his hand in greeting. "Have you had supper?"

"Not yet, General," Upton replied as he examined the table covered with food.

"Help yourself. I'm just starting myself."

Upton filled a plate before entering Grant's tent.

"That was a glorious charge today, Colonel," Grant said as he worked on a lobster. "How did you do it?"

"Nothing special, General," Upton replied. "I simply instructed the men to load their rifles but to leave them uncapped until we were in their trenches. I've seen too many attacks bog down as the men stopped to load and fire at men that couldn't be seen."

Grant nodded as he nibbled on a raw carrot. "Didn't the men protest?" Grant asked.

"No, sir. The thought of the Rebs getting off only one or two volleys actually raised their spirits." His enthusiasm rose. "You should've been there, General. The way our men reacted when the Rebs broke and ran, well, you just had to be there to see the pride on their faces."

"Come with me, Colonel," Grant said. "Bring your plate." With two aides trailing behind leading Grant's and Upton's mounts, the two men walked a hundred yards before the Confederate lines came into view. After Sedgwick's experience, Grant was more cautious, even though it was more than a mile to the nearest enemy outpost. Grant squinted as he strained his eyes to see in the dark. He pointed at the salient, its curving path outlined by spots of flickering campfires. "That's where you went in. I hear from prisoner reports that the Rebs are calling it the Mule Shoe." He leaned against the tree, pressing the sole of one foot against the trunk. As Upton thought about the day's activities, Grant lit a cigar. "Do you think your tactic would work for a whole corps?"

Upton hesitated. Being too self-assured was a dangerous practice in the military. "Yes, if the attack is pressed, General. If men hold back, as they did today with Mott's division, then I must say no."

"With proper planning," Grant replied, "that can be avoided. Thank you for speaking so frankly."

In one respect, at least in his assessment of generals, Upton had been wrong.

Grant walked to his horse and mounted. He inhaled, and the dim glow of the cigar highlighted the angles of his face. Resting his forearm on the front of the saddle, he leaned toward Upton, standing a few feet away. "By the way. As you were coming back across the field, I penned the order promoting you to brigadier general." He turned his mount and rode into the darkness. By the time Upton had praised his men, notice of his promotion was already on its way to Washington. Time would pass before the promotion became official, but Grant usually got what he wanted in such matters.

"Allow me, General," said Major Herrington, one of the aides, as he saluted. "I took the liberty and scrounged these insignia for you. You'll have to find your own seamstress."

Upton smiled. "Thank you, Major." Upton appeared embarrassed. "This comes as quite a surprise."

"General Grant is a generous man with officers who show initiative," said the major. "He expressed much pleasure with your performance today." The major saluted again as he extended the reins of Upton's horse. "Good luck, General."

Upton returned the salute, mounted, then trotted away.

*   *   *

That night Grant sent a message to Lincoln. "We have now ended the sixth day of very heavy fighting. The result to this time is much in our favor. But our losses have been heavy, as well as those of the enemy. I am now sending back to Belle Plain all my wagons for a fresh supply of provisions and ammunition, and I propose to fight it out on this line if it takes all summer." He accented the message by ordering the removal of all but one of the bridges over the Rapidan, the one remaining to be removed as soon as the loaded wagons headed south.

The next afternoon, after considering the merits of one more attack against Lee's strengthening line, Grant penned a series of orders. The first was to Burnside:

MAJOR-GENERAL HANCOCK HAS BEEN ORDERED TO MOVE HIS ENTIRE CORPS UNDER COVER OF NIGHT TO JOIN YOU IN A VIGOROUS ATTACK AGAINST THE ENEMY AT 4 A.M. OF TO-MORROW, THE 12TH INSTANT. YOU WILL MOVE AGAINST THE ENEMY WITH YOUR ENTIRE FORCE PROMPTLY AND WITH ALL POSSIBLE VIGOR AT PRECISELY 4 O'CLOCK TO-MORROW MORNING. LET YOUR PREPARATION FOR THIS ATTACK BE CONDUCTED WITH THE UTMOST SECRECY, AND VEILED ENTIRELY FROM THE ENEMY. GENERALS WARREN AND WRIGHT WILL HOLD THEIR CORPS AS CLOSE TO THE ENEMY AS POSSIBLE, TO TAKE ADVANTAGE OF ANY DIVERSION CAUSED BY YOUR AND HANCOCK'S ATTACK, AND WILL PUSH IN THEIR WHOLE FORCE IF ANY OPPORTUNITY PRESENTS ITSELF.

That night it began to rain.

*   *   *

It required all my energy to prevail against the force of the storm. Nearly a foot of snow had fallen, but gale-force winds had piled the

snow as high as second-story windows in alleys and side streets. My
hands ached from the cold. I reached for the brass door handle at 124
Grant Street and pushed my thumb against the lever. My skin nearly
froze to the metal. As I opened the door, I noticed a partially snow-
covered sign over it. Presbyterian Retirement Home. I had difficulty
seeing in the dimly lit antechamber. Shivering from the cold, with my
eyes still glazed from the chilling wind, I strained to read the list of
names penciled on the white cardboard signs inserted into the small
brass brackets. Rev. Charles Smith's name was at the bottom of the
right-hand list. I punched the buzzer button. A short, dumpy, hunch-
backed woman of about seventy came to the inner door. She wiped
away the thick frost from the leaded door window and peered at me
through the small, cleared opening.

"May I help you?" she asked in a high, squeaky voice.

"I wish to see Reverend Smith," I replied.

"Is he expecting you?"

"I'm not certain. My name is Kelly. I wrote him a letter, but he
never replied."

"Wait here," she said, "and I'll check." She turned and shuffled
slowly down the hall; then she disappeared behind the staircase. Shortly
she returned.

"Are you the writer?" she asked.

"Yes," I replied. "I wrote telling him I wanted to discuss his war
experience, for a book I'm writing."

She nodded slowly. "Come on in," she said as she opened the inner
door. She moved as if every action required concentrated thought. She
pointed with a shaking hand. "His room is at the end of the hall on
the right."

The door was ajar. "Reverend Smith?"

"Come in," said the old man, his voice no louder than a raspy whisper.

I pushed open the door and walked into the unlit room. I stumbled
over a chair as I tried to make my way.

"There's a switch by the door," he said. "Turn it on."

I moved cautiously back to the door and felt along the wall. I turned
the switch and a single fifteen-watt bulb clicked on.

"I'm blind," the old man said. "I don't turn on the light much."

I turned toward the sound and saw him sitting in a chair in the corner.
"Reverend Smith. My name is Art Kelly. I wrote you several weeks
ago."

"Yes, I remember. Miss Loomis read me your letter. I would have answered, but her arthritis is so bad she can't write anymore. It just slipped my mind."

"Do you have some time to talk with me?" I asked.

"Sure. Time is about all I do have. Come on in and have a seat."

"Reverend Smith, I'll get straight to the point. I'm writing a book about the Civil War. I'm at a difficult point. The main theme of the book is General Grant's generalship. I'm currently researching the battle at Spotsylvania Courthouse. I recently talked to two men who both told me I should talk to you. So here I am."

"You could've picked a better night for it, don't you think?" A feeble smile parted his pale, thin lips, and a thousand wrinkles crisscrossed his face.

"Yes, sir. But I was on my way home to Boston. I have a four-hour layover while they try to clear the tracks of snow. This will save me a trip back to see you later."

"What do you want to know?"

"I want your impressions of the battle," I said. "Anything you want to say will do fine. None of the men I've talked to were actually at the Bloody Angle. I understand your regiment fought there."

"Anything I want to say, huh?"

"Yes, sir," I replied.

"Why is it, Mr. Kelly, that we older, supposedly wiser, men always end up calling on our young to die to fix what we mess up?"

"A good question, sir," I replied, "but unfortunately, one asked mostly by the young. Do you think that's what happened in the Civil War?"

"I was raised in the South, Mr. Kelly. My father owned slaves. At that time, a wealthy young man chose law, the military, or the ministry. I chose law."

It was, of course, impossible for him to see the surprise on my face. "But aren't you a minister?"

"Yes, I am. But that came later. After the law, I decided to try the military. Then I became a minister. If I'd lived longer," he chuckled, "I would've tried teaching, then probably barbering. But seriously, I grew up with Negroes. As with the white population, many were dumb as posts, but many were quite intelligent and capable. Some of these people memorized the Bible, the whole thing. Can you believe that? I tried once, after I became a preacher, but couldn't get past all those names in Genesis."

"You said you were a military man. That's the part I'm interested in, sir."

"That's right, VMI, but I studied law on my own time. That's what I wanted to do, but never found the time. I was a captain in the Union Army when the war broke out. There was a strong call for a man from Georgia to go with his state. In the South, the state was everything. That's one reason why the South lost the war, but there were many more reasons. In the end, I stayed with the North."

Even in the dim light, I saw a tear roll down his cheek. "Is something wrong?" I asked.

"Sure is," he snapped. "Do you think I would cry for nothing? I had a twin brother, an identical twin. We did everything together while growing up, everything except one. Over time, I got to know some of our darkies well. I learned to respect them and how they thought. They weren't anything like what the average white man believed. It was like they were two different people, at least the smart ones. Oh, when need be they could turn on the 'yas sirs' and 'na sirs,' but they hated us through and through. In time I began to say what I thought. In the South, there was no room for variation on the nigger issue. In time my brother and I couldn't get together without it ending in a verbal fight. After I decided to stay with the Union, I never saw him again, except once, at Spotsylvania.

"By then I was a colonel commanding a regiment. Actually, the first years of the war were rough on me. The other officers didn't trust me, being as how I was a VMI graduate and all. It got worse once they learned my family owned slaves. I had to prove myself a loyal Union officer. Advancement came slowly. By '64 good officers were becoming scarce. I was still a captain at the time of Gettysburg. I did a good job during that battle and was soon promoted to major. By the time of the Wilderness I was a lieutenant colonel. Most of the officers in my regiment were killed or wounded during that battle, and I received a brevet promotion to full colonel on May seventh."

"What about May twelfth?" I asked.

He stiffened—from the memory I suppose.

"May twelfth, the day of the great battle. My division was assigned to go in on the left flank of a place called the Angle. At this point, the salient known as the Mule Shoe began to curve toward the main rebel line. It turned out to be the key to the Confederate defense. It rained most of the previous night, and the ground seemed bottomless. Shortly after four in the morning, the main attack began on the outer curve of the Mule Shoe. Just as when Upton had attacked two days earlier, we forced a breakthrough. Then the Rebs counterattacked and pushed our men back into the trenches, then over the rim. Throughout the early morning Meade kept feeding in new units. My regiment advanced about nine. We slid down the back side of the main battle line and kept working down toward the Angle. Then we tried to go in. I swear it was a hailstorm of lead. They were shooting at us from the front, side, and back. It seemed the only safe place was in their trenches. We forced our way to the breastworks just as a new Reb unit jumped into the pits. Behind us was the remainder of our brigade. We had no place to go.

"It turned into a frenzy of yelling, clubbing, stabbing, and shooting. There must have been five thousand men crammed into a two hundred-yard line. The mud was so slick we couldn't climb over the outer bank of the breastworks, and they couldn't climb out of their pits to get at us. The only option was for the men at the front of the line to kill each other to make room for those trying to come up. Anyone who made it to the top of the breastworks was certain to die, but that didn't stop men from trying. Men lost perception of their mortality.

"I found myself a place where the earth had washed away from the logs and I settled in, just like a private. I carved a hole about a foot long and four or five inches high. I found myself a broken rifle with a bayonet and every time a gray uniform came within reach I stabbed it. It was like trying to jab rabbits in a hole. I must have stuck six or more. After a while, I couldn't see anything but motionless uniforms. The bodies piled up so high they covered the hole."

"How can men endure such a struggle?" I asked.

"Crazy," he muttered. "Everyone went crazy. Life had no meaning in that place. Normal human fears and problems disappeared. Nothing else explains it." His fingers clenched the arms of the chair. His breathing grew louder and the breaths came with more urgency. I became worried, as his agitation increased, that he might have a heart attack. He must have recognized his internal turmoil, for he waited more than a minute before he continued.

"Dead men fell on me," he continued. "I shoved them away without even looking, as though they were an annoyance. All I thought about was sticking those Rebs through the hole. One time, after both sides had been thinned out a bit, a short lull settled in before new units arrived. I saw a young lieutenant load his pistol and then stand there with one knee bent, his arms relaxed, the pistol hanging in his limp hand. It just seemed as if he was waiting for someone, or trying to decide what to do next. Shortly, as if bored, he calmly withdrew a pipe from his pocket and stuffed it with tobacco from a pouch. He lit it, sat down on a rock, and started talking to a man lying on his back with a large hole in his side. He let the wounded man have a few puffs and they talked as if they were discussing the price of corn. After a while, the wounded man died and the pipe fell from his mouth into the mud. The lieutenant picked it up, wiped the mud from the stem, then stuck it in his own mouth as if nothing had happened. A minute or two later he tapped out the tobacco in his hand, rose slowly, and scraped the mud from his shoes before walking casually back into the fight. I watched it all in detached disbelief. Then I realized that what he'd done made more sense than what I'd been doing.

"I recognized him thirty years later at a division reunion. I tried to pull him into a conversation, to discuss what I'd observed, but he didn't remember a thing. It was the mind-numbing fatigue, I guess. We grew so tired we were stupid. The mind seems unable to accept such horror. After a while it just piles up, and we have to reject it."

My hands were still stiff from the cold as I wrote frantically, trying to record the minister's thoughts. I noticed the same thing with most of these old men. One look at them and it was rational to expect them to draw their last breath during the conversation. Then get them to talk about the war, and everything changes. The words flow and the color returns to their formerly pale skin. An excitement still rages down there someplace deep inside.

"I knew this one young officer, another lieutenant," he continued. "Not a day over nineteen as I remember. His men loved him. I watched him move along the trenchline; then he came back. His platoon followed his every move. I sensed his growing frustration as he tried to find a way to get at the Rebs. Twice he tried to work his way into the line and was shoved back. After a while, he put his hands on his hips, as if in disgust; then he tramped off to some open ground. His platoon, down to about ten men, followed him as usual. They all found a small patch of high ground where the rain had drained away, leaving the ground fairly dry. The men gathered around in a small circle, some sitting with legs crossed, some lying on their sides with their heads held up in an upturned hand. They ate crackers and jerky and talked as if it were their lunch break. They weren't more than a hundred yards from the bloodiest battle of the war.

"When they finished eating, the lieutenant lined them up and conducted an inspection. They looked like pigs with the mud and all, but the lieutenant tucked a collar here and brushed off the mud from a button there. They joked and bumped each other, as kids do. None was as old as the lieutenant. After examining each man's appearance, he nodded and talked with him, occasionally placing a hand on a shoulder in the process. When he'd finished, he stepped back and saluted, and each returned the salute. He pointed back toward the trenches and then started walking back toward the battle. I remembered thinking that it was as if they were on maneuvers back in Ohio and the men had not performed exactly as he'd wished, so he led them aside to instruct them on the finer points of survival.

"As they approached the line, a Minié hit the lieutenant just above the bridge of his nose. He died instantly. Without saying a word to each other, his men gathered around and said a short prayer. Then they began to dig a shallow grave. When they were finished, they gently lowered him into the ground and covered him up. Then they stood and saluted. One of the men, a Sergeant Garth, lined them up again and followed the same process as the lieutenant. When he finished, they all marched back into the line.

"A year earlier, at Chancellorsville when they were just out of training, I'd seen a cannon shell explode more'n thirty yards from those same men. They broke and ran. Now, without any thought for their own safety, they were following their sergeant into Armageddon. That's how the war and the men fighting it had changed: nowhere on earth were there ten tougher, more fearless fighting men. I wouldn't have given it a second thought if I'd been ordered to lead them to conquer Hell—but, of course, I'd done that earlier in the day without knowing it."

Never before, with all the veterans I had talked to, had a man remembered his experiences with such feeling. I felt as if I knew those men, felt their pain and emotional suffering. I sensed I was looking into the soul of a man who had died a little with each of his men who had fallen in battle. That night, I resented what Grant had put him through, but the resentment passed. If not this man, someone else would have had to take his place—quite possibly many more.

War is simply not reconcilable through rational analysis or won by the application of sympathy. Others, long before, had rejected the decisions that would have prevented the suffering. Did I think more of McClellan because he avoided battle to protect his men? No. He only assured the indefinite continuation of the killing; he passed on the responsibility to others. At least Grant did all within his power to end the war once others had decided that winning exceeded all other considerations. All that Jefferson Davis ever had to do was order the men to stack their arms. The same, of course, was true of Lincoln.

"My mouth is dry," the old minister said. "Would you be so kind as to get me a drink? There's a pitcher over by the window."

I rose and walked to the basin. "There's no glass, Reverend."

"Look in the chest to your right."

I poured the icy water and handed it to him. He drank it all and placed the glass on the table next to his chair.

"In time," he continued, "when enough bodies had been trampled into the mud, the ground began to firm up. A few men would work over the rim of the works and a terrible ruckus would follow. Then the Rebs would throw the dead and wounded over the top and things would settle down for a few minutes.

"I remember this Reb yelling on the other side. 'You stay out of this trench, Yank, and I won't shoot you.' He yelled it several times. Finally, one of our men jumped on the rim and shot him. 'Shut up that damned yelling!' the man shouted into the trench. 'Can't a man have no peace?' The rebels shot him half a dozen times before he flopped to the ground.

"I remember that so well because of what followed. A new swarm of Rebs entered the trenches just after. I suppose they didn't really understand what'd been happening. In their eagerness, they jumped on top of the breastworks and came at us. They were led by a major. I instinctively screamed, 'Get down, you fool!' The major turned to the sound of my voice and froze. It was Sam, my twin. He just had time to smile before a bayonet entered his chest. He crumpled up and the man holding the rifle stuck the butt in the ground for leverage and pitched Sam over his head. He lit about six feet from me, the broken bayonet still sticking in him. I crawled to him. 'Sam, you damned idiot,' I said as I pulled him to me, 'why didn't you keep your fool head down?' He never spoke. He placed a bloody hand on my shoulder and died."

A chill flowed down my spine. I started to reach out, but held back.

"Half a dozen of my men gathered around us," he continued quickly— I suspected he wanted to avoid dwelling on the pain—"spread out there on the muddy ground. They had to see we looked just alike. Bullets were flying all around, men were screaming, and the world seemed to be coming apart at the seams. They just knelt there, looking down as if he'd fallen from a horse while out for a morning ride. I cursed my father. I cursed the South. None of it did any good." The avoidance of the pain had only been delayed. He sobbed, and I handed him a handkerchief. "God, how I hate war," he said as he wiped his eyes and cried inconsolably.

For a long time we sat in silence. Now I knew why the others had directed me to this man. What were the chances, with a million men in the two armies, of those brothers being at the same place at the same time? In time, the reverend regained his composure.

"How long did it go on?" I asked softly.

"All day and into the night. Off in the distance, the Rebs were digging new works, trying to straighten out their trenchline. There were so many bullets flying around that many of them got shot. They had a tough time. I kept hoping they'd get done." He leaned to his left and opened a cigar box resting on the table next to his chair. He reached in and pulled out a large chunk of soft, gray metal and handed it to me. "What do you see?" he asked.

I examined the object in the dim light. "It looks like two Miniés fused together at their points," I replied.

"That's what it is. They hit head-on and welded together. They fell in my lap while I was poking with my knife. Back to my right, the way we came in, there stood a large oak that I crouched behind for a moment when we were working our way up to the Bloody Angle. When we pulled out about midnight, I noticed the tree lying on the ground. Bullets had chopped it down. It looked as if a pack of beavers had worked on it for a month."

I remembered that tree, or one like it, from my visit to the Smithsonian. I handed him the two bullets. With shaking hand, he placed the metal lump back in the box and shut the lid.

"A long time after dark," he continued, "the Rebs finished their new trench and pulled back. We let them go and were glad for it. I pulled together what remained of my regiment and we slogged back across the field, carrying our wounded. Twenty years passed before I had a good night's sleep without dreaming about that place."

"Did you ever go back?" I asked.

"Never," he said emphatically, "and I don't want to. I knew I'd glimpsed Hell that day. I wanted to guide everyone I could from such an experience. That's why I became a preacher. I don't know that I've done any good, but I've tried."

In the end, it always came back to what Reverend Smith said. I later talked with more than a dozen men who fought at the Bloody Angle. After one scraped away all the superlatives, a basic truth remained: every man devised his own way of dealing with the experience. Nothing more was possible. Some wiped it from their minds. Others, such as Reverend Smith, gave way to the profound change in their lives caused by the experience. To all of them, it was Hell. It was Grant's war at the extreme. Left unrestrained, war evolves in just one direction. Eventually, it becomes madness. It grinds and chews up anyone who gets in the way. Ultimately, the suffering is so great that the living envy the dead. That seemed to be necessary before men began to consider the urgency of bringing it to an end.

17 The Subtle Trap

The men learned much about war as they shot and hacked at each other. New measures and countermeasures emerged as a result of each encounter. Trenches were fine, even essential now, as the men were unwilling to expose themselves for more than brief periods. But Upton had demonstrated that courageous men who had it within them to brave a volley or two of concentrated fire could successfully storm the worst Lee had to offer. Lee needed something more; he needed something to restrain the progress of dedicated men, to make the cost of assault too expensive. So the war began taking another slow turn. Lee found the answer by the time he reached the North Anna River.

By nature, Lee preferred the offensive. All through the war his pattern had been to move his army to the weakest point of the Union line. Places such as the Wilderness, where men could move in secret and crash down with surprise flanking attacks, were his favorite battle sites. Now that had become impossible. The shortage of replacements for his casualties reduced his options. Besides, sweeping surprise attacks produced spectacular, long-term results only if the effort drove the enemy from the field. Grant himself posed a second problem: he was unwilling to break and run at the first sign of reversed fortunes. He seemed unwilling to run in any circumstance. Grant had time and again demonstrated a willingness to use—or even use up—his whole army. Sacrificing a portion of that army to draw Lee's divisions into battle bothered him not at all. Grant's message to Lincoln promising "to fight it out on this line if it takes all summer" would have come as no surprise to Lee.

Lee, however, had a third problem. He was running out of space.

Grant seemed determined to slug it out if the slightest chance of success existed. The mass attack on the Mule Shoe proved that. It had cost Lee more than four thousand men simply to buy time for digging new trenches to isolate the salient. But the last thing Grant wanted was a stalemate. As soon as Grant judged that future effort on a given front produced poor results, he moved his men in an effort to pull Lee out in the open. But Lee, with the advantage of interior lines, always moved faster.

At that point in the campaign Lee had three remaining options. He could retreat in measured moves in an effort to draw Grant into attacking his defenses. Failing that, he could withdraw to Richmond, where an army of slaves had constructed the strongest trench system ever. But that meant sacrificing maneuverability—that meant a siege he knew his army had little hope of surviving. Finally, he had the option of striking out across country and letting Grant have Richmond. If Lee made it into the open he might even regain the offensive. With Grant's men strung out and his supply line becoming more extended with each step south, Lee's numerical disadvantage would become less of a handicap. Grant's four thousand wagons needed protection. This left fewer men for assaults. Lee had learned the cost of straying too far from home base when he moved north toward Gettysburg. Meade had missed his opportunity to crush Lee's army against the north bank of the Potomac as Lee made his long retreat south. By now, Lee had no illusion that Grant would waste such an opportunity.

$$*   *   *$$

"Other winds were blowing," said a former senator from Maine. "Sixty-four was an election year in the North. Lincoln was under assault both from the Democrats and from within his own party. McClellan appeared to be a certain bet to be the Democrat's contender. No one dared predict how the soldiers might vote with McClellan as the challenger."

"True," I countered, "but McClellan had done poorly as a military commander. Why did the men have such faith in him?"

"That's what politics is all about, isn't it?" said the senator. "No one knew what the soldiers thought. Assessing the political situation was impossible. Everyone remembered McClellan's popularity back in '62. Had it eroded? No one knew. Although Lincoln viewed McClellan's foot-dragging as a problem, the average soldier felt McClellan's precautions kept him alive. Besides that, just carrying out a national election in the midst of a war presented prodigious problems. Then there were the numbers. Always in the back of Lincoln's mind were those growing casualty lists. By June, in a span of twenty-five days, Grant had lost fifty thousand men killed, wounded, or captured. In the process, he had moved less than thirty miles south. The loss of two thousand men a day simply could not be sustained, even with the immense resources of men and supplies available in the North. Put yourself in Lincoln's place. If McClellan mounted a strong political attack, and if Lincoln's own party split, well, Lincoln saw the possibility of the worst defeat of an incumbent president in the nation's history. In June, people were giving five to one odds against Lincoln's even being nominated. Many thought the prospect of him retaining his office was so farfetched as to be considered impossible.

"Grant couldn't operate in a political vacuum. His fortunes were linked to Lincoln. Even some of Grant's supporters in the Congress began to distance themselves from him. It had become an altogether unstable time on all fronts."

"Something altered Lincoln's fortunes," I said. "It's a matter of historical fact that the people reelected him."

"The important change came later, out in Georgia, and other changes soon followed. In truth, Lincoln's situation was so bad that any change would have worked to his advantage. Short of Lee destroying Grant's army, no one saw a way for conditions to worsen." The comment reminded me of what Grandfather had written following the first day at Shiloh. When conditions reach the bottom of the pit, something happens and everything changes. Nothing is static, least of all war. Men of destiny take fate by the throat and alter the odds. No one denied Lincoln was a man of destiny, and he had appointed similar men to implement his policies.

"So," I said, "in June of '64, the election was on the mind of everyone in the North."

"South, too. Peace with division of the country seemed a realistic possibility, if only the Southern politicians found the means to hang on until someone like McClellan assumed office. This meant Lee had to stand firm in the Richmond area. To the average citizen up North, the capture of Richmond would have been viewed as a major victory, a certain prelude to ending the war. If the war moved south, the focus of the conflict would have drifted out of sight. Lee had to keep those casualty reports flowing north. The Confederacy's best hopes lay in McClellan's winning the Democratic nomination and for a war-weakened contender to run against him. This, however, meant holding on until August. If conditions continued as during the first fifteen days of the May campaign, Lee faced the very real prospect of having no army at all by August. So Lee again retreated a short distance and set up his defenses on the south bank of the North Anna River, just north of Hanover Junction on the Richmond, Fredericksburg & Petersburg Railroad."

As if it were a dagger aimed at the heart of the South, the railroad, with its fateful list of names, pointed the way.

*   *   *

On May 20, after the fight at the Bloody Angle, Grant broke contact with Lee's army and again began to swing around the Confederate right flank.

"But Lee countered with what must've been the most brilliant defensive maneuver of the war," Brig. Gen. Clarence Fordham told me. "Only at the last minute did Grant see the trap."

I met General Fordham at an "old soldiers' home" in upstate New York. As with so many of the West Point cadets who graduated just before the war, he had advanced quickly. He controlled the fate of thousands before reaching the age of twenty-five. After the war, he reverted from brevet brigadier general to his permanent rank of captain. He stayed in the army anyway and retired as a brigadier general in 1900 following a brief stint as a staff planner for the Spanish-American War. I caught up with him as he strolled on the home's spacious green grounds.

"Why was it a trap?" I asked as we settled on a hard cement bench. "There really wasn't much fighting at the North Anna River, at least in comparison to other battles."

"Have you ever studied a map of that area?" he asked.

I confessed I had not. There were so many battles. The fighting in this campaign seemed never to end, so the battles blended together in my mind.

He picked up a long stick. "Come with me over to the horseshoe pit," he directed. "I'll draw you a map." His broad, self-confident stride reminded me of a general. He leveled the sand with his slipper. "The North Anna runs from the northeast to the southwest," he said. "Northeast of Hanover Junction, the river angles back toward the southeast. The result is a tilted, L-shaped bend." He used the stick to draw the river line in the sand as I wrote notes. "Lee placed his army's main force about a half mile northwest of the river bend at Ox Ford, the only immediate means of crossing the river without a bridge. One line of trenches stretched parallel to the river, then extended another two miles onto the open ground to the southwest. His other line stretched to the northwest and anchored on the Little River, about two miles away."

As I studied the design, I began to understand the brilliance of the plan.

"Grant placed his V and VI Corps south and west of the river facing one line of Lee's trenches. The IX Corps camped in the crook of the river. He placed the II Corps south of the river at the point where it made the bend to the southeast." He leaned back and studied the layout. "Tell me, what do you see?"

"For one thing," I said, "Lee has his army concentrated and Grant's is separated into three parts."

"Exactly," he said, slapping his leg and laughing. "Have you ever seen anything like it? It's enough to make an old military man cry with joy. No one I ever talked to believes that happened by accident. Lee placed himself in a position to make maximum use of his smaller numbers by having the flexibility to move his men to the point of greatest danger. For Grant to reinforce any part of his line, he had to move his men across the river at least once—maybe twice. Just as important, Lee had a clear view of Grant's movement. If Grant moved men around the outer rim of the arc, Lee needed only to move with him along a shorter, interior route."

The design foretold a disaster in the making. But I knew that no such disaster occurred. "What happened?" I asked.

"Well, being the old warhorse he was, Grant decided to test Lee's defenses—but only sparingly. Some minor skirmishes erupted during the next couple of days, but nothing much came of these. The Union lost about two hundred dead and fifteen hundred wounded in all of these, a paltry sum for this stage of the war. Lee had an opportunity to smash Hancock's corps during a retrograde movement by our troops, but he failed to attack. We later learned that Lee had become sick with some form of stomachache."

"So that's why no battle developed?"

"I don't know. Grant later claimed that he'd invited Lee to attack.

He said he was willing to sacrifice Hancock's corps so he could bring the army's wings together to crush Lee in between. After all that I'd seen up to then, he might've been willing to lose twenty thousand men if it meant bringing the war to an end right there."

I had no doubt that he would have done that, and counted himself fortunate in the process.

"I need to mention one condition that had changed," he concluded. "Before, Lee's trenches had always been strong, but successful assaults seemed a possibility. This time, the Rebs put all sorts of obstacles in front of their line. I saw row after row of sharp, pointed stakes stuck in the ground and pointed outward. In addition, trees had been cut down and laid end to end along the full length of the trenchline. The branches were tied together with leaves stripped off to provide clear fields of fire. A man would've had a long, uncomfortable struggle busting through those barricades to get at the trenches. Lee evidently had learned something at the Mule Shoe. He'd found a way to make it impossible to charge across open ground to attack those trenches." He smiled. "Grant can say what he wants about setting his own trap for Lee. I think Lee had moved a step ahead of Grant in more ways than one. I think Grant would've felt the worst of it before Lee's army gave up. Nobody I knew looked forward to a struggle that promised to make the Bloody Angle seem like child's play."

There are moves and countermoves in the chesslike game called war, but neither side established a clear advantage. Upton, with his new tactical vision of war, had forced it to take a more brutal—if daring— turn. Lee had wasted no time responding to the challenge. Seldom did Lee make mistakes; never did he make the same mistake twice.

The armies sparred for a couple of days before Grant concluded that another stalemate had developed. During the night of May 26 it began to rain. Shortly, the rain turned into a violent thunderstorm. By this time, the campaign had turned into a process of "shovel, shoot, and march," and the men had grown tired of it. All along the way bodies had piled up like the cordwood Grant had cut for a living during his "down days." Now, with summer approaching, the smell of rotting flesh hung low to the ground and drifted into the trenches. As one man commented: "Any man that'll take more'n one sniff of that's a hog." The next stop would offer plenty to foul a man's nostrils.

As the thunderstorm cracked overhead, the Union Army headed south—moving ever closer to Richmond. There remained one more stop along the way before the army reached the destination Grant had hoped to avoid. Just ahead loomed a hot, dry little hamlet bearing an unlikely name—Cold Harbor.

18 Cold Harbor

Time was running out for both Lee and Grant. When Grant began his spring campaign, he had hoped to run Lee to ground far in advance of Richmond. He said as much in his message to Lincoln a few days into the campaign. Lee, on the other hand, had grown accustomed to fainthearted Union generals. Although Longstreet said that Grant would never let go once the two armies clashed, Lee needed convincing. He tried everything within his power to sap Grant's aggressiveness. By the time the fighting at Spotsylvania concluded, Grant's casualties totaled thirty-six thousand soldiers killed, wounded, or captured. Lee had lost just short of twenty-three thousand—not quite two for every three of Grant's losses. The tally sheet had shifted only a little askew of Grant's prediction. This disparity provided little reason for optimism by Lee other than that his army remained alive, and every day worked to his political advantage. In the North, evidence grew daily more obvious of the people's impatience with a war that seemed to go on forever.

Still, Grant just fed more new recruits into the line and kept pushing south. Lee had one more opportunity before the barricades around Richmond came into view and the two armies would settle into a siege. The prospect of a siege was abhorrent to both Lee and Grant. Lee knew he lacked the strength to break out once Grant moved his larger army in place; Grant realized more each day that he lacked the strength to break through Lee's defenses. This would leave no choice other than to starve Lee into submission once he dug in around Richmond.

As I first moved about this barren place, I asked myself the question many of the soldiers who fought here must have asked: how did this desolate site acquire the name Cold Harbor? There is no harbor for miles, and in June the weather is sultry and oppressively hot—as was true in June of 1864. I have since learned that the name Cold Harbor belonged to an inn that provided a place to sleep but offered no fire or food. Grant, however, had another service in mind. Three roads met at this dreary village, and Grant wanted those roads. Lee had no particular need for the roads other than denying them to Grant. Those reasons were sufficient to bring the storm clouds of war rumbling south.

"Nothing could have been more different from the Wilderness than was Cold Harbor," Cpl. Gideon Arnold told me. Arnold rode with Sheridan during this period and saw godlike qualities in his general. "From the Rapidan south, all we saw were trees. It took five minutes for a cocker spaniel to find a place to relieve himself at this desolate place."

I laid my pen on my pad and smiled.

"Well, almost," he said, realizing I had caught him in an exaggeration. "But whatever Cold Harbor wasn't, it was cavalry country. Most of us had the new Henry repeating carbines. We were more'n a match for the rebel cavalry, and only if the infantry held its distance did it stand a chance. A clear field of fire gave us the advantage.

"We had the firepower," he said, "to rip the stuffin' out of any line of battle advancing across open ground. We required nothing more than a general with the will to use our power. If ever that general existed, it was Sheridan. Sheridan changed the use of cavalry," he said with pride, "and in doing so, he changed the war. We now saw ourselves as soldiers, not just scouts and outriders for the wagons."

"Did you arrive at Cold Harbor before the Confederates?" I asked.

"Just missed beatin' their cavalry there," he said with a disgusted tone, "but it was enough. They were already diggin' in when we rode up. We dismounted and charged toward them. Control of the crossroads meant we could, if it came to that, beat Lee to Richmond. We had the roads in short order, but keepin' them without infantry support might prove more difficult. We expected our infantry to relieve us soon. We never expected to have to hold the place." He laughed.

"What is it?" I asked.

"I was just rememberin'. I never saw anythin' like it. Sheridan was everywhere. I saw this new recruit talkin' to himself behind his mound of dirt and pointin' his weapon in the air and firin' at the clouds. Sheridan rode up, jabbed him in the back with his flagstaff, and yelled: 'Shoot at the Rebs, trooper, not in the air. Duck season is six months away.' That private's eyes turned as round and large as saucers. With bullets flyin' all around, he jumped to attention in plain sight of the whole Reb army. 'Yes, sir, General,' he yelled in a high, squeaky voice. 'Shoot low, that's what you said, General. I'll do it, sir.' At that moment, a bullet lifted his cap from his head. He looked menacin'ly over his shoulder. With eyes squinted and lips tight over his clenched teeth—still at attention—he turned back toward Sheridan. 'I think I see what you mean, General. Is that all?' Sheridan laughed so hard he nearly fell off his horse. 'That's all, trooper,' he said, pointin' across the field, 'now shoot me a Reb.'

"Men were more afraid of Sheridan than the enemy, but they respected him more than feared him. The man led a charmed life. All afternoon, he rode that horse in plain sight of the Rebs without so much as a scratch. I saw a man buryin' his head in the dirt for nearly an hour trying to get up the courage to look up an' shoot. Finally, he stuck his head about six inches above a rock an' a bullet drilled him clean between the eyes. I reflected on that luckless soldier an' that wiry little general trottin' about on his horse out in the open. I decided that when a man's time is up there ain't nothing he can do to stop it from happenin'. I always told the men in my squad, 'Do your duty an' trust to God.' It usually worked out. You get fatalistic after a while.

"Anyway, Wright's men finally came up. They were so tired they collapsed in sleep behind the works we'd dug. Later, about sundown, Smith's division that'd been detached from Butler marched into sight. Wright's men got orders to move. This one soldier tugged at his friend and said: 'Jim, there's a pile of troops comin'. I guess there's goin' to be a fight.' Jim rolled over in reply: 'I don't care a damn. I wish they'd shoot us an' be done with it. I'd rather be shot than marched to death.' Jim's friend was correct. The battle uncorked about ten minutes later."

To the degree that the spectacular grandeur of the field around Chattanooga is compelling, Cold Harbor is repelling. Not one soldier I ever talked to about this battle ever expressed a desire to return. Even with all the time that has passed, the place still has the smell of death. As I studied the terrain I sensed the frustration Grant must have felt. Time after time he had tried to fight Lee out in the open. Failing that, he had tried to maneuver segments of Lee's men out of their trenches to destroy his army a piece at a time. Nothing worked. The struggle had degenerated into a footrace across northern Virginia. All that had resulted were nearly sixty thousand casualties on both sides and some long, dusty marches. By now, Grant's judgment was becoming strained.

*   *   *

Old James "Ripsnorter" Devin had a vivid memory of what happened next.

"How did you get the name Ripsnorter?" I asked.

"Earned it," he replied with a gruff, defiant voice.

"But how?"

"I served in Rickett's division in Wright's corps. All I kept thinkin' about was what happened to us at the Wilderness. Longstreet's men flanked us, an' we ran like the devil was a-clingin' to our tails. Men in the other divisions wanted nothin' to do with us after that, so we had somethin' to prove. I'd just been promoted to major and was an assistant regimental commander. The Rebs were up this hill, and we received orders to go dig 'em out. More than two divisions moved up that slope. They hadn't been there long, so their works were weak, but they'd placed those infernal trees chopped from a small wood on the hill in front of their works all tangled and runnin' together. When we reached the trees we found it impossible to break through without rippin' into 'em by hand and pulling 'em apart. That's a difficult job with five thousand muskets firin' at you. But I'd made up my mind to get through or die right there. I threatened to shoot a couple of men who broke, an' when they returned the others stayed. I kept hollerin', 'Rip an' snort, men, pull these trees apart.' We ripped an' snorted at those trees 'til we nearly fell down stupid with fatigue, but we broke through an' made it into their works. We were the only ones who did. After that, they always called me—behind my back of course—'Rip-an-snort' Devin. After a while, everybody just shortened it to Ripsnorter.

"It bothered me at first," he said, a faint smile betraying his softness, "but in time I got used to it. After that, it just stuck."

As a direct result of his efforts that day, Devin lost a hand to a surgeon's knife—but not until later. "A jagged limb ripped open my hand," he said, "and blood poisonin' set in." It did not, however, keep him out of the fighting. He stayed in a field hospital near Richmond, returning to full duty before Thanksgiving. By then, as a direct result of his efforts on June 1 before Cold Harbor, he had been awarded the Medal of Honor and mentioned twice in dispatches.

*   *   *

ULYSSES GRANT TO GEORGE MEADE—2 P.M., JUNE 2
    IN VIEW OF THE WANT OF PREPARATION FOR AN ATTACK
THIS EVENING, AND THE HEAT AND WANT OF ENERGY AMONG
THE MEN FROM MOVING DURING THE NIGHT LAST NIGHT, I
THINK IT ADVISABLE TO POSTPONE ASSAULT UNTIL EARLY
TOMORROW MORNING.

Grant sent this message shortly before the planned attack on the
Confederate defenses at Cold Harbor. Thirty minutes after receiving
this order, Meade sent instructions to all his corps commanders to postpone
the planned assault on the Confederate trenches until 4:30 the next
morning, June 3. The delay proved more critical than anyone considered—it gave Lee another twelve hours to prepare his defenses. Meade's
adjutant, perhaps pondering in hindsight the result of the delay, later
recorded that "it is a rule that, when the rebels halt, the first day gives
them a good rifle-pit; the second, a regular infantry parapet with artillery in position; and the third a parapet with an abatis in front and
entrenched batteries behind. Sometimes they put this three days' work
into the first twenty-four hours." The morning of June 3, 1864, marked
the third day since hostilities commenced at Cold Harbor.

Despite the formidable line of trenches, Grant had determined to
make one more attempt to break the Confederate line in an effort to
rout the Confederate Army. The men on the line had seen enough of
Lee's work to know what this meant. Upon hearing of the attack's delay,
a young lieutenant turned to his company commander and said: "Captain,
I'm induced to think that one or both of us will go up tomorrow morning.
If anything happens to me, I want you to take care of me, and if you're
hurt and I'm not, I'll take care of you."

The captain nodded. "Yes, Jim, I'll see to that. If you're hurt, I'll
look out for you—if I'm still alive."

That night it began to rain.

*   *   *

I had been waiting for more than an hour hoping to get Capt. Johnnie
Oats to talk about his experience at Cold Harbor. Because of Oats's
poor health, the hospital's chief administrator had been reluctant to
approve my written request for a visit. Finally, on April 2, I received

a letter granting me permission to conduct my interview at 2:00 P.M. on April 9. "Your visit most likely will be unproductive," the notice advised. The short notice required juggling of my schedule, but this opportunity was too important to let pass. Now, after waiting an hour, I too was unsure that anything would result. None of the dozen or so questions I had posed stimulated any response. I checked my watch. I had only an hour before all visitors had to leave the grounds.

I sat reading the paper when, out of the corner of my eye, I detected a movement. I shifted my weight and turned toward Captain Oats.

"I served in Gen. Baldy Smith's corps," Captain Oats said without prelude. "We all knew what lay ahead. As far as we could determine, no one had even bothered to scout the rebel lines to see what we faced. Along most of the line, their trenches were out of normal line of sight behind ridges or hidden by small groves of trees." I detected no sign of emotion in his speech. The words flowed in evenly spaced, monotone syllables, as I remembered young grammar school students reading from primers seen for the first time. I struggled to maintain my concentration.

"In some places further south," he said, "there were gullies or swamps that presented nobody knew what kind of obstacles. Our orders were to move straight ahead until we made contact with the enemy; then we were to charge their breastworks. No one had slept. We had moved into a dozen battles before. Always there was fear, but it was at least masked by joking and laughter. Not this night. Seldom did the men miss the opportunity to sleep—we had gotten so little of it in the last month. There was something in the air here, but no one even tried to explain it. The men were so quiet you could hear the crackling of the fires fifty yards away. I sensed among those men a resignation to death."

As he talked, he looked straight ahead. Even when I attempted to maneuver into his line of sight, he turned away. "If it seemed so impossible," I asked, "why did Grant order the attack?"

He had an even more distant look as he pondered my question. Even more than fifty years later, the awe of the event still gripped his mind. "I don't know," Oats replied. "There just seemed to be no place in Grant's thinking for impossibilities. But Cold Harbor taught him the meaning of the word."

"Will you describe what happened?"

A wild look appeared in his eyes and the words poured out in a torrent.

*   *   *

The men of the Massachusetts regiment moved out at 4:40 in the morning, just as the first light of dawn touched the horizon. "Keep ranks closed," yelled the colonel. "Dress center, forward, march." All along the line the men of three corps moved as one. Forty thousand men were on the move along a front five miles long. It seemed as if nothing on the planet could resist such a massive assault.

"Colonel, those men are standing three deep in those trenches," Captain Oats yelled as he pointed across the field. "It'll be as bad as Fredericksburg."

The colonel shaded his eyes from the low-hanging sun as he looked across the open field two hundred yards wide and twice as deep. "It does seem like they're ready for us, doesn't it, Johnnie?"

My thoughts flashed back to the regimental record I had reviewed. One was for Oats's regiment. I had studied it carefully, even shuddered when I read the casualty count. So few remained after Cold Harbor that Meade had disbanded the regiment and assigned the survivors to other, less depleted units. The colonel had known Captain Oats since both were in grammar school, although the colonel was three years older. Most of the men in the regiment were friends, had been for most of their lives, or at least knew each other. Not even a handful were from outside a single county. There were ten sets of brothers in the regiment, three of them in Oats's company. All three of Oats's brothers had been company commanders. Only Johnnie and his kid brother, Jason, made it as far as Cold Harbor. Jason was one of those pushed into a mass grave following the battle. Later, shortly after the war ended, the government exhumed his remains—or at least the remains of someone with captain's bars on a rotting Union uniform—and sent them to Massachusetts to be buried with full military honors.

"Keep those ranks closed, men," the colonel shouted. "When we start the charge, don't stop to shoot. Don't stop for anything until we reach those trenches." The waving mass of blue snaked in vibrating, undulating lines across the green field still damp from the rain. The scattered outposts of Confederate pickets fired a couple of rounds. A few blue patches—nothing to be concerned about, there were so many available to take their place—crumpled into the grass. "Close those ranks, men," the colonel shouted again. The pickets faded back toward their own lines.

At two hundred yards, the colonel yelled, "Forward at the double time!" The men broke into a trot. At one hundred and fifty yards, he yelled again as he waved his saber: "Charge! Let's take those works." All along the front, yelling men surged forward at the command of a hundred colonels and brigadiers. Success seemed assured. An end to the war, here and now, seemed possible. Just over a hundred yards to go, then a short, sharp battle, and everyone could go home.

"Load canister!" yelled a Confederate officer on the distant edge of the field. "Fire at one hundred yards."

On the blue lines advanced, more holes appearing in their lines as they rushed forward.

"Fire!" screamed a Confederate commander. The rebel muskets exploded like a thunderclap, sending a hailstorm of lead ripping across the field, tearing gaping holes in the exposed blue lines. "Second rank, fire!" More holes appeared.

"Colonel, we'll never make it!" screamed Captain Oats above the tumult. "Their massed fire will break our back."

Following orders was all that remained. "I know, Johnnie, but we must try. We must try." A bullet bore through the colonel's neck. He fell like a rock, his spine severed. He never moved.

"Keep going, men," screamed a major; then he too fell dead with a bullet through the heart. Still, the men struggled forward.

*   *   *

"Their cannon opened up at about a hundred yards," Oats said, his voice cracking with the first sign of emotion. His speech grew even more rapid. "A complete line of men sank to the ground. I thought I'd missed an order to get down, so I dove into a small hole. All around me, men disappeared into the grass. A minute or two passed before I realized none of them were getting up. I looked around; then I realized they all were dead or wounded. A battery of cannon loaded with canister, followed immediately by a thousand musket blasts, had slammed into our ranks. With no less impact than a giant scythe, the steel and lead simply sliced them all down. A whole regiment simply disappeared.

Bits and pieces of flesh were everywhere—heads, arms, legs, bodies without any limbs at all. It was unbelievably horrible. By this time, the ranks behind us were passing over where I lay clinging to the grass. Something inside said 'get up' and I went on, even though my company had all been knocked down. As we moved closer, I saw the Rebs swing those cannon around and aim them right at me. I hit the ground again just as they fired.

"The bodies literally exploded as the shrapnel hit. Flesh, bone, bits of cloth, and chunks of rifles flew into the air; then it all rained down in a bloody deluge. A man who had been advancing right next to me simply exploded as pellets from the canister hit him full in the chest. It sounded like a rock hitting a ripe pumpkin. Three men immediately behind him went down in the withering blast. The sight and sound of it numbed me for a minute; then I began to heave. I was afraid to get up, but more afraid to stay put. If those guns kept firing, it would be only a matter of time before some of that steel got me. By then, one man more or less made no difference at all. Those who hadn't already died or been wounded were clinging to the earth or running back to our lines. The running ones seemed to attract the most attention, so I started to crawl."

His rigid posture began to slacken just a little as small beads of sweat appeared on the surface of his forehead. He crossed his legs, then uncrossed them, then crossed them again. I sensed that, from somewhere deep in his brain, a signal warned him to run, but somehow the message became garbled on the way to his legs.

"As a boy, I'd worked in a slaughterhouse in Boston," he continued. "Nothing I saw there equaled what I crawled through on the way back. I never thought it possible to slice up a man as badly as some I saw who were still alive. One man had an inch gap separating the right side of his skull from the left. He thrashed and kicked as foam gurgled in his throat before it rolled out of his mouth. One eye had been completely shot away; the eyeball in the other had rolled somewhere back in the socket. I opened my jackknife and cut his throat as I crawled by.

"After crawling about two hundred yards, I sucked in my breath and started to run. That was a lonely trek back to our lines. Out of more than a thousand men, I guess not a quarter came back whole. All morning long men kept crawling through the grass back toward our lines. Most of these were wounded in one place or another, and all felt lucky to be alive. More than a third never returned. For the better part of two days I heard men out beyond our lines begging for help before they died of thirst or life drained from their broken bodies."

I waited a minute or so, but he had finished. "Was it as bad all along the battle line?" I asked.

"From what I heard, it was bad enough, but we had it the worst. The field was so wide and open the cannon simply couldn't miss hitting someone with every chunk of steel that spewed out." He hesitated for a moment. "It's impossible to explain it," he continued. "It's something that a person must experience. By the time a blast of double canister travels sixty yards there's a steel curtain across a ten-yard front. It's almost impossible to move through that and not get hit someplace. The army lost over seven thousand men that day in a span of twenty minutes. I didn't participate at the Bloody Angle, but they fought all day and into the night before they lost that many. At least there a man had a chance. I don't think anyone in my whole regiment got off a shot. We were ordered not to fire until we reached the trenches. The closest I saw any man get to the enemy line was twenty yards, and he never came back. For all I know, we never fired a shot."

A couple of minutes passed before my hand caught up with the end of the story I had recorded in my mind. In the urgency to capture his words, I failed to notice that his mind had begun to drift away. I sighed when I turned and looked at his pale, impassive profile. His lips quivered slightly; then the most amazing thing happened.

"Johnnie will come marching home again, hurrah, hurrah," he sang.

I sat amazed at the angelic quality of this old man's alto voice. It was so different, I thought, from the mechanical tone of his speech. The melodic tone rang like a fine bell on a crisp night where not a breath of wind was blowing. Even in the long, narrow hall, the sound had a resonance equal to that sung in the most imposing of concert halls. All activity ceased as everyone turned toward the sound.

"Johnnie will come marching home again, hurrah, hurrah."

He sang the verse all the way through.

I looked on in admiration, and as the song concluded, Captain Oats's body grew rigid. Slowly, his right arm raised level with his shoulder, then his left. A vacant stare replaced the vibrant, strident image that had begun to emerge.

The sound of a woman's voice jolted me back to the present. "He was singing about himself, you know. His only remaining purpose in life is to put the war behind him, to have Johnnie make it home." The nurse gently touched his shoulder. She looked at him with pleading eyes, as if she, too, yearned for him to make it home. He offered no sign of awareness. "It's been several years since he sang that song," said the nurse. "Talking to you must have given him hope. In my ten years in this hospital, that's the longest period I've seen him sane. He goes days, sometimes weeks, without ever lowering his arms. They even stick straight up when he sleeps. It's odd they don't get tired, don't you think?" She seemed to be speaking softly to herself. "A crazy man does strange things, I suppose."

An unclinical remark for a nurse, I thought. I would have complained, but I knew she meant no disrespect. "How long has he been here?" I asked.

"I don't know for certain. At least forty years, I hear. No one remembers for certain anymore. He married and had a son after the war. One night he just sliced up his wife and child with a knife. He's resided here ever since, certified by a judge to be incurably insane. He snaps out of it now and again, as you saw, and is as sane as you and me. But it doesn't last long. He's a very old man now. Over eighty, I think. He nearly passed on three times that I remember, but he always pulls through. He's a tough old bird."

Part of him, I thought, only part of him. Another part of him is still back at Cold Harbor, living the horror of Grant's war. I wonder if anyone ever thought to count Captain Oats among the casualties produced by that thirty minutes in Hell? I doubted it. During all the war, he never shed a drop of blood. But wounds come in many forms.

I don't know how long I continued to sit next to Captain Oats, watching him, looking for some sign of life behind those cold, distant eyes. Nothing happened. He just sat rigidly, hardly even breathing. I had just finished gathering my papers in preparation for departure when a man in a white coat passed. I instinctively reached out and touched his garment. "Doctor," I said, "are you familiar with Captain Oats's case?"

"Captain Oats?" he asked, looking up from the clipboard in his hands. "Oh, yes I am. The captain and I are close friends."

"Do you have a minute?" I asked.

"What can I do for you?" he replied, still absorbed in the information on the chart he had been reading.

"Where do you think Captain Oats goes when he drifts into his trance?" I asked.

"One hundred and twelve miles northwest of here," he replied without hesitation.

"What?" I asked. The preciseness of his answer startled me.

He must have heard the skepticism in my voice. He looked up and smiled. "He goes home. Right now, he's probably lying under a tree on a hill in a small cemetery in upstate New York. He's visiting his wife and small son."

"How do you know that?"

He shrugged. "That's where he always goes."

"But he killed his wife and son. That's what the nurse told me."

"Oh, no. That's wrong. Captain Oats wouldn't hurt a fly, at least not the Captain Oats I've known for nearly thirty years."

"Then who killed them?"

"I'm not certain, but Captain Oats knows. You see, Captain Oats has another personality, one he developed after Cold Harbor. That's the part of him that killed his wife and child. At one time, we had five Cold Harbor veterans in this hospital. One was my father. All the others are dead now. My father served as surgeon in Wright's corps at the time. He collapsed after performing amputations for four straight days. He never was the same after that. These men simply couldn't adjust to the horror of that day." The doctor studied the catatonic man for several seconds. "Here, watch this." He kneeled and stretched out his arms. "Come here, Jimmy. Come to your Uncle Frank."

I wondered if I was dealing with the doctor or another patient. He wrapped his arms around an imaginary figure and pretended to lift him into the air.

"How're you today, Jimmy?" he asked, a broad grin exposing his teeth.

My attention shifted to Captain Oats. He, too, was smiling.

"He has a cold, Frank," said the captain. "Be careful you don't catch it." Oats turned to me and for the first time looked me in the eye. "That's my son, Jimmy. He just turned three. Looks like his mother, thank God." He laughed.

I had never witnessed anything like it. It seemed as if the man's mind had never moved past that time forty or more years before, when he had ripped the life from the people he loved.

"You run along and play," the doctor said. "I want to talk with your father." He turned to Captain Oats. "How are you today, Captain?"

"Good, Frank." He nodded to add assurance. "We plan to visit my brother in New Bedford next week. I'm looking forward to the trip."

"How long since you've seen him?" the doctor asked.

"Three years. I visited him in '71."

"Have a nice trip, Captain. I'll visit with you when you return."

The captain smiled; then all expression faded as his arms again rose to the horizontal.

"A man can endure only so much," the doctor said. "He thought all of his men had been killed in that attack. He felt overwhelming guilt for that, as well as for his own survival. The Captain Oats you just saw began to die on June 3 of '64. As near as I've been able to determine, that happened about a quarter after five in the morning. The man who crawled back from that battle was a different person, but it's all mixed up in his mind. He fought with his other personality for ten years before everything caved in on the morning of the tenth anniversary of the battle. The only way he knew to destroy his other self, the one that did the killing, was to bury himself in his own mind. His only link to sanity is his dead son."

"Is it possible to cure him?" I asked.

"I doubt it. Even if I knew how, I'd have no part in it. The report on what happened in '74 is an unpleasant document to read. He truly became a madman, in every sense of the word. There's no way to predict which Oats might emerge if he's cured. No. Captain Oats has made his peace. I'm willing to leave well enough alone." He bent forward and placed a hand on the old soldier's arm. "Have a nice trip, Captain." He moved on down the hall, again absorbed in the chart.

As the doctor walked away, a bell began to ring. Time to leave, I thought, and not a moment too soon. The place depressed me, almost as much as the veterans' hospital in South Dakota—but not quite.

What had the nurse said? Sane as you and me! How can we profess sanity when half a nation will do everything within its power to kill the other half? Sanity is nothing more than the state of mind of the majority that makes the rules.

I shivered as I pulled my collar to my neck. I stood for a moment looking at the skeletal growths where only a few drab leaves fluttered violently in the brisk, early spring wind. Why does life resist passing,

I asked myself, when all its beauty has vanished? Is that our strength, or is it our ultimate penalty for having been permitted to reside a brief moment on this earth? "God!" I said to myself, "I wish this war would end." It had, of course—ended I mean—more than a half century before, but it resisted letting frail but stubborn men forget its horror. The soldiers had climbed the pinnacle of war's terror on those fields surrounding Cold Harbor. The experience produced its own perverted sort of reward. Never again were the men willing to charge well-manned, reinforced trenches. Too many in the army had experienced the carnage of that day and the time before around the salient. And Grant never asked it of them, at least to the same degree. A man will move where he has a chance for survival, but where those trenches were concerned, the chance for surviving unhurt had nearly vanished.

If Lee's men were on the verge of defeat, as some papers reported at the time, few in the Union combat regiments saw signs of it. Lee, the awe-inspiring man in whom others, even his enemies, saw god-like qualities, had directed the conditions that rent from Captain Oats his sanity without so much as a scratch on his outer shell. Grant had sent the captain forward to get at Lee, if he could, to end the carnage with more carnage. The young captain had failed in his task. His sin was in surviving while having to leave his men behind on the field—some hurt, most of them dead. Confronted with unconquerable horrors, he had retreated in desperation to seek peace in a distant place beyond the general's reach. It must have been lonely there, which accounts for his unannounced and temporary retreats back to sanity. He obviously finds it equally unpleasant here with the rest of us, so he remains for only a short time. He drifts without rudder between two disagreeable worlds. There is no safe harbor where he can strike sail and find peace.

The young captain had been a pawn in a national chess game played with brutal, calculated efficiency for the highest of stakes. The king of the Southern side had knocked the captain off the board, pushed him out of the game, yet not a sign of his trauma was visible to the unsuspecting eye. The scars were inside, where only the maiming of his soul recorded the event. But for a few brief moments I had glimpsed the scars left by that cruel war. Then I realized: the scars were everywhere, just out of sight, deforming and twisting reality. My wife's wounds had healed only recently, and she had not even been born at the time of the war. Unfortunately for us all, the agony of the aftermath still festers like a grotesque, weeping abscess all through the South—where even the beginning of healing awaits new generations yet unborn.

As summer approached in 1864 the killing continued as before, but never again with the same ferocity or intensity. Grant later admitted that Cold Harbor was his single regret in that bloody campaign. Even a man who recognized the essential fact that only by killing would the killing ever end found the limit for what a nation, or a man, will endure.

As for the soldiers, they always found a way to tabulate events and record them in cold perspective, even at the moment of death. After each great battle there arrived a time for cleaning up the residue and putting it to rest. As the armies continued their movement south, burial squads finally attended the needs of the bloated dead. On one of these unfortunates, someone found a bloodstained diary. Somehow, before he died, the mortally wounded soldier had found the strength to make a closing entry: "June 3. Cold Harbor. I was killed."

For now, the war hung on like a blood-sucking leech, and all roads still led south. The next scene of the great drama lay just ahead: Petersburg, just south of Richmond.

19 One More Race to Lose

Since May 4 the armies had been locked together in an unceasing attempt to achieve mutual destruction. During that time, thirty-two days since the crossing of the Rapidan, the Union Army had lost an average of two thousand soldiers each day—sixty-four thousand dead, wounded, and missing. Providing replacements for these losses stressed even the seemingly unlimited resources of the North. Even Lincoln must have wavered, at least in his private thoughts, as the casualty reports ticked across the telegraph lines to the War Department. During this period, he spent many sleepless hours just sitting in the telegraph room in anxious anticipation of the bad news coming across the wire. No one had expected the magnitude of the cost in lives and material. By this time, Grant's aura as savior of the nation had vanished in the smoke of the endless rumbling of cannon and the sharp, deadly crack of musket fire.

The press corps had expected miracles—even predicted them—and, as usual, the reporters had established their own naive schedule for the time of deliverance. When the allotted period passed, the clamor of defeatism returned with all its shrill, sanctimonious outcry. "Peace at any cost!" the headlines blared. As a by-product of the clamor, Grant the Magnificent became Grant the Butcher. The string of horrors—the Wilderness, Spotsylvania, Cold Harbor—merged within the collective mind into one long, terrible month of carnage. Little did anyone suspect that nothing less had been intended. The battlegrounds marked a bloody scar on the Virginia map where men had been killed and maimed in unprecedented, mind-numbing numbers. "For exactly what purpose?" they now asked. No one bothered to explain. If Grant had stopped to explain, it is doubtful anyone would have listened, except perhaps Lee.

If Richmond was the objective, McClellan had been closer during the ill-fated Seven Days in 1862. To the casual observer, impressed mostly by the fierceness of his resistance, Lee's army appeared as whole as ever, the major difference being that the war had grown two years older. A man's blood had been spilled for every three yards of progress south of the Rapidan. The numbing reality of wholesale death and destruction had become too much for the mind to comprehend.

So far as I have been able to determine, Grant gave no attention to any of these concerns. Despite appearances to the contrary, he had whittled Lee's army down considerably. Far to the south, Sherman had steadily shoved Johnston south in the relentless drive toward Atlanta. Control of the Shenandoah Valley now seemed a realistic hope, if only the right general would surface to lead the way. As important as all of this, Lee had no place to retreat to except his last line of defense around Richmond and Petersburg. Time and space were running out.

"I now find," Grant wrote in a message to Halleck back in Washington, "after more than thirty days of trial, that the enemy deems it of the first importance to run no risks with the armies they now have. They act purely on the defensive, behind breastworks, or feebly on the offensive immediately in front of them and where in case of repulse they can instantly retire behind them. Without a greater sacrifice of human life than I am willing to make, all cannot be accomplished that I had designed outside of the city."

The message would have approached poetry, if it had not conveyed such gruesome tidings. Still, Grant said much in that short paragraph. First, he recognized a change in Lee, the tenacious gambler and master of the offense. Grant had concluded—subsequent events proved him correct—that Lee had abandoned all serious thought of offensive action. He had, in short, resigned himself to a war of attrition, a war he knew eventually must be lost if the North's resolve held firm.

Second, Grant had decided that perhaps there was a limit to the killing. If he lacked the capacity to gobble up Lee whole, as he hoped, then his strategy would be altered and transformed into a virtue. He solidified his position in the last part of the message. "I have, therefore, resolved upon the following plan: I will continue to hold . . . the ground now occupied, taking advantage of any favorable circumstance that may present itself, until the cavalry can be sent west to destroy the Virginia Central Railroad. . . . When this is effected I will move the army to the south side of James River. . . . Once on the south side of the James River I can cut off all sources of supply to the enemy."

In other words, siege had become an acceptable alternative—but not just yet.

Grant spent the nine days following the failed assault at Cold Harbor preparing for his next move. Then, during the small hours of June 12, Grant pulled his men out of the trenches and commenced one of the most difficult maneuvers of the war. The successful accomplishment of this withdrawal from close contact with a hostile enemy resulted in one of the few prolonged outbursts by Lee during the whole war, thereby demonstrating the significance of Grant's act to the only man who mattered.

The James River, just a stiff morning's walk beyond the horizon, was now Grant's immediate objective. Beyond the river lay Richmond's defenses, and ten miles to the south, Petersburg. Petersburg was the key to unlocking Richmond's door. If Grant could take Petersburg, Lee would retain only one railroad with which to supply both his troops and the Confederate capital. Grant's long-range plan included dismantling even that one railroad. With this achieved, the problem of supply would be added to Lee's problems of time, space, and dwindling numbers of fighting men.

*   *   *

"Few sights," said Sheldon Hanks, a retired Boston reporter whom I encountered while waiting for a Chicago-bound train, "are as grand as an army marching at full stride on a bright, clear day. I, personally, had been opposed to the war at the time, although I grew to see its necessity when I later traveled in the South. Even so, that army had a grand, noble quality about it. Grant must have felt the power of the beating hearts as he looked upon an endless line of blue-clad veterans striding toward the pontoon bridge recently constructed across the James River." He had a reporter's flair for thinking he knew what a man thought. "Within his mind must have churned the knowledge that all of these men, more than eighty thousand strong—considerably fewer than he began the campaign with—were at his call to live or die in response to his simplest command. For over a month of near-constant combat he had directed all of this power toward the formidable task of bringing Lee to heel. A less dedicated man would have given up long before. Indeed, many had, a fact more graphic than any that made necessary a commander such as Grant. In retrospect, everything that had transpired before had been necessary. While variations in tactics might have spared a few thousand lives, the essential task of cornering Lee was on schedule, even if it had always been his alternate plan."

On June 15, Grant sent another message to his old nemesis, General Halleck, a man now rendered harmless by virtue of the three stars on Grant's shoulders:

"Our forces will commence crossing the James today. The enemy shows no sign yet of having brought troops to the south side of Richmond. I will have Petersburg secured, if possible, before they get there in much force. Our movement from Cold Harbor to the James has been made with great celerity and so far without loss or accident."

Shortly thereafter, Lincoln sent a reply. "Have just read your dispatch of 1 P.M. yesterday. I begin to see it. You will succeed. God bless you all."

The message to Halleck made clear Grant's intention. Two words, however, were to prove the most prophetic. Those words were "if possible." By this time, Grant had learned to contain his assertiveness when speaking about the army's prospects for success. Although he was in command, control and command were two different qualities when managing this army's conduct. *If possible,* Grant said, he planned to take Petersburg. He might have done it, too, if he had personally led the troops in the assault. His problem was having to send other generals to perform the task.

As the distance from that deadly day at Cold Harbor grew, the horror began to blur, and the future looked brighter. Still, one central question remained unanswered: how much more bungling by the generals could the common private tolerate? Already the army was being transformed by the forces of events long past. The essential task of the men had become one of finding a way to remain alive. The best path toward that goal lay in discovering a means of being where Grant and Lee were not. Each day now, the three-year enlistments of whole regiments were expiring. The men had come into the army together, and they were, by God, going home together. They were unwilling, now that they had the chance to survive, to endure any activity more strenuous than marching to the boats sent to take them back to Washington. Many of their replacements were decidedly less dedicated to the arduous task ahead. The last of the heavy artillery units had been shipped south from Washington's defenses; most would do their duty. Of even lesser quality were the bounty soldiers who would rather desert than stand one evening of guard duty. Fighting was beyond them except when more dedicated men stood at their backs with loaded rifles, prodding them forward at the point of a bayonet. It had come to that, the theoretical bottom of the manpower pool. If I am permitted to probe Grant's thoughts, the meaning in that must have subdued his sense of well-being as he absorbed the magnitude of the force he commanded.

*   *   *

"Report, Captain," said General Smith.

"Sir, the trenches south and west of Petersburg appear nearly empty."

"Did you look inside those trenches, Captain?" the general asked, his intractable manner unmistakable.

The captain hesitated. "No, General, but for more than an hour we surveyed the line with field glasses. I estimate less than three thousand of the enemy along the whole front. I figured it out on the way back. That's hardly one man for each four yards of trench." This compared poorly to three ranks deep standing shoulder to shoulder at Cold Harbor.

"And what of the works beyond your sight?" The general was searching for an excuse, any excuse, to avoid attack. If one was denied him, he would create one.

"I could see more than a mile deep behind their first line of works, sir. I saw nothing but cooks and shirkers playing cards. Sir, they cannot withstand a dedicated attack, of that I'm certain."

"All right, Captain," he said. "I have your report. We shall see."

Doubt hung heavy in his reply as he repeated himself. "We shall see." Smith pondered the situation; then he decided to look for himself. Delay would have to do until some more substantial excuse for no action at all presented itself.

No one would have suggested that the works were less formidable than any ever made. An army of slaves had spent three years on the effort. Finally, however, even Smith had to admit that the captain's report had been correct. No more than a strong brigade manned the trenches immediately to his front, and no more than a division stood between his men and Petersburg. No such force, not even one comprising the best soldiers produced by Virginia, could hold back the force he commanded.

But caution had become a necessary ingredient in the task of staying alive, and by this time, no man felt a greater need for prudence than did Maj. Gen. William F. "Baldy" Smith. His corps had taken the worst of the thrashing at Cold Harbor, and now that battle was having an impact far beyond the immediate effect of the killing he had watched.

I have no trouble understanding Smith's skepticism. Lee's peculiar process of conditioning his enemy has become legendary. Nobody, friend or foe, considered anything beyond his capability. No one expected Lee to be in position to fight in the Wilderness, but there he beat the Union Army to a pulp. Grant had exclaimed, when a general wailed about Lee's seeming ability to have his men everywhere at once: "Don't tell me what Lee will do. Tell me what you will do. One would think that Lee will do a double flip-flop and land in our rear."

It seemed impossible for Lee to get to Spotsylvania ahead of the Union forces, but somehow he arrived just in time. To a trained observer, it appeared as though Lee had spent a month preparing the trenches at the North Anna, but he had arrived there less than a day before the Federal forces. Cold Harbor needed no explanation. Now Grant expected Smith to believe that he had beat that old fox to the defenses around his own capital! Hardly a man believed it, including the commanding general now charged with the responsibility of acting on such a preposterous prediction.

The problem was, it was true!

Other forces were at work, all of them contributing to the delay. Smith believed Hancock's corps was approaching; he expected it at any time. Smith later said that this expectation contributed to his decision to delay, but he made this statement after his removal from command, when manufacturing excuses for failure was more important than simply explaining why he had not acted promptly. Perhaps just as significant was Smith's physical condition: he suffered from a mild attack of malaria. In addition, he lacked proper engineer support to assist with a detailed assessment of the enemy works. But his own eyes told him the essential fact, and there was no way around that: too few men manned the trenches to repel his attack.

In the end, it was after 3:00 P.M. when Smith finished his personal reconnaissance and began to conclude that the trenches were, in fact, insufficiently manned to withstand a forceful attack. Then negligence factored into the equation, as it always seems to do at times of indecision. No one had bothered to inform the artillery commander that a battle was imminent, so he had sent the horses to a distant stream for water. When Smith finally decided to act, he found it impossible to put the cannon in place for a bombardment. More time slipped away as Smith waited for the horses to return.

From beginning to end, the effort to get at Petersburg suffered from "might have beens" and "if not fors." Smith might have sought vengeance for his flogging at Cold Harbor and acted with dispatch. Instead, the memory increased his caution. He might have felt better and, therefore, had the presence of mind to understand the need for moving promptly. Hancock might have better understood the urgency for moving with haste, which he did not. If not for the delay in ordering the big guns forward, all of the other conditions might not have mattered.

For three long years, the Army of the Potomac struggled with what might have been, and these justifications for inaction seemed always to be in utmost abundance when conditions rendered them least acceptable. Not even Grant seemed able to overcome this critical flaw in the army's character. He simply could not be every place at once.

So the afternoon melted away, and the early summer shadows reached out to join with dusk.

*   *   *

"Colonel Laird," said the brigade commander, for some long-forgotten reason still uninformed of the scarcity of Confederate soldiers in the trenches, "I think it's impossible to take those works, but we've been ordered to try." The general had in mind establishing an alibi for failure, even before the attack began, another symptom of Grant's most serious problem.

"My men will do their duty," Laird replied.

"God bless you and your men, Colonel," the general replied as he rode to the rear, "I wish I were going with you."

Laird scoffed at the remark, but only to his second-in-command, and only after the general had departed for safer ground. Laird knew his immediate superior. In the long month since the Wilderness, the brigadier had never been in range of a rebel bullet, not even the long-distance variety that killed General Sedgwick.

"All right, men," Laird yelled as he moved toward the departure point, "follow me." As Laird moved forward, his men reluctantly followed. Except for a few natural depressions, the ground in front of the trenches offered hardly any cover. A cannon shell exploded, and five men crumpled to the ground. Another shell landed in a gap between the onrushing ranks, but it did no harm. Momentum took hold and the men moved forward at a steady but cautious trot.

"Keep going, men!" Laird screamed. The men rushed forward after their colonel. At a hundred yards, the enemy muskets fired. A few men dropped; the remainder began to falter. "Look at the distance between the puffs of smoke, men," Laird yelled. "There's hardly any of them there. Don't tarry, men. One big rush and those trenches will be ours."

Cautiously, the men rose to a crouch and began moving forward. Laird swung his saber over his head in a broad circle, urging his soldiers across the field. Finally, the men realized that the opposing fire was thin and inaccurate. Their momentum accelerated as they approached the trenches.

"Over the top now!" Laird yelled as he climbed the earthen mound overlooking the trench. A thousand men were only a few yards behind. With bayonets extended before them, they lunged into the trenches. All along the line the rebel soldiers threw down their muskets in surrender. A few, realizing what was happening, climbed over the backside of the trenches. Now, those scattered remnants were running across the dimly lit field toward a second line of defense.

"I knew you could do it, men," Laird screamed, "I knew it! Captain Tubbs, get your company together and round up all the prisoners for escort to the rear. You other men, prepare to move forward on order."

But the order never arrived—it was never given.

When Smith finally pushed his men forward, he discovered almost immediately that they were pushing against an open door. After only token resistance, the rebels defending the outer works faded back into the twilight, leaving half their number dead or captured.

"General," urged one of Smith's division commanders, "Colonel Laird says there's almost nothing between our forces and Petersburg. We must move on! We must capture those railroads before reinforcements arrive. I recommend a night attack, sir. I recommend we move at once. Laird says he'll lead the attack if only someone will give the order."

The man was ecstatic in anticipation of final victory. His enthusiasm proved not to be contagious.

"I cannot see what's ahead in the dark," Smith replied. "Do you know what's waiting for us out there?"

Could anyone?

"General, look at these works," the subordinate said as he swung his arms about him. "These are the strongest trenches we've seen during this war. Isn't it reasonable to conclude that if they had the men they'd have been here to defend against our first attack?"

Smith shook his head. "The welfare of this army is my responsibility," he replied. "I might lose all I've gained if I attack and am repulsed." By this time, Hancock had arrived. Hands clasped behind his back, he stood silent. He in effect offered support by making no objection to Smith's argument. In this, fate played a cruel joke. Hancock, too, was ill, still suffering from an earlier wound that refused to heal. It sometimes flared up, rendering the man incapable of action. This was one of those times.

"I have information that the Confederates will be reinforced," Smith added, trying to shore up the argument for refusing to act. "How do I know those reinforcements haven't already arrived? Will you tell me that they haven't arrived?"

The officer offered no reply.

In asking the question, Smith had placed an intolerable burden on his subordinate. Obviously, no one could say if they had arrived. It was now too dark to see, but Smith had seen. Two hours earlier, at a distance as far as the horizon, those anticipated reinforcements were nowhere in sight. The essential question, however, remained unasked. Would the chances for capturing the city improve with the passing of time? The answer to that question was certain: no one doubted, now that the danger had arrived, that Lee would do everything humanly possible to get reinforcements to the site. As so often proved true, his greatest ally in his efforts to survive would be his adversary's timid response to a golden opportunity. Without the railroads, defending Richmond would be impossible. That defense was bringing Lee to this place. Reinforcements might already have arrived. They might also still be on the road, out beyond Richmond. Grant suspected, when he pulled out of the Cold Harbor trenches, that he had finally stolen a march on Lee. Now the confirmation was in hand, but Smith suffered from an illness far more deadly than malaria—he suffered from a fatal lack of initiative.

I have no doubt that Grant would have attacked, perhaps even without the earlier, detailed reconnaissance. He would have taken what the enemy gave him, or what he could have taken by force, and worried about what might happen when it happened. Of that I am certain. But the potentially fatal result of neglect and irrational caution was not yet serious. Only after a prolonged period of criminal neglect could one say absolutely that the race had been totally lost. Such was the opportunity open to General Smith.

*　　*　　*

Morning broke warm and bright. "Report, Colonel," Smith directed the commander of his dawn reconnaissance detail.

"General," replied the colonel, "there was some enemy reinforcement during the night. I estimate their total strength at no more than seven thousand. We now outnumber them about five to one, about the same as when we arrived with our lesser number against their two thousand."

A fretful man could draw much from such a remark. Smith read all that was possible. "You estimate, Colonel. *You estimate!* If it is perhaps seven thousand, might it also be nine thousand, or twelve thousand, or Lee's entire army? No, Colonel. I need more precise information than that."

More troops were on the way. He expected Burnside's corps to arrive at noon. For a man looking for an excuse to avoid action, the use of an imprecise term such as estimate provided all that was required. He would wait. Time, the only commodity ever in short supply within the Army of the Potomac (except perhaps for aggressive generals), wasted away as the generals plotted strategy and waited for more reinforcements.

Finally, Grant sent a message to Meade, who by now had arrived on the scene. "If it is a possible thing, I want an assault made at six o'clock this evening."

Hancock struck at six, and the second door gave way. More trenches and prisoners fell into Union hands. Confederate reinforcements, transfers from Butler's front at Bermuda Hundred, began moving into the rebel trenches, but not nearly enough to withstand a forceful attack all along the line.

At dawn, Meade ordered another attack, this time with all three corps—Burnside's, Hancock's, and Warren's—moving forward as one, or so he thought.

"Do you know what's happening?" Meade asked an approaching aide in exasperation.

"Sir, one of Burnside's divisions has attacked," the breathless aide reported, "but his reinforcements failed to come up in support. I've also learned that Hancock attacked, but his assault developed too late. It appears the enemy shifted troops from Burnside's front to defend against this assault. Warren reports that the force in his front is too strong to assault." The officer's shoulders slumped. "I fear nothing has been accomplished, sir."

More than forty thousand Union troops faced no more than ten thousand Confederates, and still the Federal generals were afraid to move. Another day had passed and Lee's main force still had not arrived. Meade ordered another general attack for noon the next day, June 18. Nothing much happened except for a reconnaissance-in-force to test the rebel defenses. Each corps commander waited for the other to make the first strike. Each waited in vain.

"My God," Meade screamed in anger, "is there no way to make them move? If they won't move in support of one another, perhaps they'll move on their own." Orders to that effect were given. As the afternoon passed, the generals made half-hearted efforts, but it was too late. Lee's veterans were running into the trenches as fast as they arrived. In the end, after three days of hapless effort, nothing resulted other than an increase in the Union casualty count.

*   *   *

"Somehow," a historian later recorded, "this was a time when nothing quite worked. This army had been built, trained, and used so that it would always be just a little out of control. The generals' reflexes were sluggish. Between the will and the act, there was always a gap. Now it had been demonstrated, for anyone who cared to look, that paralysis of the army's central nervous system could go no farther."

The dilemma had been, was, and would remain: what could be done about the generals? Even with the bludgeoning inflicted at Cold Harbor, the men were willing to act. Colonels were willing to lead if no soldiers of higher rank could be found to carry out the bloody act. But what about the generals who had nothing to do but give the orders?

Weeks passed before Grant learned of the lost opportunity. He should have expected it. There existed a timidity in the Union officer corps that nothing seemed able to overcome. Generals Smith and Warren, commanders of the two largest corps, always saw more than was there in the form of defenders. What was there always seemed too strong to overcome, or they thought the act required more preparation time than was available. Similar failings had led to McClellan's relief. The rough outline of defeat seemed etched into every plan. Even when Warren moved faster than expected, as when moving south out of the Wilderness, he found a way to make it work to his disadvantage.

Smith had squandered his opportunity to emerge from the war as the general who captured the greatest prize of all, short of Lee himself. Neither Warren nor Smith would hold a command by the war's end.

Meade certainly had no grounds for complaint. His success in what was essentially a defensive battle at Gettysburg had saved his reputation. Later, however, when he had Lee trapped, he let him slip away by failing to move forward decisively.

No. The fault was not in the men who did the fighting. In four days, Union losses had risen by another ten thousand. I suspect that if there had been even a sluggish effort to capture Petersburg within forty-eight hours of Smith's arrival the city would have fallen with half those casualties. The war, however, was destined to drag on, and many more thousands of men were doomed to suffer and die.

Lee filed his men into the trenches, and not even Grant, it seemed, had the stomach to press the attack.

20 The Crater

Grant pronounced the Battle of the Crater during the siege of Petersburg "the saddest affair I have witnessed in this war." Again, part of the failure was due to the generals' performance. This was as true for the decisions that were made before the battle as it was for the performance of the generals selected by fate to conduct the affair. But there was more to it than that. First, one must consider the desperation in the act, the willingness to try anything, no matter how extreme, to bring an end to the war. Beyond that, one must consider what was not done and why.

"Turk" Willcox was a practical man, and for him, if there was any fate at all in this war, it was in the selection of those who died and those who lived. He saw none of the deeper meaning in the fiasco. He simply witnessed the failure, and in that there was nothing justifying surprise.

"My God," Willcox said as he sucked on his empty pipe—he had given up the taste of tobacco in his pipe, but not all of the habit—"you'd'a thought the generals had in mind keepin' the war goin' forever." Turk was past eighty, frail, and permanently hunched from a lifetime of crawling through narrowly carved, rugged passages half a mile below the earth's surface. He had been out of the tunnels for more than twenty years, but his skin still had the persistent grimy look of a man who had spent a lifetime at hard labor in dark Pennsylvania coal mines. His lungs had no doubt filtered at least a ton of coal dust during fifty years in the mines, and his breathing had the high-pitched sound of a stiff wind straining to squeeze through a window barely cracked open.

Turk had boarded a slow freighter from England in 1849—by then he was nearly twenty and had already spent ten years in the mines, starting as a breaker boy at age nine, sorting slate and other impurities from the coal—and traveled to the "promised land." He had found less than he had bargained for.

"I was a corporal by the late spring of '64," he said. "I joined the army in the fall of '62. By then, the need for coal had reached a point that the bosses had increased the daily requirement by fifty percent and eliminated the few safety precautions that'd been in place. I figured it couldn't be any more dangerous in the army, so I joined up. I soon found out how wrong I'd been. I'd just finished what little trainin' they gave when they assigned me to a newly formed Pennsylvania brigade headin' for Fredericksburg. That was in December of '62."

Willcox suffered a fractured kneecap at Fredericksburg—he went down in the last of four futile assaults—and, as if that wasn't enough, both of his feet were frostbitten as he huddled on the field that night, west of the town, in front of the sunken road. The wound made it impossible for him to crawl back to Union lines. By midnight, the temperature dropped below freezing. To provide some minimum measure of protection from the cold wind, he pulled a corpse to either side of his shivering body. Later, rebel soldiers crept onto the field and began removing shoes from the dead Union soldiers—and some who were not so dead, Willcox included. He was rescued the next day and sent to a hospital where he recovered slowly from the frostbite and wounded knee. He rejoined his regiment as Grant's army abandoned the Cold Harbor trenches.

"We hadn't been in those Petersburg trenches more'n a couple a weeks when we all realized that unless somethin' was done we'd be there forever. I'd look out every mornin' at those Rebs in their forts no more'n two hundred yards away. A man didn't look long, though, a'fore he took a bullet in the eye. I don't rightly know how the idea got started, but someone said that we shore could make a hole in their line—if only we'd dig a tunnel under 'em. One thing led to another and, a'fore you knew it, the tunnel'd been started. Because of my experience, I supervised the midnight shift—we dug 'round the clock."

"How long did it take to dig the tunnel?" I asked.

"'Bout twice as long as it should've, if they'd given us the proper equipment. As it was, we dug about a month. A marvel of engineering, if I do say so myself. Ol' Colonel Pleasants knew his stuff. He devised a means of suckin' fresh air into that tunnel—nobody thought it'd work. As I remember, we finished about sundown on 23 July—twenty feet down and more'n five hundred feet long, with sidetunnels movin' 'bout seventy-five feet laterally in either direction from the far end. It was as pretty a tunnel as I ever dug."

"Once the tunnel was finished," I asked, "what did they plan to do?"

"To blow 'em to hell, what else did ya think? Then the army was to pour through the gap and end the war—that was the plan."

"Conditions apparently didn't develop quite as expected," I observed.

"Like I said, the generals weren't ready to end the war, at least General Burnside wasn't. If'n I'd'a thought all day, I couldn't'a thought of a more fouled-up plan for the use of that tunnel. Near as I figure, we lost 'bout four thousand that day, dead, wounded, and captured. But it wasn't a total loss. We at least had a nice big hole for buryin' the dead."

"Were you involved in the assault?" I asked.

"No, thank God, but I watched it from less'n two hundred yards away."

*   *   *

The willingness to use Negro regiments came hard for the Union high command. If in the South the Negro was thought of as little more than an animal, in the North he was thought of as something less than human. The majority in the North thought it wrong to keep him in bondage, but using him to fight for the freedom of his people stretched propriety to the breaking point. Where the Negro had fought, he had done about as well as his white counterpart, but those engagements had been limited and where they mattered least to the war effort.

The early plan at the Crater had been to use a Negro division to lead the assault. When at the last moment General Meade learned of the corps commander's decision, he substituted a different plan. At that point, the overall plan began to unravel.

Old Jack Hampton came to my attention in a most peculiar way. It was late on the second day of our journey from Hot Springs, South Dakota, where Abby and I had gone in search of Sergeant Clemmens, and I had need of a drink of water. I had noticed that when the wind blew just right through that porous old railroad car an odor sometimes drifted by my seat. I had noticed it since about noon. I discovered the source when I worked my way toward the water bucket.

There were few people on the train, so anyone who wanted one had a seat to himself. Hampton—I didn't know his name at the time—was asleep on the back seat at the rear of the car. Sitting across from him was a scarred and battered old white man who had boarded with Hampton. Hampton was as black as a December night. They had boarded about noon that day, at some desolate stop in eastern Nebraska near the Missouri border. As I stumbled down the aisle the odor grew stronger. It nearly overpowered me as I approached the back of the car. Just then the train lunged, and I lost my balance and sprawled across Hampton and his sidekick. In a flash, Hampton drew his pistol—he called it a "hog-leg"—and I found myself looking up the six-inch barrel.

"Sorry," I said pleadingly, "I lost my balance."

Hampton sighed as he slid the weapon back into its holster. His companion continued to snore.

Instinctively, my nose began to twitch and my face wrinkled in a natural reaction to that foul odor. It had crossed my mind that the odor bordered somewhere between that of a highly populated pigpen and rotting eggs, but more distinctive—and much worse.

"Skunk," he said softly, seeking to avoid a panic.

"I knew I'd smelled that odor someplace before," I replied in mild surprise, while also feeling a vague satisfaction in the knowledge that the mystery had been unraveled. With the puzzle solved, I pushed myself to a standing position and moved toward the water bucket. I drank my fill before I felt that odor moving closer.

"Any left?" Hampton asked.

I handed him the dipper just as the nausea pushed what little I had in my stomach to the surface. I barely had time to open the door and step onto the narrow platform outside the door. The wind in my face settled my nerves. Then it was there again, only less strong.

"Skunk don't set well with you, I guess," Hampton said. "Does have a right tangy kick to it, don't it?"

I turned toward Hampton, then backed as near to the rail as possible.

"Can't say as I'm too partial to it myself," he added.

"Then why don't you do something about it?" I asked sharply.

"I ain't seen no tub, has you?"

"Guess not," I replied. "How did it happen, the skunk I mean?"

"Sam an' me was ridin' up to the station this mornin' when my horse scared up a nest a them critters. The horse threw me an' I landed right on top a one a those striped cats. Sprayed me good, he did. Weren't nothin' to do but get on the train."

"How can Sam stand sitting next to you?" I asked.

"Oh, Sam can't smell nothin'."

I nodded. "I'd say he's a lucky man."

Hampton smiled; then he began to laugh. I joined him. When some things get bad enough, you either laugh or cry.

"Why is Sam unable to smell anything?" I asked.

"A Minié went through the bridge of his nose," he replied, "back in '64. Ain't been able to smell a lick since."

That explained one of the half-dozen scars on Sam's face. "Did Sam fight in the Civil War?"

"Both'n us did," he replied. "I carried him from the Crater."

"The crater south of Petersburg?"

"The same. You heard of it?"

"Yes. I'm very interested in the war. Would you mind talking about your experience at the Crater?"

"Biggest bang I ever heard," he said. He propped a battered boot on the lower rail and leaned on the top rung. "Want to go inside, where it's warmer?"

"No," I replied quickly, "I'll suffer a bit out here in the cold."

"I was in General Ferrero's division," Hampton continued, "all of fifteen at the time—but big for my age. We'd rehearsed for the assault for near a week. Excitement was runnin' high on the afternoon of June thirtieth, when the order come down. It was to be our first engagement, an' we was to lead the attack. Then a new order come down. We was to go in last, after the white divisions. Meade'd sent the order, an' there weren't nothin' anybody could do to change it— although General Burnside tried, I heard."

"Why was your division moved to the rear?" I asked.

"I heard Meade didn't trust us. Ain't no way, though, we could'a messed it up more'n them white boys."

"What difference did it make which division went first?" I asked.

"As it turned out, quite a bit. One of our regiments'd been assigned to clear the defensive tangle of obstacles that blocked the way. That assignment got overlooked in the new orders. Besides that, our orders were to fan out an' move toward the high ground. Them white boys went straight ahead, right into the crater."

"What was your impression of the explosion?"

"Gawdallmighty! That was some bang. Earth an' rock, an' more'n a few Rebs, shot a hundred feet or more into the air. Sounded like I'd always imagined the end of the world soundin'. But what goes up must come down, an' down it come with a mighty crash. Well, those white boys stood lookin' at it for a moment, then they commenced to run to the rear. Took thirty minutes or more to get 'em turned 'round an' headin' back toward the crater. I laughed 'til I thought I'd split my side."

"What happened then?"

"Since the obstacles remained in place—although they was covered with quite a bit a dirt in a few places—everyone funneled through a narrow openin' no more'n ten feet wide. This resulted in them bunchin' up at the rim of the crater. They began receivin' a pepperin' a fire from the Rebs to the north. Faced with nothin' to do but scramble for cover, they commenced to slide into that hole. This was no small hole, mind you, more like a large, deep pond that'd gone dry. Must'a been sixty or so feet across an' three times as wide, an' maybe thirty feet deep in places. One by one, then in bunches of a dozen or more, several thousand men climbed down the slopes an' commenced to dig the survivors from the churned-up ground. All a this took some time.

"My division come up 'bout midmornin' an' commenced to spread out like we'd originally planned, an' we headed for the high ground north a the Crater. Only problem was, we was four hours behind schedule. By then, the rebels had recovered an' were waitin' for us."

"Did you have a rough time of it?" I asked.

"Rough don't describe it. We lost more'n thirteen hundred men— just about a third of our division. If the intent was to keep us from gettin' kilt, that shore didn't work. More'n a third of the casualties was from my division. Even so, what happened to those men in the Crater was a sad sight to see. That's where Sam comes in.

"By then, Rebs had surrounded the hole, an' they poured a fearful fire on them boys below. You heard of shootin' fish in a barrel? Well, that's what it reminded me of. Our troops'd try to scramble up the sides only to take a bayonet in the chest or a Minié in the face. At close quarters like that, there was some of the worst wounds of the war. Anyway, Sam took one in the face. When our assault failed, I took cover just below the rim a that hole. I saw Sam moanin' an' twitchin', so I climbed down a few yards an' drug him behind a boulder as big as a small house. When things cooled off a bit, I drug him along a

narrow crevice leadin' toward the rim a the Crater an' began workin'
toward our lines."

I saw the frown and sensed a tenseness in his voice.

"What's the matter?" I asked.

"Goddamned rebels!" he exclaimed. "Men from my division was
tryin' to scramble back to our lines. More'n a few ran into the Rebs
and tried to surrender. Our men had their hands in the air, but that didn't
matter none. The Rebs commenced to stick 'em with their bayonets—
I heard one of 'em say we wasn't worth a bullet—an' when our men
tried to run, they was clubbed into the ground. It was murder, plain
an' simple."

"How did you avoid this?" I asked.

"There was plenty of confusion. Guess they didn't see me. Sam
was out cold an' looked dead, so I pulled him over me an' lay there
bakin' under the sun. 'Fore long, the fightin' moved north an' I drug
Sam to our lines. We been together on an' off ever since. We come
west after the war and punched cattle until '76. By then, we'd saved
enough to buy a small spread an' a starter herd. Been ranchin' ever
since." Hampton turned to me and smiled. "But I'm headin' home now,
back to Lu'siana."

*   *   *

I've recorded much about Civil War Union generals, a large portion of it unflattering. There was the persistent lateness when attacking, or failure to perform the preliminaries that a second lieutenant would
never ignore. Prior to the Crater, I had heard no mention of outright
cowardice, or even its appearance—although General Mott's performance at Spotsylvania came close. There was cowardice at the Crater, cowardice of the worst kind, where generals abandoned their posts
and left the men to do the dying for want of the slightest form of leadership.

In concert with the attack in the Crater area, Meade had ordered
a broad attack along the line. But everything depended on a breakthrough at the Crater. General Burnside had four divisions primed for
this initial assault. Originally, Brig. Gen. Edward Ferrero's division
of colored troops had been assigned to lead the way. Meade's last-
minute rejection of this idea forced Burnside to select another division, so the other three division commanders drew straws for the privilege.
At that point Fate joined the game of chance. The responsibility for
the initial advance passed to Brig. Gen. James H. Ledlie, the least

experienced of the three division commanders. By the time of the explosion, just before dawn, General Ledlie had slithered into a shellproof bunker and had downed half a bottle of rum. Before the attack was half finished, General Ferrero, commander of the colored division, joined him.

Something else developed at the Crater, something as sinister and deadly as cowardice. Here, the myth that the motivation for the war, at least from the Southern perspective, had been the high moral principle of states' rights, was, now and for all time, put to rest. War is bad enough in its own right, but when it degenerates to nothing more than murder, the pale luster of honor and glory fades away. Then one is confronted with the surest sign that the war must end by the most expedient means possible.

For two generals, one prominent, the other less than prominent, the war ended with the Battle of the Crater. Maj. Gen. Ambrose E. Burnside, who himself had pronounced his own unsuitability for high command before the Fredericksburg battle, was removed—for the second time—from any further role in the raging conflict. This time he would not be resurrected. A lesser man, Brigadier General Ledlie, also passed from the scene. He was summoned before a court-martial and drummed from the army for cowardice.

The idea for a tunnel had evolved more by accident than as a result of grand strategic design. It had, in fact, moved from the bottom up rather than from the generals down. Only during the latter stages of this event, when nothing better had surfaced, was any level of enthusiasm added to the scheme. But, as so often happens in war, that which appears minor in prospect becomes monumental in retrospect. In a forlorn sort of way, the Crater was an admission that all that had been planned before had not gone very well. It seemed only natural that something else might work, something more desperate, something more radical in conception and design. But that which occurred only added to the despair growing more pronounced as the long struggle continued. In its wake, a prominent general had been washed from the war forever—perhaps later than would have been best—and the attitudes that brought on the war in the first place had only hardened.

Other than the elevation of the casualty count by five thousand or more, nothing much changed as a result of this sorry turn of the war. With the explosion, a sizable portion of the landscape had been altered forever, but a hundred-mile-long line of trenches, about equally divided between the opposing sides, had done far more damage to the earth's fragile surface. Although the jagged edges of the hole have been softened by the winds of time and gently swaying grass, the scar remains. More important to the nation, deeper wounds of hate and despair remain locked in men's hearts.

In time, with the end of the war, the blight of slavery would be removed by the sting of lead and the agony of piercing bayonet steel. But in that summer of 1864, all along the Petersburg front, the men settled in for a long siege.

21 That Glorious Ride

The war ground on following the missed opportunity at Petersburg, or perhaps it is more accurate to state that the war continued to grind up the men in the trenches—on both sides. There is a commonly held misconception about siege, about trench warfare. It is thought to be a benign form of war where men languish in the comfort of bunkers buttressed by impenetrable supports. Rather, trench warfare is the height of discomfort and a process of mindless, useless killing. The deep, narrow scars in the earth concentrate the heat and cold, and dampness is almost constant. When the last drop of moisture is finally beaten from the ground by weary, plodding feet, the soil turns to powder so fine that it penetrates even sealed containers. Each shuffling step stirs up a cloud two or three feet high. The talcumlike dust drifts lazily in the pungently stale air before settling into a man's eyes, or nose, or mouth— or any other opening within reach. There it grinds into unwashed skin until a sticky plasma oozes to the surface. The dust, when mixed with the sweat produced by hundred-degree days, forms a cast that only a stiff brush can scrub away, thus irritating even more the raw, swollen skin. In time it scales off—carrying with it the top layer of a man's skin, opening the body to every form of itching agony. After more time, boil-like infections develop that, when healed, leave marks reminiscent of a reptile's scaled skin. It is worth pointing out that more men died from sickness than wounds during the war. A wounded man at least received some form of medical attention. This was less true of the men whose bodies literally rotted away from the maladies associated with the trenches.

The slow, rotting deterioration of flesh and soul was bad enough, but a more expedient death was as close as the errant lifting of a man's head to steal a look over the rim of a trench. Each side had its share of sharpshooters. For hours they aimed their rifles at a single spot, just waiting for an unthinking opponent to take a curious peek over the top. Crack! Thud! Few survived such mistakes: a Minié ball did fearful damage when it ripped into a man's head.

Just to keep life interesting, both sides regularly bombarded each other with cannon and mortar shells timed to explode in the air above the trenches. The explosions sprayed bits of white-hot, razor-sharp metal across a twenty-yard circle. At least in open battle, men had the advantage of being on the move, thus making it more difficult for gunners to find the range to time the explosion of the shell. Trench warfare offered not even this small chance for survival. Most shells were on target; seldom was the cost of steel and powder wasted.

It had become a war of attrition and hunger, of wasting flesh, of a bullet in the eye, and of deadly steel that sliced flesh from bones in no less efficient a manner than meat cleavers rending a carcass. It became an indifferent war of killing simply for the sake of killing. Neither side seemed to have the capacity to do more.

*   *   *

"Colonel," I asked, "what was the mood of the army as the siege settled in?"

"Bad," he said as he tucked the blanket around his legs, "very bad. As tiresome as all that marching was, wilting away in those trenches was worse. There was nothing for a man to do but sleep, stand guard duty, and wonder if the next shell would explode over his head. As bad as it became in the Union trenches, however, it must have been infinitely worse on the Confederate side. At least we had plenty to eat. Supplies and rations were piled high on the City Point docks. During this time, Grant and his engineers laid out the plans for supply that have been the army's blueprint ever since. They even built a railroad to haul supplies to the trenches. Ammunition was so plentiful that every man was under orders to fire no fewer than ten rounds each day. Many fired into the air to avoid raising their heads above the trenches. The average was six hundred thousand rounds each day, Sundays included. That didn't include the cannon shells. Often, a hundred guns fired for an hour without letup."

The nurse extended a handful of pills to the old colonel. "Swallow these down like a good boy," she admonished as she handed him a glass of juice.

The old soldier had passed his ninetieth year. The yellowing skin stretching across his bones reminded me of a bleached raisin withering in the sun. Each time he breathed, the air whistled across his toothless gums as he forced it over his ashen tongue.

"A year earlier," the nurse told me in private, "doctors had to remove his nose. Skin cancer ate most of it away and there was nothing else to do." The unhealed wound was only the most noticeable of his many maladies.

A week following the first shots at Fort Sumter, Col. Hiram Barlow had entered the army as a thirty-five-year-old private. His civilian experience as a railroad construction engineer, an occupation he had mastered without benefit of any formal education beyond grammar school, served him well in the military. The silver eagle on his pajama collar gave ample evidence that he had given good service to the Union cause. He had stayed with it right up until the end. Wounded for the fifth time on April 6, 1865, by a bullet that nicked his right lung, he had refused transport to a hospital.

"I wanted to be in on the end," he had told me earlier. "Lee was at the end of his trail, and I just couldn't miss out on the surrender. I munched on a stale cracker as I watched through the open door of the ambulance when that white-haired old fox walked up the steps to the farm house at Appomattox. Since that fateful day, I never again heard a shot fired in anger."

I first developed an interest in Barlow for a reason other than his distinguished military record. After the war he became a sort of political analyst. He wrote several books about the war's aftermath, becoming an expert on the disaster resulting from Reconstruction in the South. The most important of his works, from my perspective, was a short story titled "If Lincoln Had Lived." He had researched Lincoln's views on just about everything, those that had been recorded, and developed from them a hypothetical proposal of what the president would have done given the circumstances that developed after the war. I found it an intriguing analysis of Lincoln and his times. Most of all, I agreed with his conclusion, insofar as I had the background to form a judgment.

He cast a hard look at the nurse. "I'm too old for anything to do much good anymore," he growled, "so they're using me to experiment on." He brushed a feeble hand in the nurse's direction. "Shoo, you old hag," he snapped at the woman less than a third his age. "Won't you let an old man die in peace?" Still, conditioned to respond to higher authority, he pressed his hand against his mouth and swallowed the pills. He sucked in a deep breath and expelled the air slowly. The simple act of breathing caused him pain.

He must have noticed my distressed expression at the sight of his difficulty. "Just catching up on my breathing," he said with a smile. "Siege had become the predictable result of Grant's inability to bring Lee's army to bay before he reached Petersburg's defenses. This resulted from the bungling of incompetent generals when the way to Petersburg required nothing more than a gentle kicking on a series of unguarded doors. Although safe for the present, this was the form of war Lee must have dreaded. Grant's orders made clear that he was trying everything within his power to avoid a siege. It was, ironically, the one form of war Grant was certain to win, if given the time. The advantage accrued to the army with the greatest capacity to endure. In this, Grant had the fundamental advantage: he had more men to waste. He also had more supplies.

"Grant made every human effort to complicate Lee's supply problem. Lee had two options open to him: he could wait for the inevitable, ignoble end resulting from starvation, or he could try to break loose into open country and take his chances. Political circumstance compelled him to endure the stalemate as long as possible—at least until after the November elections. But in selecting this course of action, however compelling his reasons at the time, he had in fact chained himself to an irrational, forlorn hope. Before Grant would yield to anything approaching a political settlement—before Lincoln would let him yield— Grant would be compelled to attack with every man he had in one last, desperate battle."

He paused an instant. "No. Lee really had no chance. In the absence of some form of political resolution, he must have realized— he was, in my view, the most intelligent general this country ever produced—that when the time came when he could no longer endure the siege, his army would be too weak to break free. But he was loyal to his state to a fault, so he followed orders. That's what generals do, if they're good generals. They follow orders. In the end, he faced a cruel dilemma: not a man in blue had an ounce of sympathy for him or his men in gray. Our misery was directly linked to their stubbornness, and we wanted it to end once and for all."

"It seems Grant should have been content to wait," I said.

"You'd think so, wouldn't you?" he replied, his voice growing stronger as thoughts from his youth charged his aging body with new energy. "But Grant had his share of political concerns. By all measures, there appeared a better than even chance that the time needed to wait for Lee's army to waste away would never be granted. Far to the south, Sherman labored mile by mile toward Atlanta, but there the final battle was weeks away. The armies around Richmond were locked in a stalemate. Up north, conditions were deteriorating daily. The party nominating conventions were approaching, with the election just over four months away. Few gave Lincoln much of a chance to be nominated. Even if that unlikely eventuality by some miracle materialized, hope for his election seemed nonexistent." He nodded to himself. "It was, from the North's perspective, the proverbial dark before the dawn. Nothing but time could solve the problems, and there was no way to push time forward."

"Granted," I said, "there were many problems, most of them political. But Grant's concerns were military. What, in your opinion, was the central military problem, besides the fact that there was no way to get at Lee?"

"Despite everything Grant had tried," he said without hesitation, "he had been unable to stop the flow of supplies to Lee's army. Lee's defenses were much too large for Grant to surround. Every yard that Grant extended his lines required two men to occupy the lengthening trench. Over the same distance, Lee could get by with only one man in defense. Given the relative strength of the two armies, that simply maintained the balance. Each day we saw a steady flow of wagons coming down from the Valley, and each day Grant became more unsettled."

"Do you mean the supplies coming down from the Shenandoah?" I asked. I was familiar with the "Valley problem," as several old veterans had called it. There were two sides to Lee's supply problem. One was transport. The railroads were central to this issue. The other side of the problem was finding something to transport. Holding on to the railroads, or having supply outlets in the North, served little purpose if there were no supplies to transport. The most practical option available to Grant was to somehow stop the flow of supplies from the Shenandoah Valley, the most immediate source of food for Lee's soldiers and the people in Richmond and Petersburg. But that meant driving Gen. Jubal Early's army away and taking firm control of the Valley. That had been tried several times before, dating back to Stonewall Jackson's legendary defense of the Valley in 1862. Lee still controlled the Valley, or at least the army stationed there did.

"The same," he replied. "That's how I got out of those hellish trenches. I rode north with a cavalry brigade that followed after Grant when he traveled north to meet with Sheridan. That was in mid-September. After the disaster at the Crater, Grant sent Sheridan up to rebuild the small, all-but-broken Union Army cowering in the Valley. Sheridan had been up there about six weeks when Grant evidently concluded that he was taking too long to go after Old Jube, so he went up to confer. That led me to the greatest day of my life."

I stopped writing and looked up. The old colonel seemed lost in the thoughts of the past. Throughout my research, this had been the greatest test of my patience. These old soldiers would be talking about something, and then, sometimes in mid-sentence, they would just stop. It wasn't a normal pause, such as with trying to get a breath or to find the right words to make a thought clear, but a prolonged, absentminded pause that left a critical thought hanging, often never to be retrieved. This was one of those pauses.

"Why was that the greatest day in your life?" I prodded.

There was no reply. Slowly, his eyelids dropped; then his head slumped. He was sound asleep.

"He does that," the nurse said softly. "After he's awake for an hour or so, he just runs out of air and falls asleep." She looked sympathetically at him. "He's so very old, you know." She propped up his slumping head. "Come back this evening. He seems to get stronger as the day goes along."

I nodded as I watched her wheel him away.

I returned at seven. The colonel was still asleep, or sleeping again, so I set about revising my notes. I was deep in thought when I heard a soft whisper.

"That was the grandest day of my life," the colonel said. "I count myself lucky to have been there."

"What?" I asked reflexively.

He looked at me in surprise, as if I were absentminded. "You asked why it was the greatest day of my life, did you not?"

I had forgotten the four-hour-old question. "I suppose I did. Why was it your greatest day?"

He took a deep, wheezing breath before continuing. "Let me go back to the beginning. General Early had driven the Union Army, then commanded by General Hunter, from the Valley, then turned toward Washington. All through the war, that had been Lincoln's greatest fear, that a Confederate army would approach the undefended capital. Well, it wasn't undefended, but with the quality of troops on hand it might as well have been. By then, early in July, even the last of the old guard of heavies had been converted to infantry and sent to Petersburg. Most of the large guns were manned by desk soldiers and wounded infantry who didn't know the business end of a cannon from a tent pole. Old Jube danced around the outer defenses until Grant sent up VI Corps to strengthen the defenses. Their arrival was a close call. I heard that the men of VI Corps were just filing into the defensive positions as Early moved forward to attack."

From what I know of this event, I doubt that Early was serious in his efforts to invade Washington. Actually, he probably accomplished his mission by forcing Grant to move a whole corps of infantry from Petersburg to Washington. After all, reducing Grant's strength by ten thousand as a result of transfer was as effective as killing that many in a major battle. If that had been Lee's goal, to reduce the pressure on his front, he got his wish. But that was a short-term goal. What he needed was long-term relief. Moving the VI Corps north provided a solid nucleus for a new attempt to gain control of the Shenandoah. That transformation resulted in a shift in focus from Grant and returned the emphasis to the positive.

"Early was driven off with little trouble," said the colonel, "but that wasn't the real problem. The command structure around Washington was all jumbled up. It was all political, going back to the start of the war. Getting anything done meant the involvement of at least three military departments. That meant nothing got done. Grant lifted General Franklin from retirement and gave him overall command of Washington's defenses. I learned from a friend then serving on Meade's staff that Halleck sent Grant a telegram declaring that Franklin's appointment was politically unacceptable. It seems that Franklin had supported McClellan, and McClellan was nearly assured of being the Democrats' presidential nominee. Even in this dark hour, politics overruled good sense."

"What did Grant do?" I asked.

"Exasperated, Grant took one look at his generals and sent the only one he had to take charge of the defense of Washington."

"The only one he had?" I asked. "From all I've read, Grant's problem had always been having too many generals."

"There were a lot of men with stars on their shoulders, but only one real general." A bright smile lit up his face. "Sheridan was his name. You must have heard of him."

I reflected his smile. "Yes, I've heard of him."

"That's all he ever talks about," said a raspy voice from my right. "Sheridan this an' Sheridan that. You'd think he was a god or something."

Colonel Barlow stiffened. "You old coot," he replied sharply, without looking at his antagonist. "You wouldn't know a real general if he sat on your lap." He leaned closer to me. "He served under Warren. That explains his stupidity."

Men with a variety of infirmities rolled their chairs or walked unsteadily on crutches toward the fracas. Obviously, Barlow's comment had struck a sensitive nerve, and everyone within sound of the conflict and able to get about on his own power moved in our direction.

"Here we go again," Barlow said in feigned exasperation. "You're going to get your ear chewed off about who was the best general." Barlow turned toward the man who had spoken. "I'm a colonel, and you're only a major," he said indignantly. "What do you know about generals?"

"I know Sheridan disgraced Warren at Five Forks," he replied, jabbing his cane at Barlow's chest.

Barlow swatted the cane away. "Bullshit," Barlow said, "Warren disgraced himself." He turned back toward me. "We in the cavalry called Warren 'Old Slow.' He never once did anything on time." He turned back to his adversary. "As dumb as you are, if Warren had ever got you into a real battle, you'd be dead as dust nearly sixty years now."

The old major leaned forward, almost toppling from his wheelchair. "He saved the Union at Little Round Top," he countered. "If not for him, you'd be eating grits an' ham."

"That's another sin I'd discuss with him, if he were here. Grits and ham would be a damn sight better than what they feed us here."

"Whoa, men," I said smiling, unable to conceal my amusement at the first sign of vibrant life since entering this room full of forgotten men. "The war ended more than fifty-five years ago."

"That war will never end," said a new entrant into the discussion.

The others nodded their agreement. One pointed at me and said with a snicker: "If it's over, young fella', what're ya doin' here talkin' about it?"

"You have a good point," I agreed. "Colonel Barlow was just about to tell me about his association with Sheridan in the Valley in '64. Gather around." I motioned with both arms. I always learned more in group discussions. The talk was free and easy, more spiked with emotion. "Whatever you think about Sheridan, the events in the Valley played a major part in bringing the war to a close." They all knew the history, so they nodded in agreement. "Now, what were you about to say, Colonel?"

He looked around at the knot of men drawing in closer. Obviously, they wanted to hear the story, too. Even if a man had a favorite general other than Sheridan, the importance of what the man did that day was beyond doubt.

"Well, all right," he said. "It all began on September 19. I remember 'cause that's my birthday. Grant had left a couple of days before, taking with him only his closest aides. My unit was detached and assigned to Custer's cavalry division. The Battle of Winchester soon followed. After a fitful start, we rolled up Early's men and drove them from the field. Three days later, the Confederates were still running for the hills. Then we spread out and began to peel the Valley. I heard that Grant told Sheridan he wanted it wiped so clean that a crow flying over it would have to carry its own rations. By thunder, that's just what we did. Grant wanted to end Lee's use of the Valley for supply once and for all. We burned everything except the houses. On days when the wind blew, more than a few of those houses caught fire. All the livestock was rounded up and herded away. We didn't even leave cows to provide milk for the babies."

"One of those farms belonged to my parents," said an old, blind man with only one leg. Everyone turned and looked at him. "They supported the Union, but the army destroyed everything we had."

Strangely, there was an absence of hostility in his words. I thought about how I would have felt. Anger was the only emotion that came to mind. "You sound almost complacent about that tragedy," I said.

He nodded. "Each year since the war began it had been the same. The Rebs rode up the Valley each fall taking what they wanted, paying for it with worthless Confederate money. Those supplies fed the men who were killing my friends. Something had to be done about it or the killing would continue. Even so, I was young and whole at the time, still struggling to believe that wars could be fought with nobility and compassion. I became angry when I learned what had been done. I was wrong. We had to win it then and there. If doing that meant destroying the Valley that God must have blessed, well, it had to be done, that's all." He hesitated; then a tear rolled down his cheek. "Dad killed himself that winter. Mother died of pneumonia in the early spring. I have no fond memories of that war. It took my leg, my eyes, my parents, and my youth. I pray to God each night that He will finally take me and give me rest."

A solemn silence spread over the room. Each time, the same thing occurred. I always began by listening to the stories of the brave charges and the elation of victory described by a dwindling tribe of broken, old men. Somewhere along the way there always entered the cold, terrible reality that lay just beneath the surface of each such gathering. To save a nation, men had to die. It really did not matter if the bullet came from an enemy rifle or from a gun held by a despondent man after he had watched his life's work go up in smoke. The result was the same.

Soon there would be only the cold, dry words in books to speak of the glory and the terror. The flesh that had felt the wounds, heard the cries of elation and pain, the anguished emotions that no written word ever captured, would soon be lost, returned to the dust of the land where so many young men had marched innocently into battle and been transformed forever. Others, such as myself, bore the everlasting burden of reconciling the cost with the accomplishment. These forgotten old men had done all that was in them to do. It was difficult keeping that in mind as I looked at them now. Most could not even lift a musket. If there were, however, any men alive who could lay claim to giving this nation its future, a fair proportion of them were in this room.

It saddened me to see them now, broken, withering away, thoughts mired in a distant past, waiting impatiently for this great and tragic chapter of our history to end. On reflection, however, Colonel Barlow and the others were correct. This war would never end. Their sacrifice had truly given birth to a nation. Before the war, the appropriate phrase had been "these United States." All in all, that had been a contradiction in terms, and these men had set the record straight. When it was over, the phrase faded away, ever so subtly, and the nation had become "the United States."

In the dim light and silence, I thought of that. The relative merit of generals somehow seemed unimportant for a moment. Here in this room, one had only to let one's mind drift to hear the sound of reveille and the thundering boom of cannon. These men carried those sounds with them still. Even so, it was easier, looking at these old men, to realize that the more appropriate sound would soon be "Taps." They knew this better than I. They were veterans, one and all, burdened by a lonely and lasting kinship with death. They had all fought on the same side, the winning side, but individual experiences had shaped solitary perspectives. The side that they fought on no longer mattered. Even if the scars remained, the wounds had healed, both for the men and the nation, or the process was in place. The nation was one, as much as it ever could be.

There remained not a pimple of difference between these men and the men I had talked to in the taverns in Knoxville—Americans all. The men did not know each other, but those in the South would have understood the meaning of the silence in this room.

Still, I wanted to hear firsthand, from a man who was there, about that day when Sheridan rode down the Shenandoah Valley into history. It was important that I record the words of a witness. That yearning had brought me to this old soldiers' home. So I waited.

After several minutes, the old gentleman wiped away the tears with his pajama sleeve. "Well, Barlow," he said, "the man is waiting. Tell the story."

"Ahem," Barlow said, clearing his throat of the emotion that had choked him, too. "Only if you really want to hear it."

"I want to hear it," I said. I leaned forward to accent my interest.

He smiled. "It was October 19," he continued. "Sheridan had left for Washington three days earlier. Halleck had summoned him. General Wright's seven divisions were camped along Cedar Creek just west of the Valley Turnpike. It had been a hard month of fighting and cleaning out the Valley, and the men were taking a few days of rest. Then, at four-thirty that morning, everything came apart. The Rebs splashed across the Shenandoah River, just to the south of the sleeping men, and hit hard at the left flank. Surprise was total. Within an hour all seven divisions were routed and, in what can be described only as a disorganized mob, the men began running toward Winchester, ten miles to the northeast. I'd been assigned as an assistant regimental commander in Custer's cavalry. Most of the division was camped on the far right flank, away from the initial attack. I'd ridden out about thirty minutes earlier with a large patrol to keep tabs on Rosser's Confederate cavalry, which was demonstrating to our front. In no time we were cut off from the main body and had no choice but to follow the routed corps. For all we knew, the whole army was on the run.

"By nine, there was a steady flow of men moving to the northeast, us included. Some traveled along the turnpike, but most just plodded through the fields on either side of the road. They were spread east and west across several miles. We were about halfway to Winchester when I stopped.

" 'Major,' a sergeant said as he rode up beside me, 'I haven't seen a single soldier from the VI Corps.'

" 'What are you suggesting, sergeant?' I asked.

" 'Maybe they stood firm, Major. Maybe we should go back.'

"I turned in my saddle and looked across the landscape. As far as the eye could see, men were moving north and east. Here and there cavalrymen were trying to stem the tide, but with little success. What if the sergeant is right? I thought. What if we abandoned the VI Corps, leaving it to stand alone against all of Early's force? I led my men to a small grove of trees and ordered them to dismount. 'Men,' I said, 'it's been pointed out to me that none of the men we've seen are from VI Corps. That means one of two things: either the corps was captured whole, or they stood their ground and fought. I hear cannon in the distance. I think they stood. You have fifteen minutes to boil some coffee before we turn back.'

"Half a dozen fires were ablaze within a minute. I sat down under a tree with two of the company commanders and we tried to figure out what had happened. The more we examined the situation the more I was certain the rout hadn't been complete. For one thing, there were no Rebs in pursuit. They could've rounded up prisoners by the hundreds, but there wasn't a gray uniform in sight. Then it hit me: men were fighting and dying while we ran away. 'Mount up!' I yelled, and the men gulped down the warm water barely brown with the tint of coffee. 'Kick out those fires. Spread out and round up any stragglers you find. Tell them that VI Corps is holding the line. They must turn around and move to the sound of the guns. Move out at a walk.' My men spread out across several hundred yards and I moved south.

"We tried to stop the men walking north, but had little success. Some of the cavalry stragglers joined us, but mostly the foot soldiers strung along behind until we quit watching; then they disappeared into the trees and ditches. We pretended we were accomplishing something for thirty minutes or so when, from the rear, I heard a loud cheer. I stopped to look. There, moving at a slow gallop, was Sheridan at the head of a long column of cavalry. I saluted as he approached and he pulled to a stop. Back to the north, I saw former stragglers moving south toward us. Some were at a run, some at a fast walk, but all were heading south. No one seemed to be in command. They'd simply seen Sheridan heading south, and that was enough.

" 'What in hell is happening, Major?' Sheridan asked. 'Why do you think all these men are running?' I knew he already had the answer.

" 'Near as I can tell, General, the Rebs hit General Crook's flank about dawn and the whole corps ran. I think VI Corps held, though, and we're headed back.'

"Sheridan clenched a fist and sharply jabbed at the air. 'Good work, Major. Are those your men spread out across the fields?'

" 'Yes, sir. I ordered them to round up stragglers and turn them south, but we aren't having much success.'

" 'Well, by God, they'll follow me or I'll twist their tails for them. Stay at your work, Major—what's your name, Major?'

" 'Barlow, sir,' I said, 'of Custer's division.'

" 'Well, Major Barlow. I'm heading for VI Corps. I expect you to be there by noon with as many of these shirkers as you can round up. Tell them you talked to me. Tell them I need them to help me fight a battle and take back their camps. Do you think you can do that for me?'

" 'Yes, sir,' I replied with a sharp salute. 'We'll be there by noon or be dead.' I would've done it, too. I would've died for that man then and there if it'd been necessary.

" 'Good man,' he replied; then he dug his spurs into Rienzi, his horse. A short distance ahead, he ran into an infantry colonel. 'Where're you going?' I heard Sheridan ask.

" 'The army's whipped,' the colonel said.

" 'By God, you may be, Colonel, but not the army.' He shook his head as he looked at the beaten colonel. 'Turn around, men,' he yelled as he stood up in the stirrups. 'We're going to lick them out of their boots. Do you hear me? We'll lick them out of their boots. Are you with me?'

"A cheer rose from every man within sound of Sheridan's voice. 'Sheridan! Sheridan!' they yelled. All around, men began to run toward the road and the sound of his voice. Sheridan waved and yelled, and the men yelled back as they moved toward the road. You'd have thought they were all friends meeting after a year apart. 'Organize these men, Colonel, turn them south, and I'll see you at noon back where men are dying to protect your ass as you run away.'

" 'Yes, sir,' said the colonel as Sheridan rode off.

"All along the road it was the same. Sheridan rode a ways and yelled at the stragglers. They yelled back, usually screaming his name, 'Sheridan! Sheridan! It's Sheridan!' waved their caps in the air, and turned south. My men, and some of Sheridan's cavalry escort who had been ordered to extend the line, herded them along. Within an hour we had three thousand men gathered up. Those behind ran to catch up, those ahead turned when they saw us advancing. I never saw anything like it, before or after: men moving toward the battle, responding to nothing except the echo in their minds of Sheridan's call for help. And with each step, the sound of the guns grew sharper."

The old soldier seemed in a trance as he spoke. There was a reverence in his voice each time he spoke his general's name. Although most of the men gathered around had heard the story, probably many times, they leaned forward to absorb each word. Sometimes they would nod, almost as if being directed, as Barlow drove home a point. A state of grace seemed to grip them and they waited eagerly for each new revelation. There seemed to be a strange, vicarious association with what Sheridan had done that day. No one had an explanation for the electricity that snapped and sparkled in that valley; no one even tried to make sense of it. Men just don't move into a battle if there is a choice, at least not unless someone is right there to keep ordering them along. But men aren't much prone to taking orders from strange officers. I learned that in France. These men, by the thousands, moved as if Sheridan were there at their side urging them on.

"As we drew closer to the sounds of the guns," Barlow continued, "the men tucked in their shirts. With a deadly purpose of mind, they rammed the rods into their rifles to check the load. That business out of the way, they hardened their expressions into that stiff-jawed grimness so typical of men approaching death. Without orders, they began to organize themselves into squads, then companies, and, finally, regiments. Men who'd never seen each other before set their minds to fight alongside strangers and to take orders from the nearest officer. The transformation had a magical quality. The mob turned into an army in less time than it takes to tell about it. I suppose it resulted from years of training. Every man knew what to do. What struck me most was the resolve in their expressions. It was as if they all said in unison: 'By God, we ran this morning, but this afternoon we'll kick their asses.' They knew only that Sheridan needed them, and they directed every thought at arriving on time, if humanly possible.

"As the head of the column approached the hill where VI Corps had gathered, a staff general rode up. I was at the tip of a flat V of cavalry strung out right and left. 'Are you Major Barlow?' he asked.

"I saluted. 'Yes, sir.' How does he know me? I wondered.

" 'General Sheridan wants these men to extend the line to the right. Are you in command?'

" 'No, sir,' I said pointing. 'That colonel is the ranking officer.'

"The general looked sternly at the man, then at me. 'Is that the colonel who told General Sheridan that this army was whipped?'

" 'I believe he is, sir.'

"The general looked up and down the line; then he looked back at me. 'Have you been in battle before, Major?' he asked.

" 'Yes, sir. I've been with Grant from the Wilderness on. I'm on temporary assignment with Custer's division.'

" 'You're now a commander of infantry, Barlow, with the brevet rank of colonel. You take command and move these men into formation. Will you do that for General Sheridan?'

" 'YES, SIR,' I replied sharply.

"The general rode over to the colonel and leaned down and said something. As he straightened up in the saddle, the colonel had a shocked expression on his face; then his head dropped. He had the expression of a man who'd just been shot in the chest and knows that as soon as he falls he'll be dead. Then he reached up to his shoulders and tore off his rank insignia. He extended the eagles, along with his hat, which also had the insignia on it, to the general. The general snapped them up and rode back, handing me the hat and patches of cloth. 'Here,' he said, 'Now you're Colonel Barlow.'

"In the distance, sitting stiffly in the saddle, Sheridan watched this strange ceremony. As the staff general rode off, I felt Sheridan's eyes and looked directly at him as he saluted. As I returned the salute, a chill ran down my spine. At that moment, dying for Sheridan seemed far too shallow a gesture. More than at any moment in my life I wanted to live, to lead those men forward, to drive General Early all the way to the Gulf. That was the moment that gave meaning to the remainder of my life."

Colonel Barlow raised a trembling arm and, with an extended bony

forefinger, waved it slowly across his front at the men gathered before him. "Sheridan was a general," he said, his tone defying anyone
to contradict his assertion. "Many others wore stars, but with or without
stars, Sheridan was a general."

The battle was an epilogue, needing to be fought only to confirm
what seemed assured from the outset. Late in the afternoon, with stragglers
still flowing into the ranks, Sheridan ordered the army forward. As
only he knew how to do, he made the mission personal.

"Take back your camps, men," he shouted as he rode along the
line of grim-faced men. "Twist those devils' tails until they yell for
mercy."

As always, Sheridan led rather than followed his men into battle.
Early avoided being driven to the Gulf, but just barely. By nightfall,
many were on their way to Northern prison camps. Early's army never
again raided the Valley to supply Lee's army.

Maj. Gen. William H. Emory, commander of XIX Corps, watching from a distance as the blue-clad soldiers advanced, summed up
the event: "That young man has made a name for himself today," he
said of Sheridan to a man who recorded the words. Indeed, he had.

A short time later, at Grant's recommendation and with Lincoln's
approval, Congress promoted Sheridan to the permanent rank of major general in the regular army, the highest rank then available—except that held by Grant. Sheridan was thirty-three at the time. Mainly
because of his youth, men in high places had resisted his being given
command of the Valley army, but Grant knew. He had detected the
fierce spark of resolve in Sheridan's eyes, and Grant needed nothing
so much as to find a general like himself, a general who, above all
else, accepted no ending for battle except victory.

There were but few moments in the war that rank as indelible turning
points. One was when Grant turned south on a dusty road in the
Wilderness. Another was Missionary Ridge at Chattanooga, where
Sheridan led his division up an unconquerable hill and conquered it.
A third was Sheridan's ride up the Shenandoah Valley. It struck me,
as I watched the old soldiers hobble and roll back to their beds, that
greatness does not come to a man. It is within him waiting for circumstance to pull it into view. Nothing elevates circumstance, I thought,
like war.

22 Petersburg under Siege

It is impossible to pinpoint with any certainty the beginning of the end of the war. Many have proposed that this critical period began the day Lee filed his men into the Petersburg trenches. Others point to Vicksburg, noting that its capture severed all effective links to the West, thus denying the South that vital source of men and supplies. Still others point to Gettysburg, where, with the benefit of hindsight, it is evident that the battle ended the South's attempt at sustained offensive action. What historian, they say, could ever look past Pickett's charge, an event considered by many to be the "high-water mark" of the Confederacy?

Others claim that Grant's 1864 Virginia campaign is the most prominent benchmark of Southern defeat. They prefer to examine milestones from a more subtle perspective, measured by attitudes and larger world events. If that theory is correct, then certainly the Battle of the Wilderness stands out, not so much for the gruesome result of the conflict, but for the measurable change in thinking about the human savagery required to end the war. That bloody encounter recorded more than victory or defeat. Although many historians, North and South, agree that by the standards of the time Grant lost that battle, the events that followed that conflict proved of greater importance.

The transformation occurred when Grant simply refused to acknowledge defeat or dwell on transient victory or defeat and, at the Brock Road crossroads, turned his men south toward Spotsylvania. From that point forward, there was unceasing battle, with individual conflicts becoming mainly transitory means to the end—stopping the war forever. A subtle difference perhaps, but everything in the meaning of how the war was fought from that moment forward. Spots on a map lost all importance, except when the armies clashed in major battles marking a momentary surge in the casualty count. There is no denying that this change occurred, or that it evolved as the result of a specific plan. In my mind, the beginning of the end commenced at two widely separated places on the day Grant moved across the Rapidan into northern Virginia, while deep in the South Sherman began his seemingly endless series of flanking movements against Gen. Joseph E. Johnston, who was later replaced by Gen. John Bell Hood. This latter component of the conflict led to Atlanta's fall and Sherman's imposition of hard war on the states that so far had avoided the suffering that a war to eradicate ideas must inevitably impose.

If the critical transformation began with the North, there occurred an equally important metamorphosis in the South, but there it came from a different direction and had a different design. By the summer of 1864, the effectiveness of this war of attrition had reached the stage where only the most irrational Southern optimist expected ultimate victory in the field. Grant's and Sherman's forces were destroying resources and forcing Southern casualties at a pace far exceeding any possibility of replacement. Reliance on human passion to defend ideas began giving way to the cold mathematical reality of the casualty counts. All of the stamina and force of will embodied in Southern resistance could no longer alter the numbers: the bottom of the Southern barrel of resources had been reached. By the fall of 1864, with the irretrievable loss of the Shenandoah Valley, the barrel had been scraped clean. All that remained was a temporary reprieve as the South recycled aging, wartorn resources.

I believe the first sign of this evolution of events can be found in the Battle of Chickamauga, although Southerners at the time simply hailed the shift of Longstreet's corps from east to west as another example of Lee's resourcefulness. Just to eke out a narrow victory, made possible as much by Fate as by generalship, events had forced Lee to send his best corps six hundred rail miles south to establish a balance of manpower. Even with that, the victory was incomplete, largely because Braxton Bragg lacked the force to follow up the Union rout. If ever there had been justification to argue that victory delayed is victory denied, the later Battle of Chattanooga ended the debate. By the fall of 1864, when there remained no further capability for massive troop shifting to influence events, it had come down to the reality that the South would win or lose with the resources at hand. Many war-weary Southern citizens in the border states, where up to this time much of the war had been fought, were of a mind that it was high time for the states forming the core of the rebellion to join finally in their personal misery and devastation of property. Sherman's roundabout march through Georgia and the Carolinas ended this perceived slight.

Yet earlier, by the late summer of 1864, the significance of the South's plight had solidified, perhaps more so in the South than in the North. There no longer existed reasonable hope that Lee could manufacture another of his brilliant victories. Indeed, the major concern addressed the possibility of his escape when the defense of Petersburg became untenable. At this time eyes shifted North, where there would soon be a presidential election.

What had started as politics in the 1850s and early 1860s had swung full circle back to politics at mid-decade. Lincoln's election had been the catalyst for war in the first place. If Lincoln somehow managed reelection, no one doubted the war would continue. As had always been the reality, but with few other than Lincoln having the wisdom to see it, the outcome would not be determined by anything the South did. It would be by a collective decision made by Northern farmers and laborers, and, in the end, by Northern soldiers—as much at the ballot box as on the field.

I have arrived at the conviction that the South never possessed the capacity to win the war outright; it had always been a matter of Northern willingness to prosecute it. In that regard, much as the 1860 election had been a referendum on starting the war, the 1864 election became a referendum for deciding whether or not to see the war through. The result was to be as binding on the South as on the North. In that sense, at least, the schism defined by the Civil War had never been deep enough to destroy the idea of Union.

An interesting sidelight, illuminating the depths to which the South had sunk, occurred in the middle of March 1865, less than a month before Lee's surrender, when the Confederate Congress passed and sent to President Jefferson Davis a bill authorizing the induction of Negro soldiers into the army. A rider to that bill stipulated that this curious order would be executed only with the agreement of the slave's owner, although Davis had the authority to establish a firm quota of twenty-five percent of the Negro male population. In effect, the Southern Congress had launched a social revolution, nullified it to appease the fulmination that resulted, then proceeded to reaffirm the action—all in one document. A similar action, absent the required consent of any owner, had experienced difficulty even in the North. Asserting the will of a practical man, after swallowing a sizable portion of the ideals that drove him to war in the first place, Davis signed the bill and made it law.

In both North and South, this action was an irrevocable political confirmation that the Negro was indeed as capable, with proper training, of standing up to a hard fight as the most dedicated and intelligent white men. In the South, however, the action had a conspicuous anomaly: the Congress was telling the slave to fight to preserve the very social structure that presumed to keep him in perpetual bondage! Considering that the prospect of armed rebellion among the slaves had been among the few motivating forces behind Southern secession, can anyone doubt that irrationality had reached its zenith?

Nothing but the admission remained to confirm that the fighting continued with no defensible motivation other than gruesome habit.

Consequential turns in thinking seldom fail to produce pivotal results. In this instance, the turns led to a small dwelling in a backwater hamlet known as Appomattox.

If the war was in its final transformation that March, so too were the seasons. Spring, in name only, had arrived. The grim winter of 1865 hung on in a desperate struggle with the first seasonal rains as they tried to wash it away. If Lee, like the winter, would not yield, then it would be necessary to drive him from his trenches. The long fall and winter had provided Grant plenty of time to develop a plan and implement the essential changes needed to make it work.

For the first phase of operation, Grant intended to accelerate his efforts to stretch Lee's line to the breaking point. Lee knew that Grant's eventual success would require unleashing the onslaught across his whole front. He dared not wait until that happened. Lee's army of forty thousand manned an uneven, unbroken trench line that stretched more than fifty miles from the James River, east of Richmond, past Bermuda Hundred, southeast of Petersburg, and then in an arc extending north to the Southside Railroad. Mathematics defined Lee's dilemma. With fewer than a thousand troops per mile, Lee had only one man for each four yards of trench, worse even than the crisis conditions the previous June when General Smith failed to kick open the door to Petersburg with odds of five to one in his favor. The differences now were that Lee was on hand and he had considerable experience at moving troops along interior lines to shore up the points under attack. But in this there existed another mathematical impediment: moving troops to shore up weak points meant subtracting men from other sectors already near the breaking point. Grant had to find these points, strike before Lee made the shifts, and strike hard. Any breach would do if it cracked the thin veneer that held Lee's army together. First, however, he wanted to stretch the line one more time.

Lee had another idea. The condition of his army had deteriorated considerably since the first days of the siege. Animals indispensable to the task of moving cannon and supply wagons were weak from shortage of forage. Rations for the soldiers were barely at the subsistence level. Already, most of the important dignitaries had left Richmond for safer quarters farther south. It is perhaps not too judgmental to state that even the rats were abandoning the sinking Confederacy.

All in all, as the sights and sounds of spring began to fill the air, the carved-out island defining the twin cities' defenses had a dismal quality, not unlike that foretelling the advance of impending doom. Driven by sad recognition of this state of affairs, Lee decided the time had come to test Grant's preparedness. One last time, as if to show there remained a will if not a way, the old gray fox assumed the offensive.

23 Glory Lost, Glory Lost

"Looking down from a hill to the north of Fort Steadman," said the old Confederate captain in a clear, ringing voice, "Lee watched as the assault began at the break of dawn on March 25. I commanded one of the companies that assaulted the fort. Earlier, I'd escaped from Charleston before Sherman isolated the city. Leading six men, I spent the next three weeks working my way through Union lines until, wet and nearly starved, I crossed the James and scampered between Union pickets into Lee's lines. I had a burning in my soul to get back into the fight, and General Gordon gave me the chance."

"Did you really think you had a chance of success?" I asked.

He thought for a moment. "Yes, I suppose I wanted to *believe* we had a chance. At the same time, I knew in my heart that it had to end soon. I realized that at the first sight of the men holding the trenches. Gaunt beyond description, filthy to the point that skunks made wide circles around their quarters to avoid the smell, they were a sorry-looking lot. There wasn't a pound of fat on any collection of a dozen men. They were fit enough to hold a line, so long as the task required them only to load and fire a rifle. Taking offensive action, a deed demanding swift reflexes and sustained movement, was another matter. They woke up tired and their energies waned as the day progressed."

"Why, then, did Lee elect to go on the offensive?" I wanted to know.

"What choice did he have? Staying where we were meant certain defeat."

"How did you make out in the assault?"

"Just as Lee planned. We caught them by total surprise. Using the full force of the assault teams, followed by three infantry divisions, we captured Fort Steadman along with two adjacent gun batteries. Then everything came apart. After capturing the fort and batteries, we had planned to proceed south and capture three additional forts—really nothing more than built-up gun emplacements. With the captured munitions in those forts, we planned to turn the guns on the enemy flanks to consolidate what we had gained, then try to widen the breach in order to secure our escape. Trouble was, those other forts didn't exist, that is to say, they were unoccupied. There were no guns to capture and no means of providing support for what we already had captured. The Yankees had recovered from the initial surprise by the time we learned of this and had nearly surrounded our attack force. They brought a hundred cannon or more to bear—they hit us with more steel than at Gettysburg—and proceeded to pound us into the hereafter. We couldn't move forward, and retreat without being killed or captured seemed impossible."

"What did you do?"

"The men decided, mostly. They knew the war's end was only weeks away. They sensed that their deaths would be meaningless. Many surrendered. Some made it back, but more died as they tried to scamper across the field in a withering crossfire and amidst exploding shells. Later in the morning, the Union forces attacked on our right and penetrated a section of our trenches. Grant must've realized that we'd weakened our line to provide troops for the attack on Steadman. Altogether, we lost nearly five thousand men between dawn and midafternoon, losses nearly double those of Grant's force. It only confirmed the terrible cost of offensive action typical throughout the war. Our losses amounted to a tenth of our total forces. A year earlier, we would've shrugged off such losses with nothing more than normal grief for comrades lost. No longer. Those men were irreplaceable by any means."

"How did you feel?" I asked.

"Aside from the anger I felt at being among the captured, I felt numb. My efforts at getting to Lee's army had been wasted. The war had ended for me, and I knew the South was dead." He rose from the rocking chair and walked to the pillar supporting the corner of the broad brick porch. "How did I feel? Do you really want to know? That was the worst day of my life."

"Lemonade," said a soft voice at the double doors opening into the house. "Haven't you discussed the war long enough? Mr. Kelly, he'll talk your ear off if you let him. He loves the war, and everything about it. Don't let him tell you different."

The old man stiffened, as if trying to repel a difficult truth. "Hush, woman, and serve the 'ade," he said finally, with an awkward attempt at gruffness.

"He still thinks he's a captain leading troops to victory," she said as I grasped the cold glass. "But I know." She looked at him, and the love sparked in her eyes. "I know."

We sipped and rocked for a while there on the front porch of the stately stone house perched peacefully in the center of a manicured lawn surrounded on three sides by a swift-running, clear-water creek. This old soldier had gracefully weathered the years since the war. The only son of a sharecropper father, he had educated himself in the law and made the most of the meager opportunity available to him after the war. A hundred men and women, black and white, worked the cotton and tobacco fields to our front. He refused to call it a plantation, preferring instead to think of his thousand-acre domain as a farm. He and his wife had raised four sons and as many daughters, all born since the war, all successful in their own right. Three of the sons ran the farm, along with two others of near equal size that they had acquired. In addition, they managed a far-flung empire of real estate and transportation that had long since made them millionaires. The captain—Jerome was his name, but all his neighbors called him Captain—had retired more than a dozen years earlier. He seemed content to rock on the porch during the hot summer days and, in the cool, evening hours, to stroll or ride his great gray stud around this cornerstone of his accomplishment. "I call him Reb," he said of the horse with a chuckle. His boys still called him Sir, but their wives called him Dad. The grandchildren, child and adult alike, simply called him Gramps.

Here, in the tranquillity of a cool evening breeze, it occurred to me that he had been wise to curb his zeal and surrender rather than try to make it back to his lines. Much about this world would have been altered by his death. How much, I thought, had been forever altered by the deaths of the more than six hundred thousand who never made it home? How much had we given away with the loss of their energies?

Although at this desperate moment Lee's army had just two weeks to survive as a fighting unit, many of the names of the six hundred thousand remained to be written on the roll call of the dead. President Lincoln, sensing the end, traveled south to visit Grant and Sherman, the latter having recently arrived for a final strategy session with his immediate superior. Lincoln, informed by the two generals that at least one more great battle remained to be fought, suffered anguish at the thought. It must have seemed so senseless, as the outcome had become a foregone conclusion.

"Must more blood be shed?" Lincoln asked. "Cannot this last, bloody battle be avoided?"

Grant replied that only Lee could answer that question.

Lincoln responded by rephrasing his original question: "My God, my God. Can't you spare more effusions of blood? We have had so much of it."

I suppose the realization that each man killed would be a citizen of the nation bothered Lincoln the most. That, more than anything, was the cause of his anguish throughout the war. Such was the awful truth of civil war.

Grant had long since made an uneasy peace with his part in the killing. He had taken no hand in starting the conflict, but Providence had thrust him into the forefront of the effort to end it. He was determined to see it through. He had absolute confidence in the final outcome. He even viewed Lee's attack on Fort Steadman as proof of the rebel general's desperation. From a logical, military perspective the attack never had a chance of success. Lee's fortunes had sunk to the point where desperation drove him forward. He had always been audacious in battle—but never reckless, without hope or expectation of the victory. That was the difference.

The irony of Fort Steadman was that the attack had been little more than a temporary inconvenience to the Union commander. So minor, in fact, that Grant had no reservations about taking his commander-in-chief for a late afternoon visit to the site. Removal of the dead and wounded had been only half completed, and the sight was almost more than the president could endure. This undoubtedly increased his anguish when he learned of the need for at least one final battle.

*   *   *

"I was serving on Grant's staff," said Lt. James Henry, "when Sheridan came riding up in a drenching rain. Fresh out of officer training school, I'd been with the army less than a week at the time. My head was still in the clouds from the sight of all those important generals. It was the first time I'd seen Sheridan. I remembered bragging to a young captain that I, at six feet tall and half again his weight, could probably whip the general with one hand tied behind my back. The captain scoffed: 'If I was you, I'd make arrangements to send my effects home before I tried.'

"It'd been raining solid for a day. The ground was more swamp than solid earth—standing horses simply sank to the knees. The weather had brought Sheridan to talk to Grant about his orders."

"Was he upset because of them?" I asked.

"Yes, but not the way you might think. Due to the terrible weather, Grant had sent a message suggesting that Sheridan delay his attack on Lee's far right. Sheridan wanted nothing of that. Grant expressed concern that getting forage to the mounts would be impossible in that weather.

" 'Forage?' Sheridan shouted—he was the only man, Sherman included, who had no fear at all of Grant—'I'll get all the forage I need. I tell you, I'm ready to strike out tomorrow and go to smashing things!' That was the only time I saw Grant smile. They talked for a while, off in a corner, or rather Sheridan talked as Grant listened. Now and again Sheridan slammed his fist into his other hand or made some wild gesture with his arms. Grant just stood there, arms crossed, shifting his weight from one foot to the other, chewing on a cigar, and nodded his head whenever Sheridan made a sweep with his arms. I felt the excitement rising in that room, as did all the others, from generals to lieutenants. We knew the eve of the last big battle had arrived. Never once did Sheridan set about to 'smash things'—his favorite expression—but what a bunch of men died."

I knew of Sheridan's reputation, and I was familiar with the conference that Lieutenant Henry described. So far as I knew, Henry was the only man still alive who witnessed the exchange. His point of view intrigued me, as he provided the last living link to a truly historic event.

"Did he get his way?" I asked, knowing the answer in advance.

"Certainly he did. He never backed down so long as there remained a hint of a chance that events would progress as he hoped. The only way Grant could've shut him up was to say, 'Your orders are thus and such.'

" 'Goddamn!' Sheridan exclaimed, slapping his leg at the end of the discussion, 'it's time to bring this to an end, General, time to smash them up!'

"Grant said something inaudible. Sheridan nodded, then turned and walked away. 'I'll cut the Southside Railroad within two days,' he said over his shoulder as he moved toward the door. He seemed to be speaking more to himself than to Grant.

" 'Let me know, as early in the morning as you can, your judgment of the matter,' Grant said. Sheridan gestured only slightly as he pulled on his raincoat. Turning to where I stood in the corner, Grant said, 'Lieutenant Henry, go with General Sheridan to serve as courier in case there're any problems with the telegraph.'

"A sergeant's job, I thought, and I wouldn't trade the mission for a colonel's eagle. I nearly fell down scrambling for my poncho.

" 'Easy, boy,' Sheridan said, motioning me through the door ahead of him. Then I rode with the general into history, you might say."

I had difficulty imagining this noted scholar as a young man. Imagining him as an awkward, excitable shavetail proved impossible. His quarters on the top floor of the Humanities and History Building resembled more an archive than an office. Three young graduate students sat at a table nestled in a corner surrounded by broad bookcases that reached to the top of the three-meter-high ceiling. At first glance, they seemed absorbed in their research. Frequently, however, I caught them glancing out of the corner of an eye and cocking an ear to catch a phrase spoken by the professor. During my time there, all of a morning and most of the afternoon, a constant flow of students moved in and out of the large room. Henry knew them all and usually made crisp comments about papers they had written or comments they had made in one of his classes. Although now nearly 75, totally bald and blind in one eye, his mind seemed sharper than that of anyone I knew who was a third his age—including myself.

At thirty-one, Lieutenant Henry had written a book describing the behavior of different types of commanders in battle. Long before Freud published his works on psychological theory, Henry had applied similar ideas to his writings about military figures. Most of the historians I know consider his the definitive work on the subject. His thesis was that in life-and-death situations, certain types of people are most likely to be successful. Obviously, this had direct application for understanding men in military command situations. Basically, he had detected two classic types.

The first, and most obvious, are leaders who think they have nothing to lose. These are the true hero types, soldiers who throw caution to the wind and act mostly on impulse. The conditions that bring them to this action may be unique and even temporary. Henry argued that if death seems certain there is no longer any reason to be timid. When the situation stabilizes and there is time to think, the true nature of the individual reasserts itself. In rare cases, he argued, an individual will act on this plane all the time, although few survive very long. This explains, he believes, why there are so few pure military geniuses—they usually get killed before they reach the upper ranks. Also, because such leaders tend to be somewhat unconventional, they have difficulty following the rules necessary for steady movement through the ranks. Their views tend more than infrequently to offend conventional military thinking and the officers holding those views.

The second type is more complex. Lee and Grant fit this profile, as did Sheridan and Sherman, although Sheridan may have been a rare mix of the two. These men have the ability to ignore completely all the little disasters and distractions going on all about them. They focus entirely on the final outcome. Unfettered by conventional tactics, they orchestrate events with a view toward a grand strategy. They create military strategy rather than follow the thinking of others. They do this in different ways, Henry argued, but the result is always the same so long as there is any way of altering the commonplace assumption of where conditions seem to be heading. Disaster confronts such men no less than others. They simply refuse to accept it, freeing their minds to find ways around it. Such men also seem to have the uncanny ability to know what an opponent will do, often before the opponent himself knows. Lee recognized this quality in himself when he commented to Stonewall Jackson that he feared the time when Lincoln finally sent a general he could not figure out to confront him.

Longstreet knew of Grant's history as a ne'er-do-well in civilian life. Even though influenced by this knowledge, he warned Lee that Grant would come at him, and keep coming at him, until he ended the war. Lincoln, too, saw this trait when most in Washington were urging him to fire Grant after Shiloh. And Lincoln had never met the man. "This man fights," Lincoln responded when others urged him to sack the general. At the time, he needed nothing so much as a man with the willingness to fight. Such a man, a man incapable of even considering defeat, was the only type of man capable of defeating Lee.

Lee and McClellan were the most graphic contrasts in personalities. Lee acted instantly on nothing more than supposition and instinct. McClellan, on the other hand, had doubts even in the most assured of conditions. McClellan came into possession of Lee's written battle plan shortly before the battle at Antietam. He knew that Lee had split his forces and was greatly outnumbered. Still, it was beyond his capability to abandon his own doubts and bring himself to use his full force to attack Lee. He could have ended the war on that crisp September day in 1862, probably even have become president, if only he had been able to break free from his own demons of doubt. Ironically, placed in a situation where his organizational skills counted for something, McClellan probably would have been a more effective president than Grant. Instead, history has scorned him to the point that he appears to be nothing so much as a bumbling egotist long on planning and short on action.

"How long were you with him?" I inquired, still trying to catch up with my recording of his utterances. I wanted every word. The man obviously had applied his powerful intellect to looking below the surface of events, largely looking past the what and going straight to the why. I found his theories, greatly expanded since his earlier writings, intriguing and thoroughly worthy of exploration.

"Off and on, to the end," he replied.

"Were you present when he relieved Warren?" I asked.

His answer moved around the question.

"There was an urgency about Sheridan that's difficult to define," he said thoughtfully. "No matter what task he set for himself, which naturally involved those he depended upon, his thoughts seemed to be somewhere out ahead, as if the moment's events were preliminary to something yet unseen. The problem emerged when he made adjustments in his own mind, adjustments others were not privy to. I truly believe he was a man made for war, but his handicap was in having to rely on other generals to grasp developing problems and make adjustments based on initiative. When they moved more slowly than he thought necessary, he became impatient—at times even volatile."

In every sense of the word, Sheridan was Grant's Stonewall Jackson. Lee usually defined an objective in only general terms and relied on Jackson to supply the details. Grant responded to Sheridan in the same manner. This was also true of Grant's relationship with Sherman. Doing that makes one vulnerable and requires uncompromising trust and confidence among the respondents. Lee felt the pain of Jackson's loss, and the loss was evident during the last year of the war. I am totally convinced that, had Stonewall been alive, history books would make no mention of Pickett's charge at Gettysburg—it never would have happened.

"Fearless to a fault," Henry continued, "Sheridan saw only two options in battle: win or get killed in the effort. When he was cleaning out the Shenandoah, the rebel cavalry kept nipping at his heels, distracting him from the work at hand. He grew tired of it and told his cavalry commander to 'whip or get whipped.' That's a hard condition to accept for men who want to survive. It was an irrational expectation of a man such as Warren, who seldom moved without worrying about the outcome."

Henry reached toward a shelf filled with rolled-up maps. He examined them for a moment before withdrawing a roll nearly three feet long. "This is Grant's original battle map," he said. "The most interesting parts are the little notes he made in the margins." He studied the map, then looked up. "I have to say it: at this stage of the war, the army needed leaders with dash and quick reflexes. Every moment was fluid. Every missed opportunity meant more men had to die. Warren was the wrong man at the wrong time in the wrong place. Put into proper perspective, what are reputations when men's lives are at stake? Sheridan was in no mood to accept excuses. He knew what he wanted done, and he insisted on it being done right the first time. What happened to Warren probably was unfair, or would have been unfair under different circumstances. It was a case of too many times too late." He looked thoughtfully at the map. "Yes, I was there, or at least close enough to know what happened when Sheridan fired Warren."

"What exactly happened?" I asked.

"Well, after we left Grant's headquarters, we sloshed back to Sheridan's forward command post. In the dim light of a lantern, he laid out the plan for moving north at first light, regardless of the weather, to try to move around Lee's flank and capture the railroad. I have the original of that map someplace. Unknown to anyone, Lee had anticipated this move and had sent Pickett out in a blocking movement. For Lee, having Sheridan north and west of his lines meant the end. This would block his only avenue of escape, and he knew better than anyone that that route would have to be used sooner rather than later. After Sheridan solidified his plans, he sent a message telling Warren what he expected to do and asking Warren to support the right flank. I carried the dispatch. My orders were to wait to see if Warren had any questions. He said he understood his part perfectly, and I carried that message to Sheridan."

"So Warren's troops were an actual part of the operation?"

"Yes and no," the professor replied. "The next morning, Sheridan sent General Devin forward with a small force to feel out the enemy's forward defenses. Warren was expected to act independently, but in support. That was part of the problem. On the first day there really were two command structures. The fighting progressed badly that first day, mostly because the original force sent out by Sheridan was out-numbered by about three to one. Even so, he thought Warren's hesi-tation cost him the initiative. That evening, Sheridan sent a message to Grant requesting that Wright's corps replace Warren's. Sheridan had lost all confidence in Warren's leadership, if he ever had any. Grant replied that Wright had other duties, but as a compromise, he gave Sheridan overall command and, in a separate dispatch, authorized Sheridan to relieve Warren if he believed it necessary.

"In the end, it came down to a total contrast in personalities. Sheridan, the flamboyant, aggressive, hit-'em-hard-where-they-least-expect-it cavalry officer was as different as night from day to the slow, defensive-minded, cautious Warren. Warren seemed always just a step behind events. As a result, he usually found himself reacting rather than acting."

"I've never understood that," I replied. "His actions at Little Round Top were just the opposite. There, he was decisive and aggressive, actually acting beyond his authority to take charge in a crisis situation."

"I've thought about that," replied the professor. "I think I know the answer. Little Round Top was essentially a confined action. It also fit Warren's personality perfectly. His every action was in reaction to the movements of the rebels. From his vantage point he had a clear view of events unfolding all around him, a condition seldom available to him as a corps commander. Options and time were limited. But there was the added ingredient that Warren was acting on his own initia-tive rather than responding to the expectation of higher authority. If he'd failed, it would've been a noble effort that no one had a right to expect to be successful. Being a corps commander was entirely dif-ferent. There, his responsibility was firmly established. Aggressive action was more of a personal risk than passive delay. In a fixed command situation, his true, cautious nature controlled his responses. It was that inherent, plodding nature that contrasted so completely with Sheridan.

At the time, however, I thought of none of this. Sheridan was my idol, and if he called Warren unfit for command, that was all I needed to know."

"So you're telling me that the real problems began the next day?"

"Yes, right from the start of operations."

*   *   *

" 'Devin,' Sheridan commanded as the two men rode along the long line of blue-clad men organized by regiments, 'you'll go straight at Pickett. The fight's all gone from them, I sense it. Warren's men will be moving with you. If everything goes as planned, he'll swing on the enemy's left flank and block their escape route. Cavalry will screen out any reinforcements. I want them captured, all of them. Now, go to smashing them up.'

" 'Yes, sir,' Devin said; then he rode off. Devin moved the skirmishers out first; then he hit hard with everything he had. Warren didn't. Sheridan watched for a few minutes, the anxiety etched in his face because he'd received no reports from Warren. Even with the sound of Hell exploding all about, he kept looking to the east. Shortly, he broke away from his staff and rode to the top of a small knoll. Standing stiff in his stirrups, he shaded his eyes against the late afternoon sun that suddenly burst through the clouds. His aides scrambled to catch up. I brought up the rear. 'I see Ayres's division' he said, his brow furrowed. 'Where are the others?' His agitation grew. 'Lieutenant,' he pointed at me, 'ride over and see if you can determine what's going on.' Then he said as an afterthought: 'Where's General Warren?'

"I rode about four hundred yards east to the top of a rise just east of White Oak Road. Up ahead, through the woods, I saw General Ayres turning his men west—he'd moved too far east—but the other two divisions were moving far off to the east. I sensed we were heading for a disaster. I spun and rode back to Sheridan. 'General,' I yelled over the sound of the exploding shells, 'the whole corps seems to have moved too far east. From what I could see, General Ayres got his men turned back west, but the others are moving north and east, away from the battle.'

" 'Goddamn!' Sheridan exclaimed, 'I knew it. Did you see General Warren?'

" 'No, sir,' I replied. He turned and said something to a major, who then spurred his horse and rode off. He'd moved about twenty yards when a shell exploded directly under his horse. The major fell to the ground in three pieces.

" 'Lieutenant,' Sheridan said, motioning to me before the debris had settled, 'go tell General Devin that General Warren will be late. Tell him he has to drive those men and drive them hard. Tell him to keep the pressure on, and the Rebs'll break. Tell him that for me.'

"I saw the contortions on Sheridan's face. He was furious with Warren. Warren had already been late getting his men into position for the attack. This had delayed the attack for hours, and with the cloud-covered sky, daylight was fading fast. I rode off as fast as my horse would run.

"Just as my horse jumped over a trench, a shell exploded against the near bank. The force of the explosion lifted the horse's rear almost vertical, pitching me forward and to the side. I felt a sharp, burning sensation behind my right eye; then everything went black. When I woke up, my horse was screaming in agony. The shell had ripped open his belly and his guts were spread out in the mud. With double vision distorting everything around, I pulled my pistol and shot the horse; then I pulled myself to a standing position. I had only one thought: get to Devin. He had to press on, and already there were signs that the thrust was weakening. A cavalry private rode up and I grabbed his horse's reins. 'I have to get to General Devin,' I shouted. 'Get off that horse.' The private tried to pull away and I pointed my pistol at his head. 'Your way or mine,' I said, and he swung out of the saddle. I felt the blood rippling along the side of my face as I spurred the horse to a run. In the cool air, the vision returned to my left eye, but my right eye had been blinded forever." He lifted his hand to the black patch covering the socket where his eye had been. "By the time I reached Devin, with all the rough riding on the way, the eyeball hung down on my cheek.

" 'General Devin!' I yelled, 'General Sheridan says you must continue the attack. General Warren seems to have been delayed. He asks, sir, can you keep up the pressure?'

"The general just stared at me. I must have been a sight, all covered with blood, an eyeball dangling on the side of my face. 'You seem to have a problem, Lieutenant,' he said, pointing at my face.

" 'Will you be able to continue the attack, sir?' I asked again.

" 'Yes, I will,' he replied, 'but without Warren, I doubt I can cut off their retreat. Warren must block them. Tell General Sheridan that. Now, go to an aid station, sir.'

" 'General Sheridan awaits your reply, sir,' I yelled. 'I must return.'

"It must've been nearly a half hour before I found Sheridan; he never stayed in one place for long. Sheridan was in a frenzy of excitement, yet he seemed totally preoccupied. 'General Sheridan, General Devin says he has all he can handle. He'll keep going, but he says that without General Warren's men cutting off the flank, he can't give assurance he can hold Pickett's men.'

"Without replying, Sheridan grasped his guidon and rode off. Bullets were flying all around. Then he reined his horse in sharply. A sergeant, not five feet from Sheridan, cut in front of him. Taking a bullet meant for Sheridan, he toppled from his horse, shot through his temple. Then a captain fell wounded, his arm hanging by the threads of his jacket. Sheridan didn't seem to give a damn for the danger. With one man just killed, and a second with his arm nearly blown off, he looked at me curiously.

" 'There's something on your cheek, Lieutenant,' he said; then he rode off. I've always liked to tell myself that my losing an eye saved Sheridan's life, but of course I can't know that. I heard the buzz of a half dozen bullets flying by in the brief time he spoke.

"By this time, despite Devin's best efforts, the advance began to falter. Sheridan rode into their midst. Strangely, I felt no pain at all. I rode over to an aid station, where a corpsman took one look at me and called the doctor.

" 'Seems you have a problem,' he said as he clipped the strand of flesh holding the eye to the socket. He gave me a small cup of something—laudanum I think—and after cleaning up the wound, pressed a bandage to my empty socket. Feeling somewhat dizzy, I staggered back to my horse, pulled myself up, and rode back to the battle.

" 'Go get 'em, men,' Sheridan kept yelling. 'Don't delay or they'll all get away. Do your duty for me today.' He pumped the air with his guidon as if trying mentally to pry them from their holes. Slowly, they began to rise and move forward. 'By God!' I heard him say. 'Is that General Griffin coming up?' Griffin commanded the middle third of Warren's V Corps. Pointing the way with his guidon, he directed men into line. Then Pickett's men began to break and run. 'Round 'em up!'

Sheridan shouted excitedly, pointing at a squad of running Rebs. 'Don't let any of 'em get away!'

"Warren still was nowhere in sight, but as Griffin and Ayres moved their men in closer on the flank, Pickett's lines began to crumble. Rebs surrendered in lots of ten and twenty, then by companies and regiments. It was a spectacular thing to watch.

"I guess you might say, in the end, Warren got his men back on track and everything worked out satisfactorily. Actually, it appeared to me that they came up at just the right time for maximum psychological impact. I learned later that Warren was in the enemy's rear gathering up prisoners who'd broken loose from the main battle. After he got his third division moving in the correct direction, he sent a staff officer with a message that his men were closing in around the remainder of Pickett's force. My thoughts were getting a little fuzzy by this time, but Sheridan woke me up. After receiving the report, Sheridan exploded.

" 'By God, sir!' Sheridan shouted. 'You tell General Warren for me that he wasn't in this fight.' That might have ended it except the bewildered officer asked that the message be sent in writing.

"Sheridan readily complied. 'Take it down, sir!' he shouted. 'Tell him, by God, he was not at the front.' Sheridan then initialed the note and the officer rode off.

"A few minutes later, he called me over and handed me a dispatch for General Warren. He squinted and looked at my face. 'You got your eye fixed, I see,' he said, then he rode off."

The professor stopped short, pausing to catch his breath. His head turned slowly and he looked longingly at the small, glass-covered frame hanging on the wall. Strange, I thought, that I had never noticed it before. I squinted trying to identify the objects behind the glass. I had seen one before. A medal. Small, unspectacular, hanging from a blue ribbon dotted by small white stars. A Congressional Medal of Honor. This man had been more than a courier for a general, I thought.

"Have you ever been in battle?" he asked as he looked at me.

I started to answer that I had, but remained silent.

"You can't imagine," he said. "No one can who hasn't. You could spend a million words trying to describe the chaos in just a hundred-foot-square space of an all-out battle, and never capture its essence. It's all the excitement in the world crammed into a tiny space. If there're a hundred men, there're a hundred stories that would require a lifetime to record. It overwhelms the senses if you stop to think about it at the time. The miracle is that anyone survives."

He looked at the medal again, but never mentioned the event that resulted in his being awarded the nation's highest award for gallantry.

"I found out only later," he continued, precisely where he had left off, "the substance of the message. It read:

MAJOR GENERAL WARREN, COMMANDING THE FIFTH ARMY CORPS, IS RELIEVED FROM DUTY, AND WILL AT ONCE REPORT FOR ORDERS TO LIEUTENANT GENERAL GRANT, COMMANDING ARMIES OF THE UNITED STATES. BY COMMAND OF MAJOR GENERAL SHERIDAN.

"With that terse message a man's career ended. Later, the story goes—I'd yielded to the pain by then and made it to a field hospital— Warren came to Sheridan and tried to explain, asking at the end that Sheridan reconsider. 'Reconsider, hell,' Sheridan reportedly said, 'I don't reconsider my decisions. Obey the order.' "

Even though more than fifty-five years had passed, I felt pangs of sympathy for General Warren. To have command stripped away during the heat of battle, I thought, is the worst possible disaster for a general officer. Death would have served him better.

Had he been set up for the fall, or had Warren's plodding ways become so predictable that he set himself up? Grant, after all, had made a point of sending Sheridan separate and specific authority to relieve Warren—a staff colonel had delivered the message. Why had he done this? Did he know Sheridan so well, and Warren, too, that he expected something to happen to justify such radical action? Grant had ample knowledge of Sheridan's dislike for Warren. His two subordinate commanders had clashed violently at the south edge of the Wilderness, just before Spotsylvania. Grant had taken Sheridan's side in that exchange and unleashed his cavalry commander to ride off after Jeb Stuart, an action that led to the death of the flamboyant Confederate general. Warren's relief, more than any other event of the war, has left me with an unsettled feeling about Grant. Although Sheridan was the instrument, Grant guided the hand. Was he justified? I posed that very question to Professor Henry.

"Yes," he replied without forethought, "I believe the action was justified, even essential. All along, the problem with the army had been the generals. It's sometimes difficult to remember them all. McClellan, Burnside, Hooker, McDowell, Smith, even Meade—and dozens more with lesser responsibility—all had shied away when confronted with the test of fire. As a result, tens of thousands died needlessly."

He leaned his forearms on the desk and looked me in the eyes.

"What if," he said sternly, "earlier on, say in '62, a senior general had been sacked on the field for lack of fortitude? Might others have acted differently after that? Might the message have sunk in that Lee could resist, even with limited resources, all effort not wholeheartedly pressed forward? Lincoln had seen the problem. He fired McClellan twice, even as popular as McClellan was with his men. But that had been political, after the heat of battle, and meant nothing to other field commanders.

"At this time, in late March of '65, the war had been dragging on for four bloody years. Wasn't it about time to end it? Neither Grant nor Sheridan knew what lay ahead. How many times, they must've wondered, had Lee appeared defeated only to strike a fatal blow and win a battle or escape destruction? The critical battle was at hand, and Lee still had a force of nearly forty thousand of the best soldiers this world ever produced. If Lee escaped and joined with Johnston's men in North Carolina, who knows how long the war might have continued?"

I looked over my shoulder. Twenty or more eager young men and women had gathered around. They had moved in with such stealth that I never heard a sound. Even if I retained doubts, these young people certainly had none. Their eyes were fixed on their professor in glowing admiration.

"Yes, Warren's dismissal was a harsh action," Henry continued, "but a necessary object lesson. If privates were shot for cowering under fire or falling asleep on guard duty, couldn't the firing of a general be justified if he obviously, seemingly by habit, failed in the dispatch of his duty?" He looked at me with that hard, severe look that tells one there is no doubt in what is about to be said. "One fact remains clear. Warren, as a corps commander, had an obligation to check the terrain over which his men would advance. His failure was a minor one perhaps, but, based on prior experience, a failure more than sufficient to lead to another disaster. His men did arrive late, and only Sheridan's personal intervention at the front kept the soldiers moving forward. A thousand times before, in a hundred battles, similar opportunities had been squandered, and each time the casualty list swelled."

I glanced at the small framed glass on the wall. It gave his words a certain absolute credibility that I dared not ignore.

Silence. Everyone seemed to wait for the next words. I know that I did. But the lesson had ended. At last I found myself nearing the end of Grant's war, for it surely had become his war by the first of April in 1865—that part of it that did not belong to Lincoln. The relentless destruction of lives and property had been a part of the struggle from the start, but Grant had raised the carnage to a never-before-equaled plane. Sad as the prospect made him, Lincoln approved the destruction. A left turn instead of a right, back in May of 1864, would have divided the nation forever. How the world might have changed had Lincoln faltered or had Grant proved unsuited to his task! Without Lincoln, Grant would have been tanning hides back in Galena, forgotten except for a brief shining moment when it hardly mattered. Without Grant, there probably never would have been a Sherman or a Sheridan to make hard war and thus end it forever on the continent. Sherman had said, back near the beginning, that the nation faced a hard and bloody conflict, and for that the politicians had pronounced him crazy. In 1865, barely three years later, no one would even have noticed the remark. Nobody other than Lincoln, at Grant's urging, would have approved the march across Georgia.

What of Sheridan? Most in the army, at least at the time of his emergence as a historical force, considered him a brash, disrespectful, impudent know-it-all. It is difficult to conceive of a general other than Grant who would have endured his hard-charging manner—except for Sherman.

Everywhere I looked, from top to bottom, in and out, it was Grant's war. His mark had been pressed on everything, even events he never touched. What had a soldier said of him? Wherever he went, things happened! Fearless beyond comprehension, able to accept the death of a thousand men as readily as an equal number of dead leaves blown from a winter-worn tree, impervious to criticism, reserved, often embarrassed in the face of adulation, a failure—all of these, and a thousand other superlatives and detractions, described Grant.

I had to accept it. Grant had been correct in his desire to see Warren go, even if he never said it outright. Sheridan had been correct to carry out a suggestion that had only the hint of an order. Eventually, four-teen years later and three months after his death—when the act had no meaning at all—a board of inquiry partially exonerated General Warren. His statue, perched high on the rough, boulder-strewn knob of earth known as Little Round Top, now marks the place of his most glori-ous day. Many say he saved the army, and even the Union, by his prompt, unhesitating action. What ironies wars produce. A millennium seem-ingly separated the high and low points of his life. Rise slowly, if you must, but avoid the fall at all hazard. An unforgiving world recalls only the fall.

As the guns fell silent at Five Forks at twilight on that April sec-ond, the end lay just over the horizon, a long week away.

24 But They Was Yankees!

The victory at Five Forks almost exceeded Grant's expectations, but not his hopes. Pickett's force had experienced a crushing defeat. Fewer than two thousand of Pickett's men remained under arms. More than five thousand men, including the captured and maimed, had disappeared from Lee's rapidly dwindling army. Sheridan's force suffered barely a tenth of the rebel loss. The time had passed, however, when Grant was content to ponder tomorrow's events, or even to count the dead. Even before the last echoes of the late evening shots had faded, Grant walked into his tent. "I have ordered an immediate assault," he said as he emerged a few minutes later.

Less than a month before I joined the army that later transported me to France, I guided a buggy along a northern Georgia backwoods dirt road to a hamlet whose name I can't recall. Not one of the eight houses had a flake of paint still hanging from its clapboard sides, if there ever had been any. Except for its location in what seemed to be another world, it might have been where I first met with that old Union colonel on a farm just a mile from the Mississippi, a dozen miles south of St. Louis. An acquaintance had informed me that in one of these houses there lived a man who was among the most valorous soldiers in the Confederate Army. I wanted to meet him.

I pulled my buggy to a stop next to where a small Negro child was slapping a stick in a mud hole. "Do you know a man by the name of Ramrod?" I asked. The next whack of the mud spattered the horse, and it lunged forward a couple of feet.

"He lives there," the young girl said, "in those trees."

I drove on ahead and tied the buggy to the rusted chickenwire fence.

After hanging a bag of oats around the animal's head, I opened the squeaking gate hanging by one hinge. The path to the house had nearly grown over; weeds stood three feet high all the way to the crumbling foundation.

"Are you Ramrod Legard?" I asked the wrinkled old man digging worms beside the crumbling porch.

"You don't see nobody else, do ya?" he replied.

"Would you mind talking with me for a spell?" I asked. "I'm gathering information about the War Between the States, and some people I talked to said you spent some time in the Confederate Army."

"Cain't," he replied gruffly.

"Why not?" I asked.

"Goin' fishin'," he replied. "Have to eat, ya know."

I considered my options. "Here, let me help you dig those worms," I replied, hoping to loosen him up. "I've done some fishing in my day."

He placed his palm in the small of his back and pushed, as if trying to apply leverage to straighten his scarecrow frame. Sweat poured down his face and saturated the tattered, dirty garment that passed for a shirt.

He handed me the shovel. "Dig here," he said. "Worms like the coffee grounds I throw here."

He watched from his perch on the porch. I needed only a few minutes to fill the rusty can with worms.

"Hummm," he said as I handed him the can, "that oughta do it." Sliding forward to his feet, he extended his bony arm and clasped the handle of a battered old minnow bucket sitting on the corner of the porch. "Don't know what they'll bite on," he said, "so I'm takin' both worms and minnows."

Without another word, he grasped the crooked pole leaning against the side of the house, turned, and began to fight through the weeds and bushes that barred his way. His path led across a field that sank downhill toward the river flowing through the trees about a hundred yards away.

"Can you talk and fish?" I asked.

"Nope," he replied as he kicked at a 'possum scampering around a tree.

Presently, he squatted next to the bank and baited his hook with a minnow; then he let the line drop into the barely moving water.

"Got any line?" I asked after a while.

He reached into an old sack that hung from his waist and withdrew a ball of line. He handed it to me without a word. I cut a stout limb from a nearby willow and attached the line. "Got a hook and sinker?" I asked.

He withdrew a small metal container from the sack and handed it to me. "Now fish," he said.

By five that evening I had caught three catfish just right for frying and several sun perch too small to keep. He had caught nothing. The fish must have preferred worms. "Well," I said, pulling my line from the water, "I suppose it's about time for me to go. Have to get back to the hotel in town before dark." I slung the gill line with the fish over my shoulder and started to move away. Ramrod had a hurt expression, as if he could not believe I would leave with those fish. Precisely as I intended. A man has to eat, you know.

"Ya wanta talk about the war?" he asked as he pulled in his line. "If ya do, I talk better with a full belly."

A sound bargain, I thought. I handed him the three fish. "I'll gut them, you fry them," I said.

He scrunched his lips together and nodded.

*　　*　　*

"I suhved with the Army of Northern Virginia afore Lee give it that name," said Pvt. Ramrod Legard as he pushed the tin plate away from the edge of the table. "My ol' man'd sent me up from northern Georgia to southern Virginia on tobacco business. I arrived the same day they fired the first shots at Sumter." He rose and walked to where several tobacco leaves hung next to the window. He broke off a small piece from one of the leaves and crumpled it in his hand before stuffing the grounds into his pipe. "Got a match?" he asked. I handed him one.

"Aftuh concludin' my business," he continued, "I sent my father a letter tellin' him I'd enlisted in the infantry. At the time, I thought the war'd be over within six months. Down my way we didn't have much respect for Yankee fightin' ability. I figgered my four younger brothers could supervise the plantin'. The ol' man had rumatiz so bad he couldn't get 'round much." His head dropped a little. "Never saw any of 'em agin. The ol' man died a year later. All my brothers died in the war."

"I'm sorry," I replied. "It didn't work out as you planned. You were still in the army four years later?"

"Yup, an' I was prepared to stay in it for another four if necessary."

"Did your family have slaves?" I asked.

"Yup," he replied defiantly, "'bout a hundred, more or less. Does that bother you? To us, they was property, nothin' more. It'd been that way for more'n two hundred years, an' I saw nothin' wrong with it. I learned how to make love with the prettiest little ol' black gal ya ever did see. By '60, 'bout a third of our niggers was startin' to look halfway white. Lovin' those gals was common practice in my parts."

"How do you feel about all of that now?" I asked, struggling to restrain my judgment.

"How'd I feel about it?" he answered. "Madder'n hell. We was right to pull outta the Union. My people come inta the Union back in 1789 with six slaves. With careful breedin' an' good care, the numbers grew twenty times durin' my grandfather's lifetime. What give them Yankees the right to say we was wrong?"

"The Constitution," I replied. "It states that all men are created equal."

"So what? Niggers ain't men. The courts ruled that over an' over. When did they all of a sudden become men? Some Yankee sayin' it don't make it so. Still ain't."

I decided not to belabor the issue. "I get the feeling you knew what you were fighting for," I said.

"You bet. I fought ta save my country, my property, and to kill damn Yankees. The only sin was losin'."

"By the first of April, in '65, you must have known it was about over."

He shook his head vigorously. "Not me. I expected Lee ta break free of Grant an' join up with Johnston over in North Carolina. If'n that wasn't possible, I was prepared to join the irregulars and fight on. Would'a, too, if'n Lee hadn't said we had ta surrender."

"Did that make you angry with Lee?" I asked, expecting an answer in the affirmative.

He thought for a moment. "Naw," he said. "How could I be angry with the best dang soldier in the world?"

On that point, I was unsure I should take exception.

For the next several hours he outlined the war, and his part in it, from the beginning to the end. The ramblings of that old man, and those

of the people I spoke with at Vicksburg, served to form my opinion
about the way people in the Deep South looked at the war.

He had fought with Lee, in what is now West Virginia, back during the first months of the war. He had been at First Bull Run, Second Bull Run, Fredericksburg, Chancellorsville, and Gettysburg. A wound
kept him out of action at Antietam. After a severe wound at Gettysburg,
he returned to his unit in late 1863 and survived the Wilderness and
every battle following. He had risen to the rank of lieutenant before
being demoted after killing a man in a fight. Somewhere along the way,
his colonel had staged a contest to determine the best shot in the regiment.
Ramrod won hands down, according to his assessment, hitting inside
a tin cup nailed to a post eight times within three minutes—at a distance of fifty yards. As a result of having loaded and fired so fast, everyone
started calling him Ramrod. The name stuck.

By the spring of 1865, he had come full circle back to the rank of
private. He had remained a rebel through it all, right up to that day
when I spoke with him. By the time the war ended, only six of the
original members of his regiment remained alive. The long list of battles
including his name on the Roll of Honor gave ample testament to his
courage and dedication to the Southern cause. That, more than anything, probably kept him alive after he killed that other man. A man
died in the fight, but the South could ill afford to subtract Ramrod from
its ranks to avenge the death. Private or lieutenant, he still knew how
to kill Yankees. To me, his attitude and his courage formed the em-
bodiment of the fighting spirit of the Southern soldier. Still, during
my long conversation with him, I never found one point of moral
agreement with this man.

"What do you remember about the last week of the war?" I asked
as the hands on my pocket watch moved straight up.

"It was Hell on earth," he replied. "Grant come at us with all he
had just as soon as Sheridan routed Pickett at Five Forks. My comp'ny'd
been posted to guard Lee's headquarters. That mornin', even afore the
sun rose, I saw a line a bluebellies approachin' from the south. Must'a
been ten thousand of 'em. They'd busted clean through our trenches
and was closin' in for the kill. Lee come out'n his tent an' stood lookin'
at 'em for the longest time. He had a grim, hard-set expression; yet
there was a defiance in him, as if he meant ta fight 'em off by hisself.
Presently, an officer come ridin' up an' tol' Lee that Gen. A. P. Hill

was dead. Lee's chin dropped ta his chest. I think he cried. Shortly, we cooked some cornbread in bacon grease—the last hot meal I had for six days—an' then we moved out. I didn't see Lee again until the end."

"What followed?" I asked.

"Runnin'," he replied, "a whole lotta runnin'. We was plumb outta food; ammunition was low; my clothes was nothin' but threads; only one a my shoes had a sole in it; horses was so exhausted that they refused to pull the wagons—if we'd had any fit to roll—all in all we was more a mob than a army. I started out in the direction of Danville with Longstreet's corps. Our commanders'd told us that somewhere 'long the way we could expect to receive rations and supplies. 'Bout that time—April 2 or 3, I cain't 'member for certain—Petersburg an' Richmond fell to the damn Yankees. We marched near forty miles durin' that day an' the next 'fore we reached a little place called Amelia Courthouse. There we hoped ta find the rations Lee'd ordered sent forward. None'd arrived, nor were any on the way. We tried to forage, but nothin' remained."

He looked thoughtful for a moment. "Thinkin' back on it," he continued, "I think I reached a point 'bout then when I didn't care no more. Ever' muscle in my body ached—we hadn't marched much in months—an' my mind just drifted inta numbness. I tried ta sleep a bit, but these waves of pain kept floatin' up my body, endin' every second or so with a sharp pain in the back a my neck, quickly followed by the next.

"Next mornin' the army moved out. My squad was off'n the woods 'bout a hundred yards. We'd all fallen asleep by then. Somehow, with all a the disorganization, they clean forgot us. The first thing I knowed I heard this thrashin' 'bout in the bushes an' I woke up. 'Yankees comin' up!' I yelled. Everyone sprang up, grabbed their rifles, an' scrambled to find a tree to fight behind. We had no idea we was all 'lone.

" 'Surrender,' screamed this Yankee sergeant, 'yore surrounded.'

"I primed my rifle and fired. It was as good a shot as I made durin' the war. The yellin' sergeant went silent in mid-sentence as he lifted outta his saddle an' crashed ta the ground. The others in my group fired right after. Three more Yankees fell wounded. Then they blasted us with those damned repeatin' Henrys they had. They near chewed us to pieces. In a minute I was the only one left standin'."

"So you were captured?"

"Damned Yankees. They trussed me up like a hog an' led me away. They didn't even see ta our wounded. They just left 'em ta bleed ta death. Shortly, they turned me over ta some provost men guardin' other prisoners, an' after our bonds was removed, we was all herded west at a run. 'Bout noon, we stopped next ta a stream. When no one was lookin', I rolled inta the stream an' swum underwater ta the other side. Later, I joined up with some stragglers an' we kept movin' west. We hid an' ran until the sixth. Then it happened. Never saw anythin' like it an' never hope ta agin."

I leaned forward in anticipation. "What happened?"

"We'd picked up a straggler who said General Anderson's men was just ahead 'long a place called Sayler's Creek. I darted off at a run. None a the others followed. In a few minutes I heard the most God-awful firin' I'd heard in some time. I ran for several minutes 'fore I topped a hill overlookin' a valley. What I saw made me cry. Dead lay all 'long the creek an' up the hill ta the west. The Yankees was poundin' Anderson's men with cannon shot as they ran like chickens. Men was climbin' a distant hill on hands an' knees tryin' ta escape the fire. It was murder. Yankee cavalry was everywhere, roundin' up prisoners, shootin' men as they tried ta run away, cuttin' off the outstretched hands a men tryin' to ward off the saber blows, then grindin' the wounded into the ground with their horses. I swore an undying hatred for all things Yankee that day. All I can say is, it was murder."

I fought off the anger as the blood rose to my head. "You were at Cold Harbor, weren't you?" I said sharply.

"Yup," he replied. I watched as his brow furrowed with surprise at my question.

"Was it that kind of murder?" I asked.

He looked at me for a moment without speaking; then I watched his eyes as his brain formulated the only answer that made sense to him: "That was different!" he exclaimed. "Those was Yankees."

They were Americans, I thought angrily. Each one who fell, North or South, diminished the country by one. If murder is made more acceptable by war, it remains murder nonetheless. Every gray soldier who remained under arms had it in his mind to kill another Yankee. Wars never end easily. There is always a final killing ground populated by men willing to kill, men who will run to Hell to keep from being killed. Looking back on that last battle, it always seems senseless. There was a frenzy about those last few days of the war, but to the common soldier they seemed to pass in slow motion. Battles really weren't battles, not in the old sense of the term, just places where the killing and maiming continued—a hundred men here, a hundred men there. It is not surprising that when the armies finally met in force, all the pent-up anxiety finally broke loose. Shooting from his horse a man who was offering an opportunity to surrender was war; shooting a man trying to avoid capture was murder. The difference seemed to be determined by the color of the uniform, who did the killing, and who ran. A man looking for a reason to hate had no trouble finding it in Grant's war.

At Sayler's Creek, Lee looked down from a distant hill at this last great battle. "My God!" he cried as he watched his routed men. "Has the army been dissolved?"

The destruction of Lee's army defined precisely what it had been coming to all along. Lee had kept it going; his men had to pay the price. The numbing reality of hard war is that men sometimes have to endure being ground beneath hard-charging cavalry horses before it finally ends.

*   *   *

"I was in that Union force that routed the rebels at Sayler's Creek," Sgt. John Norton told me. I had told him how Ramrod had described the encounter. "Your Confederate was right, up to a point. What he didn't tell you was that the rebels had every intention of fighting a rearguard action to let the forward elements of the army get away. So long as they stood, we had to fight them." He smiled faintly before continuing. "You know what? Your angry rebel seems to think we had an obligation to wage war by his standards. There'd always been a notion in the South that the war was all chivalry and nobility on the Confederates' part and that we were the brutal, invading Yankees. They ignored the fact all along that they'd started the war, taking Union forts by force and stealing millions of dollars in Federal property. Those irregulars he talked about were murderers of the lowest sort. They captured and killed Union soldiers without giving it a thought. My brother was captured back in the Shenandoah and tied to a tree before they shot him seven times in the head. They pinned a note to his chest: 'This is what waits for all Yankees who come our way.' At least the men in this battle had a chance to defend themselves.

"In the end, thousands surrendered, but only after it became impossible for them to get away. That battle actually started when some of the rebels ambushed a troop of Sheridan's men riding along a small stream. They had more than ten thousand men ready to do battle, and not one among the Union forces expected them to give up without a fight. We had heard too many times how Lee's men were on the verge of collapse. The five hundred casualties we suffered that day did little to convince me of their desire to surrender."

Two points of view, one from the winner, the other from the loser. Since the beginning the main difference had been point of view. The rebel who looked north saw an invader. The Federal looking south saw a portion of the nation trying to break away, primarily in an effort to keep other men in bondage. Neither soldier seemed willing to compromise his point of view. Lincoln had tried to find a way. He had sent the message, in every way he could think to do it, that the only requirement was to lay aside their arms. Then the men could go back to their families. Nothing ever came of his appeals.

Shortly after Lee expressed the belief that the army had dissolved, he said to Maj. Gen. William Mahone: "Yes, General, there are some true men left. Will you please keep those people back?"

Lee seldom referred to the Union forces as the enemy. Mostly, they were just "those people." Perhaps to him they never were the enemy. Called to war, he would fight. But thinking of the men of the nation he had defended so nobly for most of his life as enemies may have been too broad a leap, even on this dark Thursday—the last Thursday of his army's existence. Still, he elected to go on, even after witnessing the worst of Confederate defeats.

Lee had only one objective: to get away from his pursuers. He wanted to join up with Johnston, but failing that, he would accept escaping into the Blue Ridge Mountains to continue the war from there, rebuilding his shattered forces with reinforcements as his men regained their strength.

But first he had to cross the Appomattox River and find his rations, the ones sent ahead, he prayed, after his bitter complaint over their not being at Amelia. Eight thousand casualties during the day had reduced his force by a fourth. That loss, added to the previous week's reduction of a third, equaled half his army in two weeks of fighting and running. The army may have been near its end, but near is not there. The man had an indomitable spirit, incapable of accepting defeat until it became absolutely impossible for his men to put one foot in front of the other. That spirit had made him the most formidable fighter of the war, surpassing even Grant in this regard, considering that he never fielded the men or possessed the materials of his opponent.

Such was Lee. Nothing would ever diminish his genius, not even the test of scrutiny applied by unforgiving historians, such as myself, who examined every move he made with the infallible certainty of hindsight. He bore no sin for his willingness to fight, but that did not apply to the cause he defended. In that, he was no different from Ramrod Legard. In that, I find no virtue at all.

25 Is It Over?

The war ground on. After more than fourteen hundred days of carnage, only two remained.

Lee recovered from the anguish he felt while watching his routed troops try to break free from Sayler's Creek. Until this day the army had endured every deprivation except one. Now, that too—the will to resist, the pride to stand, regardless of the cost—had abandoned the Army of Northern Virginia. A large portion of the army lay wasted, beyond any hope of recovery.

So much had happened since Lee stood overlooking the sunken road at Fredericksburg. There he had commented that it was good that war was so terrible or we should grow too fond of it. Although the Union Army often bent, there at Fredericksburg as on other fields, it had never broken completely. If there had been breaks, they had been in the minds of the generals. Here the opposite problem held sway. Lee still had the will to hang on, but the long run from the capital had sapped all the will within his men.

Time had become more important than rations or supplies or rest. If time had been money, Lee and his army were in absolute poverty. Lee's last hope was to capture the bridges over the Appomattox River and get his men across before the bulk of the Union forces arrived. His problem was Sheridan, compounded by Major Generals Edward Ord and Charles Griffin moving their infantry in tandem with the mounted soldiers. All along the way their divisions nipped at Lee's heels. While Lee's infantry sniped at the head of the Union columns, Sheridan's men were riding hard to get in front to cut off the path of Lee's retreat.

Finding someone to make sense out of major battles had always

been a simple task. Even if a man saw little of it himself, history served
to fill in the details. The last few days of the war were more difficult.
Mostly it had turned into a long, grueling run with no one man, or even
one corps, knowing what had developed beyond the trees. Dense woods
and dusty, winding roads were the only features, and after a time these
all appeared the same. At the outset, twenty miles separated the northern
and southern parts of Lee's army. Desperate to find rations, these parts
converged at Amelia on April 3. Grant's army traveled a parallel course
a few miles south, moving constantly westward in an effort to get in
front of Lee's men and fight the last battle. As all of the parts that
comprised the whole of these rambling forces moved west, the distance between them narrowed.

Near the end, by April 7, the two armies' parallel paths sometimes
narrowed to no more than a few hundred yards. They heard each other's
muffled sound through the trees. Dense woods masked the movements,
but at times, when the distance dwindled to nothing at all, there occurred sharp clashes as the Federal forces tried to divide the long
Confederate line. Only at a couple of places did major effusions erupt,
such as at Sayler's Creek, or when Sheridan's men clashed with a
Confederate supply train. As the armies moved westward, however,
all movement became directed at one point. The Appomattox River
was the main geographical feature in the area, and moving across it
with any significant force required bridges. If Lee reached the bridges
first, crossed them, then destroyed them, there remained an outside chance
for his men to break loose into the vast countryside.

*   *   *

"The Rebs left a rear guard to set the bridges afire," said Capt.
Frank Able as he sipped a beer following supper. "Earlier that day,
Lee's men jumped on our lead cavalry elements and thrashed them good.
We lost six hundred or more. My cavalry company formed the point
of the next element to arrive. We charged after the arsonists, and there
followed a sharp fire fight as the bridge burned. Men shoveled dirt
on the flames with one hand and fired with the other."

"See there," said Sgt. George Washington Most, a tall Negro veteran who shared with Able the small but well-maintained farmhouse
near the Gettysburg battleground, "that's what I mean about cavalry.
You can't shovel dirt and fire a rifle at the same time."

Able puffed in defense. "By God, yes you can, Most," he asserted, "if the rifle's a Henry. We didn't carry those blunderbusses the infantry lugged around. Now shut up! I'm telling this." He turned back toward me. "From the rebel position, it must've seemed certain that the wagon bridge was a goner. Flames shot fifty feet in the air, with sparkling embers drifting to the heavens and making the surrounding area near light as day. I swear it was difficult not to judge it a pretty sight. If only there'd been less lead mixed with the flames. Actually, the bridge hardly seemed to burn at all. The coal-oil-soaked splinters of the planks snapped and crackled like fury, but this caused no real damage. Thinking that the bridge was beyond saving, the rebels finally broke off, and we rushed to beat out the fire. Thirty minutes later you'd hardly've known there'd been a fire. Off to the right was this high, brick-pillared railroad bridge—near half a mile long it was. It was burning, too, and two sections finally gave way. Traffic had to use the wagon bridge."

"That's about the way it happened," said Sergeant Most. "I was with Ord's infantry, and we marched across that bridge that night. We saw the light in the sky, but all was calm when we arrived. I hadn't a notion that it'd ever been on fire."

"So both of you were there that night?" I asked.

"If you were in the Army of the Potomac," Most replied, "you probably were there at some point during that night. The whole army was on the march, or maybe I should say, in a footrace with Lee. I still remember the pounding in my head with each step. It's difficult to say that Lee's men were worse off than ours. They had no food, so they had no need to stop to eat. We had food, or rather the wagons were full of it, but we'd outrun them by miles. It simply came down to which army had the greater endurance. We'd been better fed up to April 1, so I suppose we had an advantage in the long run." He looked at the cavalryman. "Of course we had to walk. Able here had a ride. Cavalry always had it easy."

"I'd a traded my ass and feet for yours any time," Able snapped. "Did you ever sit a horse for twenty-four hours straight? Of course you didn't. You're always spouting off about things you know nothing about. The nine days from April 1 of '65 were the hardest of my life. More than once I fell asleep on my horse and woke up someplace I'd never seen before."

"See what I mean?" the sergeant interjected. "Poor cavalry. Did you ever try falling asleep on the march?"

Able did his best to ignore his antagonist. "Unlike sergeants, officers are supposed to set an example for the men, but after three days in the saddle with hardly a moment to attend to body functions, well, the body overrules the mind, and that's that."

"How much of the fighting were you involved in?" I asked Able.

"Unless I was too numb to think during some of it, I missed none of it. I was there from the first morning attack at Five Forks until the Rebs surrendered on the last day."

"Tell me about the last day."

"Let's see, that was Palm Sunday, April 9, as I recall. I hadn't had a minute's sleep or eaten anything except six hard crackers since the previous morning. Staff officers kept riding up and down the column yelling: 'Keep awake, men, keep moving. General Sheridan says we can end this right here if we just press the rebels. You can sleep in Eternity, but stay awake now.' I guess I'd've felt bad about falling asleep except I saw on that ride a general and at least six colonels sound asleep in the saddle. What bothered me was, I saw General Sheridan several times during those days. He always looked as if he'd just arisen from eight hours of sleep. The man had more energy than anyone I ever saw.

"About sundown on April 8, a staff colonel rode along the ranks yelling that rations were waiting up near Appomattox and that if we moved fast we could be there by morning. My horse was as worn out as me, but he didn't have a saddle to rest in. I knew he'd cave in before morning without some rest. About two in the morning, it began to rain. Some of the horses started giving out from the effort of slogging through the mud, and it fast became obvious that without a rest we'd all be infantry by morning. About that time, we received orders to move off the road. They told us to brush our mounts and, if any time remained, to take care of ourselves. After quickly brushing their horses, most of the men chose coffee over sleep. It wasn't long before there were a thousand little fires sparkling in the woods. Never saw such an eerie sight in my life. There wasn't hardly any noise. The men had grown too tired to talk. All I heard was the clank of tin against tin and an occasional swear word when the coffee burned a man's tongue.

"It was about that time that one of those whispering telegraph messages moved down the line of fires."

The look on my face must have communicated my confusion, for he immediately began to explain.

"Sometimes, if someone overheard something that seemed important, he turned to the people sitting around the fire just beyond and whispered what he'd heard. The message moved down the line with amazing speed—about a mile a minute by most estimates. Somehow these messages had a different ring than common gossip. Gossip usually sounded as if it was boasting and was spoken with absolute assurance, usually in a loud voice. The whispering telegraph was a certain sign that the message had the ring of truth. This message brought blood back to my head. 'Lee and Grant are going to meet in the morning to discuss surrender terms,' the whisper said. 'Pass it on.' To avoid confusion, these messages were always simple. I knew it was true, or at least wanted to believe it was true. It wasn't long before the command rolled from regiment to regiment, growing louder as it approached, then fading as it moved toward the far end of the long column: 'Prepare to mount up. We're moving out.'

"We moved immediately into a trot. About four that morning we broke into the clear on the southwest side of Appomattox and were ordered to construct defensive fieldworks astride the Lynchburg Pike. The quicker we finished, we were told, the quicker we could get some sleep. We had stout works within the hour."

"My regiment limped in about two hours after the cavalry," Most added. "What with stragglers and all, we must've been strung out for five miles along the railroad. We drew up on the far side of a gap southwest of the courthouse hamlet, just out of sight of the cavalry. All the while, the infantry regiments kept coming up and fanning out on either side of the road."

"The Rebs came down the road at sunup," Able said, "acting as if they intended to come right through us. They opened up out of our range, and men began to fall. We received orders to fall back slowly and keep firing. We aimed high so the bullets would drop on them. Then we were ordered to pull back fast. We ran to the horses and rode out at a disorganized run. It seemed a bit odd that we really didn't stand and fight behind our works, but at the same time, I had no desire to slug it out with infantry. The Rebs yelled and screeched that yell that only they could make. You'd'a thought they'd just won a great battle, and it weren't hardly a skirmish, except as measured by the numbers involved. We had twelve thousand; they had about as many infantry. We rode off down the Pike; then I knew why we had pulled out."

"Cavalry always run when the infantry came up," Most said, a faint sneer curling his lips. "That's the main reason they have those horses, to get away fast."

Able stiffened again, but held his tongue. By now it had become obvious that they had had this argument many times. They had spent a lifetime whittling it down to the essentials.

"My regiment was about fifty yards to the right of the road," Most continued. "Our line bent over this rise—my company was at the top— then stretched on another mile or so. There were as many of us on the other side of the road. Regiments were still coming up the road and filing into the line as fast as they arrived. We must have been thirty thousand strong by that time." He paused, obviously groping for the right words. He began to speak twice, then caught himself at the last moment. "I never saw anything like it," he said at last, "at least not with a rebel army. As those tattered men broke into the clearing, they were yelling and screaming as if they'd conquered Lucifer himself. At the sight of us, a hush spread along their ranks. Some of them actually seemed to recoil, as if we'd hit them with a broadside. But we'd been ordered to hold our fire. I felt that I'd just seen the last rebel charge of the war. The heart had left them. They didn't run, as you'd expect frightened men to do. They just knelt in place, rifles at the ready, and looked at us."

"We hit them at about that time," Able said. "We'd pulled back about a mile on either side of the road. When the rebels seemed to falter, we hit them on either flank. They began a slow retreat. They were trapped, and they knew it. Generals Humphreys and Wright were coming up on their rear with more men. They were chasing Longstreet and his six thousand, plus their wagons. I have to admit, our attack lacked something in the effort. No one wanted to be the last man killed. We dismounted and peppered them from a distance without either side doing much damage."

"They pulled back toward Appomattox," said Most, "and we moved forward. It reminded me of the first year of the war. No trenches, no barricades, just flesh against lead, standing out in the open. Here and there a man fell, but nothing like a real battle. The men seemed to enjoy the spectacle, as if they somehow were detached from it all. Some fired, but mostly there were just those waving blue lines, turned almost gray from the dust and dried mud, nearly two miles long and four ranks deep. Never before had I felt a sense of history about the war, but I felt it at that moment. For the first time in days, I forgot my hunger and thirst.

"Then it happened. The firing stopped, although I'd heard no command. Then a lone officer broke through the rebel ranks carrying a long pole with a white handkerchief tied to the end. In four years of fighting I'd never seen a Confederate show a white flag. We'd captured many a Reb along the way, but only when we had a gun pointing at them. This was entirely different. There was something final about that soldier's ride. The soldier next to me had fallen in the last rebel volley. I looked down at him—I saw a large, bloody hole in his side—and I smiled, trying to ease his anguish a bit.

" 'Is it over?' he asked.

" 'Appears so,' I replied.

" 'Well, help me up,' he said, gasping for breath. As I looked closer, it appeared certain that the bullet had gone into the lung. Thinking what that meant, I grimaced.

" 'I promised—my father—I'd see it through—to the finish,' he said, gasping for air. 'Now that—the end is here, I don't—don't want to miss it.'

"He squeezed the wound with his hand, and blood oozed through his fingers. Then his strength seemed to falter and he let his arm drop. As I bent over, he placed the arm around my neck, pushing against his rifle with the other hand.

" 'Can you—believe that?' he gasped. 'We beat them only once. I mean—really beat them—with white flag—and all, and that—at the last battle—of the war.' He made a strange kind of grunting sound, from the pain, I suppose, and pulled himself erect on wobbly legs. He smiled and whispered, 'Can you—beat that? It is over.' He looked at me with the brightest grin I ever saw grace a man's face. That moment of supreme pleasure froze there as I felt his soul slip away."

*   *   *

The similarities between war and chess are numerous. General Halleck, viewing it so, had sought to remove Grant from the army because he failed to demonstrate the finesse and respect for strategy ascribed to the game. Grant's approach, rather, had been to move straight ahead, directly at the center of the problem, straight for the king. "I will accept nothing other than your immediate and unconditional surrender," he responded to his friend's inquiry about the terms for abandoning Fort Donelson. There was no finesse in those words.

In light of these early events, it is perhaps ironic that the last months of the war resembled nothing so much as a chess game of epic scale.

A sequence of swift, cornering moves jumped across the landscape from the Wilderness to Petersburg, then, following a stalemate, through the valleys among the wooded hills leading to Appomattox. The king of the Southern side had slipped ever sideways, this way and that, in his desperate attempt to avoid capture. Few of his protective pieces remained at the end, the bulk having been knocked from the board over eleven months of fighting. He had lost his queen when Jackson fell two years earlier at Chancellorsville. His knight fell when a dismounted Union cavalry sergeant knocked Stuart from the game. Lesser pieces had been lost, one by one—the last, A. P. Hill, just before the final dash toward destruction.

Grant had employed a series of checking moves, first in the Wilderness, followed by Spotsylvania, South Anna, and finally at Cold Harbor. He had sent his own knight, Sheridan, up the Shenandoah Valley to secure the flank. Even during the temporary stalemate at Richmond and Petersburg, Grant whittled Lee's pieces away. Each day the gap widened between the dwindling forces of the South and the growing numbers of the North. Finally, nothing remained but the long run to Appomattox, where Lee, in a last, desperate attempt to avoid capture, sought to remove himself from the board. Finally, trapped in the corner, he moved to the last open square: checkmate.

Two days before the end, on April 7, Lee sent his first response to Grant's invitation for surrender:

GENL

I HAVE RECD YOUR NOTE OF THIS DATE. THOUGH NOT ENTERTAINING THE OPINION YOU EXPRESS OF THE HOPELESS-NESS OF FURTHER RESISTANCE ON THE PART OF THE ARMY OF N. VA. I RECIPROCATE YOUR DESIRE TO AVOID USELESS EFFUSION OF BLOOD, & THEREFORE BEFORE CONSIDERING YOUR PROPOSITION, I ASK THE TERMS YOU WILL OFFER ON CONDITION OF ITS SURRENDER.

VERY RESPC YOUR OBT SVT, R. E. LEE, GENL

The form and style of the reply was light, informal, almost indifferent. Denial, I thought. He must have known the answer before asking his question. Is it possible he expected Grant to accept an ending different from the one at the beginning so long before at Fort Donelson? I doubt it. By this time, surely, Lee had grown to understand what his opponent would do, and nothing in Grant's character or past behavior suggested he would let an opponent down easy, unless it suited his needs. Still, Grant did offer an opening, perhaps in a lapse, perhaps because he had grown to respect his adversary—the reason is unimportant.

Grant's reply read in part:

PEACE BEING MY GREAT DESIRE, THERE IS BUT ONE CONDITION I WOULD INSIST UPON—NAMELY, THAT THE MEN AND OFFICERS SURRENDERED BE DISQUALIFIED FROM TAKING UP ARMS AGAINST THE GOVERNMENT OF THE UNITED STATES UNTIL PROPERLY EXCHANGED.

Lee jumped on the opening offered by the first word in the response.

I DID NOT INTEND TO PROPOSE THE SURRENDER OF THE ARMY OF N. VA., BUT TO ASK THE TERMS OF YOUR PROPOSITION. I CANNOT THEREFORE MEET YOU WITH A VIEW TO SURRENDER OF THE ARMY OF N. VA.; BUT AS FAR AS YOUR PROPOSAL MAY AFFECT THE C.S. FORCES UNDER MY COMMAND, AND TEND TO THE RESTORATION OF PEACE, I SHALL BE PLEASED TO MEET YOU . . .

Incensed by this reply, General Rawlins earned his pay that day, although not in the way Congress had intended at the time of his appointment.

"No, sir," he said angrily to Grant. "No, sir. It is a positive insult, an attempt, in an underhanded way, to change the whole terms of the correspondence—to gain time and better terms." Then he shifted his rhetoric up an octave. "He don't think 'the emergency has arisen'! That's cool, but another falsehood. That emergency has been staring him in the face for forty-eight hours. If he hasn't seen it yet, we will soon bring it to his comprehension! He has to surrender. He shall surrender. By the Eternal, it shall be surrender or nothing else."

Perhaps it was Rawlins's lawyerly demeanor that carried the argument, or simply the soundness of his position. Then there was the uncharacteristic shrillness of his tone. In the end, the commanding general's keeper had his way. Grant replied:

I HAVE NO AUTHORITY TO TREAT ON THE SUBJECT OF
PEACE; THE MEETING PROPOSED—COULD LEAD TO NO GOOD.
THE TERMS UPON WHICH PEACE CAN BE HAD ARE WELL
UNDERSTOOD. BY THE SOUTH LAYING DOWN THEIR ARMS
THEY WILL HASTEN THAT MOST DESIRABLE EVENT.

Before this reached Lee he had already left for the meeting he had proposed for ten that morning. Instead, waiting for him was Grant's most recent response, to which he replied:

APRIL 9TH, 1865
GENERAL: I RECEIVED YOUR NOTE OF THIS MORNING ON
THE PICKET LINE, WHITHER I HAD COME TO MEET YOU AND
ASCERTAIN DEFINITELY WHAT TERMS WERE EMBRACED IN
YOUR PROPOSAL OF YESTERDAY WITH REFERENCE TO THE
SURRENDER OF THIS ARMY. I NOW REQUEST AN INTERVIEW,
IN ACCORDANCE WITH THE OFFER CONTAINED IN YOUR
LETTER OF YESTERDAY, FOR THAT PURPOSE.
VERY RESPECTFULLY, YOUR OBT SERVT
R. E. LEE

Gone was the evasive, indifferent language of the first reply. Replacing this was the formal and proper response of a man unwilling by temperament to stoop, but recognizing, nonetheless, that the end had come. Lee responded to Grant's acceptance of the invitation to discuss "the surrender of this army" by sending a rider to carry the white flag that so excited Sergeant Most.

What must Grant have thought when, all rumpled and splattered with mud, he made that ride in response to Lee's agreement? How difficult is it for a general such as Grant to set war aside? Armies are, after all, the quintessential instrument of war; yet their primary function is to prevent war, or failing that, to restore peace through war. Grant had done everything Lincoln had asked of him and more, and now the general had fought himself out of a job.

Lee arrived first at the farmhouse selected for the meeting. Grant arrived thirty minutes later. After the greetings and some talk of the past, Grant offered his terms. The Army of Northern Virginia would lay down its arms and go home. That was it. Oh, there were some details, but the Confederate Army had little that the North wanted, except the land cut off by force and considered only temporarily beyond Northern control. That temporary custody had now been relinquished. But with all of the formalities concluded, and after the generals had their say, that poor dying soldier Sergeant Most held in his arms said it best: It is over.

It had ended. True, there remained the problem of Johnston's army in North Carolina. There also remained the matter of formal surrender between governments and what to do about the politicians who led the rebellion. This all meant little to the men who now had time to lay their arms aside and eat their breakfast, a need that had driven them to this backwater hamlet in the first place. For the first time in four years, they had time to sit together, blue and gray, without fear of being shot or blown to pieces as a result of lowering their guard for a moment.

26 Perspective

And what of Grant as the last hour of the war drew to a close? First, last, and always Grant was a soldier—a perfect soldier, some might say. Little in his military action or his words about the war sounds a philosophical note. To him the nation was simply indivisible. Those with grandiose dreams of making it otherwise had no one but themselves to blame for the suffering that they and their progeny had to endure. Grant's view of events, and his place in them, was simply that of a man who performed tasks circumstance had defined for him.

Once Lincoln lifted Grant above the growing throng of generals and told him to end the war, there remained little for Lincoln to do but grit his teeth and find a way to endure the casualty count. And it was that casualty count, compressed into the last eleven months of the war, that has distorted the true meaning of Grant's accomplishment. Lesser generals had led armies south many times before. Their efforts, too, littered the landscape with youthful, blue-clad corpses, but with no other result than disillusionment and sorrow for those remaining alive. There has been no thought of calling this butchery, as has been Grant's historical legacy. It is one of the war's great ironies that during the winter of 1864, while the nation waited impatiently for a general with the will to end the killing forever, more men died of disease than were killed in battle in any comparable period under Grant's command, including the blood-stained period encompassing the Battle of the Wilderness through that dreadful twenty minutes at Cold Harbor.

It has crossed my mind that more than a modicum of misplaced romanticism has colored historical perspective as it applies to Grant.

Few except Grant—Lincoln must be counted among the rare exceptions—understood that the greater cost in lives and suffering resulted from prolonging the clash of arms.

The final judgment about Grant, it seems, most appropriately should come from the men called upon to do the fighting and dying. The common soldiers in blue who tramped the dusty roads and braved the leaden storm saw Grant more clearly than anyone. In November of 1864, guided by the only judgment that counts, then or now, they expressed their opinion in simple eloquence when, knowing that a vote for Lincoln meant the tramping would continue until their deaths or the army's victory, they voted overwhelmingly for Lincoln—and equally for Grant.

The shortest route home is usually the more difficult, less traveled road. None of Lincoln's other generals found the courage to take that route. Left to their own devices, lesser generals would have—as they had for three terrible years—strung out the casualties indefinitely. But the time for plodding, cautious ways had passed. The point had been reached where the war was scraping the raw edge of the Northern people's range of endurance. It is Grant's performance upon that stage that must be judged, and none other.

Say what we will about the Civil War, if the North had lost, a dozen or more countries most likely would now define the space presently occupied by the United States of America. Although second-guessing history is chancy business, is it far-fetched to conclude that, if the beginning of the hard business of ending the war had been delayed even a few weeks, Lincoln quite likely would have lost in the August primaries or the November election? Given the constraints and mood of the time, despite Gettysburg, Vicksburg, and all that had gone before, without Grant it is difficult to conceive of the North winning within the allotted time. I know of no available Union general who, after enduring the thrashing within the Wilderness in early May of 1864, would have turned south at the end of the third, bloody day of battle.

I must conclude, without much fear of contradiction, that the Civil War will be fought again and again by those, like myself, not constrained to do the fighting when it counted for something. But even with the myriad issues still remaining open to debate, at least one has been settled: whatever the war may have been when it began, when it moved into its last year it was Grant's war to win or lose. History records the result.

*   *   *

In a cramped Virginia farmhouse, with the stroke of a pen the Army of Northern Virginia ceased to exist forever. As the battered gray soldiers stacked their arms and marched past one last time, it was impossible to ignore the changed nature of the Federal army. Scattered through-out the Union ranks was something that a Southern soldier never thought he would have to endure, let alone accept: the sight of black men with rifles, whole regiments of them, looking into his eyes. A small thing, perhaps, but for those black men to earn that right more than six hundred thousand soldiers had died—with the wounded many times more. But in the process the nation's destiny had merged with the present.

Seventy-six years earlier, almost within the lifetime of some who witnessed the farmhouse proceedings between Grant and Lee, equally dedicated men had met in Philadelphia to hammer out a nation. The season and the tempers had been hot, and they had argued mightily about what the nation should become. They knew the words they wanted to pass on to their children and their children's children, so they wrote them down. They agreed that all men are created equal, and they said so. But they failed to agree on the precise definition of a man. Half saw nothing of manhood in a black man. The other half, knowing better, looked past that disagreement and left it to later generations to write in the details. More than had been expected had been required to seal the resolution, but the task was now complete.

Not a day had passed since the signing of that immortal document, the Constitution, that the nation had not been marching toward war. The nation had surged forward along a bumpy road, moving ever closer toward conflagration. The fire that enveloped it proved much more than anyone had bargained for. It was more than just another event need-ing interpretation in retrospect; it had rumbled forth to become a mighty explosion on the historical landscape, and everything was changed. What had changed most of all was the idea of what is right and wrong, what the words in that document really meant, what they had meant all along. Blood had washed over the document by the bucket and, when at last it washed away, the words were the same—but the meaning had changed.

It is a great irony that the Civil War, both the darkest and most enlightening moment in our history, had been necessary in the simple effort to shine a distant light, a light to dimly illuminate the meaning of justice and equality. Nothing happened to alter the heart or mind of a single human being who resisted the change. That remained the challenge for future generations. But the promise was there, and promises by a nation to its people must be satisfied.

Finding fault with what happened, and why it had to occur at all, is a simple enough task. Moral purists, who hate and reject war in all its forms, might say slavery was preferable. That would be an interesting argument to observe. Much to our discredit, however, it is an unfortunate but undeniable reality that most permanent social change has taken root only after its nourishment in blood. If we are seeking a moral imperative to find a better way, perhaps we look for more in ourselves than is there.

Select Bibliography

The following is a list of the principal sources used during my research for *Grant's War*. Each of these studies is based on extensive examination of secondary sources, as well as manuscripts containing the writings and reflections of hundreds of Civil War participants. Although I was concerned about maintaining historical perspective while writing *Grant's War*, my primary objective was to examine, from a distance, how the events of the time might have affected the war's lesser participants and how those events might have influenced subsequent history. In other words, although the sequence and general framework of *Grant's War* are based on fact, specific events portrayed by characters other than historical figures are fictitious.

Anderson, Nancy Scott and Dwight. *The Generals: Ulysses S. Grant and Robert E. Lee.* New York: Vintage Books, 1989.

Catton, Bruce. *A Stillness at Appomattox.* New York: Doubleday, 1953.

_____. *Grant Takes Command, 1863–1865.* Boston: Little, Brown, 1969.

_____. *Never Call Retreat.* New York: Doubleday, 1965.

_____. *Reflections on the Civil War.* New York: Doubleday, 1981.

_____. *Terrible Swift Sword.* New York: Doubleday, 1963.

_____. *This Hallowed Ground.* New York: Doubleday, 1956.

Cullen, Joseph P. *Battle of the Wilderness.* Harrisburg, Pa.: Eastern Acorn Press, 1965.

Foote, Shelby L. *The Civil War: A Narrative, Fort Sumter to Perryville.* New York: Random House, 1958.

_____. *The Civil War: A Narrative, Fredericksburg to Meridian.* New York: Random House, 1963.

_____. *The Civil War: A Narrative, Red River to Appomattox*. New York: Random House, 1973.

Smith, Gene. *Lee and Grant*. New York: Promontory Press, 1988.

Sword, Wiley. *The Battle of Shiloh*. Harrisburg, Pa.: Eastern Acorn Press, 1982.

Trudeau, Noah Andre. *Bloody Roads South*. Boston: Little, Brown, 1989.

Tucker, Glenn. *The Battles of Chattanooga*. Harrisburg, Pa.: Eastern Acorn Press, 1981.

Williams, T. Harry. *Lincoln and His Generals*. New York: Dorset Press, 1989.

DATE DUE

SEPT	1992		
FEB 16 1993			
DEC 0 8 1992			
SEP 2 9 1995			
GAYLORD			PRINTED IN U.S.A.